THE PENTAGRAM CHILD

PART ONE

BY

STEPHANIE HUDSON

The Pentagram Child - Part 1
The Afterlife Saga #5
Copyright © 2020 Stephanie Hudson
Published by Hudson Indie Ink
www.hudsonindieink.com

The Pentagram Child - Part 1/Stephanie Hudson – 2nd ed.
ISBN-13 - 978-1-913769-22-2

Dedication

This dedication is close to my heart and in the name of all those who make it their job in life to care for others. The deeply rooted kindness that is needed to face your days is something to be admired.

Holding the Hands of a Stranger.

We wander down this painful road,
Alone and frightened, the end untold,
We sit on a bed that we do not know,
And hold on to hope, keep letting it grow.

We fear the worst and pray for the best,
Surrounded by loved ones so we feel blessed,
But then the time comes when we're again alone,
And our fake smiles have gone away and flown.

We look around at unknown faces,
And see the same fear hidden there in traces,
Tubes and pills and injections await,
On a daily basis that becomes our fate.

But then something happens that's there to be found,
A kindness like no other that appears all around,
It comes from people doing more than their job,
Whether they're holding a mop or taking a swab.

There is kindness in nature and there for us to see,

It doesn't cost anything and welcomed for free,
Because in this place we're never without,
A stranger's hand to hold in this emotional breakout.

Thanks to all the wonderful people who cared for me and held my hand when things got painful, scary and too much to bear.

Nikki Sarimanolis, Nicola Pereira, Elias Ngonyama, Vicky Davidson, Ryan Cox, Sarah Stanbury, Ama Machado, Kevin Charles, Alex Martimez, June Bockle, Bindu Joseph, Grace Jackson, Doctor David Gore, June Saunders, Shirley George, Sajili Molethekkepurath Paulose, Jose Munar, Elicia Williams, Marisa Tavares, Carla Carvalho, Isabel Santana, Jacky Aldridge, Lorna Rolph, Sue Downer, Anne Marie, Mel Norwacki, Janice Mcpherson, Martina Bishop, Aiden Sumajit, Happy Singh, Jo Paterson, Jacque Handley.

And to the new friends I made who helped me giggle my way through six weeks in Southampton General Hospital.

Jean Parson, Carol, Lynsie Lynn, Betty Swanley, Yvonne Blake, Marilyn Mettyer, Maureen Veal, Marjurie Littleford, Heidi Rose.

WARNING

This book contains explicit sexual content, some graphic language and a highly addictive Alpha Male.

This book has been written by a UK Author with a mad sense of humour. Which means the following story contains a mixture of Northern English slang, dialect, regional colloquialisms and other quirky spellings that have been intentionally included to make the story and dialogue more realistic for modern-day characters.

Please note that for your convenience language translations have been added to optimise the readers enjoyment throughout the story.

Also meaning…

No Googling is required ;)

Also, please remember that this part of a 12 book saga, which means you are in for a long and rocky ride. So, put the kettle on, brew a cup, grab a stash of snacks and enjoy!

Thanks for reading x

PROLOGUE

KEIRA

How does the moth live in darkness when all light is suddenly ripped from its existence? Sure, the moth is safer from the flame, but dangers still lurk in the night. Eyes watching, claws twitching, feet stalking and waiting to strike under the cover of black skies.

He thought I would be safer without him but what can protect me from myself and my own dreams…dreams that won't let me go. I never thought dreaming of Draven could be classed as a nightmare, but this was now my reality.

I found myself most nights transported back to that day we first set our eyes on each other. It was just as it was that day. Me wandering too far and stumbling across the clearing like Eve finding herself in the Garden of Eden for the first time. I remember taking it all in and being sucked into the magic of it all before coming to my senses enough to ask why, what and how. And like that day…

I fell.

Only this time it was no longer the foot of my destiny there to greet me. I started to fall in painfully slow motion, watching my hair floating as if under water. Then my vision changed. It shot from one pair of eyes to another in a blink of time and I was no longer seeing the earth coming closer to meet me.

The last time I dreamt this way I was in a temple running with my chest cut deep and leaving behind bloody footprints like a pathway through deadly sand. Well now it was happening again and just like before, it shot back as I screamed ready to watch myself hit the ground.

One second I was crying out for my other self and then I cried out as I became the me that fell. I felt the moss wet and slippery under my fingers as I tried to grasp the rocks but then as I made a fist it no longer felt like anything nature would have created. It squelched into my pores and underneath my fingernails and a metallic smell wafted up to my nostrils...

Blood.

I gasped at the same time my fist uncurled. I quickly scrambled backwards and with a shaky hand moved my loose hair back.

Then I screamed.

"No, no...oh Jesus no!" I shook my head, but nothing would release me from the sight of bloody body parts that once belonged to someone breathing, living and anything but being chopped into pieces! The sound of my own frightened panting was the only noise in this now eerie place.

I managed to get to my feet and looked down to see the piece of thigh seconds ago I had had my hand embedded in. I quickly turned my head and heaved. I lifted my hand to wipe away my tears and that's when I noticed the new liquid crimson glove that now covered my skin.

More blood.

I closed my eyes and took small steps backwards, all the while chanting,

"It's just a dream, it's just a dream…wake up Keira…wake up NOW!" I shouted the ending as I backed into a tree. My eyes shot open and the first thing I noticed was no longer just the blood and gore but now the pattern in it all.

All the body parts had been arranged into some weird symbol and somewhere deeply buried was a place in my mind where a light had just been switched on. Switched on for the first time since that day. The very day I said goodbye to Draven for the last time.

"It…it… can't be…possible!" Even as I said the words my mind brought back the image where I had first seen this symbol but what did it all mean? I tore my eyes away from the butchery that lay in blood stained grass and puddles of carnage. But in doing so I now had to witness the same thing that happened so long ago. I could almost feel Draven's arm band around me to pull me closer as I watched the Garden of Eden become the Garden of Death.

The trees transformed from lush greens into grey dust, leaving only sinister looking branches that stretched out like flexing claws. The flowers folded in on themselves and crumpled like burnt paper. I clung to the tree trunk at my back but when it too started to shake, I side stepped shrieking out in surprised fright. I spun too fast and nearly stumbled into another plant, the bird of paradise.

I managed to stop just in time as I was now less than an inch away from one deadly spike piercing my eye. The once beautiful and exotic looking flower had turned into a fatal weapon. Each stunning orange petal had been transformed into a fan of blades and the central blue stems were now poisonous barbs tipped to a needle point and ready to kill.

"Ahhh!" I shouted and again scrambled back, only this time managing to stay on my feet at least. I spun back round to face what looked like a mass ritual sacrifice lay out on the floor that merely waited for its master to say the right words. But which master would it be?

This thought quickly brought on the wind and it whipped furiously around me as if disapproving of where my thoughts had taken me. But what else was there for me left to think…? There was only one place I had seen this symbol and no amount of shaking my head would undo the memory.

"WHY!?" I shouted as the wind picked up replacing my fear with anger. How could this happen, even in my dreams how could these things still haunt me?

"JUST LEAVE ME ALONE!" I screamed this time looking up at the Gods and hoping they heard the pain being ripped through me. But their only answer came in the form of the storm that battled furiously around me and the centre of the symbol circled on the ground. I raised my hands to my ears, bloody or not, I didn't care. I just needed to hold onto something. Then without knowing what else to do I let loose a screamed sentence,

"YOU DAMNED MY LOVE FOR YOU!" And suddenly the world of chaos stopped revolving around me. I was left panting into my hands and could taste another man's blood on my lips. It was a sickening thought and pulled me from my mental breakdown enough to realise the storm had passed. I lowered my arms slowly and gasped as I was now left to take in the figure that stood in the centre of the bloody symbol.

"Draven." I said his name on a breath of spent air. He didn't say anything but just stared at me from across the placed body parts. I looked around him and that was when I saw the bloodied campsite in the background. My mind took only seconds to process the memory of a newspaper I once read about missing campers found slaughtered.

Was this them?

"Draven…I…I don't understand." I stumbled out painful

words but he just shook his head at me slowly, telling me I was wrong.

"What Draven, what is it?" I asked nervously and with my growing anxiety my fingertips start to tingle.

"See me… come and see the place I go." He whispered to me and my skin prickled with fear as this was the first time I has heard his Demon voice murmur at me seductively. Draven held out his hand and again his voice unravelled my nerves and began to destroy my defences one by one.

"Come with me…come and see…"

"Come and see what?" I asked when he didn't finish. I was just about to step forward and grab his outstretched hand when his eyes suddenly changed to the likes I had never seen and his Demon voice bellowed,

"ME KILL YOU!" I screamed and fell backwards just before he could grab me. I landed painfully on my bum and watched in horror as he started laughing a dark and menacing laugh. He threw his head up to the thunderous clouds above and I now noticed the marks on his arms were still there. Only now they seemed to burn their way through his long sleeved t-shirt at the height of his demonic madness and I watched as my fears came true.

The symbols soon burned all the way through until his sleeves were nothing but charred edges above his elbows. The very same symbols that were mirrored on the ground in the form of wasted human life.

"No, Draven…what have you done?!" I sobbed looking up at the insanity that had gripped my heart's keeper. He heard me and quickly his laughter died as he lowered his head to stare down at me. He then raised his arms to the sky and all at once the limbs were set ablaze, creating a circle of fire that surrounded him.

"NO!" I shouted but it was useless. He was at once

consumed in the centre of death and he held out his arms as if embracing it.

"DRAVEN!"

"Keira." He finally said my name like a lover's whisper and for the first time I heard a slice of my Draven come back to me.

"Yes, yes it's me!" I pleaded with him, the Gods, all of Hell and anyone in between that would listen, all in hopes of making this stop. But stop it never does... because he only ever had one thing left to tell me in this dream and as I listened to the words I knew were coming, I was still left empty as always...

"The Pentagram Child, he comes"

CHAPTER ONE

DRAVEN

VISIONS OF PAIN

Ten Months...

Ten long months of agonising visions to call company. Visions of nothing but a pain so raw, it shredded my insides every time I closed my eyes. Watching those delicate fingers rip away the last part of me, as if the very memory of me was burning against her skin. I could still see it all, playing out in slow motion over and over. Her arm falling down as her muscles were spent, her fingers momentarily clenching around the necklace, as if some deep part of her didn't actually want to let go.

But then my world came crashing down around me as I watched the length of it slip through her fingers, only to find a new home in the rubble that was left of our love. A destruction I had not only caused but forced her to endure as her last moments with me.

What had I been thinking? Did I really choose all this just so that my memory could be one of love instead of hatred? Had I really put her through all I had, just so I could claim the right to be held eternally infused within a piece of her heart? But I knew the selfish answer to that question.

And so I lived with the pain from my actions every wretched minute of the day. Even now as I stood in the wreckage made that night all those months ago, I still couldn't bring myself to tear my eyes away from the spot where she had once stood, just as I couldn't bring myself to fix any of it. Because this was the one thing in my existence I wasn't *allowed* to fix. And so it became a reminder at just how real this living, breathing nightmare had become.

I walked slowly onto what remained of the balcony. My boots crunched on the glass shards like shrapnel left over from the only war I did not win. All these sights and sounds I tortured myself with everyday as punishment. A prison far more damning than one Hell could ever have imagined for me and this small scattering of evidence was a cruel reminder of my biggest failure all my years had ever known. Simply put…

This was what it felt like to die inside.

"Dom?" I heard my sister's voice behind me but my body didn't react. It remained statue still like one of the poor souls of Pompeii and not even the Wrath of the Gods could persuade me to do otherwise. This was what I had become now, this broken shell that acted like this on a regular basis. So much so that my siblings were no doubt immune to my insanity.

When I didn't answer her she cleared her throat and stepped closer, which was a brave move even for my sister, who admittedly was the only one these days that I didn't allow my anger to lash out at and attack with a venomous barb. But no one…absolutely no one, was permitted to come out here. For this was the very room where my lies finally crumbled. It had crashed down on the shores of deceit, killing all the hope my Keira had built up like a Gods be damned fortress in Heaven!

"What is it, Sophia?" I asked trying to keep the impatient disapproval out of my voice that came back at me like whiplash when I heard her quick intake of breath. I didn't mean to keep hurting those that I cared for but when you suddenly hated the world for cursing you for sins that were meant to save…well, then it was like swallowing barbed wire in aid to cure a stomach ulcer… utterly pointless.

"I came to tell you that we're leaving." I wasn't surprised hearing this. If anything, I was surprised it hadn't come sooner. I hadn't left this godforsaken villa since the day she walked from my life, leaving on the back of another man's bike. Fucking Viking! If it hadn't been for that promise I had given Keira then I would have slaughtered…no! I would not go down this dark path again. I would not sully the last thing she ever asked of me with thoughts of death and pain and revenge…not again.

I shook my head slightly as if clearing the sticky remains of my darker days and concentrated on what my sister needed, which was a reassurance she would not believe. But I was her brother and I had to try.

"I understand, you do as you must."

"By the Gods, Dom! When will you wake up?!" My sister snapped and this wasn't the first time I had heard Sophia's temper rise on the matter.

"Sophia." I said her name as a warning, one I never relished in giving to someone so dear to me.

"No! Not this time, Dom. If this is the last thing I fucking wish of you, it will be in this moment right now and in this moment Brother, I wish for you to know the depth of the mistakes you make." At the sincerity of emotion in Sophia's voice I was ripped from my private Hell to witness the unusual sight of tears in my sister's eyes. The glassy depths I saw there nearly brought me to my fucking knees.

"I am fully aware of the mistakes I have made Sister…"

"You have no clue Dom, you think because you have witnessed heartbreak from your actions that you have some right not to live with the consequences lying in plain sight… hiding here in this hole, like some punishing memory you want to live in for the rest of your days, while your Chosen One is…"

"That's enough!" This command came from my mind but through the lips of another. My Brother. The only remaining strength I had left since that day on the roof had become a constant reminder I was not alone in my suffering. I didn't understand why the Gods and their fates had seen fit to cast the two Brothers with the same infliction of loving the same woman. But the fact that they had, had only encouraged more questions than there were answers to be found. But neither of us could have her and now, more than anyone, Vincent finally understood why. No amount of love could save her from her death if fate was to put my hands as the cause.

"No, he needs to know Vincent, things have changed…she has…"

"NO!" I shouted causing some more of the stone balcony to crumble away at the edges in my anger.

"But…"

"I made one demand, just one and in return I have allowed you to continue your bond the way it was, with only one condition asked of you…Now I must ask of you again that you respect that, Sophia." I let my voice deepen with an authority that could not be denied.

"But what if she could be in danger from it?" At this question I couldn't help but let out a bitter laugh, for the very idea had quickly become ridiculous.

"As you know I don't relish in pointing out the facts for you

Sophia, but once again I will do so with the hope that this be the last time. Keira must now be one of the safest beings on this planet given the amount of loyal subjects she has gathered along the way. She not only has her life guarded from one side now but many." She went to interrupt me but I quickly shut it down when taking a step with each name mentioned. And each one felt like acid on the tip of my tongue.

"A Viking warrior King and his shadowed son. A Hellbeast ruler and his army. A Vampire overlord whose obsessions border my own, I think you see where I am going with this but if that still hasn't hit home to the extremity of her wellbeing then let me add the last to the list. My own flesh and blood who have proved themselves time and time again in adding to that protection. *The girl wants for nothing!*" I couldn't hold back the bite of my demonic tongue in this last sentence, feeling such resentment it felt like my lungs were drowning in a poison called truth.

To give credit to my sister, she held her ground well. Arms folded and looking up at me with a mixture of disappointment and undiluted anger for what she no doubt classed as my stupidity.

"And what of her heart?" She asked me causing me to take a step back as if I had been struck by Lucius' second in command.

"Who will protect that?" Only when this question forced another step back out of me could I see the anger seep from my sister's eyes.

"That's quite enough, Sophia. You've said your piece and no doubt made your point."

"No, I don't think I did, nor do I ever think I will but I can try."

"Sophia." Another warning came from Vincent but not surprisingly was also one to be ignored.

"Your respected wishes have been granted time and time again. You didn't want to know of her life, a life she has been forcing herself to live, then that's fine. But what will happen when she no longer chooses to live the right life...? What then, Brother? Are you telling me that just so long as she breathes that will be enough for you? What becomes of her when that air becomes too tainted by your decisions, by a past love that crushed her enough not to care for any love at all? Can *you* live with that? Can *you* really live how you lived without knowing if she was safe, knowing that death hunted her with or without you by her side?"

"Sophia, that's enough" Sophia whipped her head round at Vincent and shouted,

"IT WILL NEVER BE ENOUGH!" She then aimed her rage back at the rightful person who warranted it and said her final words.

"I don't know the reasons Dom, but I know fear is one of them and I also know that fear should never conquer over love. You're choosing fear, she didn't choose it for you. But you know the biggest disappointment in all this..." I couldn't move waiting for the biggest hit yet to come and knowing that I deserved every word of it didn't make it easier to swallow.

"...she did something you never did...she conquered her fear for love and you...well... you gave your love away out of fear." If I thought that preparing myself for her words was going to protect me against the blow, I was mistaken. My foot went back one last time until I found myself standing in the exact position Keira had that night she had found me. Sophia was where the bed once sat but now what was left, like the pieces of my broken soul, was in ruins pushed back around the edges of the room, mirroring the insides of my vessel.

"Come Sophia, say goodbye." I noted for the first time during her speech that tears were streaming down her porcelain cheeks and the sight made me want to plough my fist into something unshakable. She looked me in the eyes as if searching for something, anything to indicate that what she had said would make a difference. She found nothing. Because she simply didn't understand.

I saw one last tear fall to the floor where it had all began and then she turned away from me wrenching at my heart painfully. Vincent took note of my feelings and gave me what he considered as a 'stay strong' nod before escorting our sister out of the door. She was just walking through the broken frame when her hand shot out and gripped the splintered edges as if needing to hold on. It was as though she had just been shocked with information that had her locking down her vessel.

"It's just as he said it would be...selfless acts, the fates... Keira's heart finding..."

"What?!" I shouted and at the same time my back straightened in response to my veins igniting with raw power.

"He told me..." Sophia was talking to herself and on hearing my growl of frustration finally looked up at me.

"Who?" I demanded.

"He said it would happen this way and that only when you started to seek the truth would you realise..."

"Who, Sophia?" I asked again feeling something other than pain for the first time since I left her that day. Since I left her to go and die. Since I left her with nothing to do but mourn me.

But with the next words out of Sophia's mouth, I knew the balance in my future was about to shift once more and with it, Keira had no choice in following me down fate's path, whether I liked it or not.

"Who Sophia?" This time it was Vincent who asked the question but the answer that came was a shock to no one...

"Our father."

CHAPTER TWO

DRAVEN

HELLS LASTING FOOTSTEPS

As I took my first steps in a place I was long overdue in visiting, I did something I had never done here before and that was simply to stop and take a moment to think. I looked around the vast wastelands that bordered my father's kingdom in the Second Circle of Hell, noting how little had changed.

Whenever I travelled back through the portals, I felt the Demon side of me sigh its relief in coming home. Being this close to one of the life forces that made my unique mix possible was difficult to deny, even if I was seriously pissed at the reasons I was even here in the first place. However, this didn't mean I could stop myself from raising my head and taking in the constant storm that lashed around me, gifting me with an essence of power I could absorb.

Of course, this meant my father knew I was here. He always

did. I circled my neck and inhaled the scent of the red sand dunes that went on for miles.

What humans didn't realise was that Hell was far greater in size than both the surface of the Earth and Heaven combined. This was due to the great depths in which it was forged. Layer upon layer and kingdom on top of kingdom lay in hiding, waiting for the unsuspecting souls to be cast down here from a lifetime of sins accumulated. Some layers even had their own atmospheres producing its own gases and storms like the one that endlessly raged overhead, whipping sand around in little twisters.

But it was the endless sea of dead trees that howled like tortured souls from the wind travelling through their hollowed insides. Their tops were void of any leaves or reaching branches, that earth boasted a beauty created throughout the seasons. No not here, not in this place. Instead there were twisted roots that held the remains of broken bodies and limbs that were no longer needed but had grown from the lower layers of Hell, like demonic seeds of the dead.

At least some humans had some things right when describing Hell, I thought dryly. Although granted, these were always ones to have been under the influence of my kind at the time. I thought back to the English poet John Keats and his sonnet 'On a Dream'. His version of the Second Circle was correct when he wrote of this place but for me, personally it was punishing in more ways than one.

I closed my eyes as I walked, striding towards the large castle I knew was being hidden by the very sands that belonged to my father and with each step recited the passage…

"But to that second circle of sad Hell,
Where in the gust, the whirlwind, and the flaw
Of rain and hail-stones, lovers need not tell

Their sorrows—pale were the sweet lips I saw…"

Then, just as the storm started to gravitate tighter around me I let loose my wings. The feeling of liberation stole the breath from my lungs when they surged from my confining vessel, giving birth to the very meaning of the words 'to be free'. My body shot into the air through the funnel of sand until I burst from the torrent of power continually displayed in my father's realm.

It was once I was free of the storm's reach that I could see the towering mass of imposing black stone that had been carved into my father's giant sentinels. The whole castle had been built from the belly of one of Earth's most volatile volcanoes Mount Merapi, situated in the centre of the island of Java, in Indonesia. I remember hearing the last time it had erupted there knowing this was down to my father's famous rage upon hearing of my mother's refusal to see him once again. It was easy to say that I definitely received my temper from the Demonic side of my parentage.

Funny then that it would be my Angelic brother who also received his fair share of our father's character, only in the form of his lustful ways. Not that many would have the chance to see this side of Vincent, but I knew of his inner struggles at calming his sexual urges of dominance. This being something any Angel would find difficult given that their natural tendencies were usually the opposite.

But I made it my business to know my kin, even if they continually tried to hide aspects of their lives from me. For years even Sophia was naive enough to try and hide her involvement with a certain Albino from me, thankfully though, *he* knew better.

It didn't take me long to reach the highest battlements that were nestled nicely into the sentinel's carved helmets of the centre tower. I let my wings level out and let the air carry me until my landing came into view below. Then with little thought, my wings folded and I dropped the remaining forty foot to land with one knee to the ground. I bit back a smile when all the sentinels guarding the roof scurried back a few steps. I then rose to my full height, briefly taking note of the broken stone my landing had caused before facing my father's guards.

I turned my head slightly letting my senses take in the amount of demons that now surrounded me and again had to hold in a smile. Good, I counted twenty. Now if I could just get the bastards to react aggressively towards me, then I was finally in for a chance at a good fight. I really needed a good fight. I cracked my neck to the side and waited for the bravest one to step forward first...

He didn't disappoint.

This time I couldn't hide my grin as I sidestepped his charging form and released my blades at the same time. I arched my torso backwards, slicing one flaming blade upwards and ripped through armour made from the carved bones of others. I allowed myself the pleasure in seeing the new jagged hole that was left down the spine of my opponent.

The sound of my father's foot soldiers all moving as one dragged my gaze back round to face what looked like their general barging through the centre. It was easy to tell the difference in ranks among my father's army. There was really only one rule that applied in this place and that was the bigger you were, the higher up the food chain you became... and didn't I just get a sick kick out of teaching these assholes a new lesson, one learnt by annihilating that rule in the form of broken limbs.

The general was at least twice my size and that wasn't including the added height gained by his helmet, one that was raised in the centre with a deadly shard of raw black metal. He positioned himself in front of me in such a way I knew he didn't know my identity and I was glad for it.

So my father had received some new recruits since the last time I was here. Well in that case it would be rude of me not to put them through their paces now wouldn't it, I thought with another malicious grin curving my lips.

"AMMENI ISU SALMAT QAQQADI ALKA ANNA ANNU ASRU" ('Why have Mankind come unto this place') The ancient Sumerian spoken was of a basic kind, which wasn't surprising even for a general and I very much doubted the others even knew what was said.

"EZEBU MA BALTU U LU TAHAZU MA ANA SIMTIM ALAKU" ('leave and live or battle and meet one's fate') I replied, making my warning clear enough even for the likes of an uneducated demon pawn at my father's hand. His reaction to this threat didn't surprise me... if anything I was counting on it.

A roar was released into the endless storm and there was a wave of growls that echoed around me, providing a dramatic effect. They were like the drums of war. They were never needed but fuck if the power in my blood didn't hum and dance along my veins with the sound made. And right now, I relished in the surge of power I could feel building.

"ALAL DAKU! ALAL DAKU! ALAL DAKU!" The rest of the sentinels started chanting his name and with the surge of adrenaline flooding my senses I could only hope they didn't stop. The word 'Daku' in Sumerian meant 'Kill' and as they asked so nicely, I didn't want to disappoint.

"Your name is Destroyer?" I asked in English, not expecting him to answer. Instead he slowly raised a heavily armoured hand to the visor on his helmet and slid it up. It made me wonder what I would have thought if I had been the weak and low ranking humankind, he obviously mistook me for. Now no longer faced with row after row of jaw like bars that covered his face and provided protection, I could see what a lifetime of Hell could do to what was once the face of a man.

Tortured souls never lasted long with their skin attached. It was always the first thing to go. Lips and noses would rot away and depending on how long your sentence was, extra demonic senses would form. From the looks of the general in front of me now, he had been here for quite a while, having too many extra teeth to count, no eyelids to speak of and more cracked bone than smooth. Most of which had been crudely stapled back together with claws of some long gone beast, whose decayed corpse no doubt now rested within the sands of souls.

"I ALAL!" He thundered in response and my smile was the last sight he saw before my warning rang true.

"Not anymore!" I said and swung up my sword quicker than any demon could boast. I watched with sickening satisfaction as only the tip of my blade now rested on top of his head, after being speared up through his neck. I watched the crimson spark in his eyes die before dislodging my blade with a slicing motion, causing what remained of his face to fall to the ground with a thud.

All at once the soldiers took a step back.

"Now come on, don't be like that." I said before pushing on my swords so that they formed a different shape. The grips folded inwards fitting my fists like liquid steel and the blades readjusted themselves so that they no longer pointed to the ground. Now they both curved up against the length of my arms, so that when they charged at me, the close proximity wouldn't hinder the fight.

I extended my arms and spun on one foot taking down the ones in closer range to then flick out the swords once more, taking down another line at the back. I was granted a moment to take in the carnage caused with the bodies lay lifelessly at my feet but considering my mood, it wasn't nearly enough. This wasn't a fight, it was a slaughter and now where was the fun in that.

"ALKA INA!" ('Come on!') I roared at the ones left that were no longer so brave and had started the retreat after witnessing so many fallen in just two moves with my blade.

"FINE! I will just have to bring the fight to you then!" I could no longer hear my other self reasoning with my inner battle. All that was left was a rage that had been burning into me ever since I heard the Oracle speak those haunting words of death so long ago. I wanted to kill. I wanted to punish. And I wanted someone to blame. So when I lifted up my swords to strike I wasn't surprised that a red river of death flowed steadily through my veins, with no heavenly essence in sight.

I ran at the unprovoked beings that I centred this all on and propelled my body from the back of a slumped demon. I landed with my blades held with the sole purpose to maim, to detach limbs from torsos and heads from necks. I sliced my way through the crowd, kicking the ones near the edge from the battlements and taking in their descending cries until they were too far to be heard.

"Enki, batiltu...Kataru...Kataru!" ('Lord of Earth, stop... Alliance!... Alliance!') I heard the voice break through the massacre and finally dragged enough air into my lungs to get my rage under control. At the sound of the title my father's people had named me, what was left of the sentinels guarding this tower fell to their knees. Wrath or not, they knew their place.

"Kataru." The newcomer said sidestepping amongst those still breathing and those who weren't. I took in the smaller demon and knew from his plain attire that he was a low-ranking servant. Something they call a 'Rakbu' which means messenger in this ancient language.

"Yes, yes, Nahu." I told him to calm down in the only tongue that would be understood by his kind thanks to it being over 5000 years old. They usually stuck to old ways of a long since dead world they no longer knew anything about.

I let my blades retract into my body and calmed my blood, letting my demon side know it had enjoyed enough fun for today.

"Ammeni Enki, alka anna annu asru?" ('Why Lord of Earth, come unto this place?')

"Sar Sha Hatti." ('The King of Sin') He lowered his head in respect and held out an arm for me to precede him through the open doorway. I walked through the stone arch and came to an abrupt stop at the edge of a spiral staircase. It tunnelled so deep it became the epitome of the term 'bottomless pits in Hell' and I had neither the time, nor the inclination to descend its many steps. If anything, I had just come to the realisation that my actions just now had more likely put those guards out of their misery, if this was what faced them in getting to their post every day.

What was I thinking? I knew my father never wasted a good soul and those guards were like no other, even if now their bodies were rendered useless. There was always an endless supply ready to take possession of a strong soul needing a purpose and in my father's kingdom there were always those ready to reward such services. It was the Kingdom of Lust after all.

"Asar?" I asked him where and he pointed down the centre, off to the right.

"Elenu dimtu, isten baba ina pilus duru" ('Upper tower, first gate on tunnel wall') I took in my directions wondering, in all the times in my life I had been here, if I had ever revisited the same place twice. The castle was easily the size of New York City, which was why I always chose some place high to land.

The fight had just been a bonus. Usually my identity was found out a lot quicker and nobody wants to find themselves in a battle with their King's son. But I hadn't been back here in a long time, which meant Asmodeus had indeed been recruiting.

I didn't reply, nor did I bid the servant any parting words as such things weren't done in this realm. I simply stepped off the edge and only let my wings unfold when I saw the first gate he spoke of. The air resisted against each feather as I slowed enough to grab a hold of one of the pillars and hoisted myself over the side to the steps. I ruffled my wings until comfortable again before pinning them back out of the way.

Like most of my kind, our wings were not only an incredibly sensitive part of our bodies but also something we showed with pride. It reflected our important status within the supernatural world. Those who had been punished enough to have their wings removed were normally shunned from our kind and never granted another chance at getting them back. It was one of the reasons I reserved the punishment for those who were foolish enough to really piss me off. Tipping the scales in a way that affects greater numbers, or simply like the day at my warehouses when hunters tried to take Keira from me. Now that thought had me grinding my teeth and cracking my knuckles, desperate for another fight.

These murderous thoughts were enough to last until I was close enough to feel my father's presence within the castle. I followed the static air as it became thicker, something that always happened when you put two alpha males with such raw power in the same vicinity as each other.

I walked into the last room where I knew I would find my father but frowned when I heard the sound of clapping and someone playing the Spanish guitar.

"Ah the prodigal son returns!" I rolled my eyes at my father's humour and came to a stop at the sight that met me.

Asmodeus lay sprawled out on top of an island of piled furs, cushions and naked bodies all entwined in sexual acts. My mind flashed back to Keira's family traditions and seriously doubted that this was one sight she would have witnessed upon her homecomings.

"Abum," I replied using the old word for father knowing how it irritated him so.

"Now, now my Maru, is that anyway to greet your old man?" He asked throwing back the word for son in the same way.

"And this is a way to great your son, with your cock firmly embedded in the hole of a restrained mouth?" I asked back, folding my arms and leaning against a pillar that for once wasn't the statue of a naked being.

My father's smile turned wicked and pulled back on the hair he had fisted to lock the mouth in question to his erection.

"It's a hot mouth at that my dear but one that will have to wait." He then released the female causing her to fall back and I couldn't help but shake my head at the outfit she wore that he was getting off on.

"A nun…really?"

"A *naughty* nun son, so don't kill the illusion." I ended up needing to hold the bridge of my nose at the re-run of events we always seemed to play out. The sound of his deep laughter right in front of me had me opening one eye to see if he had done with this game yet. He slapped me on the back and said,

"Come, I want to show you my new toy."

"I don't have time for this." I said to his back as he walked from me into the room. He looked over his shoulder with a smirk and said,

"But yet you found the time to play with my soldiers…um?"

"Trust me, soldiers like that needed the time taking and I

would hardly call it a fight, more like playing dead without waiting for the command. Is this what your army has been reduced to?" I saw only a brief flash of fire in his eyes to know he had taken a hit to his ego with my last comment. Of course he quickly reined it in and said,

"Please, they were merely younglings and now this way when their souls are recycled, they will have learnt a valuable lesson."

"So you're thanking me?" I asked wryly making my father laugh.

"From the looks of things you need to be thanking me for the relief… I bet your demon certainly enjoyed himself for those few short moments you allowed it." This time it was the fire I could feel flash in my own eyes as my demon responded in agreement. Again he laughed, making me growl.

"Come." He nodded to where the music still played.

"You have got to be kidding me?" I said after pushing my body from the pillar and following him. I could barely believe the new level of insanity my father had succumbed to.

In the centre of the room was a naked man on his knees and hog tied in such a way he looked close to toppling over. His face was locked in a device, looking straight towards a large white sheet that was held at the wall by two servants. His eyes had turned milky white and his blank expression told me he was under the influence of my father's demonic power.

"I always wanted to watch this film." He said as he petted his new toy's arched back and then smacked his ass. In doing so it made the vision of the movie playing from his eyes jump, like a reel of film skipping a scene.

There were two females fighting in a winter garden with samurai swords and I had to admit the sight looked appealing enough to hold my interest for a few seconds.

"Apparently it's called 'Kill Bill', but I am yet to find out who this Bill character is, so if you happen to come across a sinful soul who has seen the sequel, then do send them my way won't you" I raised an eyebrow at my father's new toy and wondered how much the poor soul being used as a projector thanks to his memories, wished electricity existed in Hell.

"I have important matters to discuss with you." I decided to get straight to the point.

"Oh in that I have no doubt, come…sit." He held out an arm for me to follow him to the orgy that continued even in his brief absence.

"Alone." My order rang clear and one I knew he wouldn't deny me.

"Very well." He said not even bothering to keep the humour from his reply. The Demon was insufferable!

"You know the last time I saw you, I remember you still found pleasures in thrusting your cock within the warmth of a willing vessel."

"Things have changed." I snapped not being able to keep the memory of being told my Chosen One had finally been born from influencing my response.

"That they have indeed." He muttered and for once he didn't lace the comment with flippancy.

I followed behind him as he walked through a large archway and further away from the events I had first walked into. We walked in silence and only the sounds of our footsteps echoed the halls that normally held noises of a very different kind. If anything it only managed to enhance the sincerity of the conversation that we both knew would be shortly taking place.

If I was honest, it had taken me all of ten months to calm enough to this point so that I didn't end up having this conversation with my father's neck at the end of my blade. Irrational thinking I know, considering it had nothing to do with my father's decisions when a very unexpected guest turned up on his doorstep. But just the thought of them being in the same room together had me balling my hands into fists until I heard them crack once more.

My father led me down a long hallway and to a door at the end. The size of the entrance and seriousness of the locking mechanism told me this wasn't a room he shared often, if at all. It most certainly wasn't a room I had ever been invited into and when he opened the door, I quickly knew why.

Never once in all my years had I been inside my father's private chambers and I only knew of one other soul who had…

My mother.

The large space was sectioned off into different areas and the one he led me to now was clearly used as his office. I found myself rolling my eyes behind his back as my father's warped sense of humour even reflected in his private life. He walked up a few steps and turned back to smirk at me as I took in the church altar he was using as a desk.

It was a handcrafted solid piece of oak, only there was nothing holy about it. It was heavily carved, with four panels cut at the front, each one displaying their own sexual scene that would make any pastor blush. Not surprisingly carved apples were the fruit of choice to frame the whole piece.

"Won't you take a seat?" He nodded to the chair in front but I ignored him, knowing what I had come here to say was best said standing.

My father took his seat behind the altar in what could only be described as the most egotistical throne I had ever seen and I had sat in a quite a few in my time.

"Nice chair." I commented dryly on the matt black stone statue that was my father's exact image of his Demon self, created in such a way it could be sat upon. The three famous sides of his personality sat at the top of the throne, the first being that of a ram. Lucifer always did say his humour would

27

butt heads with his fellow Kings of the other circles… he was right of course.

There was also his incredible strength in the form of a bull and lastly that of his hot-headed temper which was a man breathing fire. Again, I thought back to the erupting volcanoes and suppressed a knowing smile.

"It is becoming of me is it not? Hand carved by Jainism monks…under the influence you understand, but I had hoped it would have included a naked form of some kind, however I thought best not to push my luck."

"And that would be a first." He smiled back at me and then his fingers tapped against the serpent's tail that acted as the arm rests.

"But while we are on the subject of your true form I must ask why you still continue to choose that one in particular." I nodded to the body that unnervingly looked like an older version of myself, wishing more for the demon depicted in his throne to be facing me instead.

"Ah my son, your dear mother loves this form for a reason." He threw back at me and I sighed, reconsidering my decision to stand. I used my power without much thought to move the chair back and answered his comment with a cutting one of my own.

"Why, has she been down here recently?" I saw a flash of my father's rage before it simmered. Good, I wanted that rage so I had something to battle. Just the very thought of Keira in this place twisted my insides like one of Vincent's blades. Had she come into this room? What had she been forced to witness?

"Touché Dominic." He said fighting with his temper enough to force out his next question.

"So tell me, how is my dear wife these days, does she still favour the sun?" I snapped out of my own ire and looked up at him, noting how his muscles had tensed. His skin had tightened to what looked like a painful degree. I shook my head at the same question I received every time. It was always about *his Sarah*.

"She is very well but this is not news." I replied the same as always.

"You know it has not slipped her notice the obsession you still hold over her." I added.

"One night with a Goddess will do that to you son but this you already know...tell me Son, how is your own Goddess doing these days?" I growled low in my throat and crushed the arms of the chair, knowing I should never have sat down. I stood perfectly in sync with one single pound of my heart as I let his words ignite my temper. I kicked the chair back hearing it smash into the furniture behind me but not taking a second of care to look.

"Fuck you! Do not play games with me old man for you know she isn't *mine anymore!"* The last words came through in my demon tongue, as it was as angry with his last comment as I was. However, my father barely flinched at my outburst but merely made a tutting sound before speaking.

"Now, now Dom, you know she will always be yours...a being of your birthright and keeper of my blood doesn't lay claim to the other half of their soul and then truly walk away from it." His voice became harsher with every syllable that left his lips, showing his mounting impatience.

"And mother?" I pushed back, as was my nature. He surprised me when instead of mirroring my anger he simply relaxed his features, features that so resembled my own. Then he grinned that fucking grin of his!

"She will always be mine, even as she sits in her gleaming tower of purity and thinks otherwise."

"And if your decision meant her death, what then?" I snapped making his fist come crashing down on the wood.

"The idea's painful isn't it father?"

"Fucking fates! Now you listen boy and you listen good. If I had taken any care in words spoken by any ideas the Gods had seen fit to say, then you and your siblings would never have been born!"

"And if you're wrong? Or *I* am wrong…?"

"Or the fates are wrong." He interrupted me and I closed my eyes at the hope in his words, ones I always carried buried and locked away in my heart.

"I can't chance her life, I won't!" This was not an option for me!

"Where is my son Dominic? Where is the fearless King I know lives inside you?"

"Don't play that card and don't gamble with my pride, for you will lose!" I growled back at him knowing what he was doing.

"But you let the Fates play and gamble with your very life, yet you are not brave enough to snatch back control. To take what you were destined to take…to demand and to OWN what is rightfully yours!"

"I WILL KILL HER!" I roared in his face over the altar, throwing my arms back in my soul-destroying confession.

"If you truly believed that then why are you even here?" I took in his question and the anger started to seep from my blood, making me pant like a wild beast that roamed my father's lands. Fuck, like this I was no better than that damned Hellbeast Cerberus!

"You spoke about this to Sophia?"

"I did."

"So you think me a coward?" I asked bitterly.

"No. Trust me, I know of the strength it took for you to walk away from her but understand my son, that it took that very same strength in her coming here looking for you."

"You think I don't know this!?" I ran a frustrated hand

through my hair and then let the anger boil once more, only to slice my arm down and shout,

"I know this! I am reminded of the fact every damn day I breathe on Earth's plane, but I am also reminded of what it feels like to have nearly lost her. You have seen her scars and you know the truth…where was my protection then?"

"Where was the protection of the Gods? Where were the self-righteous Fates guiding her then… guiding her to you? You put too much on yourself when only the ones above us are to blame." He argued and I knew this conversation was getting me nowhere for I would never feel differently on the matter. It was a simple fact that where Keira was concerned, I could never seem to do right by her.

"It no longer matters. I am removed from her life and therefore have removed the threat of taking her life."

"You're making a mistake." Why wouldn't he just give it up!?

"You mean to torture me, is that it?!" He simply shook his head at my questioning.

"Then you say these things only because you don't understand." At this statement something deeper passed through my father's eyes and if I had to choose the emotion, I would say it was nothing less *than* understanding.

"Come, I wish to show you something." My father stood and walked up to the arched balcony that was joined from two small staircases either side of his altar. The walls on these sides were covered in books crammed so full they looked close to bursting from the shelves. I followed him up the steep staircase and saw that what originally looked like only enough space for one person to stand there was actually another room beyond its darkness.

"Immaru!" My father spoke the word for 'light' in Sumerian and I sucked in a quick breath at what he had hidden there.

"You see son, we are not without our similarities."

"Does she know of this place?" I asked in astonishment as I took in the cavernous space where every inch was filled with my mother's image. It was a space so big that it looked like a hollowed-out mountain and was impossible to see an end, even given my enhanced abilities. Her beauty shone from every surface in the room like a silent prisoner of Heaven lived down here.

"No one but I knows of this place…and now so do you." I shook my head as I was assaulted with an image of my father that I had proceeded to get wrong on so many levels. Yes I knew of his obsession with the only woman he really truly loved but for a being of his stature, then this news was a revelation. Understanding quickly dawned on me.

"You keep this place hidden to keep her safe" I said trying to take in the hundreds or maybe even thousands of statues, sculptures, paintings and real-life drawings of the woman that gave birth to me. It was a hauntingly beautiful sight to behold flickering in the firelight.

"I have many enemies." Well I knew of that fact as it mimicked my own in the central realm.

"So you do understand?"

"What I understand is that if the other half of your soul chooses *not* to be with you and therefore shuns your protection, then to protect her you must let her go." I frowned and turned from the treasures my father held dear to look him in the face.

"But you have been trying to…"

"You misunderstand my meaning. Keira did not shun your protection Dominic. She did not shun your heart. She fought for it… now don't you think it is time to do the same?" He added this last part as he paused at the door before turning from the room to walk back the way we came. I lowered my head to scowl at the floor, taking in everything he had told me. Was it possible that I could better protect Keira with her by my side, than from a distance? But that wasn't the question that needed answering the most. It was could I really protect her from me?

"Wait, how did you know?" I asked storming back into room and feeling the surge of power as he locked the invisible vault door behind me.

"Know?"

"About my own obsession, about my own room dedicated to Keira's image?" I said pointing back at my father's hidden room. I watched a genuine smile curve his lips before he answered with a simple…

"I have met her son, trust me…"

"…*I know.*"

CHAPTER THREE

DRAVEN

SOMEBODY ELSE?

I watched my father descend the steps and retake his seat on that ostentatious throne of his. Of course, he was right, everyone who was ever lucky enough in life to meet Keira instantly knew there was something special about her. There was something that drew you in and captured you. It then held you prisoner and you simply smiled as she unknowingly swallowed the key for the rest of your eternity.

That was her greatest gift and she didn't even know it. Armies would line up from one smile, ready to fight to keep her safe. She would have the underworld kneeling at her feet with the power of her soul, one that could brighten any dark realm without much thought. And all this power and not one fucking clue!

And she was once mine.

I had to shake my head to hold these thoughts from injecting me with a murderous rage as it usually did. You know not of the treasure you hold when looking into the eyes of true love until those eyes become forever closed to you. If it is true what the poets say, that the eyes are the key to a person's soul, then looking into one as pure as Keira's was like being able to gaze through the keyhole to Heaven's door for a mortal.

"So, my Maru, the question remains…are you really going to trust in the Fates when the Fates not only obviously lied to you but to her as well?" ('Son' in Sumerian)

"You know of their lies?" I asked my father after sucking in a defeated breath.

"I do indeed and from the perfectly formed lips of your Electus." I couldn't help the growl that sounded at the back of my throat when hearing my father talk of the very same lips I craved like salvation to a dying man. However, my father simply smirked and ran a fingertip across his own lips in order no doubt to goad me further.

"If you want a fight old man then you only need to ask." I commented dryly knowing my father was good for it, never being one to pass up the chance of a challenging fight.

"But of course my child, if you think it will help." He lowered his head to me in respect and rose gracefully from his seat. I watched as he held out an arm and nodded in the direction I was to follow. I felt my blood start to heat under my confining skin in anticipation. Yes, this was what I needed, a man who didn't fear giving me his all. A worthy opponent and one so equally matched to my own skills.

I waited as he approached a pair of double doors and briefly took note of my surroundings. The large open space was sectioned into different areas and each had its own carnal influence. There was a raised platform at waist height that was obviously where he slept. This was a combination of fine silks in the colours of a sunset he never saw and twisted raw iron arms and hands set in crude ways that formed the bed frame.

It was as though medieval England had clashed against an Arabian harem. I rolled my eyes as I turned away and watched as my father pulled both doors back dramatically.

"Ah, now this will do nicely!" He said taking in the room beyond where he stood with his arms outstretched. I shook my head at my father's theatrics and followed him through to see for myself what the mad King was up to this time.

"Let it be said Father, that your imagination knows no bounds." I said wryly as I took in the new space.

"What can I say, I felt inspired…it really is a very good movie." I supressed a groan at his outlandish ways and responded only with a grunt. The room we now stood in was a large hall that had been converted for a short time into a Japanese training room. Of course this one had a few significant twists. For one, it was snowing and covered the ground in a blanket of crisp white that crunched with each step I made.

"Only you could make it snow in Hell." I commented wryly shaking my head at him. His only reply was to laugh vigorously.

The other aspects of the room included the wall at my back and the one directly opposite me both made from thick dark blocks, reminding me we were still in my father's castle. The ones at our sides were in keeping with Japanese architecture as the walls were fusuma, a paper and wooden frame that let in lots of light. In this case however, it created a perfect stage for the shadow puppets that were putting on a show behind it.

"I don't remember that in the movie." I nodded to the Japanese Demon warriors that were battling it out around the room behind the walls. My father smirked at me before saying,

"So you *have* seen it?" I merely answered him with a shrug.

"Well, this is *my* version." He said before facing the centre

37

of the room and lifting up his arm bringing his outstretched fingers to a fist. I waited knowing this was what was done when bringing forth power from the elements around you and in my father's case, something volcanic.

I heard the floor groan and split before I saw the cracks emerge. Once again, and something quite common in my father's presence, was the urge to roll my eyes as I watched the floor open up. A clay furnace then rose from the depths like a sarcophagus on fire.

"A Tatara...? This is your idea of a suitable environment for a fight?" I asked frowning and unable to resist the urge to rub the bridge of my nose in frustration, a habit I had never had the inclination to correct.

"I thought it rather apt as I hear your skills with the Katana are quite legendary." My father said walking to one side where two long, thin wooden boxes were waiting. I grunted at my father's twisted logic. Yes, it had to be said that it was in this clay furnace that the combination of iron, sand and the carbon from coal made the right steel known as Tamahagane, one that was needed to make the formidable Samurai. But did it really need to act as centre piece for this momentous event? Granted that there was only one other time I had fought my father and it had also been about a woman back then...

My mother.

"Well, the last time we used Bardiche, so I thought something a little less barbaric this time, don't you think?" I nodded briefly reminiscing back to that day and how it felt to hold that long poled axe firmly in my hand as it travelled towards my father's head, his famous smirk wavering just before he dodged the deadly blow.

"Besides, I didn't think you would object to such a weapon given your acquired skills in the art."

"I had a good master." I said, thinking back again on fond

memories of blood, sweat and tears of those I was taught to defeat.

"Ah yes, how is Takeshi, still a member of your council I presume?"

"And has been since his rebirth in 1630." I added as he flipped back the lids of the two boxes that lay situated side by side. He raised his head up and spoke his thoughts,

"You never could let go of the good ones could you…? Enlighten me, what was he called before his…"

"Grand Master, Miyamoto Musashi." I answered, interrupting him, letting him know the depth of respect I felt for the man both back when he was human and now as he still stands at my side.

"But of course, 'men of the waves', one of the Ronin… pray tell me my son, how did you manage to ensnare him in your powerful clutches?" I growled at his pointless questioning of times long past. Why my father always had this maddening effect on me I couldn't fathom but I knew it had something to do with his endless questions about my time on the central plane. Curious was too simple a word to describe my fathering blood bearer.

"He committed seppuku at my request." At this my father smiled, just loving the dark side to any story.

"Oh such loyalty… to fall on one's sword until disembowelment, I wonder though at their last thoughts." He said looking thoughtful pushing up his bottom lip momentarily.

"It is part of the Samurai Bushido honour code and one he took gladly knowing what I had in store for him in his next life…now are we going to fight, old man or do you wish me to regale you of all my council's tales of woe and how they came to be?" I said crossing my arms and leaning back on one of the wooden pillars that were spread out throughout the room.

"Now, now, Dominic there is no need to be so touchy…I

brought you in here for a fight and a fight I shall indeed give you!" He finished by throwing me a sword, one he had taken from the box. I caught the sword and for a moment I was stunned at what I now beheld in my grasp.

"This…why, this is a Masamune sword." I almost stuttered in my awe. I was not lying when I told Keira that day of my passion for collecting weapons.

"It is not only a Masamune sword but *the* Masamune sword." My father said in pride causing my head to shoot up from staring at its perfection.

"Surely you jest? It can't be the…"

"It is the one and only Honjo Masamune." I couldn't help but gasp, even though I suspected it the moment my skin made contact.

"So this is where it has been hiding." My father smirked as he took his own sword and released it slowly from its encasing.

"This is where it is *waiting*, not hiding." He counteracted.

"Do you know how long I have been searching for this sword?" I asked him barely concealing my irritation.

"Quite a while, I imagine."

"You imagine right, now explain yourself!" I snapped.

"Careful Dominic, you are in my domain now and here I rule!" My comeback was a confident smile as I took in the evidence that I'd finally started to crack his armour of indifference.

"Yes and maybe you're losing your edge."

"Ah my child, now you start to show your own weakness in your need for this fight…did my soldiers really do so little for you?" He came to stand opposite me and all at once he and I were clothed in Japanese robes better suited for fighting.

"They were nothing, barely even an appetiser." I responded pulling out my own blade, taking beautiful note of some of the old battle scars the sword held. I grinned bringing it up closer to my face before resting it at my side in a ready stance, thinking it was only to be expected when you were over 700 years old.

We started to circle each other slowly making a meal out of who would be the first to break in battle.

"And your own Samurai?" I asked nodding to his weapon.

"Fudo Masamune and one of the few signed by the man himself." Again I was impressed. My eyes widened as I realised this fight was more evenly matched in more ways than one.

"My sword's brother, and no less than two five body blades fighting against each other." I said referring to the highest measurement that can be considered for such a weapon, as to slice through five bodies in one isn't an easy feat to accomplish.

"Vincent would be jealous indeed."

"Now that I would like to see, my Angelic son does tend to keep his emotions in check doesn't he and so like his mother." I nodded in agreement and waited for the first move I knew would not be long in coming.

"Rules still stand, we fight as men." I said this time making my father roll his eyes.

"Now where is the fun in that exactly?"

"Scared of the challenge Abum?" I answered with a taunting question of my own. ('Father' in Sumerian)

"Quaking in my fucking boots!" He mocked before he charged at me just like I knew he would. He ran at me with his sword held high and I saw a flash of the burning rage flare in his eyes as it reflected in his steel. I blocked the attack and the sound of our swords clashing echoed, drowning out the sound of flames crackling from the centre of the room.

I spun on one foot and landed low to the ground holding my blade above me as I fended off another blow. I grinned at the feel of my father's strength, relishing in it and the feeling of a worthy fight. Normally fighting against those so low beneath my own abilities was nothing more than an annoyance for my wasted time. A mindless chore that required very little thinking but this, well now, this was nothing short of a gift!

I swiped my foot out taking him by surprise and to the floor. I spun back up and attacked the best way that the sword was made for, slashing downwards using brute strength thanks to its curvature shape. My father not surprisingly blocked my attempt at getting at his heart and flipped upwards horizontally, using the motion to push me back with his sword.

I had barely taken a step back and he was once again coming at me. I met him head on and our blades collided. We became locked together with little space between us and our match in strength didn't go un-noticed.

"How's your Demon holding up…clawing to break free yet?" He asked pointing out the obvious, that yes, my Demon was riding me hard wanting to take over the fight as was its nature.

"My Demon is lucky enough to have such control in a Master such as I!" I snarled back and pushed harder against his blade. He laughed as I gained one inch at a time, forcing his body to bend backwards.

"My son, the controlled Master indeed…should daddy be proud?" He taunted and my Demon growled at the insult, trying to force its way to the surface. Just before my father's wish was granted in releasing my Demon, I pushed off his blade and spun catching him at the side, leaving behind a slice of blood.

"At last! Well done my Etlu Maru!" He shouted joyfully and I tried to conceal my shock at finally being able to leave my mark for the first time. Never before had I ever drawn my father's blood and up until now, I wasn't sure if he was even human enough to bleed after all this time. ('Warrior son' in Sumerian)

"I see now that your Grand Master taught you well, which makes me wonder…" He paused as he took further steps backward putting more space between us. I circled around him and swiped my sword forcefully in front of me. My father's eyes took in the line of his blood that now marked the snow in a sprayed line from my actions.

"You wonder…?" I asked dragging his angry eyes back to my circling form.

"Who would win in a fight between two Grand Masters, as I too was taught by one in the family… tell me, does Takeshi know his father Munisai resides down here?" I didn't even bother hiding my astonishment and my father used the moment to his advantage.

I found myself near to being overwhelmed from blow after blow of attacks my father rained down on me and only just being able to hold his blade at bay from making deadly contact. I forced myself to snap back from the information I'd just learned and could once again hear my old Master in my head.

'Attack the arteries here and here', he would say mock slicing at the inside of my arms and legs. 'Then go for the engine, for fuel cannot travel the body without its pump', he would add, while aiming the blade's tip at my heart.

Finally, I used my Master's old words to centre me enough to regain the upper hand. I watched as my father's moves became more predictable now that I was accustomed to his style and I waited for just the right move I knew was coming. So I prompted the action by leading him into a false sense of security and I wasn't left disappointed.

He played nicely into my hands as I brought him closer into the centre near the furnace. Again Takeshi's words rang true… 'The best warrior is the one that can turn circumstances to his advantage in a fight and use the elements as an extension of his weapon'.

With this in mind I kept the flames to my back and purposely made a mistake in my defence, letting my father drive me to my knees. The heat at my back felt strangely comforting to my Demon that knew what was coming and I could feel him seep through enough to make me smile.

"Grinning whilst on your knees is a sign of insanity, son." He said pushing down on my blade that was inches away from my face.

"And you would know!" I said just before I used all of my strength to push up and at the same time caught hold of the end of his sword next to his hands. I locked myself to him and swiftly stood taking him off guard. I then spun around and used my body weight to spin him around and let go, propelling him into the furnace.

He crashed into the centre and split open the clay sending sparks of amber skittering across the snow and into the air like deadly fireflies. A burst of steam clouded the room as heat cooled against the icy floor and momentarily blinded me. I held my arm across my eyes for a few short seconds and waited for the destruction to calm.

I looked amongst the wreckage and quickly noticed a flaming shadow climbing from the piles of glowing steel. I was not surprised to see my father emerging in his true form but I was surprised when he bothered to change back once more. He started his steps as a Demon ruler and finished them jumping down from the remains as a man.

"That wasn't very sporting of you, Dominic." He said dusting off the few burning embers that smoked on his shoulders. His attire was nearly completely burnt off but my father never remained dishevelled for long. The material soon started to regrow back into its original form and with an aggravated motion he dug his hand deep into the belly of the broken furnace and retrieved his now glowing sword.

"Means must, old man." I replied making him grin as though an idea just lit up his mischievous side.

"So that's how we are playing this? Very well Dominic, just remember that you erased the first line of conduct." I frowned at what he could mean.

"You know your sister came to visit me recently." He said as matter of fact and throwing me off guard.

"This isn't news to me." I remarked trying not to lose myself to the urge of grabbing him by the throat and roaring at him to get on with it!

"No, I gathered not, only I would wager the topic of conversation would interest you greatly." I growled low in my throat knowing there was no way I would be able to refrain from taking a bite out of the bait he dangled in front of me.

"Play your games with another fool, Asmodeus and say what you intend to say!" I snapped feeling my fist clench to near breaking point around my blade's handle. He lifted his head to the side, gave me an evil grin and my breath caught, for I knew the information he had was of the sort that made him believe he would win. The only way that would happen is if I went into a blind rage and lost my head in allowing my Demon to make decisions based on its wrath.

My blood started to run cold.

"I do believe Sophia is meeting with her now as we speak and with her…" He paused for dramatic effect and I let my eyes flash red in warning. Again with that fucking smile!

"…her new supernatural *lover!*" At the sound of his words my blood didn't just turn cold, no, it turned glacial!

My Demon erupted and this time, down here there was no Angel in sight to hold him back. I roared at my father, shaking the foundations of his castle and for a fleeting moment it looked as though he knew he had gone too far.

"YOU LIE!!!!" I screamed at him before letting go and charging at him like a crazed battle horse. My reasoning all fled and left a husk of a man fuelled only with the desire to kill everyone and everything in its path. It wanted its mate back! It wanted its calming solace and the other half of its soul back just as much as I did but unlike me, it had no logic in its quest to get it back!

To get *her* back.

I ran at him and at the last second instead of running him through with my blade I used what was left of my inner self and twisted my body, so my shoulder hit him square in the chest. He was once again flying backwards and travelling through the remains of the furnace. I watched as his body landed against the far wall of stone but before he could be allowed to slump down to the ground I was there at his side.

I raised my sword to slice into his side but then caught a flash of raised steel in my side vision. My father was bringing his weapon down at my head and I made a quick decision to bring up my sword and block the blow to my head, instead of causing his body damage.

In the seconds this all happened I also witnessed his eyes flash to their Demon side before he used his powers to cut through my blade. This gave me only a fraction of time to prevent my head from being slashed open as my free hand shot up and gripped his sword. I had to transform part of myself into my Demon as a means of protection from losing my fingers in the process.

"You cheated." I said stating the obvious.

"What did you expect?" He asked laughing.

"What you never did…My turn!" This was the only warning I gave him as I reversed his sword so that I now held the handle and the tip was left pointing at his throat. My free hand came back to his side as I held my remaining blade at his gut, ready to see what a demon King was really made of if he didn't answer my questions.

"NOW TELL ME!" My Demon roared at him, only my answer came from behind me.

"I tried to tell you, Dom." Sophia's soft voice was a cruel music that filled the carnage of the room, giving it a gentleness that didn't belong.

"Let him go Dom, I asked him to do this."

"WHY?!" I snarled turning my head towards her.

"Because you needed to know, and you wouldn't listen." She reasoned.

"Listen to what, these lies!?" It couldn't be true...she wouldn't...she...wouldn't do that...would she?

"That's just it though brother, it's not lies... and it's about time you saw the truth for your own eyes." I shook my head and only when I felt my father's hand rest on my shoulder did I realise I must have lowered my weapons in the ultimate defeat.

"It's alright son, there's still time."

"He's right Dom, come with me." Sophia said softly as though she knew how my heart was being shredded apart by a truth I had pushed Keira into.

"Go where Sophia, back to claim what is no longer mine to claim?" I asked bitterly. She shook her head making the halo of loose dark curls bounce.

"No brother, come back with me to Afterlife and claim what is rightfully *yours to claim.*" I closed my eyes at the sound of her hope and every fibre in my body hummed with tension knowing Keira was with someone else.

I needed to see. I needed to witness this with my own eyes.

I needed to go back to...

My Afterlife.

CHAPTER FOUR

KEIRA

BACK TO AFTERLIFE

"It was over ten months ago, Keira…get a grip!" I said to myself in the mirror, after first looking round to check no-one else was in any of the cubicles. I washed my hands again in the lavish sink that one would never expect to see in a Gothic nightclub, but then again this wasn't just any Gothic nightclub…

This was Afterlife.

It was the first time I had come here since it reopened back in October last year and now we were in June. It felt as if so much had happened since then and yet nothing at all. Well, nothing at all compared to how my life usually went. For starters, there were no kidnappings, no attacks, no battles of any kind, not unless you called trying to change Ella's nappy a battle…that kid just hated being still for more than a second!

I could even say that not one single person had tried to drug me yet and I was starting to feel…well, I guess a little bored with normality. Even my boyfriend, who I should probably mention was at least slightly supernatural, was as normal as they came. Sure, he was gorgeous and amazingly talented when it came to design, but he was an architect for God's sake…I mean how normal could I get after dating Mr D. (I had forbidden myself from saying the D word not long after I arrived home). I mean, he might as well have been a dentist or an accountant!

But he was a good guy and after the emotional rollercoaster I had been on, then I needed a good 'normal' guy. And Alex Cain was more than a good guy, he was a friggin' saint!

But don't get me wrong, it's not like I met him on that flight and 'bam' we started dating…not even close. It was actually at college that I bumped into him again when he was giving a lecture for the architectural department and when I say bumped, I mean in true Keira fashion, I fell into him.

You know how it is. It was after a depressing Christmas and New Year where I was about as happy as a two-week-old turkey sandwich! I tried not to let it be known, putting on a smile for my family's sake, but there were certain things I couldn't do, no matter how traditional they were in the William's household. For one thing, everyone got their gifts from me in gift bags instead of wrapping paper because it was too painful a memory of when Draven and I were in my old room wrapping gifts together.

Oh and I stupidly crammed in Christmas pud, just because last year we declined it after dinner to go back upstairs. Poor Frank had to go out in the snow and get me a packet of Rennies from the only place he could find open.

So, by the time I went back to college I was in desperate need to focus on anything that had nothing to do with a certain someone. I can't say it didn't still hurt, oh hell no, it hurt every damn day! But as the days went on and as the time passed, it just hurt a little less. That was ok of course, until my friends had finally ground me down into going back to Afterlife to see them and I'm not talking about just Jack and RJ.

The main difference this time was that 'he who shall not be named' had kept to his word. I spoke to Sophia and Pip almost every day, but I always refused any information they had offered about their King. I'd even met up with them both a few times since, along with seeing Lucius when he was near Portland, which granted was only once and that was because I quote 'Squeak nagged me'.

I had even seen Vincent on occasion and once we even went for a ride on his bike to nowhere in particular, just somewhere and anywhere we could be alone. There was never anything in it, but spending time with someone I loved like a brother and always would, meant the world to me. He had tried to tell me about his brother a few times but after I made it more than a little clear (I was loud), he gave up.

I had even received a postcard from Sigurd, which was funny as it had on it a man's naked behind with a tattoo on one cheek that was stamped 'Pain in the ass women belong here'. I had tears in my eyes that day and laughed until it hurt. But I had to say the biggest shocker of all was when one day Jared showed up at my door. Frank nearly had a heart attack at seeing a biker on his doorstep asking for me.

He told me he was just passing through and wanted to know if I fancied getting a drink with him. It took me three days to convince Frank and Libby that I wasn't going off the deep end and becoming a biker chick or a Hell's Angel's old lady! (Which had me once again in stitches laughing when Libby had said that's what they call them).

I think that was why they seemed so relieved when I finally introduced them to Alex. Libby had to fan herself in the kitchen when she heard his French accent. I just laughed and shook my head knowing my family was nuts, but I loved them.

Alex was originally born in America, but he was brought up mostly in Bordeaux, in the South of France, to then study in Paris. Both his parents were dead, but that was about as much as I had been able to get from him, as it was clearly a touchy subject, which was fair enough considering I had quite a few of those myself.

He travelled quite a bit, which was also alright with me as I wasn't ready to jump into a demanding relationship just yet. But the strangest thing about our relationship, which had been just over six months, was that we had not once had sex. We had done some stuff together but the actual act was not on the cards yet and I found myself conflicted, wondering if I ever would be able to. I was happy this wasn't just down to me as he was deeply religious and didn't believe in sex before marriage.

I couldn't believe my luck. I had found the one guy out there who was old-fashioned enough to think this way and I couldn't have been happier for it. After that last night with Mr No Name, I couldn't seem to be able to get past it enough to even try, but thankfully with Alex I didn't even have to.

Which brought me back to now and why I had been in the loo for the last ten minutes having a series of mini panic attacks. Sophia had convinced me to come to Afterlife tonight as she and Vincent were coming back for a few weeks. My first question had been answered even before I asked it.

"Don't worry Keira, Dominic won't be there." The relief was obvious in the whoosh of air that came from my side of the phone. Sophia just laughed at me and then talked my ear off for an hour and half until I caved in. So now, for the first time in over a year, I was back and weeing my not so big girl knickers!

"Yo Bitch, your yummy French pie told me to come in here

and get you…oh and he told me to say 'Surprise'!" RJ said coming to jump up on the sinks to face me.

"He's here?! He said he couldn't come." I said letting a new panic set in. I had told him my plans and silently thanked my lucky stars when he said he would still be in Portland, where the main office for the company he worked for was located.

I had told Vincent and Sophia about Alex and even though they didn't pass judgement, you could see they weren't about to do cartwheels over the fact any time soon. But I guess who could really blame them? I had dated their brother and was supposedly destined for him by the very Gods, who had buggered things up for us in the first place!

"I think that's where the whole 'Surprise' thing came in." RJ said smirking.

"Oh God!" I said running the tap again to wash my hands which I had done about six times now. I mean, Afterlife offered nice soap in the ladies, but it wasn't that nice!

"Oh come on, it isn't that bad… and besides, you were the one who said Draverlicous wouldn't be here…right?"

"I wish you would stop calling him that." I grumbled, bracing my 'very' clean hands on the sink and focusing on the ring of bubbles I had created by the plug hole.

"Hey Kaz, you know he is fair game now, not that that would ever help any of us commoners or the fact that the guy has done a Houdini, as he never comes here anymore, is despite the fact."

"Yeah well, you're all welcome to him!" I commented bitterly, something I obviously didn't mean but it was just easier acting this way. No one seemed to ask questions when I played the bitchy sour Ex…and I was getting oh so good at it!

"So, you coming or what, 'cause I got to say, you hide out any longer in here and Cassie bitch features is gonna get her claws in your man, and this year's fashion choice is seedy strip joint." I laughed at the thought of Alex dealing with that. Hell, one conversation with my boyfriend and this summer's fashion would soon be Sunday school or slutty nun but if I was to bet on just one I would go with the first for sure!

"Fine, let's get this over with." RJ slapped me on the shoulder and said,

"Now that's the spirit…wow when did my optimistic friend get to be so much fun?" RJ asked sarcastically, causing me to check my fingernails only by keeping the middle finger extended her way. She just laughed and grabbed my hand to pull me from my hiding place.

"Come on blondie, time for the VIP treatment once again." At this I groaned making her laugh, when really all I wanted to do was run screaming from the doors, in a comical, girly dramatic fashion like you see in the movies. After all, I remembered all too well what happened the first time I got suckered up into Afterlife's VIP. I had not come out of it the same person that was for sure, which just begged the question… what would happen to me this time?

"There you are, Catherine." Oh yeah, and ever since Alex got introduced to me via a snooty hostess as Catherine, that's what he continued to call me. Or sometimes even Cathy for short. It didn't bother me. No, if anything it felt nice being called something different that didn't just end up reminding me of a certain someone whenever we were kissing or just spending time together.

I think the biggest appeal to Alex was that nothing he ever did reminded me of him. There was not one ounce that could even tie the two men together and other than first meeting him on my way back home last year, there was nothing that tied him to my painful memories. Of course, it helped he was hot, handsome and as smart as they came.

He wasn't especially tall but with me being only 5' 3", he

was still going to be taller than me at 5' 10". He had a slim build, which was refreshing, given the bulk I was used to being around and when he hugged me it didn't feel like he could ever forget himself and crush me to death! See, I had developed the happy knack of turning things that once would have turned me on or made me happy into a negative and an added pile of shit that I continually collected in my memories. This was something I didn't need any expert to tell me was a coping mechanism.

But don't get me wrong, he was still fit, only he had more of a swimmer's body. All lean muscles that tapered down into a slim waist, hidden behind his usual perfect clothes. Alex was a man who prided himself on looking smart and professional at all times, whether it was his styled back dark hair that sometimes looked slick with the aid of products or his smooth moisturized face that smelled of one clean male.

He had a set of piercing grey blue eyes, but a lighter shade to mine. His features were pointed, with a sharp nose and chin to match which gave him an air of authority, but one very different to the owners of Afterlife. And when he smiled it creased his cheeks which gave him a dangerous edge that I was yet to find.

Which is what he did now as I went into his open arms for a hug.

"Hey, I thought you said you couldn't make it." I tried to sound light-hearted but it was hard when my heart was pounding at the thought of introducing my new boyfriend to my 'other' family.

"The meeting finished earlier than I thought it would…it's not a problem is it? I thought you would want me here for support."

"Of course it is…I mean isn't…umm…let me start again…" I mumbled making RJ roll her eyes at me behind him, when he laughed. I don't know why but I always got the impression from RJ and Jack that they didn't like him as much as they had… erm… you know who.

Although of course they never said so in as many words, but I guessed it was because there were just so many differences between them. I mean, take now for example. We were in a Goth club and Alex was wearing a suit without the tie. Okay, he had probably just come straight from the office but still, he stuck out like a sore thumb…which made me wonder what he saw in me sometimes?

Like now, I was wearing a pair of grey skinny jeans that I could only wear under something that covered my bum or they would be classed as indecent, given the extra pounds my chocolate habit had managed to put on. I matched this with a tight long sleeved dress in cherry red that was just like an overly long t-shirt with a bit of flare round the bottom, which kicked out like a skirt. My sister had bought it for me because it had a black lace back in the shape of a massive skull that showed off most of my skin underneath. We both agreed it would be perfect for Afterlife should I ever have the guts to go back there again, which brought me to my outfit choice.

"You look different honey, what is it?" He asked, holding me back at arm's length to take me in.

"I dunno, maybe 'cause I left my hair down." I prompted as this was something I still rarely did, but even more so after that night.

"That's it, so this is a special occasion then?" He asked giving me that look. Alex didn't think it healthy that I was still in such tight contact with my Ex's family, but other than a few snide comments, ones I ignored, it hadn't caused too many problems…until now.

"They're my friends Alex and I want to look nice for them." I said keeping my voice low. I saw that little tensing of his jaw that told me he wanted to say more, but then just like that he was back to smiling and kissing me on the forehead,

"Of course you do and you look lovely." I smiled back up at him before taking his hand.

"Well, we might as well get going." I said knowing that I couldn't prolong it any longer. So, with my hand in his, we snaked our way through the crowd until coming to the left side of the double staircase. The guard at the end nodded to me, no doubt remembering me and moved aside to let us go on up. If I thought my heart was pounding in the bathroom, then now it was jack-hammering itself against my chest cavity, trying to break free. Maybe it was scared about what going up these steps again would do to the remainder of it, as the last time didn't go so well.

As we got up to the VIP floor, the sight took my breath away and Alex had heard it.

"You're sure on this, we could go back?" I felt his hand at the small of my back and the feeling gave me comfort enough to do this. I shook my head as my answer and continued to walk through until I saw the top table coming into view, as for some reason, everyone seemed to be up out of their seats standing.

When I saw Vincent and Sophia I couldn't help the massive beaming grin from forming. I pulled Alex a little quicker, trying to get through the unusual crowd who looked as though they were all waiting for something.

"Sophia!" I shouted making her turn her head and find me. I saw her lean over to Vincent and whisper something, making him turn my way, but what surprised me the most was the expressions on their faces…*worry.*

"Hey, sorry we're…late…" I stopped dead in my sentence as I came to the front of the top table just as another was coming to the head of it. Everyone around us sat down at once with just a nod from the man now stood in front of me. I wanted to cry, I wanted to shout and I wanted to throw something or self-combust taking half of the room with me!

But I didn't do any of these things…no, for all I could do was let my mouth drop for a few seconds before letting out a breathy name, one not said in far too long…

"Draven"

CHAPTER FIVE

KEIRA

BACK TO THE BEGINNING

"Draven." I swallowed hard and managed to say the name I had avoided for all this time. I even had to lock my knees together to prevent myself from breaking down and falling to the floor. I felt completely disarmed and stripped naked of the armour I had erected around the broken remains of my heart, trying in vain to preserve all I had left.

"Keira." He spoke my name as though it was being ripped from his soul where his voice was thick and hoarse. My breath actually hitched as I took in too much air whilst trying not to cry. It was as if for these first few seconds we were the only two people in the room and meeting once more after all these painful months apart was obviously taking its toll on both of us. I barely took in the rest of the room watching us as I was caught in the most deadly trap alive...two burning purple eyes that held me captive.

Then the spell was broken as Alex cleared his throat next to me and I felt his hand slide round my back and flex against my waist. Draven's eyes became that of a hawk and snapped to my side to take in the sight of another man touching me, clearly claiming me as his own. I wanted to cry as I felt a surge of guilt I knew I shouldn't feel infect my soul. He threw me away and damned my love for him...what more could I do? So I cleared my throat also and shut down my emotions from seeping onto my face, like they had no doubt already done.

"Hey everyone, this...uh, well... this is Alexander Cain... my boyfriend." I added 'my boyfriend' in anger when I saw Draven raise an arrogant eyebrow at the stumble in my introduction. I knew it was petty but I thought given the situation and the immense hurt I still felt at the sight of this man, he was just lucky I hadn't grabbed Alex by his shirt and kissed the breath from him out of spite.

I was still so attuned to Draven that I couldn't help but note the hardening of his jawline as he ground his teeth and the punishing grip he had on the back of his chair where he stood next to it.

"So I'm told...both of you sit...if you please." Draven said adding the 'please' as an obvious unwelcome afterthought. However, his words held a venomous edge before the room echoed with the sound of his chair being scraped back along the floor ready for him to sit. Everyone in the room looked too scared to make so much as a sound and I couldn't help but bite my bottom lip as my anxiety grew. I shouldn't be here. I should just make my excuses and leave before my winning streak of a disaster free life took a tumble in the form of one dead boyfriend.

"I think we'd better..."

"Sit down, Keira." This was an order from across the table and came from a different Draven. I was actually surprised at hearing Vincent sounding so cold towards me. Draven nodded to someone behind me and by the time I turned my head, two extra chairs were being placed where we stood ready for us to fill. I looked to Alex and was surprised to see a slight smirk grace his lips as he looked at Draven. I couldn't believe the balls he possessed and never would have thought Alex had it in him.

"It's alright Catherine, let's sit shall we?" He nodded to my chair as he took my hand to lower me down and I tried not to notice the sound of the gasps around the table as he said my given name. I swallowed down another difficult hit to my guilt and sat trying in vain not to look at Draven. God though, he'd looked so hurt and angry it felt like bile clogging my throat making it hard to get air to my lungs.

"So Keira, how have you be…?"

"Tell me Alec, where are you from?" Draven snapped out his question, interrupting Sophia abruptly.

"It's Alex actually or Mr Cain, whichever you prefer." Alex said smoothly not only coating his words in his French accent but also with confidence.

"I don't give a fuck what your name is but only care for what your intentions are with my…our *Keira.*"

"Draven!"

"Dom." both Vincent and I reacted to Draven's outburst but whereas I shouted his name in disbelief, Vincent's was a warning for his brother to try and remain calm. I just couldn't believe the nerve of him! He didn't get to do all that he had done to me and then act like this!

"I knew this was a mistake! Come on, we're leaving!" I snapped standing up and reaching for Alex. He simply laughed and said,

"Come now ma chérie, I am not offended…sit back down, Catherine." I did as he said with a huff, shooting daggers at Draven, a look he ignored I might add.

"I am from Bordeaux, monsieur." Alex said answering Draven's question calmly and I couldn't believe how he could act so cool in the face of Draven's obvious hatred.

"But you weren't born there." This was said as a statement not a question and once again Alex smirked.

"No, I was not but I call it home." He turned to me and smiled, taking my hand in his to bring it to his lips to kiss. I blushed fuchsia knowing the look of death we both received because of the act. I could have sworn I heard wood splitting. Jesus, what had I been thinking coming here!

"And your parents, what of them?" Draven growled out the question and my head snapped back to him.

"Draven stop it!"

"Dead. Now if you will excuse me, I must make a phone call." He rose from his seat after answering his question just as abruptly as it had been asked.

"Wait, I will come with you." I said rising but he put a hand on my shoulder and said,

"It's fine, I will only be a moment…stay and talk with your friends." I bit my lip again worrying about what to do but in the end I just nodded and let him walk a few tables away to make a call.

"Subtle as always I see." I said looking back to Draven making him cock an eyebrow at me.

"I think I have a right to these answers, Keira." He replied arrogantly.

"No, if I remember correctly, you in fact gave up that right, Draven." I replied trying to keep emotion at bay. I wanted to appear as though saying this didn't shred at my soul like claws from a bitter beast. Well at least he had the good grace to flinch at my words as he knew them to be born from the truth of his actions.

"I…" Draven started to say something in annoyance but Sophia quickly interrupted asking me if I had heard from Pip lately. I was more than thankful for her change of subject and started to talk about the last time I had seen her, when Alex came back. He bent down and gave me a quick kiss when Draven barked out an order,

"Drink!" making us both jump and ruining the moment. Loz quickly came over to the table and I gave her a little wink when she smiled at seeing me again.

"Set up a fountain for the table, Loz for I think our Lord is in the mood for something a little stronger this night." Sophia asked referring to absinthe. She nodded and was about to walk away when Draven called her back.

"And for Keira, she will have a Corona…"

"Red wine," Alex interrupted and poor Loz looked lost and torn between the two men.

"It's alright Loz, a Corona will be fine." She looked relieved and quickly made her escape to get the drinks.

"I thought you never cared for red wine?" Draven asked and even hearing his abrupt, harsh voice gave me goosebumps as I was flooded with too many memories to cope with.

"Tastes change, Draven." I replied quietly knowing he would get the inner meaning to that statement.

"That they do." He gritted out his reply and I bravely raised my eyes to see him glaring at the new taste in question.

"Catherine, I am afraid I have to leave you sooner than I thought." I looked to Alex and realised what he was saying.

"Why…is everything alright at the office?" I asked knowing Alex was working on a big project and would often have to leave suddenly.

"Leaving so soon, how disappointing." Draven commented

dryly gaining another filthy look from me. Loz came then and placed an elaborate green glass fountain on the table. She turned to take the black, gothic looking crystal glasses from Rue's tray that were just the right size to fit under the four taps that spouted from the centre. The fountain was in the shape of a giant teardrop and topped with a beautiful dainty glass fairy that looked like she was being chased mid-flight.

"I have to get back to Portland and get these new designs ready for a meeting that has been rescheduled for tomorrow." Alex said ignoring Draven's snide comment and turned to the rest of my friends to add,

"I'm an architect in the city." Draven rolled his eyes and said sarcastically,

"Sounds thrilling," before downing a full glass of green liquid just poured by Loz. I, like everyone else, ignored Draven and turned to give my full attention to Alex.

"I will come with you."

"No it's fine. You stay and be with your friends, I know how much you were looking forward to it." I blushed again as of course he was right, apart from seeing Draven I had been dying to see Vincent and Sophia again and also I thought I would get another chance to see my old bodyguard Ragnar but as of yet he hadn't appeared.

"But…"

"It's fine Catherine, really… but you got a ride here, correct?" I nodded as Frank had dropped me off so I could have a drink.

"Then how will you get home? Is he picking you up?" I hadn't arranged anything as I just gathered Sophia would try and convince me to stay or if not at least arrange for her driver to take me home.

"Your concern isn't needed. Keira, will of course be taken home and get there safely in my care." Draven's cutting voice was once again invading my senses and making me want to both cringe in frustration and curse my heart for taking notice for the first time in over ten months.

"But that's where you're wrong, as she is *my* concern now and not yours any longer." Alex said bravely and you could almost hear the entire room suck in a sharp breath of disbelief.

"Say that to me again." Draven threatened transforming the air in the room to thicken making it harder to breathe.

"Brother." Vincent was once again the voice of reason, placing his hand on Draven's shoulder and trying to get him to remain calm and stop him from what he looked like he wanted to do and that was rip my Alex to bloody shreds and bathe in the pieces!

"Enough, Draven! He's right, I'm not your concern anymore…"

"You will always be my…"

"*And* to answer your question Alex, I can call Frank or get a lift with Jack." I said interrupting him before he finished that sentence, for both his sake and mine as I knew the argument would just escalate. I also ignored Draven's growl of frustration.

"Very well, I will see you in a few days at the airport."

"Airport…Keira are you going somewhere?" Sophia asked making me wince. She had told me they were coming back for a few weeks and we were going to spend some quality time together.

"Erm…well Alex kind of surprised me and…"

"Yes I did, as I thought she could do with a break and get away for a while." Sophia nodded her head but I could tell she wasn't happy with the way Alex put it or it could be that she wasn't happy with the plans he had made for me.

"Where?!" Draven asked shrugging off his brother's hand from his shoulder. Obviously, he had calmed enough from his last outburst to ask but I was now fearful that the answer to this question would just bring on a new rage.

"Uh…well see we thought…"

"Italy." Alex butted in and I frowned at how thoughtless it was regardless of Draven's behaviour.

"Italy…really Keira?" He said looking even more hurt and I once again wanted to cry from the guilt I felt. It was like being torn in two. One side of my broken heart wanted to scream 'YOU BASTARD, YOU LEFT ME!' and the other wanted to quietly beg for forgiveness that I was now sat here with another man.

"I…"

"I planned our trip, as it was on a flight back from there last year when we first met. However, from what I heard, the trip didn't exactly go to plan and left a sour taste in Catherine's experience of the country. I thought this time I could show her the real beauty of Italy and that it has so much more to offer." I closed my eyes when he finished and banged my head back on the chair before turning my face to his.

"Alex…don't," I whispered on a sigh but didn't know why I even bothered as the damage had already been done.

"Right…right…" Draven for the first time looked dumbstruck as he tried to find his words and Sophia had her eyes closed as if feeling her brother's pain. I thought back to how that sounded and wondered if Alex had said it that way on purpose. Christ, but it had made me look like the biggest, most heartless bitch in existence!

"Draven I…" I started but as before I wasn't going to be able to get a word out.

"Well I'd better get going, Catherine." He nodded for me to get up with him to say goodbye in private and I happily complied just so that I could have a minute of freedom from being crushed to death by my guilt. When we were out of earshot I frowned up at Alex and said,

"You didn't have to say it like that!" He simply smiled down at me making me for once want to slap that handsome face.

"Catherine, I understand that I don't know exactly know what happened between you two but I do remember the hurt I saw etched deep there when I first met you…don't forget what he put you through, ma chérie." He said running a perfectly manicured fingertip down my cheek.

"I haven't forgotten Alex, I just choose not to be a bitch about it!" I snapped back turning my face from his caress. God, I was so frustrated and just wanted to stomp away from both of them and drink myself stupid till I forgot either of their names!

"Forgive me for being protective of my girlfriend's pride but I guess with dating a man like that you were used to being walked over." Now it was Alex's turn to get snappy. I took a deep breath and tried to remember that there was little doubt that we were being overheard, even this far away from the top table.

"Let's just forget about it. Text me later?" I asked not wanting to say goodbye on a disagreement. That was the other weird thing about me and Alex, we very rarely argued, and I think the only major one was when I tried to press for information about what happened to his parents. He had walked out and not called me for three days making me wonder if it was over or not.

His eyes softened and when he smiled, he got that trademark line in his cheek.

"Don't I always?" I smiled back at his answer.

"Alright then, I will see you in a few days." I said leaning up and kissing him on his cheek. I then turned to go back to the table but was halted mid step with a hand on my arm.

"Alex?"

"Don't I get a real kiss goodbye?" He said laughing.

"I…I don't think that's a good idea, not with…" I never got to finish as Alex pulled me to him and crushed his lips over mine before I could utter another syllable. He tilted my head with his hand on my neck and deepened the kiss. My hands fisted in his shirt as I held fast the urge to push him away. It didn't feel right to me rubbing Draven's nose in it and I started to feel sick. Luckily Alex let me go but not before kissing my neck, which I knew was so he could look at Draven over my shoulder. I felt him smile on my skin at whatever he must have seen and that sick feeling doubled.

I stepped away abruptly and muttered a goodbye before rushing back to the table, only chickening out halfway there and running for the balcony instead. It was admittedly one of the last places I ever wanted to see again, knowing how many painful and delicious memories it held for me but what choice did I have.

I felt my phone ping in my pocket, and I groaned when I saw it was a text message from Alex.

'Sorry, I know it was wrong but I needed to stake my claim. Please don't blame me for being an overbearing asshole Miss you already. X'

I released a sigh and quickly texted back my reply,

'Not cool but I forgive you, you big jerk hot head! ;) C ya soon x'

I just couldn't bring myself to say I missed him too, as right now I most certainly did not. The last twenty minutes had been some of the most difficult in my life and that was saying something considering all I had been through in my twenty-four, soon to be twenty-five years!

"Argh, bloody men!" I growled walking closer to the edge rubbing my arms in the cool summer night.

"Amen to that, sister!" I groaned out loud before turning around to face the smallest Draven.

"Sophia." I said her name as a warning making her laugh nervously and holding both her hands up in surrender.

"I know what you're thinking."

"Murder?" I asked sarcastically making her grin.

"Well I didn't think it went *that* bad." At this I burst out laughing but wasn't completely convinced it was in humour.

"You were there at that table right?" I said dragging a hand through my hair and holding it at my neck in frustration. Even this action reminded me of the man I had tried so hard to forget.

"Keira…" She said my name softly making me wince.

"No Sophia! I told you…I bloody told you! All this time… Jesus, I mean nearly a bloody year of not wanting even the tiniest bit of information about him, and you what…thought that actually meant I wanted to see him again!?" I was ranting I knew but I felt so betrayed and after last year then this was a massive issue with me.

"I know you're hurt sweetheart but just listen to me for a second…" I felt her hand curl around my wrist as she pulled me to face her. I couldn't help but bite my lip when her eyes took note of the tears that were threatening to spill over.

"Oh Kazzy, please don't blame me, I didn't know he was coming here…it happened before I could even warn you about it. He knew I was meeting you and up until the last minute he refused to come with us but then…"

"Wait a minute…*you tried* to get him to come with you?!" I screeched out this new information making her blush for once.

69

"Uh…ooops." She made a cute as all Hell scrunched up face and shrugged her shoulders.

"Ooops!?"

"My bad?" She tried that one and sounded just like Pip!

"Arrrrh! I take it back…bloody *Dravens!*" I shouted knowing I was never going to trust any of them again!

"Ok, ok…so I know I was in the wrong but Keira, you both can't see what's going on around you and you are both so damned stubborn! You needed to at least start seeing each other again or the Proph…"

"Don't! Just…just don't Sophia. I can't hear one more word about some damn Prophecy that is dead set on ruining my life… it did it once but not again…you hear?!" Now the tears were falling and I wiped them away angrily knowing I had spent far too many seconds of my life crying over what the fucking powers above had deemed to be my future. But not anymore!

"Alright Keira, I understand but please…please just try to understand me. What would you do for a brother you love…? What lengths would you go to if it was Libby's happiness at stake? I didn't just do it for him." I sucked in a jagged breath, widened my eyes to try to hold back the tears and once again bit my lip all in vain of trying to keep my emotions in the prison I had constructed from hurt.

"Just come back inside and be with us…that's all I'm asking…we miss you, Keira." I turned to look at her and could no longer hold back. I ran the distance and threw myself into her body, wrapping my arms around her and holding her close while the dam broke. She was shocked for a few seconds but then I felt her arms go around me to hold me closer. She waited for my silent sobbing to calm, all the while stroking back my hair and saying soothing words in another language.

I could feel my tears soak her beautiful dress that would probably make some ridiculously expensive designer weep at the sight but I couldn't help it. She was like a sister to me and it had been hard to keep up this act around her for so long.

"I'm sorry. I know you only did what you thought was best but just seeing him again…it…it *hurts,* Sophia." My voice broke on the word 'hurts' and I pulled back to wipe my tears away for hopefully the last time tonight.

"I know honey, and I am so sorry you're in pain but Kaz, did you really think that was it…that you would never see each other again?"

"But he was the one who did this… he was the one who threw away my love, Sophia not the other way around." Sophia took a deep breath, closed her eyes and released it slowly.

"One day you will understand and when you do it will mark the day of change for us all but until then, all I can say is it's not my place *or* my story to tell." She had said something like this before or at least tried to but like now I had brushed it off as an excuse. I mean really, what could there possibly be to have made him act the way he did?

"So what changed his mind?" I asked hating myself for needing to know what had changed.

"Why he came back?" I nodded at her question. She gave me a mischievous half smile that screamed the Sophia I knew and loved.

"Why do you think?" I turned to look back at the view of the national park lit only by the moonlight and felt my heart getting heavier by the second. Of course, I knew why he had come back and I hated the feeling of self-loathing it created.

"He heard about Alex." It wasn't a question as it didn't need to be. There was no doubt this was the only reason Draven was back and the idea hurt me more than it should after all this time. He wasn't back for me…to see *me*…no, he was back to see *me with Alex*.

"Right, I get it."

"Do you?" I shook my head, begging her silently for her not to continue, one she thankfully took on board.

"So what do you say to just one night…that's all I'm asking for?" Could I really do it…? Could I really go back to those days knowing how it would rip me apart for many months to come? It was like being offered the sweetest torture, one you knew could destroy all you have left but leaving you dying with the most blissful memories to hold your hand. I sighed as I knew before I even asked myself this, what my answer would be.

"Have you ever known me to say no to you?"

"I dread the day." Sophia said laughing and walked past me giving me a pat on the arm. I continued to look out at that view even with Sophia by the door at my back. I focused on the moon as I would often do since all that had happened last year and it took me back to how I did the same when locked away in that filthy prison thinking about my mission...

My mission to save Draven.

I heard the whoosh of the door and my voice broke free, saying words so painful they hurt making their way out.

"He died, Sophia." I felt her freeze without even needing to see her but at her reply my body turned to ice.

"Yeah, and without you…"

"He still is, Keira."

CHAPTER SIX

KEIRA

THROUGH DRAVENS' DOOR

After that bomb, kindly left by Sophia, I had no choice but to remain frozen, suspended in time alone on this balcony with nothing more than her words to haunt me. It was like being slapped across the face and then trying to ignore the action of it coming from your best friend. Why had she said that? Why would she tell me something like that knowing how I felt? It was like dangling one bloody carrot in a pen of starving donkeys with all my emotions trying to latch on to that one sentence. Was he really hurting that badly?

No! No, I couldn't think about this. I couldn't obsess over this one question as I had done for nearly a year. I'd spent too many minutes of the day sat staring out into the world through my window, wondering if he was missing me as much as I was him. Wondering what he was doing right at that precise moment in time and if, like me, he was thinking back to our time together.

That's the problem with blissful memories, they were never going to be as great or as wonderful as that exact moment when you created them. There was no scent to breathe in, there was no touch to experience and there were no words to hear by the voice of those you loved. They were just black and white grainy photographs void of real life.

That's how my memories felt.

I don't know how long I had been out here but it must not have been that long as I didn't get another member of the Draven clan to come in search of me. And my guess was that Vincent wasn't far from standing up to the task. If I was honest with myself I wasn't entirely sure if given the chance I would have left this balcony to walk straight out of this club and never look back.

Even the club itself felt like I was coming home and that hurt just as much, knowing half of me wanted to leave it behind me forever. But I just couldn't do it. Call it weakness or call it a craving but it was the same reason I couldn't walk away from this situation I now found myself in. I knew what was good for me but when did that ever stop me from making crazy decisions? Christ, most of last year was one giant crazy decision and look how that turned out. If going to Hell and back wasn't bad for me then I don't know what was!

So with my mind made up I sucked in a big girl breath and turned to go back into the unknown.

"You can do this...it's just one night, Keira...yeah right, who am I kidding?" I said to myself as I walked through the sliding doors.

I couldn't help but look to the bar and the same pain clinched in my chest when I still expected to see my friend Karmun at the bar. I bit my lip for the millionth time trying to eradicate the picture of him fading away in the arms of his lover. It was always a painful memory, like so many others this place held. Which made me wonder, if all the memories I had of the place were placed on a scale, which way they would tip…good or bad?

I shook those depressing thoughts away and walked round back to the top table feeling both ease and unease at now doing it alone and without Alex by my side.

"There you are, your seat's waiting for you." Sophia said making me fail my mission in getting to my seat without looking at Draven, only in the end it didn't matter…

He was gone.

I again mentally cursed my stupid heart for the disappointment I felt and tried to kid myself into believing it was a good thing. I went to the end of the table when Sophia said,

"Not there silly, up here." I looked up to see she was motioning to Draven's empty chair. I looked back to the seat I was first sat in at the other end, only to find it had been taken away, so there was no escape for me. I tried not to make it obvious that I was dragging my feet as I had no wish to ever sit in that chair again, knowing how painful the last time had been. I winced as a flash of me with short black hair, sobbing into the frame pierced my brain, adding to that invisible scale and not tipping it in Afterlife's favour.

"I don't think that's a good…"

"Keira, it's fine. I doubt Dom will be coming back anytime soon if that's what you're worried about." Sophia assured me but considering her past assurances I wasn't entirely convinced. In the end I just let out a sigh and sat down but I couldn't ignore the shiver that ran the length of my spine and coated my skin with chilled bumps.

"Hi." I said turning to Vincent and beaming at him when I saw he was finally smiling.

"Why, hello beautiful." He said winking and making me blush.

"How have you been?" He asked and Sophia, who was sat next to me, nudged my arm laughing,

"Come on, you can say you missed us." I laughed once trying in vain to force back the emotion that was building thanks to that simple, light hearted question.

"Hey." Vincent said sensing the change and pulling me into his arms for a hug. I felt a single tear fall and I watched a drip of colour darken on his faded black t-shirt, one that said 'Indian Motorcycles' and was obviously vintage.

"I'm sorry, I guess…well, being back here after all this time…"

"Keira you don't have to explain, it is perfectly natural that you are finding it difficult…and I think you gathered by now that you're not the only one." I pulled back and wiped my eyes again, hating the fact that I had cried twice now and not even been back a full hour. The night certainly wasn't looking too promising for my sanity that was for sure!

"So, that damn temper of his got the better of him again, didn't it?"

"Almost." On hearing the deep voice reply right behind me, I ended up making Vincent chuckle when I mouthed the F word before turning around to face the man in question. I gulped when my eyes finally made it all the way up his expensive suited body to a pair of frowning eyes of black.

"Uh…hey…*my bad?*" I said lamely and followed Sophia's lead when dealing with being caught out. I braced myself for his reaction and released my held breath when I saw a small smile playing at those perfect lips of his. His eyes also softened before he said,

"That chair suits you," then nodding down at me. I bit my lip and quickly stood almost making the chair fall backwards.

"Oh shit! I mean…I erm…well sorry, I will just…" I fumbled with the back of the chair that had been saved by Draven's quick reflexes from crashing to the floor and bending at a funny angle to do so. I heard Sophia snigger at my comical actions, and I shot her a death ray glare that did nothing but make her giggle more.

"Keira, its fine, please sit down," Draven ordered softly using his reasoning voice that was always hard to resist, damn him. I sat back down and wondered for half a second if he wasn't staying but then that flew right out of my head when he turned to face me. He casually leaned his weight against the table, turning his back to the rest of his council to stare down at me after crossing his arms.

O…k…talk about making a girl feel uncomfortable, jeez, I felt like I was being stripped naked and examined with a magnifying glass! 'Don't bite your lip…don't bite your lip… don't bite your lip.' I chanted and kept rolling my lips back in my mouth, probably looking like a fish just from trying to hold back the urge that intensified tenfold whenever Draven was around.

"You're looking well, Keira." Draven said after giving me an extensive once over, one that had my heart pounding like a juiced-up kid after a Halloween's worth of sweets. I mean Jesus, did he just purr that sentence!

"Thanks, you…you too," I murmured turning shy and brushing the shorter side parts of my hair behind my ear just for something to do.

"Hell yeah she does! Just look at all those curves." Sophia shouted enthusiastically and I was once again begging her with my eyes. Oh this was another set up alright. One look into her gleaming eyes dancing with mirth told me as much.

"I'm looking, Sophia." Draven said still looking down at me and I quickly started to turn a very unattractive shade of burnt Brit sunbather! Was it just me or was it baking in here?! I turned to Vincent and caught him smirking, with a half-smile hidden behind his hand. What was this, a damn conspiracy?

"So did you all just get in or have you been here a few days?" I asked after wracking my brain to find small talk but really, in this situation there wasn't much to go with.

"We arrived early this morning." Vincent said softly and obviously my best Draven choice for aiding with my small talk plan.

"Yeah but Dom here got back from Hell, what about two hours ago?" Sophia said looking up at Draven and gaining a look of disbelief back.

"Sophia!"

"Sophia!" The two brothers scolded their sister at the same time, whilst I was left looking like a fish gasping for air.

"Did…did she just say…*Hell!?*" I couldn't help it this time when my voice grew in pitch by the end of that sentence.

"What? Why can't she know that? You only went to visit our father!" Sophia whined like a petulant child.

"Oh…you saw your father?" Draven was still scowling at his sister but at my question he dragged his gaze from her to me. Thankfully he swapped his burning annoyance for something softer before he turned it on me.

"I did." Draven said, as always a man of many words I thought sarcastically.

"Well that's cool…how was he?" I couldn't help but ask thinking back to very fond memories of the King of Lust…well that was minus the reasons I was there in the first place but man, the guy could give a mean foot rub!

"Keira." Draven actually groaned at my question before saying my name like he was now dealing with two naughty

children that he wanted to send to bed without supper. Ok, Keira, for your sanity you must remember never, NEVER, to think of another analogy where Draven and the word bed are in the same sentence!

"What? He was nice to me." I argued making Vincent burst out laughing, Sophia grin like a mad woman and Draven roll his eyes and mutter what I presumed was a swear word in another language.

"Well he was." I muttered reaching for the glass in front of me and forgetting what was in it. I took a gulp and quickly reacted as if I had just swallowed acid. I started coughing and spluttering in a very unladylike fashion and I felt a pair of hands pull me forward and start patting my back.

"Holy mother of Hades! What is that stuff, paint stripper and liquid nitro?! Jesus!" I complained as the large hand at my back stopped patting but instead continued to rub large, soothing circles around my back. I looked up, parting my hair and expected to see Vincent there as the one who had been helping me but couldn't help but inhale sharply when it wasn't.

"Hey," Draven said kneeling down to my level and half leaning over me as his hand was still at my back. The feel of him touching me again was as if a live wire straight to my heart had been switched back on, jump starting it back to life.

"Hey," I breathed making him smile.

"You good?" I nodded biting my damn lip again. He gave me a cheeky half smile and shocked me by taking my chin between his thumb and finger before giving it a playful, little shake then saying,

"You're good." He then stood up and shouted to Loz to bring me water and a bottle of what used to be my usual. I sat back up and gave his silent council a little embarrassed smile sending up a prayer that a certain someone was no longer at the table. I would have to remember to ask Sophia about that when we were next alone. What had happened to Aurora?

"It sure has been boring without you around, Keira." Zagan said surprising us all...well everyone but Sophia that was. Draven frowned at him but he just shrugged his shoulders giving us a small glimpse of his pale eyes and tattooed scar underneath his hood. Sophia however beamed at him lovingly as though he was her hero for saying that.

"Then here's to missed human entertainment." I said raising my new bottle, forgetting about the water Loz had also placed before me. I then took a long swig letting the cold beer cool my burning throat and noticed over my bottle everyone else had raised their glasses too.

"Missed indeed." I could have sworn that was what I heard Draven whisper over his own glass, the very one I had stupidly drank out of. Did he really say that or was I just imagining the words I secretly longed to hear?

"So, was it just a catch up?" I asked Draven.

"Something like that." He answered after first needing to think about it. Sophia on the other hand snorted like I would have and once again she was having her name said in warning, this time though it was by her own partner Zagan.

"Alright, alright, I won't mention anything about the fight."

"What?" I shouted in response.

"Ooops." Sophia said not looking sorry in the slightest.

"You had a fight with your dad...as in a fight, fight?" I asked and it was only when I put my hand on his folded arm that he looked away from Sophia but not before he said,

"We will be having words later, Sophia." Then he turned to first look at my hand, making me quickly pull it away and then back down at my expectant face.

"We fought yes but it is not your concern." Wow that stung,

but I guess I now knew how he felt after what Alex had said to him.

"No…of course not." I couldn't help but keep the resentment out of my voice.

"Keira, I didn't…"

"Its fine, I mean you're right…but, well I just hope you sorted it out with your dad." He smiled at that.

"Let's say that we came to a compromise."

"That's good to know." I replied quietly, feeling shy again under his watchful gaze. This meeting was definitely going better than it had earlier that was for sure but still it felt weird. Like I was transported back in time, back to the beginning all over again and trying to find safe footing when it came to speaking with him. I was confused, I was intimidated, I was hot and bothered at being this close to him and I was angry that I was feeling any of these things at all. I always said that if I ever came across Draven again, I would just act cool and play the emotionless ice queen. Well there went that plan out the window…Ha, me ice queen, what a joke. Yeah I think being caught in his chair, nearly knocking it to the floor and half choking to death was a sure way to burn that ice queen routine to cinders!

"So how's the new job, Keira?" Sophia asked making Draven's eyes widen for a moment.

"New job?" Ah so at least I now knew that like me, he hadn't being keeping tabs on me via information provided by his siblings. Again I would be lying if I said that also didn't sting but really, what did I expect? The guy had pretended to be dead and made sure every aspect of the life I had allowed to grow around me, thanks to his own seed planted, was dead too. That wasn't ever going to be the actions of a man who also wanted to know about my wellbeing. Take last year for example, all those things that happened to me and where was he…where was his protection…it was dead by choice, that's where it was!

"Yeah, life goes on Draven, did you really expect me not to get another job?" I snapped unable to help myself after these painful feelings I had just dug back up. He had the cheek to look taken aback by my snippy reply but then masked his features better than I could with a look of indifference.

"To be honest I gave it little thought considering the decision made to financially see to your future." Oh no he didn't! Was this guy nuts? I even heard Sophia and Vincent groan at the obvious mistake he just made by saying that shit.

I stood up quickly, this time not giving a shit about whether the chair made it or not. I took a threatening step towards him and poked him in the chest as I proceeded to give him a piece of my mind,

"Alright Daddy Warbucks, time to give you a little insight. See I don't give a flying shit about your money, never have, never will! Although I bet the badgers loved it, oh and that guy I sent on holiday. So with that said I DO NOT appreciate you thinking you can buy me off and send me on my merry way so that what exactly…you can sleep better at night? How dare you! Who the Hell do you think you are you?!" I shouted up at him and continued poking him with every point made.

"Badgers…?"

"Yeah badgers, you know, nowty little buggers with stripy heads!" I said motioning with my hands as I got more animated and my Liverpool accent came through thicker.

"I know what a badger is, Keira now 'nowty' on the other hand…"

"It means angry, annoyed, irritated, fuming, livid, foot stomping mad…pretty much all the things I am right now!"

"Right, if you are quite finished shouting at me I will expla…"

"Oh no, I am not finished, not by a long shot you bast…!" I started shouting at him only to be interrupted just like I had done to him, only his way was far more effective.

"Alright, have it your way!" He said before bending suddenly and jamming his shoulder in my belly before hoisting me up and over his shoulder.

"Hey! What are you doing? Put me down right now!" I shouted bent over with my hair trailing down the back of his legs. I tried to push myself up, shamefully loving the fact I had to use his beautiful behind as leverage. I managed it for only a second or two before slipping on the smooth material of his suit trousers.

"You can't do this, Draven!"

"I think you will find I am doing it just fine!" He snapped back as he continued to carry me to somewhere, I couldn't see.

"Are you guys just going to sit there or are you going to help me?!" I said looking sideways and upside down at Vincent and Sophia.

"Nope."

"Nada." They both said at the same time making me growl.

"Fine! Traitors!" At this I started to shake on Draven's shoulder as he started to laugh. Bloody laugh! The audacity of this man knew no bounds!

"Come now, you really think either of them could stop me…have you forgotten all of your time with me already?" He asked still clearly amused. I tried to fold my arms in frustration but in the end I had to use my hands to brace myself as I just looked like one of those nodding bobble heads that was all the rage years ago.

"A girl can try," I said acting bitchy but his continued laughter told me I didn't quite pull it off. I huffed at the sound and listened to a pair of heavy doors opening. This was when I really started to panic. I started to tug on his shirt in desperation.

"No Draven...wait, just wait a minute!" He immediately stopped laughing on hearing my pleading.

"You're fine"

"No! Where are you taking me...please...please don't take me back there." I said feeling myself losing it quickly.

"Keira, what is it...what's wrong?" I heard another door being opened and my heart sank as I closed my eyes not wanting to see it again. I couldn't. It would kill me! I felt him lower me down his front and another shiver shot through me.

"Keira, open your eyes." He ordered gently and I dug my palms over my eyes and shook my head feeling the tears forming beneath them.

"Tell me what is it...? *Talk to me.*" I felt him reach up and try to pry my hands from my eyes and when I put up a resistance, he simply pulled harder. My strength gave in knowing there was little point when up against someone like Draven. Still, I kept my eyes firmly shut.

"I don't understand why you won't...wait, what is it you said before we came in here...don't take you back there...that's what you said." He was starting to piece it together and it suddenly felt like my heart was lodged firmly in my throat, ready to fall at his feet.

"Keira, where do you think you are?" He asked me this as though he was talking to an unstable mental person with a gun in her hand.

"Your bed chamber." I whispered shamefully trying to pull my arms from his hold but it was useless. For long moments there was an overwhelming silence between us, and I knew Draven was using this time to think about why I would feel this way about going back to that room. It was when I heard him

exhale a heavy sigh that I knew the truth of the matter had hit him.

I was terrified at what going back in that room would do to me. Afterlife was one thing and seeing Draven in it another, these were all different levels of torture in their own right but that room…that room held all the *good* memories. There were no weighing scales of good and bad in that room. There was nothing to tip the balance enough for me to not be haunted for another ten months of beautiful and perfect moments of what I thought was pure love. And I had so long now been hanging on to a thin thread that was created of nothing but bitterness. It had to be if I was to survive each day.

I couldn't think back to those days. I couldn't think back to before those words. The most painful words to ever be spoken from the man you love.

"Keira, open your eyes and trust me."

"But I don't…*not anymore.*" I whispered again, only thankful that I couldn't see the hurt I could have inflicted with my truthful words. I heard him clear his throat first before speaking again and his next words were hoarse and tense,

"That is something I have to accept due to my actions…I understand this but Keira, if you won't trust me then trust in yourself." He said and before I could ask what he meant he started to move me around the room and led me over to different pieces of furniture there.

I knew he expected me to feel the curves, textures and objects he placed my hands on but all I could feel was his solid presence at my back, his arms around me from behind and hands on top of mine with our fingers entwined as we touched each piece together.

"See…it's all different," he whispered soothingly at my ear making me quiver. My eyes flew open and I waited for them to focus.

"Your office." I muttered and I felt him smile before moving from my neck.

"Yes." I took in a deep relieved breath and felt my back brush against his chest from the movement. I had to get out of his hold, and I had to do it right now before it got too much. If I thought that room would bombard me with painful memories then what was being in his arms again going to do to me in the long run? I tried to pull away and his hands quickly shackled my wrists.

"Wait! Not yet…just…just a little longer." His desperate sounding request shocked me enough to gasp. He wanted to hold me longer!?

"Tell me."

"Tell…tell you what?" I stuttered feeling him lean down to my neck once more.

"Tell me why you were so scared to go back there, Keira."

"I…I…can't." I felt him rub his nose along my neck and inhale my skin, taking in my scent in deep breaths, hypnotising me and luring me further under his spell. Why hadn't I remembered what it was like? Did I really forget about all those times back then when his spell would weave its way around my senses, moving and twisting them into doing his will? Where was my resistance now eh? It was blown to smithereens that's where!

"Yes you can, just speak the words…just say the words I need to hear, Keira and I will release you from my arms." It didn't escape me that he never said the words 'I will let you go' and I couldn't help but wonder why…why he worded it that way and why he 'needed' to hear the reasons why. Didn't he already know?

"I couldn't do it…I couldn't see it again and not be…" I hesitated making him grip me harder to his unyielding frame.

"And not be…?" And with this he sealed my fate by

whispering the last of the magic needed to get me to open up to him like a flower blooming at night. Magic spoken against my skin and once I felt his tongue momentarily make contact with my skin I knew I was lost.

"And not be…"

"…loved by you."

CHAPTER SEVEN

KEIRA

TRUTHFUL TRIP DOWN MEMORY LANE

"Keira, I still…"

"NO!" I shouted, wrenching myself out of his arms and almost falling forward with the force of my actions. Draven tried to make a grab for me but I staggered forward, thankfully finding my footing before he needed to touch me again. I couldn't listen to anything he had to say. I couldn't take any more from this man, not when his words had already destroyed me once.

I couldn't give him that power again…*never again.*

I felt so ashamed by what I had said and so angry at what I had been coerced into saying. Well, one thing was obvious and that was all this time apart had killed any resilience I once had to Draven's power of manipulation.

I walked further away and held my arms protectively around myself, rubbing the thin sleeves of my cherry red dress wishing

I was wearing something thicker. Something more protective from the touch I could still feel on my body from a pair of strong male hands I craved on my skin.

"Just…" I took a shuddering breath before I could carry on.

"Please… it's all I ask, Draven."

"Please what...? Not touch you, because I will never agree to that, Keira." I turned around in shock at his words.

"You think you have the right after what you did?!"

"I know that I don't but that doesn't change what my soul knows." I frowned at him from across the room and then shook my head in frustration.

"And that is?"

"That you are mine and always will be." I sucked in a sharp breath and even staggered back a step as though he had just pulled a trigger.

"This can't be happening." I muttered in disbelief now really convinced this must be a dream. One of those dream scenarios we play over and over in our minds until at some point there's the fear it will cross over into reality and leave you more confused than ever…like now.

"You doubt my sincerity in that statement?" He asked coming closer.

"Oh no, you stay there!" I said knowing if he touched me right now, I would be a gonner!

"Answer my question." He demanded getting angry…an anger he had absolutely no right to I might add.

"Screw you and your orders! You don't bloody own me and you have no GODDAMN right to say that to me!"

"Keira." He warned but again I held up my hand.

"If you're gonna lecture me about cursing the Gods then save it! As far as I am concerned they hate me anyway so they can just go ahead and strike me down if they dare… but I am telling *you* now, they would bloody regret it 'cos the way I have

THE PENTAGRAM CHILD - PART 1

been feeling this past year I want to rip the fucking place apart!" I shouted, panting with my rant and shaking with my lack of control.

Draven's eyes closed as if in pain and he ran both his hands through his hair that I'd only just noticed looked a little longer. Actually everything about him looked more unkempt than usual. His stubble was the longest I had ever seen it, close to becoming a full beard and he had darker circles under his eyes as if he hadn't slept in weeks. It was only his suit that was as impeccable as always.

He seemed to be fighting with himself as his chest heaved and his hands remained locked at the back of his neck. If anything, he didn't seem to be dealing with our situation any better than I was. I took a deep and calming breath, feeling bad for letting out my anger now that I saw how he was taking it. It was as though I held a whip in my hand and had just kept lashing out at him but really, what was he expecting from me... a loving and open arm reunion?

"Look, I...I think I should just go..."

"No!" He shouted and I was surprised to see a moment of panic cross his features as he looked back at me. He, like me, took a calming breath and continued,

"Please...stay." He said these words as though he no longer gave a shit about pride and was not above begging me to stay. This for a man like Draven was monumental. After all he was a King and Kings beg to no man...but I wasn't a man now was I.

"Alright." As soon as I said the word his shoulders sagged and his tense body visibly relaxed.

"Thank you for staying, for I know I do not deserve it." I bit my lip and nodded knowing I couldn't say anything to that for more reasons than one. It was clear he knew he deserved my anger and in most ways had accepted it when my emotions had got the better of me. However, that didn't mean I wanted to be intentionally cruel, no matter what he had put me through, I still didn't feel right about hurting someone that I still cared for... would *always* care for.

"Will you sit with me?" He asked motioning to the teal velvet couch that I remembered seeing once in less than perfect condition. It was back when I was held captive by Lucius and Pip was once again performing her mumbo jumbo on me, sending me back here like a ghost. Draven had practically tore the place apart in his rage to get me back, which was just another memory that created more whys and buts. The lengths he went to back then and all for what, to just throw me away at the end of it all? It just didn't make sense...

It never would make sense!

We sat down and thankfully Draven kept some reasonable space between us, knowing now how much I needed it.

"Tell me about your job?" He asked making me snort in disbelief.

"You're kiddin' right?" I said referring to such a mundane question after what had just happened between us. He just shrugged his shoulders and then gave me a small laugh before saying,

"Well I think it's a safer subject...unless you're about to tell me you're now working as a Demon hunter or even worse, for Lucius!" He said looking at me sideways, smirking. I laughed trying to hold back another snort and failed.

"Well he did offer me a job as his personal masseuse."

"He what!?" Draven shouted and I smirked back at him before assuring him with,

"Teasing," making him relax again.

"Not funny." He warned even though he was smiling again.

"Ah come on...it was a little." I said nudging his shoulder and my heart couldn't help but soar when his smile grew into a full-blown grin.

"Ah don't tell me, the new job you have is as a comedian." He teased, nudging me back.

"What, you don't think I could be? I'm funny!" I said pretending to be offended. He straightened his face, but he still couldn't keep the humour from showing by the cute creases by his eyes, as he leaned in and whispered,

"Hate to tell you this sweetheart but you are more goofy cute than funny." I shrieked dramatically as my mouth formed an 'o' and slapped his muscle-bound arm for effect.

"You lie!" I hissed not wanting this teasing to ever end. He then nearly stopped my heart as for the first time in what felt like forever he graced me with that trademark bad boy grin of his before leaning into me again and saying,

"I lie." To which we both burst out laughing.

"Well it just so happens that I have repented my wicked ways by becoming a very respected pillar of the community, therefore giving up my life of sin working for the *Prince* of Lust…" I said waggling my eyebrows at him when calling him 'Prince'

"Nice." He said laughing at my dramatic pause or from what I called him.

"…and I have become a Librarian." The look on Draven's face was priceless as he nearly choked.

"You've what?!"

"It's true, they were hiring at the Library next to Wakewood Hall so I applied." Draven took all this in and I watched in fascination as his face changed with an emotion I couldn't describe as it was one I hadn't seen on him before. If I was to guess though I would say he looked uncomfortable and I had no clue why.

"Draven are you…blushing?" I asked in shock as he had indeed turned slightly red on his cheeks.

"Of course not." He denied shifting his weight on the seat. I couldn't help but giggle at the sight and proceeded to tease him further…what can I say, it was just too good an opportunity!

"You so are! Oh my God, it's the cutest thing…" I got so excited I got up on my knees on the couch and then said in a deep voice with a pretend microphone in my hand,

"This just in, Dominic Draven, Master of the Universe has been witnessed blushing like a girl with her knickers showing and…" I tried to carry on but Draven quickly made a grab for me and I found myself giggling once more into his hand that he held over my mouth. He leant down to my ear and whispered,

"One more word and I will have to punish you." His eyes were bright with delight as they stared down into mine and I couldn't stop laughing into his hand. He lifted his other hand in warning, hovering it over my side and I wrestled to get away from him in excited panic. His hand kept coming closer and closer, clearly enjoying me squirming and it was only then that I realised I was nearly fully beneath him. Unfortunately, this was also the time when reality kicked in and I realised we weren't back over a year ago when this playfulness was the norm. No, I knew I should put a stop to this but oh God how I wanted this to never end.

"Do you surrender?" He asked just before his fingertips were about to make contact with my sensitive sides and begin his tickling torture. I nodded frantically making his grin deepen and when they touched me I screamed out in laughter. He then stopped just as quickly to say,

"Sorry what was that?" Turning his ear to the side and listening to where he still had his hand over my mouth.

"I mmm said yeesss" I mumbled out.

"Nope, sorry didn't get that." He said and then went to tickle me again. I scrunched up my face waiting for it and when he burst out laughing, I opened one eye a crack to see him staring down at me with a soft look in his eyes…oh and they were also ringed with purple. Shit, but I knew what that meant. Draven was getting turned on.

I decided enough was enough before it went too far and from that one look alone, I would say we had crossed that line at the first round of teasing. So to get him to release me I licked his palm, shocking him enough to pull back.

"That was a sneaky trick." He said shaking his head slightly as if trying to get rid of some inappropriate thought.

"When means must." I said straightening up and smoothing back my loose hair that had gone crazy in the fight.

"So are you gonna tell me what you were blushing about?" He raised one single eyebrow at me and Jesus if it wasn't one of the sexiest sights alive!

"I don't know, do you want to be writhing beneath me again?" He countered and soon I was blushing scarlet. Was it just me or did the air get thick in here damn fast?

"Now who's blushing?" He stated and was soon staring at my bottom lip held captive by my teeth.

"Draven, I don't think we should…"

"So tell me, exactly how exciting is life as a librarian?" He said interrupting me and I knew he did it on purpose. Well if he wanted to change the subject first then I was happy to comply.

"Oh it's thrilling, no honestly…one minute it's all Economics 101 and Moby Dick the next…I really don't how I endure all the excitement. You know I sometimes find myself going home giddy." I said making him roar with laughter.

"I can only imagine."

"Oh and I really must thank you."

"And why is that?" He asked, again raising a sexy eyebrow my way.

"Because you gave me a glowing reference."

"Oh did I now?" I nodded making him chuckle and once again shake his head at me.

"Now that I would be curious to read."

"I bet, it was a doozy and very gushing with praise, if anything you were a fool for letting me go." I said before I realised what I'd said. His smile dropped and he looked down at the floor for a silent moment before raising his eyes to mine once more.

"I'm sorry, I didn't…well…ok you know I have no filter from my brain to my mouth right?" I said trying to lighten the mood after my slip up. What was wrong with me? What was I saying, I knew what was wrong with me and so did my subconscious that wanted to continue to make him suffer for ever leaving me! Yeah, that was it.

"I am fully aware I deserve far worse, Keira. There is no need to hold back in sparing my feelings, as you could not say anything that I have not already tortured myself with."

"Draven…" He silenced me with a slight shake of his head and a smile that this time didn't reach his eyes.

"What are we doing, Draven?" I bravely asked after I had given him the minute he needed. He lifted his head to look at me and raked a hand through his hair to push it back from where it had fallen.

"I don't know but if I was to venture a guess, I would say finding a truce." He said softly and I could tell he was testing the waters with his reply.

"So, friends then?" I asked not being able to help sounding hopeful. Because as crazy as I must be right now, I had no wish to behave in a way I was completely entitled to. Yes, I could have been a bitch and yes I could have told him that I hated him and cried about it for the rest of my days. But where would that have left me when all my tears had dried up…?

Regrets, that's what. Burning regrets that I could never take back. No matter what this man had put me through he had still saved my life. He had brought me back to myself after I left a part of me back in the cold damp prison all that time ago. He had shown me a love I knew I would never find again and so what if he never followed through with it and fought till the end for it. Because the reality of it all was a question I asked myself once. Was it really better to have loved and lost or never to have loved at all?

Well, I had my answer then and I had my answer now. Because you don't go to Hell and back for a man and ever… EVER… stop loving him, no matter what he did to you, it just wasn't possible. And trust me I had spent the last ten months, all three hundred and fourteen days to be precise, trying to do just that. And one look at Draven again and I knew that I had wasted every single minute trying.

So with all this in mind and even with the broken heart and hurt that had all but ripped me apart, I still couldn't fully give him up when given the chance. So I would take it. I would take it even though I knew we would never be to each other what we once were. Because at the root of it all, I would never be able to forgive him, and Draven would never *want* me enough for me to be able to forgive him.

"If that's what you can give, then that's what I will take." He said replying after processing my question. I smiled up at him and held out my hand.

"Then let's shake on it." His lips twitched as he fought a smile and took my smaller hand that was quickly dwarfed in his own. He slowly shook it all the while locking my gaze to his with an expression I couldn't read. I sucked in a shaky breath at the intensity of his touch and his look combined then quickly tried to take my hand back. His fingers tensed as I pulled and for a minute it felt as though he would never give me up but then the reality of that statement was like falling through the cracks on an icy lake. The look on my face must have registered because he let me go and he didn't look happy about it.

STEPHANIE HUDSON

I cleared my throat and tucked a stray bit of hair behind my ear before trying to find equal ground between us again.

"So…you saw your dad, how was he?" I asked before quickly remembering that they'd had a fight and asking this probably wasn't the smartest of questions. Thankfully though, he didn't look too pissed off.

"Let's just say he was definitely better before I turned up and kicked his ass." He responded dryly. I slapped him on the arm and scolded,

"Draven!" To which he just raised his eyebrow at me.

"You shouldn't be fighting with your dad." I said frowning and deepening that frown when he smirked at me.

"You know having a powerful Demon King for a father isn't ever gonna mean we go fishing, fix cars together and drink beers over talking about life…right?" I narrowed my eyes at him and then snapped,

"Oh but it means you have to beat the crap out of each other, trying to prove something with your dicks instead of your heads uh?" One side of his mouth quirked up at my response making me want to smack him upside the head.

"Firstly, he most certainly did not 'beat the crap out of me' and secondly, I believe I haven't thought with my dick since I last had you naked beneath me." He added seductively and then had the bloody cheek to wink at me making me roll my eyes purely to cover up the reaction I wanted to give him, which was to fan myself at the bittersweet memory. I couldn't think of anything witty to say so in true Keira fashion went with something lame instead.

"Whatever…and anyway, since when do you ever say words like 'Gonna'?... Carry on like that and people will get the mistaken impression you are down with the humans and becoming a cool dude." Ok so it might have been lame, but I

98

felt a little skip in my heart at how good my come back sounded.

"What can I say but I must like you rubbing off on me in a way that *sticks.*" He said in a purr that growled the last word. I gulped at how it made me tingle in all the best places. Of course, this feeling was enhanced by the way he ran a single fingertip down my arm when he spoke these hypnotic words. I should have pulled away from him and from his dangerous touch knowing what it would do to me when I no longer had it again. But the simple fact was it was next to an impossible task. It was as if just as soon as I was in his presence he had me, held tightly and bound in a net he cast just for me.

Instead of doing what I should have which was flee, I was simply left with a nervous laugh that told him all he needed to know…He had caught me and caught me good.

"So what's next, talking Scouse and wearing shiny trackie bottoms?" I asked just for something to say as I tried to process all his unrestrained flirting, flirting that if I had half a brain I would have put a stop to already…well nobody could say I had done everything the smart way when it came to Draven so why start now?

"If it makes you bite your lip at me then I will even perm my hair." He commented making me burst out laughing to the point I had to hold my ribs and tears formed. He laughed with me and as I bent over rocking as the laughter wouldn't leave me he took the opportunity to rub my back softly.

"You like that idea I see." He said and I started snorting in between my madness at the very idea of him in a shiny shell suit from the eighties and a mini afro!

"Oh please…" I could barely speak though the giggles making him smile down at me.

"Oh please?" He asked making it sound so sexual that it sobered me enough to get the words out.

"Oh please tell me that you have a hideous purple, pink and green shell suit hiding in the back of your wardrobe along with some used hair curlers?" At this his eyes widened, and he shocked me when he said,

"Fuck no!" Then he looked at me sideways, a bit sheepish at swearing in front of me so freely, so he added a quick,

"My apologies." I smiled at him and patted his thigh without thinking and said,

"I think that response was more than warranted…I mean what were we thinking wearing those…? I even think Libby has a picture at home with all four of us wearing matching ones at the airport before going on holiday!" I said shaking my head thanking the powers that be that I was only a toddler at the time and liked to think I had no say in the matter!

He nudged me making me look up at him and for a minute he looked lost in some emotion I once again couldn't place but just as quickly he recovered before I could place it.

"I bet you looked adorable." At this I released another very unladylike snort and replied,

"Draven, nobody looks adorable in a shell suit…in fact I am pretty sure it's illegal to look serious in one." I joked and silently blessed this witty banter for granting me the opportunity to see Draven's devastating grin that was nothing short of breathtaking. That was the thing with Draven. Around everyone else he was such a serious character most of the time so that when I got to be the one to make him smile like that, it felt like I had achieved nothing short of greatness…well now, wasn't that just a foolish thought to be thinking?

I dragged my bottom lip between my teeth and decided to punish that, seeing as smacking myself on the forehead was far too obvious. What was I thinking feeling like that? He wasn't mine anymore and more importantly, which I really needed to keep reminding myself, is that he never would be again! His smiles weren't mine any longer and my need to receive them should remain dead and buried where he had placed them and I was now keeping them.

"Hey, what is it?" His voice wasn't the only thing to bring me back to the now as I felt his fingertips under my chin pulling my gaze up to his.

"What are you torturing that poor innocent lip about this time, huh?" He asked searching my eyes and without taking his touch from my face his thumb gently prised my lip away from my teeth.

"I…I guess…" I tried to find the words to speak my mind and be brave enough to be honest without bringing back the pain.

"Tell me, Keira." His tender coaxing was too much to beat back the truth…so the truth is what I gave him.

"I guess…like this…It's just easy to forget, that's all." I felt my shameful blush bloom across my skin, skin he was still touching and made no move to stop. He let his hand glide from my chin down the column of my throat, feeling my heavy and nervous swallow for himself under his strong and determined hold. I watched as he closed his eyes as if in pain but not before seeing the flash of purple flames ignite. I wondered briefly if he had tried to hide it from me?

"That it is." He said so softly that it crushed something inside of me enough to make me wince at not being strong enough to get a lock down on the pain. He dropped his hand and I couldn't tell you if I was relieved or close to begging for it back.

He suddenly got up abruptly as if he needed to put space between us and my paranoid mind flooded itself with self-doubt and was plagued with the question 'could he no longer stand to touch me?' Jesus! But what was I doing to myself with these thoughts? This was precisely why it was far easier to muster up the hatred for what this man had put me through and focus solely on that! So with that in mind I straightened up and took a few deep breaths to get my emotions under control and in check.

"I have something I need to talk to you about, Keira… something of great importance and something I will have to ask of you to listen to until you fully understand its seriousness." He now took on this other side of Draven that was so much a part of him it would have bled from his pores if it could have and that was pure, raw and commanding… *power.*

I just nodded having one of those 'oh shit' moments that made me wonder after only hours of having the Dravens back in my life, what shit they had brought with them this time?!

"Alex Cain isn't the man you think he is, Keira." Draven stated folding his arms across his chest and standing there looking very much like the living God and King he was. This, however, had absolutely no effect on cooling the blood that now start to boil beneath my skin. I closed my eyes and threw my head back against the couch and started to laugh with not one shred of humour creating the sound.

"So now the truth comes out." I said trying to keep the utter rage from making those words come out in a scream of frustration and anger an inch from his face.

"And what is that supposed to mean?" He snapped.

"Only that I should have bloody seen it a mile away…Hell, I am just surprised it took you this sodding long…! So come on, who was it…? Oh wait, but of course, now it all makes sense." I said working it out in my mind until the supernatural puzzle pieces start to fall into place.

"What are you talking…?"

"So that's what the fight was about with your father, wasn't it?" He took a step back looking shocked that I had figured it out before replacing his surprise with a frown.

"Give me some fucking credit Draven, I think by now I know how your family operates." At this he growled at me but I just ignored the signs of his rage building, not really giving a shit about it anymore.

"I don't care for that statement."

"Well I don't care if you do or not, it's the truth and you know it! Christ but will I ever *not* be played by one of you!? Do *any* of you know how *not to lie?"* Ok, so I might have screamed this last part but I just knew there was no way around it feeling the way I did right now.

"Stop being so dramatic Keira, no one has played you." At this I scoffed,

"Oh really…" I asked sarcastically before snapping,

"So the only reason you came back here tonight wasn't because you heard about me and Alex…?" He tried to interrupt me but I was quicker with my rage than he was,

"…Oh and you didn't run to daddy dearest to find out this information and end up ripping into each other…?"

"Now just wait…"

"…Oh and I guess Sophia had not one thing to do with this, huh?!" I added knowing without his answer that of course she did. From the very beginning her, Vincent and even Pip had tried to grind me down to a point of hearing how Draven was having such a tough time being without me but to me, after what he had done, well it was all bullshit on sale and I wasn't buying it for a second!

"You need to keep my family out of this." He struck back causing me a second of pain at having it confirmed that I was no longer classed as family in his eyes anymore. Well that was just fine by me! I got up and stormed to the door ready to shake some hinges after slamming it on his arrogant ass!

"What do you think you're doing?!" He snarled in his anger and stormed towards me.

"I am getting the Hell outta here, that's what!"

"Oh no you're not!" He grabbed me by the arm and whipped me back around to face him and I wish he hadn't done it without hurting me so I had another thing to be pissed about. But wasn't that just the kicker, I gave Draven my body and he would never harm it but I gave him my heart and he fucking destroyed it!

"Screw you!" I shouted trying to get free from his grip briefly wondering in my red haze how we managed to do a complete 360 in no time at all. He ignored my verbal lashing and instead threw me back over his shoulder. Before I could scream a single complaint he threw me back down so I landed hard enough on the couch to bounce. He then caged me in with his arms holding his body above me and his face was a breath away from mine, killing all notion of personal space.

We were both breathing heavy and staring at each other with a scary and potent mix of anger and lust clogging the air around us.

"Now, are you going to get control of your irrational anger…?"

"Irrational! Why you…!" I started to shout but his hand came out of nowhere and clamped tight over my mouth. He shook his head slowly and said more calmly,

"Now let's try that again should we…I call it irrational because no matter what you think of me, I have left you alone all this time for what I believed to be for your own good. Now, however, after what I have learned it is no longer the case. So yes, although it may hurt your pride, I came here to rectify an issue I have with who you have unwisely chosen to…" He looked off to the side like he wanted to crush something but his hands were closer to a gentle caress in spite of his anger. Then through gritted teeth he continued with,

"...date" in more of a snarl than an actual word. I narrowed my eyes up at him.

"Now if I let you go are we going to talk about this like adults or are you going to scream more abuse at me like some unruly teenager?" I growled beneath his hand making his eyes once again flash purple but like before I couldn't tell you why.

He widened his eyes down at me as if asking if I would behave or not, making me just roll mine and nod in a silent and begrudging yes.

"Good girl." He said and released me, allowing my first response to be,

"Don't patronise me, Draven, after last year I stopped being a good girl after going to Hell and back!" I snapped and could only hope it hit him like a whiplash. Well at least he flinched. He inhaled a deep and frustrated breath before moving off me completely, finally giving me the space my traitorous body needed to calm down from having Draven nearly on top of me.

"Yes and you'd have thought that trip would have taught you a thing or two." He threw back at me making me sit up and cross my arms across my chest.

"And just what is that supposed to mean exactly?!"

"Only that you should know by now who is your friend and who is your foe."

"According to you everyone I meet outside of your family is the enemy, Draven...so tell me, who is it this time you have come all this way to warn me about?" I asked again unable to leave the sarcasm from turning my voice ugly.

"Alex Cain." His voice sounded strained saying the name of my new boyfriend and for a second I couldn't blame him as I too had problems saying a certain Goddess' name on occasion.

"Oh wow, now I am so shocked to hear that." I said rolling my eyes and shaking my head.

"I don't think you're getting what I am trying to tell you, Keira."

"And what's that exactly?"

"He's not human, he's…" He looked pained for a moment as though what he was about to tell me might crush me further than what his action had already done. I was tempted to put him out of his misery but then he beat me to it and continued with what he knew was the truth,

"He's a… Nephilim." I closed my eyes as the weight of what I was about to say bore down on me like one of those cartoon anvils, only there was not one single thing funny about it!

I took a deep breath in the face of the locked cage I was about to open and said the words that would release the beast…

"Yes, I know."

CHAPTER EIGHT

KEIRA

SECRETS ALREADY KNOWN

"WHAT?!!!" And there it was, Draven erupting from the cage I had opened with my last statement.

"You did not…" He had to stop what he was saying, holding up his hand at me like he was trying to process it all over again before carrying on and in an attempt to rein in his fury.

"…did not just say what I think you said." He finished with not much more restraint than before.

"Well, if you're happy thinking that, then you go right ahead but in reality then this is how it goes…*yes*, I know about Alex. I know because he told me, unlike other people I thought I knew, *he* doesn't lie to me!" I fired at him like venom hissing from my lips.

I then jumped back further into the chair as I witnessed for the first time in what felt like forever Draven explode into his demon side. His wings extended fully to the sides and I watched as though in slow motion as the purple veins under his skin started to glow and pulse in his exposed neck.

"The truth hurts doesn't it, Draven?" I snapped making him snarl at me and I wondered if I didn't have a few screws loose considering it wasn't exactly the smartest thing to do was add fuel to an already out of control blaze.

"You think you know his kind?! YOU DON'T!" Draven roared at me making me shoot to my feet in anger.

"No, that's where you're wrong because the only Demon I don't know IS YOU!" I screamed back taking a step closer to him and clenching my fists by my sides, wanting nothing more than to lash out at him.

"He will hurt you!" He told me with pain and rage mixing, giving his eyes both a strong resolve one minute and then an erratic kind of panic, making them look everywhere at once.

"No, no he won't." I said a little calmer this time in the sight of how he clearly wasn't coping with this news.

"HE WILL HURT YOU!" He roared at me and this time I flinched back with a shock of fear I very rarely felt around Draven but it was enough to get him to simmer slightly. He took a deep breath that he wouldn't release until after he closed his eyes. I took another step back and with his eyes still closed he then cut me up inside with one order spoken,

"Leave!"

"What?" I whispered in shock, never before hearing this demand from Draven before.

"LEAVE! NOW!" He bellowed igniting his body in a red flame making me almost fall over myself to get away. I scrambled to the door and was just about to fling it open when I heard a broken voice from behind me,

"Keira, I…please, please…just give me time…forgive me… I…" I stopped and looked down to watch a tear fall and land on the floor passing where my death grip pulled the handle down, ready for my escape. I sucked in a shuddered breath and turned to face him over my shoulder.

"He can't hurt me, Draven…no one can… not…not after what you did to me…" I said before pulling down on the heavy iron and walking through the door right before I heard the destruction I now left in my wake.

After leaving Draven to his rage I leant back on the door to let the tears fall freely. I banged my head back on the wood and forced myself to listen to his pain rip the room apart behind me. I didn't know if he even realised I was still out here but with each sound of devastation, with each thunder of pain I heard, I felt it like a blade to the chest. I couldn't help but think that if he didn't love me why would he be reacting this way. Would anyone who didn't feel like their life was being ripped apart at the seams react this way? So why…?

I jumped when I heard the cracking of wood and moved away from the door to see it too was now being punished with the wrath of Draven and when an almighty demon roared into the night I started to run. I just let my legs take me somewhere, anywhere deeper into the fortress that was now closing in around me like the wall of souls down in the temple.

I was panting and trying in vain to take in great gulps of air that burned my throat as though I was breathing in thick black smoke. I wanted to wake up from this nightmare but when I slipped and landed painfully on my knees I knew then it wasn't ever going to be the kind of pain I could just wake up from. I pulled my legs under me and cried like the child I felt as I let the combination of mine and Draven's pain overwhelm me. It felt like I was drowning right here in this hallway and each end of it only held more heartache I wasn't ready for. His room was right there. So damn close I could almost touch it and then pretend that the last year had never happened.

"Keira?" I didn't even look up at the sound of Vincent's voice but just managed to sob harder, rocking myself faster and holding myself tighter.

"Oh, Keira." He said touching me and gently prying myself from my protective ball that wasn't doing shit in protecting my already damaged heart. He pulled me into him and his hand held the back of my head to his chest. I felt him shaking and realised it was because I was trembling in his hold.

"I gather that didn't go too well." He said softly and I could no longer hold it back, saying the words I had denied myself in so long, it felt like fingernails were tearing at the words that were glued to my very soul,

"I still love him, Vincent!" I cried out, after looking him in the eyes and seeing the clear blue concern sparkling back down at me as if I was looking at the ocean under the moonlight. I saw pity just under the surface but there was something else there I couldn't reach. He looked back over his shoulder at the door to Draven's office as though listening to something. Then he closed his eyes and let his head hang, looking at the floor before allowing his gaze to find me once more. His eyes were filled with a mirrored pain and I wondered what he had heard coming from behind that age old oak?

"I know, Keira, as does he with you." On hearing that I tore my watery gaze from his, not allowing myself to truly believe his claim.

"Take me away, Vincent…take me away from here…take me anywhere…*please.*" I pleaded and only felt myself breathe normally again when he nodded and pulled me to my feet. Then without warning he swept me off my feet and carried me away, saying the only thing I needed to hear right then…

"Let's go for a ride babe."

DRAVEN

"DAMN HIM! DAMN THE FATES! DAMN THEM ALL!" I screamed out all my frustrations with the help of my Demon side that could not be tamed. My voice felt raw and ragged with the pain I felt coursing through my blood like a toxin that would surely eat away at my soul! I wanted to damn the world and every bastard in it until they all felt this agony but what use were any of these emotions? They got me nothing fast and they got me nowhere even faster.

"It has all been in vain." I said out loud slumping back against the pillar, one of the only things in the room I had not destroyed in my uncontrollable rage. In that moment I wanted to lash out at her, but not physically...*never physically*, by the Gods but that thought brought me indescribable pain. No, I wanted to mentally shake her, take over her mind and let her see her stupidity for herself! Let her feel all the reasons why I had protected her in the most brutal way a person could protect someone. Yes, I had lied. I had lied in the worst possible way another soul could but why, for the very life I hold above my own, above any other life on this Gods forsaken planet!

If only she could see all that I had done, all I still do in order to keep her safe and not just from me. If only she could see the endless nights I had locked myself away in a prison only made for the Gods, just so that I could stay away from her. And all for what, so she could move on with her life with a fucking Nephilim! A half breed only allowed to continue life thanks to the punishment of the supernatural side, the punishment of my own kind, and one that I had to enforce with my own hands!

Oh yes, the Nephilim were a sore spot with me indeed and now I had to stand back and watch one date my woman, the other half of my soul and my intended Queen! My Electus.

I would rather roast another thousand years in Tartarus and cool my charred skin in the flaming river of Phlegethon that flows into its very depths of the prison. These thoughts caused me to bring my solid desk once carved with such skill and care to fly across the room and crash into the wall opposite. The action left me bent over double and panting into my hands.

I was in half a mind to journey back to Hell and prompt another round from my father, or at least take on one of his many legions. But then I heard her in the distance crying out. She was down the hall after I had ruthlessly forced her from the room with my harsh demands. I didn't want to, but I had no choice. It was that or let her see the extent of what my rage reduces me to. I couldn't let her see me this way…this broken shell of a man whose only useful emotion was the rage and bitterness that kept me moving my body every damn day. Any other emotion that I allowed to seep in would render me useless for days, even weeks on end.

No, right now I needed this anger to help me to act because the reality of my situation had being staring at me across the room when the bastard had kissed her. I had never wanted another being dead right there and then more in my entire life. I wanted to walk calmly up to him and take his head in my hand to crush his skull until his brain matter covered my arm as the only evidence that he could no longer touch her.

I heard another cry and any thoughts of death swiftly left me. I stumbled to the door ready to go to her. Ready to take her body in my arms where it belonged and comfort her. I couldn't stand hearing her pain, hearing what *I* myself had inflicted. But what was worse, hearing her sadness at my cruel dismissal or seeing the fear in her eyes again. That was my personal Hell right there in that one look. That one flinch and step back she took as if I had struck her…when in reality she had struck me with the sight of her fear. I knew then I had to get her to leave me because tears I could deal with. Her fear of me I could not.

My hand touched the handle and noted the great crack I had created in the door just to get her to finally leave. I knew she was there, right behind the door listening to my outburst of rage but before I could really let go I needed her to get away from me and with more than just a flimsy piece of oak between us. If not I would have let my Demon take over, ripping the wood like paper only to haul her back into my arms and never letting her go again.

But instead of my arms I could now hear it was my brother's arms which had come to her aid. I opened up my senses further and listened to what was being said whilst holding my forehead against the broken door. I held my fists at the same height as if waiting for another knife she unknowingly would be plunging in my heart. And then it came soon enough…

"I still love him, Vincent." By the Gods! There were no sweeter words spoken and no harder words heard in all my years taking breath!

This was when my knees hit the floor, cracking the stone with the pent-up power that was just begging for an even greater release. I closed my eyes as I'd done in front of her just to try and calm the flames I knew consumed my irises.

"As do I my love…as do I, *my Keira.*" I said letting my head hang and the burning tears form under my lids that I refused to let fall.

I don't know how long I continued like this, knelt by the door but it was a while after that I heard Keira's plea to be taken from this place. And hearing my brother take my heart into his arms and carry her off, was like trying to swallow a bitter pill the size of my fist. I wanted to take back what was mine, and demand he hand her to me to care for but I knew this was not what she needed or more importantly, what she even wanted. So, as I don't know how many times before…

I let her go.

At the distant sound of Vincent's Dyna wide glide Harley Davidson purring down the road, I rose from the floor and launched myself up and twisted my wings to curl round me as I flew through the arches in the balcony and out into the desolate night. I let gravity take me as I free fell before then spreading my wings out to catch the air that pushed against each feather, taking me upwards. I tilted to one side to turn before using my strength to take me further up the building Keira had ran from.

I pushed myself to rise higher. Beating my wings was definitely easier than beating back my anger. I quickly reached my intended perch at the highest point of Afterlife and landed not caring for the cracks I created with the force. With one knee to the floor I looked up in time to see the light of Vincent's bike manoeuvring along the winding road with Keira gripping onto his body like she feared she would fall off with every turn.

I stood up to my full height on the small stone platform and watched until they went out of sight, torturing myself. I was tempted to follow them but then I knew it would only serve as yet another mistake in a very long list of ones already committed. No, my time was best served deciding what my next move was in getting rid of one Alex Cain. In the very little time I knew of him I hadn't been able to find anything about him, other than his human life. He was off the grid in my world and this was what worried me the most.

Nephilim were created when the Fallen of Heaven would fall from grace even further, taking that extra step when sleeping with a human and producing a child from that forbidden union. This was the reason they were punished. Angels who passed on their powers and longevity through to humans who couldn't be controlled. They were a dangerous breed for one reason and one reason only… they were exempt from my interference in regard to the law. The Gods believed they had enough human nature inside their veins that they were allowed to live in the world with the same free will granted to each human soul. They themselves walking as immortal Gods amongst mere mortals and having no one to answer to.

This meant they held no loyalty to me and nor were they expected to. I could only get involved if they broke one of my laws that tipped the balance enough to be classed as interference with another human life. They could literally walk into a bank, break every person's bones with their superior strength, killing them and then take every penny to then get away with it. But if they happened to kill an old lady by sucking the energy from what was left in her fragile body, only then could I bring them to justice. The reasoning behind this was that every human had the free will to do good granted to them in the hope that they would walk this path. But it worked the other way also, the ability to bring about destruction in the form of a knife, gun or bomb, killing without thought and no remorse. This was also their own free will and path to choose if they so wished.

The world was filled with killers and dark tainted souls anyway, so what if half of the Nephilim were that way inclined? However, this reasoning never sat well with me and was a decision that I never happily accepted. But it was one that I had no choice but to abide with. That was my own law to adhere to.

And now that Heavenly decision was made even harder to

accept thanks to one of their kind, that for reasons unknown, had insinuated himself into Keira's life. This caused me to think murderous thoughts indeed. If only I could get away with breaking my own rules and take this cretin out of the picture, oh what fun I would have ripping him apart with my bare hands!

I don't think I will ever forget that moment when seeing Keira again after all that time. The pictures I have of her are but a miniscule of the beauty she possesses, and its shine equalled that of the sun, blinding me when gazing upon it after so very long. It was as though we were the only two people that existed at that moment, so much so I didn't even give the parasite that stood next to her a second thought, hell even a first thought when seeing her.

She, as always, was my only.

I ran a frustrated hand through my hair, pushing it back like I was close to ripping each fucker out from my scalp if it would only bring me relief from this burning wrath. And by the Gods but what it had felt like when I finally touched her for the first time. I thought I would come out of my skin, that or embarrass myself like the unruly teenager I had accused her of acting.

When she had mentioned about my temper getting the better of me, what she didn't realise that up until that point I had still not managed to regain my control over that 'famous Demon temper' of mine. But one look at her sat in my chair was enough to heat my blood for very different reasons. I hadn't lied when I told her that it suited her, however what I would have liked to have added was a whispered fantasy in her ear about how I had always felt a desperate need to make love to her on it.

The sight of her blush again, one brought out even more in that delicious cherry red dress that clung to even tastier curves. But by the Gods she was sin and bliss combined, wrapped in the softest skin alive. It took me back to the days and the perfect hours spent tasting every inch of her.

I huffed out loud, wondering what she would really think of me if she knew the level of my obsession… well, before she thought me a ruthless bastard who stomped all over her heart, with no explanation given. This was just yet another punishing thought that had plagued me for what felt like eternity.

But once I started I couldn't stop as I thought back to her sat in my modern day throne. It engulfed her in its size enough that I wanted to scoop her up and lay her over my lap before kissing the past behind us and effectively numbing the pain for us both. I wanted to hold her and keep her safe like I needed oxygen to travel my body to keep it living. I had almost groaned out loud when she rolled her lip nervously as I blatantly stared at her. It was almost laughable how much she wanted to bite it and I think I would have done if I hadn't been more concerned about my growing erection at the time.

But when she forgot herself and gulped back the Absinthe, then there was no way in Hell or out of it, that I wasn't going to touch her. If Vincent hadn't given me a look and shake of his head when I went to pick her up then I would have snatched her to my arms before she could get her next spluttering cough in. Instead I had to satisfy myself with rubbing her back and holding back every instinct that was ingrained in me since the day I first saw her.

I shook my head, trying to steer my mind away from these thoughts when I noticed Ava flying towards me from a distance. She, like my other family members, had not been happy with my decisions in leaving Keira and had even been openly hostile towards me at times. But as usual she came to me when she felt my pain, offering me a comfort we both knew I didn't deserve.

She dipped her wings in a graceful swoop until she was close enough to land on my outstretched arm.

"Ah my Rara Avis, how are you my precious one?" She ruffled her feathers like she always did when hearing her pet name of 'Rare bird' in Latin. She nudged my hand and squawked at me, with her head tilted. I knew this was her way of asking me what was wrong.

"I saw my heart again tonight and she…she was not happy." I never had any problems speaking so freely to my pet and I put this down to so many years of sharing her body when needed. Let's just say it was certainly an ice breaker.

She shifted on my arm getting closer to my neck, where she rubbed her satin feathers under my chin in an affectionate manner. I laughed, stroking her and basking in a moment of freedom from my worries.

"I need you to keep an eye on her for me… can you do that, my girl?" She looked back at me and made a piercing call before she took off towards the direction Keira and my brother had taken. I instantly breathed a little easier for it but that was short lived when I felt I was no longer alone.

"Feeling any better after your little chat with bitchy feathers there?"

"This is not a good time, Sophia." I said without looking at her but knowing she was sat on the wall of the roof garden behind me.

"Has it ever been a good time over this last year, Brother?" I didn't reply but instead watched my bird until she flew out of sight.

"Say what you came to say and have done with it." I almost cringed at the sound of my harsh demand but not being able to help it feeling the way I did.

"Something needs to be done about this Alex Cain." This finally made me turn around and I noticed Zagan in the background keeping a watchful eye on his own heart. I nodded to my commander at arms and he nodded back respectfully before leaving us alone.

"Something will be done, have no doubt in that, Sister." I

promised jumping down from my view point until I was at the same level as my small sibling.

"You know most of what she says is because she doesn't understand why…you realise that, right?" She said and I cracked my knuckles when they both flexed at my sides. This reaction couldn't be helped when I thought back to all the hurt in her voice and the spite behind each and every word she lashed out at me like a weapon…Her greatest weapon against me.

"And she never will know."

"Dominic…"

"NO!" I barked at her and then took a deep breath to calm myself before continuing on with what I needed to say.

"No, Sophia, for this she can never know."

"And why not?" I was walking past her when I stopped. I shook my head and then turned back to her to hit her with the truth just as the Oracle once did with me that day.

"Because if she ever knew the truth, then she would never let me go."

"And that's bad because…?" My reaction to these thoughts was always the same. My panic at it ever coming to pass was soul consuming and made me close my eyes tight to hold in the greatest fear I had ever known…my one and only true fear.

"Because if she never let me go, then she would never let go of her destiny of death…"

"But…" I held up my hand and my eyes snapped open to express the seriousness of my next words, the only words that mattered when it came to my future and preventing it with my last breath…

"A death…Sophia,

"…at my hands."

CHAPTER NINE

KEIRA

PITY FOR YOUR BROTHER

I can say there is nothing quite like escaping your past whilst holding on to an Angel taking your breath away on the back of his bike. I clung onto his hard body in front of me and as I lay my cheek to his back, I let my tears run down his leather. I didn't know if he knew as I silently sobbed at his back, but I would feel his abs tighten each time I inhaled sharply. I would feel bad if he did but I knew it couldn't be helped. The dam had broken. It had crumbled beneath the weight of a year's worth of tears and I didn't know how I was ever going to fix it again.

That's what Draven did to me. That's what an immeasurable amount of love did to you. It was infinite, it was vast and it was endless. It was an ever-burning flame that no matter what Draven did wasn't ever going to extinguish, lighting his face even in the darkest of hours. And the painful truth was that I knew that I would grow old and blind well before I no longer saw him.

So I cried. I cried for the man who held my heart in his hand and crushed it right in front of me. I cried for the man who still held it in his fist and even though broken, still wouldn't let it go. I watched the world go by feeling as empty as the road we travelled down and could only muster up enough thanks that I wasn't alone in this.

I felt like I had been alone for so long now it was like standing at the mouth of a bottomless hollow in the earth looking down. Wondering all the time when a hand would come over the edge of darkness to grab me, pull me under and drag me into my own misery deep enough that I would never be able to claw myself out again.

My mind kept up with these depressing thoughts all the way, up until a point I hadn't even realised Vincent had killed the engine.

"That's quite a heavy mind you've got there, Beautiful" He said as he raised two gloved hands to my face and used his leather covered thumbs to wipe away my remaining tears. I swallowed what felt like a heartbroken lump and looked up at him as he twisted round to face me. I felt my bottom lip start to vibrate and quickly pulled it into my mouth to try and stop the next round of tears from falling.

"Oh sweetheart, come here," He said pulling me to his chest after shifting fully on his bike. I went to him willingly and let it all go. I cried until I shook and hiccupped every breath I needed to keep going, dragging it painfully into my lungs. I don't know how long we stayed like this, but he only allowed me to pull away from him after he was sure all my tears were spent.

"Feel better?" I nodded at his question and wiped my eyes with my long sleeves.

"Good because we need to talk." He said letting go of me

and getting off his bike to walk to the edge of the cliff face. I looked around and thanks to the full moon was able to make out where we were. I sucked in a startled breath as the last time I had come here I was also with Vincent but under very different circumstances. He turned to look at me over his shoulder and said,

"I could not think of a better place to have this conversation that would prove my point more," and then he looked back over towards the rugged mountains where I knew Draven's cave was hidden away in the jagged rock.

"I can't go back there." I even shuddered at the thought, hugging myself.

"And I would not expect that you could but being here, as close as we are, will be enough I think." I took in what he said and for long moments didn't move. Thankfully he seemed to know that I needed the time, waiting for me silently with his back to my internal struggles. Finally I nodded to myself and got off the bike to walk slowly over to him. I saw him lift his head to the clear summer sky above as if basking in the moonlight that gave his perfect skin a divine quality. He had never looked more angelic than at this moment.

"Vincent?"

"Umm." He made a noise almost like he was letting me know he was still with me but was also half consumed with absorbing some kind of energy from above. I placed my hand up on his shoulder as I asked,

"Are you alright?" finally making him break his invisible connection to, I didn't know what and look down at me stood at his side.

"Truthfully?" I said and I nodded ready for whatever he had to say…or at least hoping that I was.

"I don't think I ever will be alright until my brother is also." I winced at this.

"Vincent I…"

"Before I begin, I want you to know that you have not one thing to be sorry for… do you understand, Keira?" He asked interrupting what was going to be an apology on my part in what happened tonight.

"Do you?" He pushed again making me nod, if only to make him feel better. He took in a deep breath and nodded back at me.

"You and your sister are close, are you not?"

"Yeah, we're close." I said quietly, having a very good idea where he was going with this.

"And when you hurt, she hurts doesn't she?" My breathing hitched and I felt the watery film over my eyes suspended there as I tried to gather my emotions back, willing them not to fall again. I thought back to being taken and seeing her for the first time at the hospital.

Many times since I had shamefully thought how I would have handled it if our situations had been in reverse. How I would have felt seeing my sister in that hospital bed, the one broken and not only bleeding on the outside. How hopeless I would have felt for weeks after, seeing her close in on herself. Witnessing more and more with each passing day you lose the sister you once knew. The pain and the anger that flashed across her eyes, all as though she was trying to absorb the hurt right out of me and take it on herself.

It was all there as plain as night watching it passing through Vincent's eyes. The pain and the anger as though he wanted to take the same hurt from his brother just to ease his suffering…a suffering that by me being here was only adding to the weight of them all. Three close siblings who although so very different were also so very similar. If one of them hurt then all of them hurt and it was only now that I was discovering just how much that hurt had cost them.

And now it was time for my brutal truth.

I didn't need to word my answer to him as he saw it all play out across my face as the realisation came to pass.

"So now you know."

"Yes…*now I know,*" I whispered turning away from him, the view and the place where I knew his cave lay waiting, everything that held me hostage in this hopeless situation.

"It was all his choosing, Vincent." I said letting the agony transform my voice to one of torment.

"But see, that's where you're wrong, Keira…this…this type of pain is never anyone's choosing. You think he wanted to hurt you this way…? By the Gods, Keira even I didn't understand it but now…"

"And now…?" I snapped, swinging back round to face him again.

"And now I know that he really had no choice at all." I shook my head and said bitterly,

"But let me guess, it's not your place to tell me why."

"It is not my place, no. Just as it also isn't Dom's." I let out a frustrated huff and raised my arms dramatically only to fall back again.

"Right! How perfect! This is my life and the decisions made that affect it I not only don't have a say in, but I don't even get to bloody know what the reasons are! You can surely see where I would have a problem with that…right?!"

"I do." He agreed calmly in spite of my mounting rage.

"As does Dom," he added when I let out a sigh making my mouth nearly drop open in shock.

"What?!"

"Did you really imagine Dom was finding any of this easy? Did you really think making any of these decisions, decisions that he knew would break you *both*, came easy to him?" He asked his voice getting hard and I stuttered for a moment,

125

"Well I…well, no but…"

"And did you really think that bearing the weight of these decisions was going to be easy to live with, knowing it was for the rest of his days?"

"I…no of course not but…"

"No! No they were not. I even admit myself that up until I finally knew why I could not understand the level of love needed in making them but make no mistake Keira, that was exactly what it took." On hearing this I fell back a step unable to believe his words.

"What…what do you mean?" I asked on a whispered breath. Vincent looked away from me and looked down at the ground as if needing to compose himself before speaking again.

"Answer me something, Keira, you were angry at my brother when hearing why he came back here, were you not?"

"Yes I was because he didn't come back here for me…he… he came back because of Alex." I said straightening my back and clenching my fists at my sides.

"See that's where you're right but also very, very wrong." He looked back up and then turned to me again to take in my defensive stance. He shook his head in what looked like frustration and then hit me with the painful truth.

"So you're angry at that but tell me, how painful would it have been for you to know that Dom knew of you and this Alex but did nothing… simply because he didn't care." At this my shoulders slumped, and I bit my lip as all that he said hit its mark with deadly accuracy. Thinking this would have indeed been far, far worse. Him knowing about us and doing…*nothing,* God but that thought alone nearly brought me to my knees!

I had spent so much time being pissed at Draven that I didn't think for even a minute what him acting this way really meant. How I would have felt if he had done nothing, reacting as if he didn't care but he hadn't done that now had he? No, he had acted in the complete opposite. So that could only mean one thing…

"He…he still cares for me?" I said shocked that I could even make the words pass through my lips. Vincent's lips quirked into a small smile before saying,

"But of course he does. There is not a being alive that would not act that way unless there was love driving their actions."

"But if he still cares then why doesn't he just try and get me back…why has it taken this long for him to…?"

"Don't do that to yourself, sweetheart." He interrupted quickly.

"Do what?"

"Hope for what he can't allow to happen." He finished sadly.

"So that's it! He breaks my heart for reasons I will never know and you not only tell me his own heart is breaking from his decision but also that he can never do anything to fix it!?" This time it was Vincent's turn to sigh and clench his gloved fists.

"That's what I am telling you." I sucked in a sharp breath surprised at what I should have been ready for.

"So that's it for us…there's…there's no use fighting anymore is there?" I tried to get it out without letting the tears fall but what was the use, they were already streaming down my face in an angry flow that I hadn't even realised until now.

"Oh, Keira… haven't you realised it by now…?" He waited for me to look back up at him and when I did he held out his hand to me. I ran to him as I had no strength in me to fight against my need for his comfort. He held me to him and I looked up to see him looking directly at the cave I knew was hidden there. And when looking there I saw we were no longer alone as Ava was seen circling overhead watching us, making me wonder if Draven could also see us?

These thoughts evaporated when he finished with the most important statement of all,

"…You don't have it in you to ever stop fighting for him." And I answered him the only way I knew how…

With the truth.

"I know."

We were now on our way back with me as before, clutching onto Vincent as we sped down empty roads. We didn't have much more to say to each other after that, as what else was there to say. It was obvious the pain Vincent endured watching his brother walk this lonely path that the Oracle had sent him down. It was also obvious that no matter what either of us said or did, that he would continue to walk it even if there was no point to the destination at the end.

This was what I just needed to accept. Even if what Vincent had said made me face the truth. That I would never really stop fighting for him but the difference was that sometimes even as we continue to fight the good fight it didn't mean that the war hadn't already long since been lost. I didn't say this to Vincent, but I didn't need to. All he needed to do was look at it written there, etched deep in my anguish of someone already beaten. But he surprised me. The last thing he did was look back to the cave one last time and say,

"You know of the truth untold but now… well, now I think it is time for his own truth to be found." And without explaining it fully he took my hand and led me back to his bike.

It was as if nothing more needed to be said. And as I held on it gave my mind plenty to think about as I watched the road unravel ahead. It was time to be honest with myself and finally let go of the past. I had been hurting for so long now it was easier to feel bitter than to hold on to hope. It was easier to be angry at Draven than wonder too deeply what his own feelings could be. But really, where did any of that get me? It didn't make me feel better, if anything it made me feel worse. And my cutting words to him, that nobody would deny he deserved on some level, but what did they really achieve? They just ended up hurting someone I loved and that wasn't what I wanted.

I think I could safely say that he knew how much he had wounded me and for reasons, it was obvious I would never find out, he felt like he had no other choice to make. So why make him suffer more? No, from now on I wasn't going to do that to him. I was going to let go of the past year and look to the hard reality of a future that didn't include him and me ever being together again. But that didn't mean we couldn't still be friends now, could it? Well, I was definitely going to give it a try because Vincent was right, I wasn't going to give up on him.

I didn't have it in me.

These tangled thoughts brought me all the way to our destination, and I frowned when I saw it wasn't the one I had been expecting.

"Err…Vincent, why are we back here?" I asked as he shut down his bike. He kicked down the stand and looked over his shoulder to wink at me.

"No time like the present to start turning over that new leaf of yours." He said smirking.

"You were listening?!" I screeched in panic.

"Honey, your mind was screaming at me so loud I could hear you over the engine." I groaned as I realised my mistake. It seemed like all that time I spent guarding my mind in front of Draven, that when I was no longer in his presence my exhausted brain just flopped down in front of the telly, to put her feet up and let any bugger in!

"Great." I responded dryly making Vincent laugh.

"We don't even know that I will still be welcome after…" At this Vincent burst out laughing stopping me in my tracks. He was still chuckling as he pulled me off his bike and walked me back towards the building…

Back to Afterlife.

"I don't think we need to worry about that." He said nodding ahead of him and my eyes followed to find Draven stood there waiting and leaning against the stone wall next to a side door that Vincent used as our exit earlier. I would like to have said I was cool as a cucumber but with a faltered step that nearly made me trip over myself and my face no doubt sporting an attractive puffiness from crying, well… that cool wasn't even in the building to start with, let alone given the chance to go flying out the window!

The closer we got the more my palms began to sweat praying I wasn't about to walk back into a showdown. I noticed he had changed out of his suit and to say the sight of him didn't affect me would have sent me straight to Hell as a sinner. He now had his strong long legs encased in faded denim that moulded to him in a way that you couldn't help but notice the size of his powerful thighs. Christ but even the slight rips at his knees that showed that slither of skin made my girly parts tingle.

My eyes shamelessly did an all body scan and when I reached his chest my mouth went dry. Well, I was only human! But come on, the sight was just too unfair for words. He wore a tight, long sleeved t-shirt that was a dark grey with a design etched on the front that was the back end of some vintage car.

It was rare to see Draven wearing anything that allowed you a glimpse into his personality other than his power suits that screamed an authoritative, 'don't mess with me, or I will crush you'. So it brought a small smile to my lips just seeing that rough pencil drawing of a car I couldn't place, sitting there across his chest. Oh, and the muscles I saw outlined under the material certainly helped that smile form!

What had he been doing all this time, bench pressing trees and running up mountains with log cabins on his back?! I mean the guy had what looked like a friggin eight pack beneath that shirt and I am pretty sure I only counted six the last time I saw it. And I didn't even want to get started on those arms, not if I wanted to be able to form words that weren't just a series of grunts and bumbling murmurs.

"Keira, you're bac…"

"I'm sorry!" I blurted out before he could finish. He closed both his eyes for a few seconds longer than a blink and shook his head slightly, as if clearing his mind of an action he wanted to follow through on. He then flashed his brother a look, communicating something between them that only family blood would pick up on.

"Well, as always it's been eventful, Beautiful but best I leave you two to it…*remember what I said, Keira."* He whispered this last part by my ear as he gave me a half hug goodbye. I nodded and whispered a,

"Thank you" back before letting him go. He winked down at me in more affection than just being cheeky and I gave him a little shy smile before he turned back to his brother. As he walked past Draven he grabbed his arm and held him immobile for a second. And what he said next both shocked me and filled me with such peace it made my heart soar for a few blissful beats.

"Thank you for bringing her back to me, Brother." Vincent lowered his head in a sign of deep respect and then clasped Draven on his shoulder, giving it a reassuring squeeze.

"As I always will do, Brother." And then he left us alone, making me jump when the heavy door slammed behind him. I giggled nervously, trying to ease the tension at how frazzled my nerves were.

"Uhh…so what now?" I asked after a minute of awkward silence that was most likely only fifteen seconds.

"Now…? Well, I think now we could both do with a drink, don't you?" He said and I smiled, feeling the last of my tension leave me, being replaced with relief. He held out his hand to me and said,

"Shall we?" And like my body was made of metal, I went to the magnet that was Draven, instantly feeling the tingles wrack my body at his touch. If he noticed me shudder then he didn't say anything and I was more than thankful for it.

We walked back through his fortress and when we turned a way I hadn't been before I frowned looking back behind us.

"I hope you don't mind but Sophia kind of had something planned for you." He asked me softly whilst pulling me along with him. Didn't he realise that when he spoke to me like that it felt like his fingertips were running tantalisingly along my spine and I would have done anything he asked?

"Okay," I said feeling the heat in my cheeks at how breathy it sounded. He simply grinned down at me and then looked ahead, allowing me a chance to mouth the words 'Oh my God' to the floor. I had to wonder if there would ever be a time when Draven and I weren't playing cat and mouse on a rollercoaster that was our lives. One minute we were screaming at each other and the next…well, the next was far more dangerous. The next was us holding hands and speaking in beautifully soft words combined with gentle forbidden touches. Like what his thumb was doing right now, rubbing delicious little slow circles over my index finger that was the equivalent of putting me under a spell. It was beautifully torturous.

I had a single moment of guilt thinking about Alex and wondering if this could be considered as cheating. I really hoped not as I thought if me and Draven really could get beyond our turbulent past then I doubted we could ever have the kind of friendship that didn't include touching. It just didn't seem possible to me and with the way Draven was acting it didn't seem like it was possible for him either.

We soon came to a winding staircase that was quite narrow and he held the door open for me.

"After you my…" He started to say his pet name for me and then had to clear his throat after stopping himself. I felt bad for him so said,

"I would say age before beauty but you're like a beautiful old man, so where does that leave me?" The smile he gave me was just as I had described him…beautiful.

"That leaves the beautiful girl before me going first so this old man can catch her if she falls." And there it was, a perfect answer formed by a pair of perfect lips smirking down at me.

"Oh boy, you are goooood." I said stretching out the end when taking the first steep steps up. Draven waited for it to bring us to the same height and then leaned in so his lips were at my ear.

"I certainly never remember any complaints." He purred and I stupidly inhaled a good amount of his intoxicating scent, amplifying his sexual words tenfold. It nearly rendered me incapable of using my legs but when his hands gripped my sides in a possessive hold, they nearly gave out altogether.

"Let's get that drink should we?" He whispered and gave me a little push to get me moving again, not taking his hands from my waist. I quickly found myself torn between running up the steps to get away from his deviously tempting touch and falling backwards just so he could catch me. In the end I just walked to the top feeling the sexual tension tick up a notch with every step we took. I turned round at one point, not being able to resist any longer and found him staring at my behind as though my cheeks were jiggling in time to some cheesy disco beat that had him hypnotised.

I cleared my throat and he knew he had been caught, making him for once be the one to bite his lip. And if that sinful bad boy grin was anything to go by then it was in no doubt to help hold in his laughter.

When we finally got to the top, he artfully slid passed me, making sure that there wasn't an inch between our bodies. I had to look away as the feeling was nearly overwhelming. His hand on my side became an arm around my back, whilst his other hand reached for the door. The move caused my breasts to press up against his hard stomach muscles, having nowhere else to go and if I turned my head to face him, I would have ended up brushing my nose against his defined pecs.

There was no way in Hell he wasn't doing this on purpose and I let out a frustrated growl letting him know I was on to him and whatever precarious game he was playing.

"Just being a gentleman," he said full of humour and letting the door swing open. I huffed and walked out of his hold, which was something I wanted to do about as much as piercing my tongue with a rusty nail!

"Smooth," I hummed with a smile and patted his chest trying to give the appearance of confidence to mask my pounding heart as I went past.

"I do try," he replied close to my back and I was glad he didn't see me biting my lip for...oh I don't know, the gazillionth time tonight! I felt his hand at the small of my back putting a nice amount of pressure there as he led me forward which was clearly not needed, as what Sophia had planned was there right in front of us.

"It's stunning," I said taking in the gorgeous rooftop garden that was illuminated by what looked like thousands of tiny fairy lights. They were wrapped around everything, from tall sculpted ferns and wrought iron furniture legs to arched wooden pillars that also made the frame for the deep crimson canopy that was stretched above its massive hexagon shape.

"I am glad you like it and it's about time you two stopped arguing and joined us." Sophia said from inside the Arabian night scene, looking like a royal Goddess being worshiped by a silent Zagan. They both lay lounged out on a sofa that put them floor level and their backs were leaning against massive stuffed tube shape cushions that were covered in shiny satin material, with different shades of rich red stripes. Small carved tables were also dotted about and large square scatter pillows were strategically placed around the fire pit in the centre. There was also an elaborate carved stone chimney above it that gave the canopy a classic Moroccan tent shape at its centre.

The summer air was alive with the scent of exotic flowers that I had no doubt were only able to grow in this part of the world thanks to a little supernatural mojo sent their way. I could only sympathise as I knew exactly what the Dravens favour of mojo could do to a soul.

"Helpful as always, Sophia." Draven said leading me through the twinkling arch and into the sensual space that screamed 'not a good idea!'

"I do try," she said mimicking what Draven had said to me and smiling that cat like grin over her glass. This made Zagan smirk at her like she was both his entire world and a woman he wanted to bend over his knee and spank. Ok, no more thoughts like that in this place or more importantly being in the same building as Draven…or maybe even the same state… Yep, that might be safer!

"Ah now, I definitely want to know what that blush is all about?!" Sophia said excitedly clapping her hands. I rolled my eyes trying to play it cool but of course it didn't help when I heard Draven murmur,

"You and I both."

"So I guess Zagan is the only one that's going to behave, is that it?" I asked raising my eyebrow at first Draven and then down at his sister.

"Not if I can help it." Sophia said turning to Zagan and he winked at her after she flicked his hood up revealing a little more of his pale but handsome face. I couldn't help smile at the sight of them both but this was short lived as I let out a yelp in shock as Draven fell backwards, taking me with him.

He landed on what looked like a matching couch on the floor, opposite to where Sophia and Zagan sat. He landed first and then I followed, only unlike him I didn't land on the soft bed sized cushion. Oh no, I landed right on top of Draven with my butt to his groin, making him groan in what I hoped wasn't in pleasure...well, only half hoped anyway.

I scrambled off him all red faced and embarrassed when trying to find a place to put my hands. He finally took pity on me by lifting me off him and shifted me to his side. I didn't fail to notice how his hands lingered longer than needed either.

"I guess there's my answer," I commented, referring back to him misbehaving and this made Draven's head fall back as he burst into roaring laughter. I'm not gonna lie but I was momentarily transfixed by the glorious sight.

The way the soft light reflected off his midnight dark hair making me long to run my fingers through it just once more to see if it was as silky to touch as I remembered. The way I could have reached out if I was just brave enough and run my fingertips over the cords in his neck and then down to his bunched strong shoulders. Was his skin still as smooth and were his muscles still as hard as they looked?

Sophia cleared her throat and I snapped my gaze from Draven and saw her give me a hidden smile, as if she knew exactly what I had just been thinking about. Draven had finally composed himself with a grin and sat up a little straighter before he clapped his hands. A servant came from behind a wall of green foliage with pretty orange flowers blooming like stars in clusters.

"A bottle of the White Gold Jeroboam, oh and lo si può entrare ora" ('You may let him in now' in Italian) Draven said leaving me wondering yet again what he said. Sometimes I don't think he even realised he started speaking in a different language.

When we were together I would often wake up to him whispering words I didn't understand over my skin or speaking to me while making love and having to ask him afterwards what he meant. Of course it used to frustrate the bejesus out of me when he would just smile and make a motion of sealing his lips at me like it was his little secret.

"He's here?" Sophia asked which certainly got my attention. Draven nodded not giving anything away so I grabbed his arm and asked without restraint,

"Who's here?" To which I received my answer from the deep gruff voice behind me that I would have known anywhere.

"Oh my God!" I shouted excitedly and bounced in my seat turning around to see if my mind was playing tricks on me. But no, thankfully it wasn't.

As there behind me was my past and he was certainly a beautiful sight to behold…

"My friend."

CHAPTER TEN

KEIRA

LITTLE APPLE OR LITTLE BEAR?

"L ille øjesten." That deep rumbling voice said and my heart leapt at the sound.

"Ragnar!" I shouted as my only warning to the man who I was now throwing my body at. He let out an umph sound at the impact, but his colossal arms encircled me all the same.

"Hello, little one." He said looking down at me trying to fit my arms all the way around his waist with no such luck. I felt my throat start to thicken with the emotion that built from seeing my old protector once again. It had been so long and I understood why. As Draven's head of the guards Ragnar rarely went anywhere without his King. So because of this I knew why I hadn't seen him since that painfully fated day when I left Italy and its agony behind me.

"You're a sight for sore eyes, big guy." I said laughing and trying to wipe my damp eyes without being caught. Of course as I turned my head to the side to use my sleeve I couldn't help but notice Draven's eyes on me, watching my every move with great interest. He gave me a small smile at my reaction to seeing my old bodyguard once again. I gave him a shy smile before mouthing the words 'Thank you' at him, to which he nodded his head and mouthed back 'You're most welcome'. Of course I blushed but thankfully had the perfect reason to turn my attention away from him.

"I must say little human that I am surprised you have managed to keep yourself out of trouble all these months." Ragnar said, teasing me which was like old times once again.

"Oi! As shocking as it sounds I am sometimes capable of taking care of myself you know." I replied crossing my arms and looking up at this seven foot giant with not one ounce of fear making him laugh down at me. At one time this rough looking beast of a demon used to freak the F words out of me but now, well let's just say that I wasn't sure some of those massive muscles weren't filled with marshmallows!

The rest of the night went by without a hitch. Though most surprisingly was how comfortable it all felt. It was a cruel and dangerous thought to allow myself to have but it felt like old times. It also became very clear that trying to sit without being next to Draven wasn't an option. So after he grabbed my hand, when I was trying to pass him, and quickly yanking me down without a word, I thought it best not to protest and make a scene. Ok, so being honest here… did I want to be away from his side for even a second…? Hell no! But glutton for punishment remember.

I don't know what was going through his head and if he even realised that given the circumstances shouldn't he be pushing me away? I mean I was more than thrilled he wasn't but this didn't mean I wasn't spending half of the evening confused as pumpkin in a pie…and just like my analogy, it didn't mean I didn't like the taste, it's just that I didn't get it!

"So, off to Italy then, Keira?" Sophia asked just as she was pouring another drink from the shiniest silver champagne bottle I had ever seen. It was only when it was on its way round to me that I read the label as Dom Perignon and I gulped thinking Christ only knew how much that cost per swallow.

"Keira?" I heard my name being called and I heard Draven chuckle next to me as he no doubt saw the look on my face as I followed the bottle around the tent. I felt a bit like a magpie attracted to something shiny but given that the bottle looked like it was silver plated I could only look on in awe.

"It's Dom Perignon Jeroboam White Gold and a 1998 Vintage, you should try some." Draven whispered with his lips at my ear. Bloody Hell, but I was sure he even licked them first! How on earth was I supposed to sit here and take this kind of attention from Draven without my heart stopping? Then he reached out and found my hand that held onto my champagne flute in something akin to a death grip.

His fingers artfully closed over mine and he extended my arm out for our server to fill my glass. I had to wonder what he thought when my hand started to tremble in his as there was no way to miss it. Well, if the way his grip tightened on mine was anything to go by, then yeah, he most certainly didn't miss it. I turned to face him when he winked at me before letting me go finally allowing me to breathe again.

He nodded to my now full glass and I knew he wanted to see what I thought. I took a tentative sip and couldn't help but moan as the gentle hints of grapefruit and almonds danced along my tongue. I was no wine connoisseur by any stretch of the imagination, hell I bet I could barely even say the word without it sounding funny in my Northern accent, but I knew what I liked and this was freakin awesome!

I looked up to find Draven watching me with a hungry expression. This meant that I had to look away quickly to hide my blush but in doing so noticed how his hands had fisted at his sides enough to be turning his knuckles white.

"Eh…sorry, I guess I missed that…what were you saying?" I asked turning back to Sophia who had called my name yet again.

"Italy with your new Boyfr…"

"Sophia," Draven warned cutting her off.

"Uh…it's ok…really, I mean, I guess it was only a matter of time before the elephant walked back into the room…right?" I said, trying to defuse the tension that was mounting between brother and sister. Sophia gave Draven a look I couldn't place before turning back to me to smile.

"So you were saying." She prompted again with her hand rolling at the wrist in one of those 'I am getting impatient gestures'. I squashed down the urge to roll my eyes and cleared my throat instead ready for the awkward bit of the evening that was obviously going to happen at some point.

"Alex has some work thing out there and …was, erm… he was picked to represent the firm at some event, so he decided to surprise me and make it a holiday." I said trying really sodding hard to keep my voice even but I cracked half way through when I felt the air crackle with Draven at its centre. I wish I could say I was brave enough to look his way but I totally chickened out with that one.

It wasn't hard to catch the look Sophia shot her brother before continuing with her Spanish inquisition…Monty Python would have been proud!

"And when is it you are being whisked away?"

"In a couple of days." I said murmuring the answer over the rim of my glass.

"Where in Italy?" This question came directly from the brooding man to my left and I suddenly wanted the building to cave in on itself just to get away from being everyone's centre of attention.

"Uh…I'm not actually sure, he wanted to keep it as a surprise."

"Of course he did." Draven replied severely and I winced before finding my back bone.

"And what is that supposed to mean exactl…?"

"I am sure you can understand our worry and concern Keira, after all, what do you really know about this Alexander Cain?" Sophia interjected quickly. I folded my arms across my chest and snapped,

"Yes well, you weren't exactly forthcoming yourselves when I met you all, now were you?"

"Point well made." Sophia replied taking a sip of her own drink.

"Look, I know this is…*awkward*. But it is what it is. I am with Alex now and what happened is in the past, where I think you can all understand I would like it to stay. I am just trying to take this one step at a time and keep you all in my life as much as I can. So all I am asking is simple…please don't make this any harder than it has to be." I ended my plea by turning to the main culprit in all this and Draven looked less than happy as he gritted his teeth.

No one responded to my outburst and I sighed feeling my heart grow heavy.

"I'd better just go." I said putting down my glass and getting ready to heave myself from the cushioned floor.

"Don't." Draven's voice sounded like a soft command but his restraining hand on my arm was anything but. He didn't hurt me but it was firm enough for me to know that I couldn't pull away, even if I wanted to. I first looked down at his hand on my arm and then looked back over my shoulder at him ready to give him a glare. However, I didn't expect the hint of vulnerability I found there and it was enough to get me to soften my expression.

"Yeah, come on Kaz, don't go yet... it's still early." Sophia said jumping on the guilt inflicting bandwagon.

"I guess I could stay for a little while longer." I said quietly and Draven let go of my arm only to reach across me to reclaim my glass for me. The feel of half his hard body leaning over me was too much of a temptation to pass up on and I inhaled a lung full of his incredible scent to a point that I almost felt lightheaded.

"Or you could just stay." I would have thought this idea would have come first from the prettiest member of the Draven clan, but I was wrong. Draven had said this whilst looking down at me and holding out my glass for me to take.

"I...I...couldn't" I said hearing for myself the disbelief in my breathy response.

"And why not? I think we have the room, Keira" Sophia added laughing. I bit my lip and as I looked up at Draven some of the shorter parts of my hair fell across my left eye thankfully hiding some of my blushing skin. It was all down to that heated look he kept giving me and when the telling ring of purple pulsated through the black I knew what it meant.

"You have nothing to fear being here, Keira." He said as he gently caught my fallen hair between his fingers and pushed it back behind my ear, proving just how wrong his statement had been.

"I will have to text Libby so she won't worry."

"Excellent!" Sophia shouted, clapping her hands together

once as if she knew I would be unable to resist. And if you're gonna add a Draven to the mix then God wasn't that the truth!

———

Not long after I had stupidly agreed to stay the night Draven seemed to relax on a greater level, as did everyone else, including Vincent who also joined us shortly after. I on the other hand was still at the point where I wanted to smack myself for being suckered into doing something as foolish as sleeping under the same roof as Draven. What the Hell had I been thinking? Could I even do something like this? What was I saying…? If I could be lounging around on a day bed/couch with Draven by my side, touching me at every chance he got, then sleeping in a spare room under this immense fortress should be a piece of cake. Yeah right!

"So Keira, a big brother birdy told me you were the new Librarian on campus, is that true?" I laughed and thanks to four glasses of beautiful golden bubbles I followed it with a trademark snort. This made Draven laugh and I shot him a dirty look, one that did nothing to wipe the grin from his handsome face.

"Yep, that's me! I can't hook you up with The Gutenberg Bible but if ya fancy a bit of Harry Potter then I'm your girl" I said with a wink at Sophia that ended with my mouth dropping open like a guppy when she said,

"We already have a Gutenberg Bible, oh and a first edition Harry Potter, signed of course by the talented J. K. Rowling herself but I am holding onto that for Pip's birthday…"

"The Gutenberg Bible…? Wait, Pip's birthday is coming up?" I asked deciding this was more important than the five-million-dollar book that was one of the rarest out there.

"Yeah and she has a massive crush on Harry Potter, which is

only because he reminds her of Adam." Now this made me smile and because of my tipsy state I thought it a good idea to turn back round to face Draven and say,

"It's Pip's birthday soon!" with possibly the biggest grin in history that I could feel almost crack my lips.

"Yeah sweetheart, it is." He replied giving me a warm look that almost made me melt…what am I saying, almost my ass, I was already melting like a cherry flavoured ice lolly in the Sahara!

"Oh shit!"

"What?" Draven asked concerned with my dramatics when throwing up my arms.

"What on Earth am I going to get her!?" I said thinking it best to cut the 'Bloody Hells' whilst around the Demons in the room.

"Are you kiddin me, she is like the easiest person to buy for! For starters just think of something you wouldn't be caught dead wearing, add a rainbow and some Gothic skulls, black and white stripes and there you go!" Sophia said making everyone laugh, as yeah, she was pretty spot on with that one.

"I think I know what we can get her…" I turned to Draven oblivious to the fact that everyone was now staring at us and silence had washed over the tent.

"…I saw this girl when I was back at home for Christmas and she was wearing this Fraggle Rock t-shirt, she would go mad for it and…" I trailed off when I saw his brief expression of pain and it took me a while to realise my slip up until it was far too late.

I had said 'we'.

"What's a Fraggle Rock?" This question came from Zagan and thankfully it broke the tension my mistake had caused. I gave him my thankful eyes and he winked at me when no one was looking. I was just happy that my little mishap had quickly been brushed over and having me explain the old puppet show known as Fraggle Rock was enough to get us to the next topic without incident…

That was until I started to fall asleep.

I don't really know what was happening but I felt deliciously safe with a pair of solid arms wrapped protectively around me. I think I even released a contented sigh as I snuggled closer to the warmth and my hands fisted the material I was already clutching on to. It was like my body was scared of losing the blissful cocoon it had encountered and was acting on reflex.

"Leave them be, it's about time they found some peace for once." I heard a distant voice speaking in hushed tones and I wondered what perfection the next part of my dream would hold. But then my body quickly tensed at the horrible thought that threatened to turn this beautiful dream into a nightmare. What if someone tried to take me from these arms or worse still, what if these arms suddenly pushed me away?

But then something glorious happened, almost as if my dire thoughts had been heard. The arms that held me tightened around me and pulled me flush against the body lying next to me. I could feel my nose touch the softness of a t-shirt that covered the hard planes of a strong chest and I could hear the steady heartbeat behind that strength. I flexed my fingers out from the tight fist and spanned them across a man's lower back feeling for the skin I knew was hiding there.

I moved so slowly, knowing somewhere in the back of my mind that if I woke him up this would all end and I couldn't allow that to happen… not yet. So with painfully slow movements I pulled at the material ever so slightly and sucked in a breath when my fingers finally felt the warm skin beneath.

It was as if my body craved the connection, even in sleep. I was drawn to this man in such a way it was like my body needed to be locked down to keep me away from it…

Like I needed to be imprisoned.

But wait, why was that thought such a sobering one? Why did my heart jump as though an understanding just rammed me in the chest?

"Ssshh now, I've got you. Go back to sleep." A deep and powerful voice spoke softly, one that vibrated through me thanks to my close proximity. I felt a large hand smooth down the back of my hair and the action made me moan without shame. Well if I was going to enjoy this dream I might as well… *really* enjoy it.

I let my head fall back and this soothing hand suddenly gripped my hair at the base of my neck, igniting a blissful bite of pain. This caused a captivating tingle to course down my spine and come to rest in between my thighs.

My eyes fluttered open to find the most intense purple gaze staring back at me from above. For long moments we both seemed frozen, suspended in time from the force of what our bodies were desperate to do. But it wasn't only our apprehensive minds that held us back… *it was also our fragile hearts.*

This was when everything became as clear as the morning sky overhead and it took me a while to bravely find my voice.

"This isn't another one of my dreams, is it?" On reflection I could have just said 'I'm not dreaming am I?' instead of alerting him to the fact that I obviously dreamt about him often.

"By the Gods I hope not." He replied in earnest and my breath caught as my fingers twitched against his skin. We were still connected in a loving embrace and it looked as though neither of us wanted to change that anytime soon. I shamefully took the time to bask in the glory of it and absorb all the sensations I possibly could before my personal Heaven was ripped away from me as it usually was. I knew it was wrong and so did Draven if the pained expression on his face was anything to go by. However, his arm still remained around my body like a vice and his fingers were still embedded in my hair, if a little less forcefully but no less possessively than before.

It was as though we were both scared to move, bringing with it the end of the first connection we had felt in so, so very long. In the end it was my body that ruined the moment and growled angrily at me to feed it. Draven's eyes widened at the noise and I felt the heat of embarrassment show on my skin. Then he leant closer to me and for a wonderful moment I thought he was going to kiss me.

"Is there a bear on the roof?" He said after comically looking off to the sides. I laughed and then brought my arm around to slap him playfully on the chest. He smirked down at me and I rolled my eyes at him making him throw his head back and laugh. I can't lie and say it was the worst way to wake up in the morning, but it painfully took me back to those perfect days when this would never have been awkward. Back to the days when he would have simply pushed me firmly to my back and woken me with his hands worshipping every inch of my body, getting me ready to take him. The thought was sobering enough for me to push out of his hold and for a moment it felt like he didn't want to let me.

I sat up and stretched out my arms, no doubt looking like I was trying to direct traffic. I looked down halfway through when I heard a chuckle and saw Draven had turned to lay fully on his back and put his hands casually behind his head. The sight made my mouth dry and it felt like a bucket of hot sand had been poured down my throat. Jesus, but could this man get any hotter?

The sight of his biceps bulging from this new position made

it look as though he had been injected with rock. The material strained around them and it was only after minutes of staring at him silently did I realise he had finished his chuckling long ago. My eyes shot to his and once again I found the purple fire licking at the edges of his irises.

"For your best interest, I strongly suggest you don't look at me that way again, Keira." Draven almost growled at me and this shook me enough to do a double take.

"Uh...Sorry?" I whispered as his perfection had once again stolen enough of my breath to speak normally. He bolted upright so quickly I gasped as he grabbed onto my arms and pulled me roughly to him.

"Let me make it even clearer for you, my little beauty... my restraint around you hangs by a single thread but giving me those 'make love to me' eyes of yours, well let's just say that acts as a knife's edge held to that thread...do you get me?" He said frowning down at me and looked both seriously frustrated and utterly turned on. I looked down before I could stop myself and saw the unmistakable bulge painfully tight, locked underneath the denim and running down his thigh. Christ, but was he always that huge!?

"Eh...I...yeah I..."

"Yeah, you get me now, sweetheart" He said after seeing where my gaze landed. He suddenly got up from the floor bed and I was left still searching my blank and useless mind for some words when he said my name,

"Keira"

"Yes?" I replied softly and turned to find his outstretched hand waiting for me.

"Let me feed you." He ordered and nodded back down to his hand making me hesitate no longer before taking it. He hauled me up and then had to steady me with his hand at my waist due to his strength that made me fall into him. Was that on purpose? I pulled back and then said,

"Alright hunter man, feed me," in a teasing tone. He laughed once and then replied with a sweet…

"With pleasure, my little blonde bear."

CHAPTER ELEVEN

KEIRA

BROKEN TIME SHATTERED

The rest of the day continued on in some kind of euphoric blur that only broke when someone would need me to scan a book or do a search on the computer screen in front of me. I would have liked to have blamed it on the late night but that would have been the biggest load of BS to enter my mind this year! No, it was all down to one man and shamefully I wasn't talking about my current boyfriend.

I felt so conflicted but more than anything else, just downright confused. I knew better than most the painful reality that Draven and I could never be together again, not in that way. But that didn't mean that the love you hold on to just disappears with the first sight of clarity. And evidently it also didn't mean that you stopped obsessing about them at your place of work, after waking up to find their arms around you!

I shook my head and tried in vain to concentrate on anything other than a particular someone with the initials double D. In theory this was a good plan, however in actual Keira lifetime drama, not so much. Well this was what you get for thinking your life boring for the last ten months, dumb ass! I thought scolding myself and banging my head on top of a stack of books.

"You know, I don't think that's part of your job description." On hearing that particular voice I think I actually groaned 'why me' into the books I had attractively face planted.

"Unless of course it helps to get the job done," he added with a barely contained chuckle at my expense. Not that I minded of course, as it was worth making a fool of myself just to hear that deep and attractive sound vibrating from that muscle-bound chest.

"Uh…what are you doing h…?" My question ended as the pile of books I had been using to hide my shame crashed to the floor, echoing around the large space. Of course, causing a loud ruckus in a silent and crowded Library wasn't exactly the best way of hiding anything, let alone my shame…which also brought lots of notice to the living God that was now stood before me.

Every eye in the building had now turned to witness Draven grinning down at me as I fumbled around holding onto the few books I had caught, with my legs bent at a funny angle.

"Need help with that?" He asked biting his bottom lip again to hold in his laughter. Damn him but he was right, doing that just made you zone right in on a person's lips. I think it was about time I tried to break that bad habit of mine, because it was downright distracting. But then to be honest, this was Draven after all. I mean if the man had been doing something creepy and cheesy like flipping over a cocktail stick with his tongue then it would have been drool worthy!

"No, no, I'm good," I mumbled quickly dumping them on the reception counter before bending over to pick up the rest. I could only hope that the blood rushing to my cheeks had moved on by the time I looked back up at Draven.

"You alright down there?" Draven asked and was clearly enjoying himself if the amusement in his voice was anything to go by. I was taking my time trying to calm myself and regain some cool composure for when I faced him again. 'You can do this' I mouthed the words on bent knees before taking a deep breath, feeling somewhat better…well, that was until I stood up again and banged my head on the lip of the counter!

"Oww!" I moaned, holding the top of my head with one hand and taking an unsteady step backwards.

"Whoa there, easy now." Draven said as he was suddenly on my side of reception and pulling my hands down so he could take over my care. What had he done, vaulted over the counter in front of everyone?!

"And you call me smooth…" He laughed softly as he tilted up my head to get a better look at my forehead.

"…Are you feeling faint?" I shook my head as much as his hold would let me and then said,

"I'm fine, just the usual case of the clumsy Keira syndrome."

"Is it weird to say I kind of miss your clumsiness?" He asked making me laugh nervously.

"A bit, yeah…why I have no clue though." This turned out to be a bad thing to say if my sanity was anything to go by. He leaned down to my ear and once again gave me his hypnotic velvet voice.

"Having a clumsy Keira, means I get to catch you and be your saviour."

"Draven I…we…?" He pulled back on hearing the desperate confusion in my voice and quickly interrupted me.

"Not here, but later, we can talk then and I …"

"Keira, what do you think you're doing?!" I groaned out loud as I turned to my new boss and all round ball buster of the highest form, and that was saying something considering he had balls himself! Ok, so they might have resembled hazelnuts but still, the guy could be scary when he wanted to be. Oh, and it just so happened that he hated me.

I pulled away from Draven and turned to face what I thought resembled an angry English bulldog. It was the lack of an actual neck and his baggy cheeks that seemed to glow as though someone had gone apeshit crazy with a brush full of blusher. But to be honest, that wasn't exactly fair on all those cute dogs out there.

"Er…Mr Coc…Cox." I said nearly slipping up with what most people actually called him. Although I was trying to get people on board with an epic rename to Jaba. It was after seeing him eating in the cafeteria once and man alive but that tongue of his had a disgusting mind of its own!

"This doesn't look like work, Missy" I wasn't sure if Draven could feel the revulsion coming off me in waves, but I am sure my shudder wasn't hard to miss.

"I am sorry Sir, it won't happen again and…" I started to say and felt Draven turn solid next to me which I didn't take as a good sign. We might not still be together, but I think it was safe to say that with all the evidence displayed last night that Draven still felt protective over me.

"Yes and see that it doesn't! And what is this…*person* doing behind your station…um?" He said as he motioned his hand up and down at Draven like the man next to me was riff raff and I think I came close to swallowing my own tongue. It was a definite 'Oh shit' moment.

"Mr Cox this is…"

"Mr Draven, and this college's benefactor." Draven said in a commanding voice that clearly wasn't down with me being spoken to like that. He also came forward and positioned himself slightly in front of me, which I had to admit, I really liked. But what I liked way more was looking back at Mr Cox aka, Jaba flappy tongue, and finding his face almost turning purple in the face of what was the biggest screw up of the day. I would say of the year but hey, the man screwed up a lot!

"Mr Dra…Draven, Sir, but of course I know who you are, I just…I didn't expect to see you here conversing with our lowest member of staff, please let me help…"

"What did you say?!" Draven snapped losing his cool pretty damn quickly at his direct insult. The difference of course was that one, I was used to it and two, I couldn't snap the guy's neck with just a thought…although I had to wonder if even Draven would strain a little at the thickness of that thing? It's not like you could get your hands around it.

I decided to defuse the situation by stepping around Draven and in what I hoped was a calming influence, placed my hand on his stomach to also hold him back in case it didn't work.

"Mr Draven here had just requested a tour before helping me with some books that had accidently fallen."

"Ah, well…" He huffed before adding,

"I would be more than happy to show you around Mr Draven, as I am sure you would want someone more experienced in the field and higher up in the ranks… and being as I am the library director, I would be more than happy to…"

"I think not." Draven retorted barely holding himself in check and I knew this because I could feel his stomach muscles tighten further where I still had my hand on him.

"Keira here is more than proficient enough to show me around. However, I will make the point that you are currently keeping me from my business, and I am an *extremely* busy man. So needless to say I don't appreciate delays in any way, shape or… form." Draven stated in that toe curling dominant tone of his and I had to bite my lip to keep from laughing at the distasteful look he gave my boss when saying the words 'shape' and 'form', clearly finding him as repulsive as we all did.

"Are we clear?" Draven added and I suddenly wanted to kiss his feet for turning Jaba baggy cheeks into a spluttering mess who couldn't form his apology quickly enough.

"Yes, but of course, please forgive me, Mr Draven I…"

"You are still keeping me from conducting my business." Draven interrupted and then simply turned his back to him to face me.

"Shall we?" He said softly and obviously reserving his gentlemanly ways just for me. I had the biggest impulse to pop my head round Draven and stick my tongue out at him, but I doubt that would have been considered as professional enough for our little business ruse we had going on. So instead I went with a beaming smile and said,

"Yes of course Mr Draven, if you would like to follow me this way we can now begin." I tried to hide my smirk, I ready did…ok, who am I kidding, I didn't hide it, not even close and Draven's bad boy grin came out to play when he saw it. I did at least manage to wait until we rounded the corner and out of sight before I almost launched myself at Draven in gratitude.

I turned and playfully grabbed at his jacket before jumping up and down a few times in my utter glee.

"Oh you are good! That was brilliant, just bloody brilliant! God but you are like a freakin Jedi Knight at intimidation!" I decided to stick with my Star Wars analogies making him beam down at me.

"I thought he was going to pee himself! And he was so rude but you just swooped right in there and wham, you put him in his place! Oh the girls are gonna love this when I tell em." I carried on like this barely being able to keep still in my excitement. The guy was a nightmare to everyone, not just me and at any opportunity to make someone cry he did more than just take it, he enjoyed it!

"Keira, please calm and have some pity." Draven said in an almost pained way and all of a sudden I felt bad. I didn't want Draven to think I had become a bitch or anything, so I quickly spun on my heel back to face him.

"Oh, no, no...see, you're getting this all wrong, I'm not being a bitch...well maybe just a little but that guy is horrible to us all, there was this one time when Jessica's Nan got ill and she needed to leave but he..." I started talking so fast that I barely noticed the soft smile he gave me before placing both his hands intimately on either side of my face. He bent his knees and levelled his eyes with mine. This action shut me up pretty damn quick as I soon got lost in his beautiful deep eyes.

"I didn't mean pity for the vile creature, Keira I meant pity for me." He said gently making my jaw go slack.

"Uhh...Okaaay... what do you mean?" I asked thinking I was missing something here. He laughed once and then shook his head as if trying to find the strength for something.

"If I took my clothes off right now, would it be difficult for you to turn away, given our attraction to each other." He said and if I thought my jaw went slack before then now it was about to hit the floor! Did he really just say that?

My eyes travelled the length of him and now all I could imagine was peeling off his long sleeved dark red T-shirt, flicking open that heavy belt buckle and popping open those dark denim jeans to reveal what I knew he was packing down there. But wait a minute...why did he always seem to be wearing long sleeves lately?

"I will take that heated look in your eyes as a yes." He all but growled and when my eyes shot up they found the same heat staring back at me.

159

"Then you will understand when I ask you to please try and stop being so delectably cute all the time." His voice had grown deeper, more hoarse with his obvious arousal.

"Cute?" I whispered feeling my breath quicken. His eyes erupted into purple fire and I stumbled back a step. He in turn took a step towards me in a predatory manner causing me to retreat until my back hit against one of the tall aisles of bookshelves we were hiding along. Then his hands came up to cage me in and grip onto the shelf either side of my head.

"Yeah…*cute,*" he said coming closer on the bloody word that had caused all this. But hold up, what was I saying? It wasn't like I was doing something on purpose to end up in this position and as belly melting as it was I still had to find out what was really going on here. In fact, it sounded like a great plan. Only actually trying to put it into action was a little more difficult than just thinking about it. What with him looking down at me like that as though he wanted to devour every inch of me after first tasting me with that perfect mouth of his.

"I…uh, don't know…what are we…Draven?" I said or at least tried to say anyway. Surely, I got points for that…right?

"Keira, I…" He started, leaning down further and my heart started to run, even if it was in a race it couldn't ever win. I felt the emotions build and tried desperately to keep them locked away but then lost the battle when I received a soft command from Draven.

"Look at me." I did as I was told and felt the tears coat my eyes without falling. His own eyes flashed a deeper purple as he took in my inner torment and one hand left the shelf to come to cup the side of my face. His thumb gradually started to move until it swiped across my lips causing me to suck in a shuddered breath. I closed my eyes for a second in a pointless attempt to escape the raw intensity I felt coming from him in devastating waves. Then I opened my eyes just in time to see him coming

closer and I knew that this was it, this was the time I would finally feel his lips again after all this broken time.

I wanted this kiss. I knew I shouldn't but I did. I knew I should tell him no and walk away to save the hurt that I knew would all but kill me later, but I couldn't. Because it wasn't just about walking away from a man like Draven, no it was about not being able to give up *on a man like Draven*. A man, I was still very much in love with. So even knowing what Vincent had said, about us never being able to be together again. I could only hope that he was wrong about some things because in the other thing he was dead right...

I would never stop fighting for Draven.

I just simply didn't have it in me.

But with the next words out of Draven's mouth, I now knew for certain that one of us did and that broken time...shattered...

"I can't do this anymore."

CHAPTER TWELVE

KEIRA

AWKWARD MUCH?

O n hearing this I quickly ducked out of his hold. My heart pounded with both anger and humiliation, which was an ugly mix. I was just taking a minute to decide whether to storm off or give him a piece of my mind. Maybe it should have taken me longer, then to go with option two and not act on impulse. Either way I didn't get very far.

"Draven, you can't just do…!" I started but was cut off mid rant when his hand clamped over my mouth and an arm snaked around my body to pull me back to him.

"Ssshh, we are being watched," Draven whispered, and I followed his eyes to the end of the long aisle to an extremely tall, hooded figure. I frowned at Draven's paranoid tone and shook my head, managing to dislodge his hand in the process.

"Yeah and I would have thought by now you were used to it." I retorted dryly but he wasn't listening.

"Go back to the reception and stay there until I return." He ordered quickly after he saw the man disappear out of sight and took a step to follow him.

"Draven it's just a student…"

"Do as I say Keira, now!" Draven said, barking at me in a forceful tone, one that brooked no argument.

"Fine!" I snapped back, turning on my heel and leaving him to whatever freak out he was having. I looked back over my shoulder just in time to see Draven's form rounding the corner in hot pursuit.

"Whatever," I muttered as I looked back and bumped straight into someone and that someone was my boyfriend!

"Alex!?" I said his name more in a panic than shock and I found myself trying to lock down the urge to look around for Draven.

"The one and only…but hey, are you alright? You look flushed?" Alex said holding onto the tops of my arms and rubbing them as if he thought I was cold.

"I'm fine!" I said in a high pitched squeal that sounded anything but. He raised one eyebrow at me like I was fooling no one.

"So, what are you doing here? Not that I am not happy to see you of course, I just thought that I would only be seeing you at the airport." I was rambling and I knew this but when you are having a mini meltdown at the idea of your current boyfriend seeing that he wasn't the only one to have 'popped in' to see me and that my ex had supposedly also had the same idea…well there was only one word for it…

Awkward!

"I wanted to surprise you." Yeah and he wasn't the only one, I thought on a wince I hopefully hid. Well given I was just nearly caught kissing my ex I thought I was doing ok so far. Now I just needed to get rid of him before Draven came back.

"Oh you certainly did." I muttered under my breath as I started pulling him closer to one of the aisles in case an angry Demonic/sometimes slightly Angelic lord came back. Oh who was I kidding, I hadn't seen Draven's Angel side in quite a while and there was definitely nothing remotely Angelic in that smouldering look he was giving me only minutes ago. That was right before he dumped a bucket of icy cold water over me and extinguished any flames he had ignited.

Alex laughed at my strange behaviour and luckily, I had one of the best excuses considering who my boss was.

"Sorry but I just don't want to get caught…you know, with my boyfriend…"

"Making out?" He whispered leaning into me. Oh God but right now that was the last thing I wanted to be caught doing and not just by my pain in the ass boss! Not good Keira, so not good!

So what did I do to get out of this situation? What I usually did in all the rest of the awkward positions I managed to get myself into…I snorted, and it wasn't pretty.

"Sorry about that, I'm just, you know…uh…"

"Keira, it's alright, I know." At this I think my eyes bulged a bit when I blurted out in panic,

"You do!?" To which he laughed.

"Yeah ma chérie, and it's alright, I find it cute." Ok so we were totally not talking about the same thing, 'cause I was pretty sure that no one would find nearly kissing their ex cute!

"I like that you are excited about our trip. I don't know about you but what I look forward to the most is spending some quality time together. I feel between your college work and my hectic schedule that we hardly see each other lately." He said wrapping his arms around me and pulling me into his embrace. I tried not to let my body go stiff and to relax but knowing

Draven was only around the corner this wasn't so easy to accomplish.

I would have asked myself what was wrong with me but I think it was a little more than obvious and I felt like a horrible person. Here I was with a loving, sweet and caring boyfriend who had surprised me and was whisking me away on a romantic getaway and how was I acting…? Like a love sick teenager with a crush on her ex! Ok, so granted it was a little more complicated than that, but the outcome would be the same. Draven wouldn't allow himself to have me but it seemed he wasn't opposed to torturing me with those facts when almost kissing me and then kindly informing me that 'he couldn't do this anymore'!

"So that's why I wanted to surprise you by taking you out to dinner and somewhere nice, not that vile diner you took me to once." He made a face as though I had once made him eat Oliver Twist style gruel there. I just laughed and pinched him playfully on the sleeve of his expensive suit jacket.

"It wasn't that bad!"

"Keira, I am pretty sure my burger had a face on it." I rolled my eyes as I giggled, thinking it was funny watching his face as he lifted off the grease-soaked bun and flicked it to the side. However, this thought just brought me back to one even funnier and that was the sight of Draven in Burger King that time we went Christmas shopping in Liverpool. It was such a perfect day that it just made this last Christmas gone all the more harder to deal with.

"So dinner, what time do you finish today?" Alex asked shaking me from my depressing thoughts and also reminding me that the man I was once again obsessing over was also in the same building. And this was definitely one showdown I didn't want to witness again, not after last night.

"I don't know as Jessica said she might be running late, and I have to wait for her to get in before I can leave."

"That should be fine as I have someone to see here anyway, I can just pick you up from home later, about 7:30?" He said this and then automatically looked over my head, making me paranoid for a second thinking that Draven was stood directly behind me. Thankfully though he wasn't but there was still something about that look that didn't sit right.

"Yeah, that sounds good." I said vaguely, still deep in thought.

"Great, oh and wear something nice, it will be expensive." He added eyeing my outfit like I had on a prison jumpsuit and was rocking orange. I frowned down at myself and wondered briefly with comments like that what exactly it was he saw in me? Ok so I was dressed casually for work by wearing a faded blue T-shirt with an old-fashioned typewriter printed on the front in black but I thought considering I worked in a library it would be quirky. This combined with slightly frayed jeans and my usual black long fingerless gloves I fit right in with everyone else. So what if some of the other girls looked a little more professional in their tight skirts and frilly shirts but management hadn't said there was a dress code so I didn't think it an issue…until now that was.

"I'm sure I have a dress somewhere." I said trying not to sound too disheartened. Of course, I wanted to smack myself upside the head when I thought about Draven liking my style… or lack of it apparently.

"Excellent." He replied suddenly beaming at me making me feel bad for giving him a hard time in my head. So he wanted me to dress up, what was the big deal? I needed to relax and forget all about a certain dark haired, muscled God who wanted to torment me.

"Great, I look forward to it." I said feeling a little more

upbeat about the night ahead of me and then I remembered something.

"Oh, but I kind of promised Sophia this morning that I would have some girly time with her later." And I had, simply because she had given me very little choice in the matter. This had happened over breakfast which strangely had been like a small family affair. It had been held in the stunning marble dining room and the spread laid out on the table looked like someone had robbed the whole bakery before then moving on to a diner for the meat and dairy products. There was enough to feed the army that I'd had Zagan send back to Hell for me!

Draven had sat at the head of the table and I still remember staring at that strange symbol just showing on the high back above his head. It was the same as my birth mark and to this day I still didn't know what it meant. Sophia had interrupted my thoughts when she thrust a loaded plate in my hand with what looked like two of everything on it, before manhandling me until I was sat down on Draven's left.

I think in all the time I had been in Draven's life it was the first meal I had seen them all sit down together to eat. Vincent had given me a wink as he bit into his cinnamon roll and then made me laugh when moaning out loud and slowly rolling his eyes in obvious pleasure. Sophia just rolled her eyes for a different reason before throwing a sugar cube at him.

"You look like a pig." She had chastised and I couldn't help but burst out laughing as Zagan grabbed his own cinnamon roll and did the same as Vincent, only louder.

"Ah pigs!" She complained dramatically, only it would have been more convincing without her fighting a grin.

"Well at least one of the men at this table is behaving himself in front of the ladies." She said nodding at Draven, who I had not been able to look at until now.

"Yeah, but he is trying to impress someone, so it doesn't

count." Vincent said mischievously winking at me again and igniting my blushing cheeks.

"You need not try and impress me my Lord, I have seen you devour your food many a time." Zagan said nodding at his lord and the whole table erupted into laughter, even Draven. It was such an unusual but wonderful experience that I couldn't help but instantly file the memory away as one of my favourites.

After such an easy going start to the day I thought that having Draven drive me home to get ready for my shift would have been the part where it got bizarre between us but I was happily wrong. We just chatted about the new things going on in my life and obviously avoided Alex's name like the plague. However, I did get the impression Draven was holding himself back on asking me about him.

At the end before getting out of the car I turned to him and said,

"I'm not gonna lie and pretend it hasn't been nice seeing you again Draven…I'm… I'm glad we can still be…be friends." I stumbled a little bit before forcing the words of friendship past my lips. It was almost as though I was pushing against some invisible force of blasphemy just thinking them, let alone saying them out loud. I didn't miss the way his eyes had flashed with purple anger, one he hid just as quickly by looking out of his window for long seconds. Had he been trying to compose himself? Had my words of friendship hurt him and if they had, then what was it he wanted from me if not friendship?

"Catherine?" I shook my head and focused back on the man in front of me. Alex laughed and commented,

"I think I lost you there, you looked miles away."

"Sorry, I guess I just have a lot on my mind…erm you know, packing, passport and stuff." I said rushing out the last part to hide my slip up about what was really going on in my jumbled messed up head.

"Don't worry about a thing, ma chérie, soon we will be on a plane together and leaving behind any of life's distractions." He said pulling me to him and brushing some of my hair behind my ear. I didn't have to look up as much as I did with Draven and I tried to turn this into a positive thing. However, my mind quickly rebelled against me, reminding me how much I used to love the feeling of Draven's massive body towering over me, making me feel both consumed by his presence and immense safety from the brutal and raw strength he possessed.

"Distractions would be a good thing to lose right now." I mumbled truthfully, looking down to the side and feeling lost in the depths of my confusion.

"Great, then I will say goodbye for now my darling and I will see you later." He said cupping my face and bringing it back round ready for, painfully, my first kiss of the day. The only thing I was grateful for was that it was a little more than a brief joining of our lips before it was over. The whole thing left me feeling cheap and conflicted. I didn't want to be that woman who took advantage of a good man but on the other hand this was Draven we were talking about. How could I ever find enough restraint around him? No, there was only one thing to be done about it…

I needed to stay away from him.

Yeah, this was what I would do, I would make it so I didn't see Draven again before I went away with Alex and then I could use the time to figure out where my relationship with Alex was going without being reminded of what I once had. I needed to focus on the future and who I wanted to spend it with, not the past and who I had lost back there.

This was a good plan but like most good plans putting them into action was often harder than thinking them up. This was proved even more so when I turned back to the reception after Alex let me go and bumped right into the man himself, blowing that plan all to Hell!

"Draven?!" I said looking up at him and finding his eyes rooted to the figure behind me with nothing less than murder in his eyes.

"Keira." He said without even looking at me but still managed to make it sound like he owned the rights to my name. It wasn't hard given our height difference for him to continually stare at Alex right above my head, so I moved back a step to fall in next to him and no doubt making it clear that I didn't belong to Draven anymore. This was finally when Draven's eyes found mine and narrowed as though my action at choosing Alex over him was alien to him.

"Wh…what are you doing here?" I said hoping, or more like praying he wouldn't let on to Alex the real answer to that question.

"You know full well why I am here." Well there went that burning hope I thought with Draven's blunt answer.

"And that is?" This question came from Alex who stood calmly next to me, folding his arms.

"To see Keira, which I very much doubt is the same reason *you* are here." Draven answered arrogantly, folding his own arms, which I had to admit was way more intimidating than when Alex did it.

"Draven!" I hissed looking round to see we were starting to draw attention to ourselves.

"It's alright, Keira, I am not insecure enough to let time spent with your ex-boyfriend worry me in the slightest. Not when I was the one to bear witness to the effects of what his cruel dismissal did to you. Thankfully though, time heals all wounds and certainly continues to do so with the help of others." On hearing this coming from Alex, Draven actually snarled at him, which sounded terrifyingly like his Demon side was breaking through.

"Please don't do this." I whispered, pleading with both of them. Just then I was thankful when Alex's phone started ringing in his pocket. He didn't look like he was going to answer it for a second, not wanting to break eye contact with Draven first but it must have been important because he swiped his thumb across the screen to accept it.

"There is no need to say anything as I will be there in a moment to meet with you." Alex said quickly and it was more than clear by his tone that he didn't respect the person on the other end of the line, as he hung up before the person even had a chance to say anything. Draven raised one eyebrow as though he had detected something odd in this, which wasn't surprising given that he was probably looking for any reason not to trust him. What was surprising however was that he didn't look smug or in any way happy that he had been right, because unlike Draven, Alex hadn't made the trip just to see me and that phone call had been his proof.

"It pains me to have to go Catherine, but like you I have to finish my work." When Alex said this he looked over to the reception area and nodded as if silently reminding me too that I should be working. It was subtle enough that I could have been being paranoid but for some reason I didn't think so. However, it could have been because Draven looked like he too thought the same as me and as a result wanted to choke the life out of him.

"Its fine, it was nice of you to come and see me before your meeting." I said hoping this would be the right thing to say for the one person who was supposed to matter to me the most... whether it was Alex was still shamefully debatable though.

"Until tonight, ma chérie." He said before bending his neck to kiss me and at the last second, I turned my head so his kiss landed on my cheek. I wasn't sure what other people would have done in my position after all the hurt Draven had inflicted on me and with the bitter taste of rejection I had encountered not moments before. But for me, I just wasn't cruel enough to ram it in Draven's face that I was with another man, even if Alex could.

"See you later." I said with my face still turned away and my line of sight made it so I couldn't help but notice Draven's hands clench into tight fists at his sides, only relaxing when Alex moved away from me and walked away.

"I know you don't want to, *Keira* but at some point, we are going to have to have a conversation about…*that."* Draven said affirming both the name he obviously preferred I be called and what he also preferred to call my boyfriend.

"That, is my boyfriend and *that* is who I choose to be with, so if you stopped acting like an ass around him then it would make it a Hell of a lot easier for me to be around *you!"* I ranted up at him before trying to storm off but not getting very far from him. He followed me close enough so that I could feel the angry heat at my back and I knew if I stopped for a second he would run right into me.

"And that is precisely what we need to discuss." He growled in my ear making me spin back round to face him.

"No, we don't! You have no say in who I date Draven and the sooner you come to realise that the better!" I said feeling so angry it was like my heart was going burst out of my chest any minute, so it too could slap him!

"And just now, when I had you trembling in my arms with just the thought of when I was about to kiss you?" He said with his face getting closer to mine as if aiding him whilst making his point. I on the other hand could feel my jaw go slack in utter shock.

"Uh…sorry?" I whispered completely dumbstruck.

"You want me to say it again or follow through with my desires to drive my point home, because I am pretty sure either way it gives me a damn right in who touches you!" Okay so he was definitely angry now, but I was still left playing catch up on what the hell I had just missed!

"I…uh…but you said…uh…okay Draven, now I'm confused." I admitted letting my shoulders slump and taking a much needed step back from all this and not just physically.

"What I said?" He looked just as confused for a moment before something must have registered when he looked back at me.

"Keira I…" Draven started but was abruptly cut off when I heard my name being called from the front desk. I looked over to see RJ waving me over like a mad woman, with Lanie stood next to her wearing her usual shy smile.

"Look I have to go." I said feeling like some sad, deflated balloon that had been left out far too long after the celebrations had all ended.

"Just give me a minute to explain, that's all I ask."

"I can't," I replied softly trying not to look him in the eyes, knowing I would crack if I did.

"Can't or won't?" I could tell by the way he asked me that question that he wasn't happy about being told no, but what else could I do? I had to make the decision at some point that this needed to end before it began, because no matter what Draven really felt or wanted, it wasn't ever going to be enough to go back in time. I couldn't allow him to have that power over me again. I couldn't allow him to kiss me and then eventually take it back.

For no matter what I wanted in the heat of the moment I knew in the long run I had to keep my heart safe and guarded because at the end of that kiss was the inevitable waiting to happen…

Rejection. Pain. And then devastation with Draven walking away...*yet again.* No, I couldn't let that kiss ever happen no matter how much I wanted it...craved it and normally would have fought tooth and nail to get it.

But not this time.

So with that in mind I answered him before walking away with a decision that felt so wrong it was lodged in my throat, making this one word all the more harder to get out...

"Both."

CHAPTER THIRTEEN

KEIRA

IN BAD TASTE

W alking away from Draven wasn't easy, not by a long shot but I knew it was better for me in the long run. Having Alex turn up when he had was the wakeup call I needed. I didn't mind being friends with Draven, as it was better than nothing, but I was going to have to put a stop right now to all the mixed messages I was receiving. It wasn't fair to me and my fragile heart to keep putting me through this. It was confusing enough just trying to find the right balance to be friends but having him backing me into a corner and nearly kissing me was taking it to a whole new level of cruelty.

I knew enough about Draven that if he wanted something he would simply take it, which included me. If something had changed in the fates that meant we could finally be together then I couldn't imagine Draven taking his time in letting it be known that he wanted me back. But that hadn't happened. And unless I missed the memo, nothing had changed and nothing ever would. No, I couldn't do this and I quickly realised something when I had turned round to see Draven with Alex still at my back. If it hadn't been for him knowing about Alex, then Draven wouldn't even have been here let alone nearly kissing me, which only meant one thing…

Draven was only reacting to this because he felt threatened.

The thought was a depressing one but there was no other explanation for his behaviour. Vincent had been right that night on top of the cliff. I would have been devastated to find out Draven hadn't cared when finding out that I was with Alex but what Vincent didn't realise was that Draven's reaction to it was just as devastating.

Of course, just because I had made up my mind didn't mean I could let it go. It didn't mean I didn't start obsessing over every little detail in the last twenty four hours! Because let's face it, that's what us girls did. We analysed every single thing and looked for the hidden meaning as if we were cracking that damn Da Vinci Code of men!

Which brought me to now and standing in front of the mirror staring at the borrowed dress I wore wondering if it was good enough for Alex. I think in the long list of differences between Alex and Draven one thing always stood out the most and that was how unsure I now felt about myself. I knew Alex liked the finer things in life as blatantly did my ex but unlike Draven Alex seemed to find them far more important than they were ever meant to be. He cared about the designer names and the flashy cars, always explaining how much things cost. And yes, Draven had all of this but never once did he ever make it seem that important to him. It was always just stuff to him, stuff that could be replaced or even forgotten. Surely that's how it should have been…right?

So that was why I now fidgeted in my high heels that pinched my little toes and rubbed the back of my heels to a point I knew I would need plasters at some point this evening. But yet here I was, wearing a dress that wasn't mine just because it had an expensive label and shoes that were too tight because they were designer. And I was staring at a girl I didn't know. So I guess the right question was… if Draven hadn't cared what I wore back then, then why did *I* care about what Alex thought about what I was wearing now?

I didn't have an answer.

"Wow, you look amazing, Kazzy!" Libby said pulling me from my depressing thoughts. I looked down at the clingy navy dress that was long sleeved and finished a few naughty inches above my knees. It was made with the most beautiful and intricate lace and had a simple satin ribbon around the waist like a thin belt. The underneath was lined in the same colour navy but had a sweetheart neckline so the lace showed my skin above my breasts and on my shoulders and arms. This meant I could just get away without wearing gloves and not worry about my scars showing due to the many flowers and swirls laced together.

"You don't think it's too much?" I asked playing with the loose curls that spilled over the up do Libby had helped me with earlier.

"What? No, of course not…and anyway, Alex did say he was taking you somewhere fancy, right?" I nodded not trusting my fragile state of mind right now from blurting out about how I had seen Draven. I knew at some point I wouldn't be able to keep it from her but right now…well let's just say ignorance was a blissful state I could only wish for but at least it was something I could give my sister. I knew she would be worried about me considering the Zombie Kaz she'd had to deal with last year.

God, but I wanted to cringe when thinking back to how I was when I got back from Italy. But if the past had taught me anything, then I knew I would only end up hurting the people who cared for me more by keeping them in the dark and not letting them in. Of course there was more I *couldn't* say to Libs than what I could, but it hadn't mattered. All that was important was at the very core of my problem and that was that Draven had lied and left me. Full stop. That was the root of my pain and in that she could help, not with words but with just being there. So I might have been a Zombie but this time I was a Zombie with a partner in crime…just not the flesh eating variety!

"I know you will be jet-setting off tomorrow but it's still about time you had some fun and you look knock out in that dress!"

"Thank you for lending it to me." At this she scoffed and said,

"Well I don't think I will be wearing it for a while, not unless it looks good with baby puke and sticky handprints." I laughed at my sister's no doubt correct assumption to what would happen. Even now she had a stain on her t-shirt that I couldn't tell whether it was juice or drool.

"Well at least that's one promise I can make when wearing it, unless Alex's dinner habits have drastically changed… Eeew." I added making her laugh with me.

"Kazzy, your date's here!" We both heard Frank bellow from downstairs, and I winced at the sound of his tone.

"Don't mind him, he just liked Dom is all and you know how weird men can be with these types of things." Libby said referring to the fact that Frank obviously didn't like Alex. It wasn't that he was openly rude or anything but he did always lay the whole big brother act on a little too thick whenever he stepped through the door. Also, for some reason he outright refused to call him my boyfriend, even though we had been dating a while now. However, I just shrugged it all off like I usually did.

We both left what was now my new room, as I still couldn't face the one I had before, what with all the painfully beautiful memories it still held. Downstairs I was met by one handsome Frenchman who was wearing a different suit to what he'd had on earlier. He gave me the once over and my heart almost stopped waiting for his reaction. It was only when I saw one side of his lip tilt up that I knew I had got it right.

I always thought that when he smiled like that there was a dark sinister side to him lurking just beneath the surface but then I always felt guilty for thinking so. I think it was because he had such strong angular features, like now, the way he got a crease in his cheek with that one sided grin. His high cheekbones and defined straight nose that others would have called 'beak like' if they had wanted to be cruel. But I just thought it suited the rest of his face. Yes it sometimes gave him an air of arrogance but I think that was just down to his upbringing in France and coming from a different culture.

"You look lovely." He said reaching out for my hand as I took my last steps from the stairs.

"Thanks," I replied softly. Frank cleared his throat and I mentally rolled my eyes before facing him with an amused smile.

"Will you need me to pick you up again tonight?" Frank asked and I grimaced at how it sounded. Okay so there had been that time when Alex was called in for an emergency meeting and Frank had to pick me up at the restaurant because it would have taken Alex too long to drop me back home. I knew Frank hadn't been happy with his behaviour, but I understood that work sometimes got in the way. I mean, he was just trying to build up his career, so why should dating me put a stop to that?

Frank hadn't seen it that way at all, which was why the next time it happened I had called RJ.

"She will be fine, Frank." Alex said in a tone that clearly meant his patience was cracking and under Frank's intimidating look I got why. Frank had his arms crossed and looked anything but friendly which I still wasn't used to considering Frank was normally as friendly as they came. Needless to say, Alex hadn't been invited to dinner like Draven had.

"Come on Catherine, we have reservations." Then Alex led me through the door with only enough time to grab my purse from Libby. She didn't look too pleased and I didn't know who it was aimed at this time, so I just mouthed the word 'Men' at her and rolled my eyes.

"Call me if you need me, Kazzy!" Frank shouted through the door and to try and lighten the mood I shouted back,

"Thanks dad!" Making him chuckle at my light hearted banter.

"Sorry about that." I muttered as Alex opened the passenger side door for me.

"Forget about it, I am not concerned if he likes me or not, Catherine." I didn't really like the idea that Alex didn't care what my family thought, but I guess now wasn't the time to discuss it.

"Oh I forgot my jacket." I said before getting into his shiny new Porsche 911, which I knew had cost him over a hundred thousand dollars thanks to being told a few times. I don't really know where he got his money from exactly as I doubted it was something he could afford on his salary…but what did I know.

"You won't need it," he replied and nodded for me to get in, which I did hoping the night wouldn't turn chilly later. Well I suppose if we actually managed to make it through to dessert then it meant I wouldn't be needing one, seeing as he would be able to drive me home this time.

We sat in what I hoped was comfortable silence for most of the drive and it was only when taking the freeway, as they say here, that I recognised we were headed into the city.

"So where are you taking me?" I asked trying to sound more excited than I actually felt. I didn't really know why I had started to feel this way but if I had to venture a guess, I would say all answers began with a D.

"To this new place called One Eight Seven, my friend is a chef there so he got us the table, otherwise the waiting list is months." My eyes widened and I started to play with my sleeves again, as I always seemed to do when nervous. I wasn't great in posh situations and the waiting list told me exactly what type of place this would be.

"That sounds nice." I said trying to sound more positive than I felt. The last thing I wanted to do was embarrass him by doing something daft like dropping a prawn down my top or snorting in my soup.

The rest of the way there zoomed by like the cars on the opposite side and the closer we got, the more I wished I was zooming that way with them. I was still in this weird funk until I jumped when the door was opened for me. Alex stood there holding out his hand and I got out of the car to see the imposing modern building and its stylish logo. It was the word 'One' and 'Seven' with the number eight slanted between them. The building was all frosted glass windows that produced a warm glow behind them from what I guessed was the ambient lighting.

I was all for romance and everything, but I was one of those people who liked to see what I was actually eating. Okay, now I just sounded like I was picking and bitching for no good reason.

"Shall we?" Alex said after handing the valet his keys. I nodded and put my arm in his, thankful for it so I didn't stumble in these heels. The door was opened for us and just as we reached the gorgeous looking hostess Alex's phone started to beep. Dread filled me as he reached into his pocket and read a text message with a frown. The hostess looked me up and down like I was wearing something from her granny's wardrobe and then turned her eyes to Alex with a smirk. I instantly hated her and her ultra-modern hairstyle, that if you asked me looked more like she was getting ready to be shot out of a cannon than a bob cut.

"Do you have a reservation, Sir?" She purred but Alex wasn't taking any notice. I would have liked to have said it was because he had me on his arm but no, this time it was his phone that was getting all the attention.

"Alex?" I whispered and gave him a nudge.

"Yes, we have a reservation, it's under the name Cain." She looked down her list and then with a nod asked us to follow her. As we walked through the open space that was clearly an expensive interior designer's wet dream I leant into Alex and whispered,

"Is everything alright?" The look he gave me was all the answer I needed. I had a feeling I was going to be in need of that jacket after all. We let the hostess seat us in the middle of everyone else, which was another small pet hate of mine. I liked my food and wasn't one to pick at it like a mouse, so this just meant I sometimes made a pig of myself, which needless to say doesn't need an audience.

The hostess started to hand us our menus, but Alex put his hand up to stop her.

"I already ordered us both the chef's tasting menu when making the reservation." He told her and I wanted to cringe at the thought of getting something I knew I wouldn't like, for example oysters. Why anyone would eat something that just tasted like swallowing a mouthful of sea water was beyond me!

"Very good Sir, your waiter will be with you shortly to take your drinks order, here is the wine list." She handed him the thin leather book and wished us a pleasant evening like a drone sucked of any personality. It made me wonder if she had to practice in the mirror before work or if she just woke up that fake?

"So the chef's tasting menu sounds interesting." I said taking my origami napkin from the table and laying it smooth over my dress.

"Umm?" Alex said taking out his phone again and frowning into it.

"Alex, is there something wrong at work?" I asked the same question I did all those other times.

"I'm sorry Catherine, I am going have to sort this mess out, it should just take a phone call... can you excuse me for a moment?" I wanted to roll my eyes and tell him to just get it over with but I didn't. No instead I smiled and played a good girlfriend by saying,

"Of course." He smiled at me and then rose from his seat. He came and kissed the top of my head and said,

"What did I ever do to deserve such a beautiful and understanding girlfriend?" It wasn't a question I could answer, especially not considering what this girlfriend nearly did with her ex only a few hours ago. I shrugged my shoulders and gave him a smile I knew didn't reach my eyes.

"I won't be long, do you want to order a bottle of the Pinor Noir Copain, Tous Ensemble 2011?"

"Eh...the what now?" I said knowing I would mess it up royally if I even attempted ordering that. I could tell Alex wanted to be the one to roll his eyes at me this time but thankfully our waiter came and saved the day. Alex ordered his fancy wine and gave a nod when asked if we were ready for the first course. I wasn't so sure I was ever going to be ready when the first course turned out to be...yep, you guessed it...

"To begin Miss Williams we have the raw oyster on the half shell." He said and I tried not to throw up in my mouth. Bloody oysters! I gave him a small smile as he placed the oversized plate in front of me before then placing one opposite. I thought it best to wait for Alex and in doing so delaying the slime I would have to put in my mouth. That or I could convince Alex to eat mine. But he always had a habit of making me feel guilty for not trying new things, no matter if it looked like a giant's snot ball that had been chewed up and spat out on a shell!

Thankfully I wasn't left alone for long as Alex came back but I frowned up at him when he didn't retake his seat opposite.

"Let me guess…"

"Catherine, I'm so sorry." This time I did roll my eyes.

"It's fine Alex, I know you have to go…*you always do.*" I added this last part muttering under my breath, no longer caring if he heard me.

"It's not fine Catherine, I don't know how this happened but if I don't go and sort this out then we could lose this client…"

"Alex I understand, you've worked so hard on this project." I said trying once again to be the good girlfriend and not throwing the hissy fit of all hissy fits.

"Yes and it just feels as though in these last few days that someone is working against me. These orders have been coming from the top, from my boss' bosses, which never happens. But I promise you Catherine, that when we leave tomorrow, I will make it up to you." I smiled at his sincere promise and said,

"I look forward to it." He gave me a half smile back before leaning down to kiss me on my cheek.

"You are too good to me." He whispered softly before pulling back.

"Why don't you enjoy the meal before Frank picks you up."

I tensed hearing this thinking Frank was the last person I wanted coming all this way to pick me up.

"You can't take me home?" I said feeling the whine in my voice. He at least had the decency to look sheepish.

"I wish I could ma chérie, but I am so close to my office, it would mean taking that time away from sorting out this mess in time to travel tomorrow." I lowered my head in acceptance making him groan.

"I am sorry, you make me feel so guilty." I wanted to frown at that. It wasn't my fault he asked me to get all dressed up and brought me all the way out here only to be dumped without a ride home.

"It's fine, I will call Frank." On hearing this he looked happier and after giving me a quick kiss goodbye he was off and I was surprised I didn't see him running for the damn exit. I let out a sigh and felt like banging my head on the table. People were starting to look at me and I suppressed the urge to stick my tongue out at them and say 'What, have you never seen a girl stood up before?!' But instead I grabbed my glass of water and downed the lot wishing it was a lot stronger and burned on its way down.

I tried to think what I should do now and how embarrassing either choice would be. Do I sit here and eat a meal I wasn't interested in eating alone or do I ask for the bill and leave? And that's another thing, what would I end up paying for this fancy meal? I wasn't sure I groaned out loud until it was confirmed from a voice behind me, making me only groan again,

"That's not a happy Keira sound."

"This can't be happening." I could actually hear him smile and then I felt it for myself when he leant down and kissed my cheek.

"Keira." He said my name in that seductive drizzle that he coated his words with when he wanted me to know exactly

187

what he was thinking. It made me shudder and I felt his smile widen on my cheek before pulling away. Then my heart fluttered a wild and unruly beat as he took the seat that was meant to be filled by my boyfriend.

I took a deep breath and said his name, no doubt taking him by surprise by the one I chose…

"Dominic."

CHAPTER FOURTEEN

KEIRA

A DATE TO REMEMBER

I could not believe Draven was here right now! For starters, how did he know I was going to be at this restaurant? Which was precisely what I asked him…well, in a roundabout way of course.

"What are you doing here?" I asked, trying not to stare… or drool… or beg! I mean come on! It was so not fair for him to be here right now, looking that damn good he could melt my knickers off with one head nod!

He wore a pair of charcoal shaded jeans that look sculptured to his strong thighs and a crisp white shirt under a dark navy suit jacket. He also had the top two buttons undone allowing me to fantasize about kissing my way up that golden skin of his, which looked even more delicious against the white of his shirt. And then there was the dark stubble that made me want to rub against him like a damn cat! See, totally not fair!

He just raised one eyebrow at my question asking me a silent 'isn't it obvious?' with just one look. However, I didn't want to assume anything so carried on questioning him.

"Are you here with someone?"

"I am now." He replied smoothly, giving me a bad boy smirk.

"Draven, I don't think…" I was cut off when Draven raised his hand to get the waiter's attention. The man actually left another person's table to come rushing over. Did everyone in this state know the importance of the Dravens?! I almost expected the flustered waiter to bow when he got to our table… oh wait, not ours, more like mine!

"You can take that away now, the lady doesn't like oysters." Draven said motioning to my plate.

"And can you have a more private table set up for us." It wasn't said as a question but more like a politely given order. The waiter nodded profusely, saying,

"Yes Sir, right away Sir."

"Draven you can't just come in here and…" I started to say when the waiter left but Draven cut me off.

"What, ruin your date…? I think you would actually have to have a date stick around for more than five minutes for that to happen." Okay, so that stung, so much in fact that I picked up my napkin and threw it on the table as I stood, snapping,

"Screw you!" in my anger. He had the audacity to look shocked for a moment before his face got soft and regretful. The waiter came rushing back telling us that our new table was ready.

"It's alright, he will be eating alone, oh and he loves any dish with cucumbers!" I said turning and giving him a smarmy look over my shoulder. I heard him burst out laughing and even though I would have loved to have basked in the sound, I was far too busy storming out of the restaurant. No surprises when I didn't get very far.

"Hold up now, Beautiful" He said wrapping an arm around my waist and putting an end to my dramatic escape…damn him!

"Draven," I warned him but then sucked in a breath when I felt his face come to my neck. His lips hovered over my skin and I squirmed under his hold.

"Easy now." He said as his hold tightened around me. I couldn't believe he was doing this in the middle of a restaurant full of people.

"Draven let me go, people are watching us." I hissed with my head down trying to hide my flaming face.

"Let them. Come and have dinner with me." He was doing that seductive thing again and it felt like I was drowning under his spell.

"No." I felt him chuckle at my ear.

"Ah come now…even if I say *please?"* I shuddered again when he whispered that word 'please' along my skin and he knew he had me.

"Fine!" I almost growled the word and once again felt him smiling at my ear.

"Good girl." He replied kissing me quick on the neck and then letting me go. I was so embarrassed to see that our little exchange had been witnessed by not only half the restaurant but the waiter as well. I bet he thought I was a right floozy coming here with one man and then getting all cuddly with another five minutes after he left. This was what made me whip round and say,

"But only if you apologise for what you said." He looked taken back a moment before schooling his features and crossing his arms across his chest.

"I am not sorry that the fool left you for the simple fact that

I can now be here in his place…" I was about to interrupt when he quickly carried on,

"…However, I am sorry if his stupidity hurt you and my insensitivity to the fact brought forth those hurt feelings."

"*Brought forth*…really Draven it's like living in a period drama with you." I said almost giggling.

"Keira." He said my name with a frown and this time it made me smile, only after throwing up my hands saying,

"Alright, alright, apology accepted." Then I let our poor confused waiter lead us to a secluded part of the restaurant. One look around at the private space and I was soon nervous once again. Now no one could see us back here and I didn't think this was a good thing. I sat down and tried not to notice the way Draven folded himself into the seat like he commanded the room. What was it about this man that seemed to suck the energy from any space around him and use it as a weapon to bend all those to his will? I could barely take my eyes away from his body, taking note of his every movement and storing it away like some naughty little secret.

"Should I serve the next course, Sir?" The waiter asked Draven as it was obvious who was in charge at our table.

"The next course?" Draven inquired frowning and I felt my cheeks heat up knowing what was coming next.

"Yes Sir, the gentleman before you pre-ordered the chef's tasting menu to be served." He said and as Draven's eyes grew darker, I quickly felt sorry for the poor man as he squirmed uncomfortably under Draven's obvious displeasure. He then turned his gaze to me and it took all my control not to flinch back he looked so angry.

"Did the lady first see this tasting menu?" He asked without his intense eyes leaving me.

"I don't believe so Sir, no."

"Draven, its fine, I…"

"Bring us the menu." Draven snapped interrupting me and I really didn't know what the big deal was.

"Yes Sir and should I still serve the wine that was ordered?" At this he raised an eyebrow at me and I quietly shook my head as I still didn't really care for red wine. The only reason I ever drank it in the first place was that it was Alex's favourite and he was always trying to get me to detect the hidden flavours in them, which I found was endearing of him…obviously Draven didn't.

"Which bottle was ordered?"

"The Pinot Noir Copain, Tous Ensemble 2011, Sir" At this Draven scoffed and made a motion with his hand like he was batting away a fly. One look at the waiter's face and he knew where this was headed. It was blatantly obvious this was some posh version of a macho man's pissing contest.

"No, definitely not, the lady doesn't like Red… so you can bring us the wine list as well."

"Very good, Sir" I frowned at Draven and quickly said,

"Thank you," to the waiter before he left, to which I received a small smile that I knew meant he was grateful for my little show of kindness.

"You know you could be more polite to the working man, Draven." I scolded crossing my arms across my chest and momentarily forgetting I had a tight dress on. Well that was until it drew his gaze to my breasts and now instead of angry Draven I got hungry Draven. I instantly lowered my arms making him smirk but he didn't make eye contact which I was grateful for. Thankfully the waiter returned with the menus, giving me a small but much needed break to slow my pounding heart.

"Do you always let him order for you?" He asked completely ignoring my last comment.

"There is nothing wrong in him wanting me to try new things." I argued and resisted the urge to pout.

"And these new things include oysters, which I know for a fact you hate and can't understand why anyone would, considering you think they taste like seawater?" Oh Lord he was so very smug...but just so happened to be very right, the jammy bastard!

"I hadn't mentioned it." I said which I knew was a lie because I had in fact mentioned it once.

"It's nice to know that your lying skills are as fine-tuned as ever." He said sarcastically and I think my face said it all but he got the verbal lashing anyway.

"We can't all be experts at it, Draven!" As soon as I said it I wanted to take it back as I watched his face drop and pain replace any other emotion.

"Touché, Keira." He said and I wanted to bang my head against the table. This night was not turning out how I hoped at all.

"Look, I'm sorry I said that."

"Why when it's the truth...I did lie... to protect someone, just as you're trying to lie to protect someone now." He said leaning forward, putting his elbows on the table.

"It's not the same thing." I said trying to defend myself.

"No, you're right, it's not but that is because this person..."

"Alex."

"Asshole..." He corrected firmly before carrying on his rant,

"...is not worthy of your lies. He orders you food he knows you don't like, he orders you wine *I know* he knows you don't like and then leaves you sat in a restaurant alone when he hasn't even had chance to warm his seat and then.. pray tell me...how exactly were you going to get home, Keira, because I am pretty sure I didn't see a blue truck pull up from where I was sat?"

"You've been watching us?!" I half whispered, half screeched leaning across the table. He just gave me a look that said his own version of 'well durr!'

"Raising your eyebrow at me Draven isn't an answer!"

"Well it's a good job I was here don't you think or you would be eating alone now wouldn't you?" He said calmly and it grated on my last nerve.

"I wouldn't have stayed you big ox!"

"Big ox?" Okay so as far as insults went I will admit it wasn't my finest.

"Yeah, big ox!" I said having no choice now but to roll with it.

"Well this big ox is very interested to know how you were planning on getting home this evening?" He said looking mildly amused no doubt at my ridiculous new name for him.

"I would have just called RJ or Frank like last time." I said sounding smug but then quickly changed that to an 'oh shit' face as I saw the angry purple flash in his eyes.

"Like last time?" He asked this in such a way I knew that most of it was controlled by his demon side. I quickly picked up my menu and used it as a barrier to Draven's dark side.

"Erm…Oh look here comes our waiter, let's order should we…? Umm I am starved, what looks good…have you been here before… recommend anything?" I jabbered on in the hope of moving on but when our waiter came closer only to be turned away by Draven, I knew it was no use hiding in my menu.

"How many times, Keira?" He growled the question at me and I wanted the chair to swallow me up and walk me out of here like a scene from Beauty and the Beast.

"Draven it is none of your…"

"How many?" Okay so this time it definitely was his demon side and I knew better than to poke at it with my attitude stick.

"Fine! Three times okay, now will you get off my back?" I said reopening my menu with enough force I nearly snapped the spine.

"Three times!? And you put up with that?" Now it was my turn to growl out,

"I have put up with a lot worse before him!" Again it was below the belt and I knew this when I saw his face fall but I just couldn't seem to help myself. I think if the most obvious fact didn't exist and I wasn't still in love with Draven, then I would have just let the past go. But we both knew that wasn't the case and unfortunately with love and when it is unreturned, well it makes you do stupid shit and lash out in horrible ways. It pushes you to limits you never knew you had and drives you to hurt others in ways that you never knew you were capable of.

"I wish I could deny that statement…I wish it like you wouldn't believe Keira, but I can't, because you are right." The way he said this made me feel only pain and I couldn't have helped my reaction even if I had wanted too. I reached out my hand and grabbed tight onto his, looking him straight in the eyes and holding his gaze.

"I am sorry, that was unnecessary and cruel. But Draven, you have to stop this with me and Alex. We both made our choices and now we need to live with them…the only question now is if we can live with them and still be in each other's lives?" He first looked down at our hands and he turned his slowly. I started to pull back but his other hand flashed out and gripped my wrist, anchoring it in place so he could turn his other hand fully without me fleeing. He then interlaced his fingers with mine and squeezed them before releasing my wrist. It was only when he knew he had a firm hold of me that he finally raised his gaze to mine.

I didn't know what to make of his expression but there was only one word I could find to describe it and that was intense.

The purple flames licked the edges and although this was something I was used to, the burning crimson in the centre wasn't. It was the first time I had seen the mixed parts of his soul conflicting with his demon side but that was what must have been happening. What other reason was there? But more importantly, why now?

"You are so very pure…it still takes my breath away, little one." I swallowed hard, trying in vain to get the lump that just formed to drop back to my stomach like a lead gun ball. We just seemed to stare at one another for endless minutes until our poor waiter could be seen hovering around. At this rate we would end up being the only ones left and this poor guy would still be trying to get us to order. I was just about to speak up when my stomach decided to do it for me.

Draven let me go and finally I got his beaming smile back.

"Let's feed you, shall we?" I gave him a shy smile making him laugh. He motioned the waiter over, and I heard Draven chuckle. I was just about to ask him what he found funny, but it had to wait as the waiter was now at Draven's side.

"What can I get for you, Sir?"

"To begin with something to drink…" Draven said opening the list and scanning the pages for what he was looking for.

"Ah yes that will do, a bottle of the Krug, Clos d'Ambonnay 1995." As soon as the wine was mentioned the waiter's eyes bulged, which told me all I needed to know…the wine was going to be ridiculously expensive.

"Oh that's alright I can just…uh…" I stopped mid flow when I saw Draven's pointed look and quickly shifted gears to his preferred speed,

"…What he's having" I finished dejectedly.

"Uh sir, please excuse me for saying so but it's part of my job to warn you it's six thousand dollars a bottle."

"That's fine I will let you know if we need another and we

should be ready to order by the time you return." Draven said with an authoritative air that only came from people who had an extortionate amount of money.

"Of course." The waiter replied and promptly left the table to no doubt start hyperventilating.

"What were you laughing at before he came over?" I asked dying to know.

"He was thanking God that we were ready to order." I couldn't help but find the funny side too, considering who Draven really was. Draven seemed slightly transfixed as he watched me throw my head back and start laughing. I only noticed he was still staring at me or more like my neck, when I had finished with my outburst.

"What is it?"

"It's just, it's still strange seeing you without it…that's all." I gave him a confused look and my hand automatically reached up to touch my neck but before I could ask he said,

"Your necklace…the one I gave you." He said this last part into his menu and I knew then he didn't want to say anymore on the matter, which I was more than happy with. The whole comment had floored me and I decided to follow his lead and hide behind my menu. I mouthed the words 'Oh my God' and shook my head in vain but it did nothing to help my racing emotions. I had to wonder, like I had shamefully done many times before, if he still had it.

"So what would you like?" Draven's voice sounded slightly strained and he had to clear his throat after asking me that question.

"Umm…to be honest I haven't a clue what most of this stuff is." I said on a laugh making him smile at me.

"I am sorry I never brought you to places like this." I was a little taken back by Draven's confession and I dropped my menu to look at him.

"Why...? I mean you shouldn't be as they're not exactly my thing." I watched him take a deep breath and lower his own menu.

"Honestly...?" I nodded and couldn't help but bite my lip as I waited.

"Because I always wanted to keep you to myself." He said shrugging his shoulders like the weight of his words hadn't just added to the rest of the conflicting emotions raging within me.

"Draven I can't..." I started to say but was cut off when he raised his menu once again and I knew this was his way of telling me not to finish that sentence.

"Do you want me to order what I know you will like?" He asked after a few hopeless minutes of silence.

"I think that would be safer." I said trying to lighten the mood when really all I wanted to do was excuse myself, lock myself away in the safety of a cubicle and cry like a little girl. I wasn't exactly sure why he was doing this to me and I wanted...no, almost *needed* to find some anger in the cruelty of it all, but the simple fact was that I couldn't. Because it suddenly occurred to me that although what Draven had done was in fact very cruel and very wrong, it didn't mean he had done any of it with the sole purpose to hurt me.

Like now, he wasn't sat there saying these things to rub it in my face, he was simply saying them because he *needed* to. Don't get me wrong, it didn't stop the pain but it just meant absorbing it wasn't quite as...

Painful.

CHAPTER FIFTEEN

KEIRA

I SEE FIRE IN YOUR SCARS

Thankfully the rest of the evening took a turn for the better and soon we both relaxed enough to fool ourselves into believing nothing had changed. It is amazing how you allow your mind to do this and find a comfortable balance when hiding the truth. I wondered half way through my meal if this was how people lived their turbulent lives, through a window of fogged glass. Did they just think if they thought hard enough then their problems would just go away or was it a case of if you couldn't see them, then they couldn't see you? And then blissfully you don't have to acknowledge what you don't see hidden in that part of your mind you call hope.

But I wasn't naïve enough anymore to place things hidden there. That hope was no longer a blooming flower I watered daily. Because no matter what Draven did or said now, he had crushed that hope to its roots. And yet despite all this it still didn't mean that I wasn't going to take anything I could get and right now I wanted to pretend for just one night.

So that's exactly what we did. We ordered our food and chatted the night away as if we were the only two people in the room. He asked about the minute details of my life, making me laugh when he asked if I'd still tried on all my Christmas presents this year, like I had done the year before. I told him how disappointed my grandmother had been not to have any 'beef candy' to prey on and he had thrown his head back and roared with laughter when I added,

"Her words, not mine."

All in all it was shaping up to be a lovely evening, minus the hiccups at the beginning. But now it was coming to an end and I found myself wishing I liked coffee just as an excuse to have that extra time.

"Shall we?" Draven said standing after paying a small fortune for the meal. I nodded and stood, reaching down to where I had stowed my purse. When I straightened again, I almost cried out as I looked up to find Draven stood right next to me.

"You look truly magnificent tonight." He said in a voice so deep I had to wonder how many levels to this man there really were. I started to smile up at him but was stopped abruptly when I saw that same mix of fire in his eyes as before. It was like looking into a different Draven and it scared me.

"Are you...okay?" I asked quietly trying to pull him from whatever emotions had him locked in place. I tentatively placed my hand on his forearm, and it was like my touch was enough to douse the crimson flames that were battling against him. He flinched and looked down at my hand on his as though he too was trying to figure out what just happened. I slowly pulled back and tried to take a step away, suddenly needing that space between us but Draven had other ideas. His arm came around me and pulled me from my escape and up against him.

"Don't!" His warning rang clear and I knew this wasn't the time to push him. Something was going on with Draven and it seemed by his facial expression that he was just as much in the dark about it as I was. So I let myself be led from the restaurant with his arm draped possessively around me and I had the feeling if he could have got away with carrying me in his arms he would have.

We walked past the hostess and I had to supress a wicked grin at seeing that perfect façade drop at the sight of a man like Draven walking away from her without so much as a glance. She looked him up and down like a shopaholic at a summer sale. It made me want to cosy up to him and take a possessive claim but that was until I reminded myself. Draven wasn't mine and I had in fact walked through these doors with another man at my arm. The thought made me want to pull myself from Draven, but he must have felt me tense at his side.

"I wouldn't, Keira...remember the knife you hold." I looked up at him, frowned at his warning and was just about to ask when it dawned on me what he meant. I held the knife to the edge of his thread. I was almost tempted to slice forward and watch as it broke. What would happen exactly? Was that the line we just couldn't cross? But more importantly...what would happen if we ever did?

I didn't answer him but instead let him lead me outside to a parked black Rolls Royce with the passenger door already being held open. I had the sudden urge not to get into the car, fearing this new mood of Draven's. I felt once again out of my depth and it was a feeling I was no longer used to.

"Just get in the car, Keira...you have nothing to fear." He said obviously being able to read some of my emotions. I mentally pulled up my big girl pants and with Draven holding

203

my hand was helped into the car. I was quickly followed by Draven folding his large frame in next to me and without a word the car pulled away.

Most of the journey was spent in silence as I watched the world go past without really seeing it at all. My mind was awash with all that had happened over the last few days and it almost seemed like some cosmic joke as to where I now sat. I looked over to Draven and saw he too looked out of his window. I wondered what he thought about right now…was he thinking the same as I? I couldn't help but notice how he had one hand over his forearm…the one I had touched and one he still kept hidden from me. It took me back to that day once more at the villa when I saw those ugly burns that looked so raw and fresh. I was just about to ask him about them when he suddenly turned to look at me.

"We're here."

"Oh…that was quick." I said lying but not knowing what else to say. I looked away from Draven and saw the mighty and imposing Afterlife come into view. I couldn't help but smile at the sight.

"Why do you always do that?" Draven's question startled me.

"Do what?"

"Smile in sight of my home…you always did that, and I always wanted to know." I gave him a small grin and hoped my response would mean he would drop the subject without me having to answer him.

"It's not like you to wait so long till finding out something you wish to know."

"Consider it as me choosing the importance of my priorities." I gave him a little shake of my head and a raised eyebrow, silently asking him to explain the cryptic statement.

"My enjoyment at seeing your happiness outweighed my

curiosity." He said making me turn my head away so he couldn't see how much his words affected me.

"So are you going to tell me?"

"Not today." I replied softly to the night at my window.

"Why not?" He asked pushing the subject like I knew he would. So I turned my body to face him and nodded to his arms before arguing my point.

"Are you gonna tell me about them and why you're obviously hiding them from me?" For the first moment he looked taken aback and even shifted his body further back in his seat as if he was afraid I was going to reach out and touch them.

"That's what I thought." I said when I got no reply but a frown.

"Some things are meant to be left in the past."

"Including us?" I asked quickly making him wince at the power of my question.

"I…Keira, you must understand...this…"

"Oh I understand, Draven, you want all the answers but with no questions asked. Well I am afraid it doesn't work like that, it might have done at one time but let's just say I learnt my lesson. You can't go through life without ever explaining yourself, not to the people you're supposed to care about…*well, maybe that's your lesson to learn for next time.*" I added this part looking back out to the night in a whisper I knew he would still hear.

"Next time?" He asked as I reached for the handle of the door now the car had just come to a stop. I didn't turn to face him, I couldn't with what I was about to say…

"Yeah, the next time…" I took a deep shuddering breath, released it and pushed open the door…

"…you fall in love."

I shifted on the bed but then stopped abruptly as the sensation that I was on a float stopped me. The rocking my motions caused felt like I was bobbing along the water in little waves lapping at the shore. I wanted to bolt upright but remained frozen in fear. It even took all my mental strength to brave opening my eyes slowly to what new horrors now faced me.

But what I was expecting exactly I couldn't say but the misty dull grey sky wasn't it. It was like no other sky I had ever seen, being void of all variants of colour. There were no clouds, no differences in space and distance. There was no sun and no life discovering its vast space. It was...empty.

I decided I needed to move if I was ever going to try and understand this lost place. I slowly moved my hands to my sides and pushed myself up. It was as though I feared any sudden movements were going to send me off into a never-ending ocean or floating off into an eternal abyss.

"What is this place?" I whispered to no one as I took in my strange surroundings. I looked around and the first thing I noticed was the strange black mattress I was sat upon that floated calmly on top of the deadly still lake. The water had that unnatural quality to it, almost like a liquid mirror that was smoky grey like the sky it reflected. There was no distinction between water and atmosphere creating an eerie vast space that could have gone on forever. It was almost like being placed in a box of fog and the only things you can see are the things that are immediately around you.

The black mattress crept along at a snail's pace almost as though it knew where it was going, as there was certainly no current aiding our progress. I placed my hand down and felt the strange looking black material that almost looked like thick webbing. Like some giant demonic spider had covered the bed like a cocoon with miles of the rubbery cord the same thickness as my finger.

But what was even more startling about the sight was the

blinding contrast my white dressed body looked against it. Even the difference in materials screamed out as the soft delicate folds of the skirt folded in ribbons and fell against the harsh unbreakable shell. The dress looked as though it had enough material to cover ten bodies as it overflowed the sides of the bed and floated majestically in the murky water. My hand went to my stomach and pulled at the thick, satin ribbon that was the exact colour of blood. It had been wrapped around my torso, crisscrossed over and over in tight constricting bands, almost as though someone had wanted to keep me restrained.

Even now I noticed the same ribbon binding my arms to the very top and across my shoulders ending with a bow to one side of my neck. I tried twisting my upper body and felt a tugging sensation straining against my skin from every point.

"What the ..." I said but stopped as something caught my eye to my left. I left trying to tug myself free for the moment and watched as a shadow started to emerge from the mist. At first I thought it was a long thin bridge to nowhere but then I squinted my eyes and could make out it was a small rickety dock that looked ready to fall at any moment. The thin planks ran width ways, held up by thin bent poles that looked as though any weight would make them snap like twigs.

The entire dock looked black and I couldn't tell if it was because it was burnt or just appeared that dark against the foggy backdrop. My unlikely little boat still bobbed closer to it and soon the very end of the dock came into view. I sucked in a sharp breath as I quickly realised I was not alone anymore.

The new body was only but a glimpse of limbs that could be seen sat there, facing out into the grim nothingness. I didn't know what to do...did I call out, did I remain silent or did I try and pull myself up against the dock when I got close enough? Was this all a dream, like so many others or was this the other world's way of trying to warn me of something? These were all great questions but all just as pointless as the energy put into thinking them.

I don't know how long I took wondering what the next step to take was but when the time came I reached out and grabbed for it in the form of the dock. I stood on the shaky mattress and only just managed to heave myself up and over onto the dock before the mattress continued on past. The massive weight of my dress dragged out of the water with its ridiculous length and I slapped it behind me as I stood. I felt the old wood groan beneath me and looked down through the gaps with trepidation. Well I had made my decision now and I had to follow through with it.

The body on the chair didn't even stir as my footsteps grew closer and with it the noise that the person was obviously now no longer alone. I didn't know whether to take this as a good sign or not but still I continued on. If only the fog would lift just enough to make out some features so I had some clue as to what I was dealing with and then maybe I wouldn't have to go as far. I looked down at the dock and saw my bare feet after having to grab handfuls of useless fabric so that I wouldn't trip. I shuffled along trying not to step on the large gaps big enough to get my foot stuck sideways. In fact I was making good progress considering I was terrified but when I looked up to see, I had to clamp my hands around my mouth to lock away the scream.

The body was now stood and it was clear it was the strong powerful body of a man. He only wore black trousers that were frayed in patches like they were hundreds of years old. His bare top showed square shoulders and muscled lines down his back which then tapered down into a V-shape. But all these factors were insignificant. They were cast back into the shadows of my mind as my eyes homed in on the many black chains that wrapped around the forearms of the man. There should have been too much weight for him to even hold his arms up but this was precisely what he did.

My eyes travelled the length of the chains that bound him so crudely and followed them to the chair that stood suspended on its back two legs. It only took a few more steps on my part to see the chair itself was actually made up of the same lengths of chain. Twisted and coiled around to form the shape until it got to the bottom of the feet, where it then spread out like roots of a tree. Whoever he was, he was well and truly trapped to the end of that soulless sight with no means of escape.

I couldn't help but feel for the prisoner, for to be cast into this place to suffer the emptiness for any length of time was a cruel punishment indeed. I wasn't really sure though how long I stood, stock still, watching his silent torment in sick fascination but eventually it came to an end in the most brutal of ways. It was when I couldn't wait any longer and I took my last and final step, coming within touching distance of the man. I then reached out my hand before I even knew what I was doing. It was in that exact moment my fingertips came into contact with the first link of metal in his chains that everything changed.

I thought in this cold place I would feel the icy touch of iron against my skin, but I was wrong. It burned me, scalding my flesh as if I had just touched burning coal. That's when I knew it wasn't metal at all. Because his chains weren't manmade and they weren't of Earth, no… they were made from Hell's own rock.

The impact of my touch caused a domino effect of reactions but the one most profound was when the man before me whipped his head around to face me.

"NO!" I screamed looking up into the eyes of purple flame, only this time, as I had first witnessed today, Hell's fire raged there in the centres.

"Draven?!" My raw and pain laced voice spoke his name like it would somehow help in releasing him.

"You shouldn't be here, my Keira." These words weren't spoken aloud in Draven's voice but that of his controlled Demon. It was growled without malice and it was snarled without threat. It was just spoken from another part of him that didn't know how to be gentle with me but still had enough thought not to want to frighten me. I don't know how I knew this as fact but it didn't matter, what mattered was that I did and I wasn't afraid.

"Why are you here Draven…what…what is *this place?"* I asked whispering the last few words as the emotion at seeing those chains around him got to be too much for me to handle. I noticed how where I had first touched had now started to glow, like the centre of a log fire where it's at its hottest. The heat started to travel quickly along the links and I watched on in horror as it got closer to his arms.

"Draven?!" I said his name again in panic, madly thinking what it was I could do to stop it from burning his skin.

"This place is my prison of choice." His Demon said looking back over the fog and when I followed his gaze, I could see it had finally started to lift. Only now, I quickly wished it hadn't, for all at once the last of the links quickly erupted around Draven's arms and the rest of the vile world came crashing into view.

"This is… TARTARUS!" His demon side erupted fully and I took a step back in fright. He motioned an arm out in front of us and I turned to see a very different kind of Hell.

We stood at what seemed to be on the edge of a chasm in Hell and it opened out into a cavernous space filled with row after row of soldiers. There were thousands of them all stood to attention in too many lines to count, all in formation and ranks. But wait, there was something different about them, something not only demonic but something more. I wanted to step closer but Draven's burning arm came up, reminding me of what was more important.

I looked down and noticed the chains barely hid something attached to his arms. They were wrapped around some sort of metal plate with symbols on there. It was a circle with words around the edge and in the centre… was that…a star?

"Who is doing this to you? Who is keeping you here, Draven?" I asked looking up at him so he could see the level of pleading in my eyes. But no matter what I expected him to say, it would never had prepared me for the blow he was about to deliver, not to my mind nor to my heart but this time…to my very soul…

"You are, Keira…

Only you."

CHAPTER SIXTEEN

KEIRA

TERRIFYING LITTLE PEOPLE

I woke with a jolt that felt as though my heart had actually stopped for a short time. Of course, now it was thundering within my chest like a jack hammer. I took in the dark room that only let in a thin slither of moonlight where the curtains hadn't been closed properly. I scanned the room and it took my fragile nerves a minute or two to calm enough to realise where I was.

My mind took me back to the night before after getting out of the car with Draven. Sophia had been there to meet me ready for our 'girl time' and thankfully I hadn't seen Draven again that night. I didn't think I could face him and I think Sophia could tell something had happened as for once she didn't ask. In fact she didn't mention her brother at all for the rest of the night. Instead she just made it her mission to distract me with what deemed her version of a sleep over and made me laugh at every opportunity.

By the end of the night I think I was well on my way to being drunk after all the champagne she made me consume. But if I had to choose the highlight of our night, it would be seeing Zagan's face when he walked in and looked on in absolute horror when seeing his wife with a lumpy pea green face mask on. I actually spat out some of my drink I laughed that hard. It was only after Sophia tried to drag him in the room to paint his toenails that he fled in fear.

So now here I was, in some guest room I had never seen before, lying upon an elaborate metal bed that looked like some black iron rose garden, shaped so at least four bodies could sleep amongst it all. I vaguely remembered being shown this room after I continued to nod off on Sophia's gothic pink and black couch...but wait...I was missing something. The more I thought about it the more I didn't think I was led to this room but more like carried to it.

"Draven." As soon as I whispered the name the sound of someone inhaling sharply sounded in the room and my gaze shot up to a shadow of black I now knew belonged to a man's frame. I held my own breath as I watched him take the first steps from the shadows and into the line of moonlight, bathing his features in an ethereal glow. My eyes scanned the length of him and I could just make out on the side facing the window where his long sleeves looked charred along his forearm.

"The chains." I said before I could stop myself and watched as he tensed his fists at his sides.

"You had a nightmare." He stated with his voice sounding gruff.

"You carried me in here last night...didn't you?" I asked as the snippets of last night came back to me.

"Go back to sleep, Keira."

"Do you know what I dreamt of?" I asked ignoring his demand.

"Don't over analyse what you don't know." At this I scoffed, making a little snorting sound in disbelief.

"Well what else am I to do, when you obviously won't tell me the truth…? Hell, I'm not sure you even know what that is anymore!"

"What I do know is that the truth will never be something you could handle knowing, so it would be wise to leave it at that." Draven snapped back taking another few steps toward me.

"Oh right, I forgot…I haven't had to handle difficult shit before…nothing like say, my boyfriend faking his own death just to get away from me!" I threw at him like a verbal slap. He actually growled at this and looked like he was fighting shaking me or storming out the door.

"Yes and can you possibly imagine the level of severity which caused such drastic actions…? Can you even grasp what would drive a man in love to do such an unforgivable act?" He shouted down at me as he was suddenly at my bedside, but it wasn't in anger. No, it was nothing short of undiluted pain.

"Why can't you just tell me…does it have something to do with…" I took a deep breath knowing the explosive side of Draven that would probably erupt when I finished that question…

"…*Tartarus?*" and just as I thought it would, as soon as the name passed my lips, Draven ignited into a purple fuel that coursed through his body like an uncaged beast running riot beneath the surface. His wings burst forth and spread out, plunging the room into darkness. I shrank back against the metal roses at my shoulders and I suddenly felt trapped as he slowly leaned his frame in and over me. It was only the current of his other self that I could see traveling his veins that lit up my startled features.

"Dra...Draven...move back." I said nervously and suddenly desperate to get back that space between us. Because I was a coward, and this was a very different kind of fear screaming out at me to get away. This was the fear of need...of want...of all-consuming desire at it rawest form...

This was terrifying.

Draven, despite my fear, continued coming closer until his wings came forward and their tips held all his body weight off the mattress either side of me. His hands then came up and gripped onto the metal frame either side of my head.

"My...An Angel shouldn't know of that place, let alone utter its name." He said and he couldn't have missed the way I sucked in a quick breath from what his slip up meant to me.

"What are you doing?" I asked as he started to shift one arm beneath me, and I wanted to moan at the feel of his hand gliding down my spine. He moved his head closer to my neck and I felt his lips smile against my skin as he felt me swallowing down the hard lump he caused. I tried to shift out of his arms but it was quickly becoming impossible when his wings started to move under me. Then he finally answered my question...

"I'm giving an Angel wings to sleep in." He whispered and then in one move simultaneously wrapped my body in both his arms and wings, spinning me so I now lay on my side next to him, wrapped in a feather cocoon.

"Draven!"

"Ssshh now, you need to sleep and last night you slept so well in my arms...don't fight me, Keira...now rest." He ordered softly into my hair and I felt his wings curl round tighter as if to prove a point. I had to admit that the fear making me want to run away was slowly morphing into that of a much greater need...

216

The simple need to stay.

The next time I woke I was alone and feeling foolish. I wasn't sure if all of last night had been a dream or just the frightening parts. Had Draven really been there or had my mind conjured up that part as a way to deal with my nightmare? Either way, he had played the part of my hero and either way it had once again messed with my head.

I sat up and stretched, then rubbed the sleep from my eyes. The room looked a lot softer in the morning light and without the presence of the masterful figure of Draven to command it. If anything, now the room looked far too girly for Draven to even step foot in it. I giggled at the thought as I took in the large rose patterned wallpaper that looked like velvet on one wall. The other walls were neutral with black painted vines spreading out from the rose paper as if they were alive. It was beautiful and it was all Sophia.

I whipped back the covers that were most likely a zillion cotton thread count and got out of the enormous bed that, knowing Sophia, was made just for mad orgies. I stretched again and realised for the second morning running I had once again slept in my clothes. Well at least I knew for certain this would be the last time as I was off to Italy later today…

"Oh god! Shit...! I have to pack!" I shouted frantically as I started the mission of looking for my shoes. Ok, so they were borrowed shoes but still, I was more than thankful not to still be wearing my sister's dress. That had been the one snag in last night's dramatic car exit. I had been hoping to go home first and at least change before my plans with Sophia. But just as always Sophia being as fabulous as she always is, was ready and prepared with a change of clothes in my size. She even assured me they weren't what were left over from my side of Draven's wardrobe. Which did make me wonder, what happened to all those clothes? Well as long as I wasn't wearing any of them then I was happy, as that would have felt too weird and too...*familiar.*

So now I was on my hands and knees looking for the pair of skull converse Sophia had given to me giggling. I didn't care as they were comfy and I thought quite cute despite the theme. Plus they reminded me of Pip and anything that did that was never a bad thing.

"I can't say that's a bad sight to walk in on." I heard said from behind me and I looked back over my shoulder to see Draven leaning casually against the door frame with both his arms and legs crossed. Before I could think about it a beaming smile spread out across my face at the sight of his own smile.

"Yeah well if you could use your demon mojo and find my shoes I would be more than grateful." I had only just finished my request when the pair of shoes shot from under the other side of the bed straight to my hands. I smiled down at them before getting up to sit back on the bed to put them on.

"You're up early." Draven stated making me wonder if he was hoping to catch me still asleep.

"Well I have to get home and pack, so I gotta go." I said in reply as I sat back up after pulling the backs up on my heels after I had kicked them on.

"I will drive you."

"Draven you don't have to do that, I can just grab a taxi and…" His face said it all but if that wasn't enough he interrupted me by saying,

"Nonsense, now are you ready to leave?" I rolled my eyes at him and then giggled when he mimicked me by doing the same.

"Yeah, I'm ready."

The drive back to my house was mostly taken in silence and I think this was because we both knew this was the end. I was to go off to Italy and by the time I got back the Dravens would have no doubt moved on. And even if they hadn't what would have changed really? It wasn't like I could make a habit of seeing Draven like this…no that would never work and in the long run be far too painful. Even just after this small amount of time, it was seriously messing with my head.

These thoughts assaulted me all the way home as Draven silently manoeuvred us in one of his shiny sports cars through the winding country roads. It was only when I heard the crunch of the wheels hit the gravel driveway did I realise I was home.

"That was fast." I said finally looking at him. He just raised an eyebrow as if to say, 'this is me we are talking about'. The man couldn't go slow in a car even if he had an entire state police department travelling behind him and a funeral procession in front!

"Well I guess this is it…I will say…uh…what are you doing?" I stuttered off mid my goodbyes as I saw Draven opening his door and exiting the car. He came around to my side and opened my door for me. I was allowing myself to hope this was all he was going to do before getting back into his 'death defying speed' motor and zoom on outta here. But of course, this was Draven we were talking about and therefore in that statement meant Draven was completely unpredictable.

So I should not have been surprised when after slamming my door closed behind me he then continued to walk next to me up to the house.

"Draven, I don't think this is a good…" I started only to once again be interrupted, only this time by Libby and Frank coming out of the front door.

"Oh great…perfect, just what I need." I muttered making Draven cough back a laugh.

"Kaz I was wonder…ing…oh…" Libby soon trailed off that sentence when she saw who was stood here with me. Frank also did a double take and unlike Libby's scowl, he had a beaming grin.

"Dom, my man! How are you?" Frank said taking Draven's hand and giving it a firm man shake.

"Frank!" Libby hissed at his side making him drop Draven's hand as though Libby would whip out a cleaver and chop off his balls if he didn't.

"Eh…yeah…well...obviously you're good." Frank said taking a step back and therefore effectively coming to heel next to Libby.

"Mr Draven," Libby said in a snooty 'I hate you cause you broke my sister's heart you bastard' kind of way. I was just about to speak when Draven beat me to it.

"Frank, Libby, as always it is a pleasure but I was wondering if you wouldn't mind giving me a moment of your time?" He said this last part directed at Frank and I was once again left looking for the right words of dissuasion against this little man chat only to be left alone with Libby with my mouth open.

"What the hell, Kaz!?" Libby snapped dragging me back to the twilight zone part of my day.

"Uhhh…"

"Oh no, you're gonna have to do a lot better than Uh!" I turned away from where Draven and Frank now stood to face my sister's understandable wrath.

"Ok, ok…just keep your voice down." I pulled her arm round so we were facing the other way in hopes this would help Mr Super Hearing over there in not hearing us.

"Kazzy, explain what he's doing here before Ella is old enough to be asking you the same question."

"Where is she anyway?" I asked looking through the open front door.

"She's in her playpen watching Bubble Guppies." I couldn't help the shiver of revulsion to shake my frame at the mention of that show. I'm sure it was fine for kids, in fact Ella clearly loved it but for me I ended up singing 'It's time for lunch' in my damn sleep!

"You mean she's actually staying in her playpen?" I asked both stalling for time and really curious considering the child was like the reincarnation of Houdini!

"Kaz" Libby said in warning.

"Alright fine, but it's nothing really."

"Uhh uh" She made that 'yeah right' sound whilst crossing her arms.

"Ok so I went to Afterlife that first night to see Sophia and Vincent and he was there."

"I gathered that part…so let's skip to the part where he is now *here."* She said hissing the word 'here' and looking back over her shoulder at him. I followed her gaze and watched the two deep in a conversation I really wanted to be a part of, only what he could be telling Frank I had no clue.

"He gave me a lift after I spent the night with Sophia doing girly crap…we…uh…well we decided we are going to be friends." At this Libby's eyes got wide as she gave me an incredulous look.

"Friends?"

"Yeah"

"As in, friends, friends?" I laughed and said,

"Yeah, is there any other kind?" Now it was her turn to laugh.

"Yeah, there is the type of friends where both parties are

trying to fool each other into believing they just want to be friends, when really they want to get back together but both said parties are too damn stubborn to admit their true feelings!" I rolled my eyes and said,

"That's not what's happening here."

"Ok, so I don't know about him but you...come on Kaz, I saw you...that man crushed your heart, I know he did and you cannot stand there and tell me that him being here and back in your life isn't messing with your head!" Ok, so she had me there but that didn't mean I wasn't going to deny it till the cows came home.

"I'm fine, besides...I have Alex and he knows that."

"Oh I bet that went down well...*not.*"

"Libby." This time I was the one to say her name in warning.

"So how did last night go?" She asked thankfully changing the subject and therefore getting off my back about the whole situation.

"He stood her up again!" This answer came from Frank as I hadn't realised they were back.

"He didn't stand me up...well...not exactly, he just had to work that's all." I defended clenching my fists at my sides.

"He was there all of enough time to be led to the table before swiftly leaving." Draven put in and I shot him a nasty look, one that obviously didn't faze him in the slightest.

"Oh Kazzy, he did it again?" Libby asked giving me a slight head tilt in pity.

"It was fine...Jesus, the only people that have an issue with it is you guys!" I said letting my voice rise with my frustration.

"He's a douche bag." Frank muttered crossing his arms.

"Frank!" I shouted his name, but he just shrugged his shoulders and retorted,

"Well he is! Let's face it Kaz, you can do better than that arrogant French pric…"

"Frank!" This time it was Libby's turn to reprimand him.

"Look, all I'm saying is that no real man leaves his woman like that!"

"Right, fine…I get it, you don't like him…now can we please get off the subject!" I was just starting to get to a whole new level of being annoyed when the most perfect being alive toddled out of the front door.

"Daddy!" Ella cried out in excitement and both parent's faces dropped.

"What the heck, Frank! You said she definitely couldn't get out this time!" Libby said rushing over to her escape artist daughter in hearts and rainbow covered dungarees. She had a riot of red curls like a sun halo waving round her head as she was swept up into Libby's arms.

"You little rascal! I don't know how you keep doing it, little Miss," my sister cooed and Frank looked on adoringly. I smiled at my niece and then looked to Draven to see him staring at me in a way I had never seen before. It was so different that I don't think I could have described it even if I had all day to analyse it.

"Erm…so, this is my niece Ella." I said and like perfect timing Ella thrust her little chubby arms out at me to take her.

"Ok baby girl, come to Auntie Kazzy." I said taking her from my sister and also taking note that Libby too was watching Draven. I heaved her up in my arms and turned to face Draven myself.

"Ella belly this is…uh…Dom." I said thinking this would be the easiest name for her to say. Of course, I didn't want to think too much into it as to why this was so important.

"Dom!" She said repeating me in her little cute voice that made you want to say 'Aww' to every single thing she said. I swear she could make the words goat herder or car transmission sound adorable.

"Hello there, little one." Draven said after first needing to clear his throat.

"Libs, can I borrow you for a sec." Frank said putting his arm around Libby's shoulders and steering her into the house. I raised my eyebrows at Libby but she just shrugged her shoulders as if to say she had no clue but if I was to venture a guess I would say he wanted to tell her what Draven had told him. As soon as they went out of sight Ella started wriggling in my hold and at first I thought it was to get to them.

"I don't think that's a good idea, Keira." I looked at Draven's almost panicked face and back to the source of that panic as Ella was now reaching out to him. I couldn't help it but I laughed. This mighty King of Demons and Angels on Earth, faced God knows how many armies and enemies but in the face of one little girl barely a year old and he looked ready to run and hide.

"I think you can handle it, Draven." I said still chuckling as I passed her over to Draven not giving him much choice in the matter. He gripped her little body with his large hands overlapping and held her away from him like she was a ticking time bomb. I shook my head still laughing softly and said,

"Like this, cradle her to you." I then motioned for him to hold one hand under her bum and the other around her body to hold her against his chest. Once he did this something in him just seemed to change instantly, like flipping a switch and one I suspected was wired directly to his heart.

"Dom, Dom!" She squealed in delight making his eyes widen.

"See, she likes you." I said nodding as she planted both her tiny hands on his cheeks and getting closer to his face.

"She does?" He asked in wonder and I couldn't have

stopped the ache in my heart from mounting at the sight of Draven falling under the spell of my niece and becoming quickly and utterly smitten.

"Totally." I whispered trying to rein in my emotions and the thickness in my voice.

"Well you are certainly a rare beauty, aren't you?" He said to her and she giggled before she pushed his cheeks together in the way she does to everyone.

"Chummba cheeks." She said mimicking the way her daddy did it to her when she sat on his lap. Draven burst out laughing and then shifted her further up in his hold, obviously getting more comfortable with holding her now. He then both made my heart soar and crash at the same time when he bent his head and kissed her nose. She wrinkled it up and then poked him on his own and shouted,

"Nose! Nose!" I think it was at that precise moment I witnessed Draven fall in love with another human being and it was the single most beautiful moment in my life so far. But with its beauty came with it the devastating truth that up until that moment I had never fully let myself believe. I had kept it locked away all this time to a place I never wanted to unlock because to unlock it and set it free meant one haunting truth...

I could never have that beauty with Draven and that beauty was one only found when creating a child and inevitably was the kind of beauty…

I always craved.

CHAPTER SEVENTEEN

KEIRA

ALMOST LETTING GO

"**D**om, Dom!" Ella shouted as she was still being carried around by Draven and I don't think either of them was ready to give up the other any time soon. Libby's icy demeanour soon thawed, and I wasn't sure whether this was because of the obvious adoration Draven was showing her daughter or from what Frank had told her. Well whichever one did it, Libby was now back in full welcoming mode and currently bringing through a tray of tea and biscuits making me want to groan when I saw her fancy china set, that I believe was a wedding gift never used.

"Well I'd better go pack," I said as everyone else seated themselves in the living room.

"Oh don't be daft, you have plenty of time," Libby said setting the tray down as Ella shouted,

"Candy!" Which was what she called anything that was

sweet. She then squirmed on Draven's lap and started trying to reach out for a biscuit. Draven not even thinking about it reached out and grabbed one to hand her but what shocked everyone was that he first took a bite as if testing it for himself before letting her have it.

"Uh…are you still ok to take me to the airport?" I asked trying to move past the heavy sweet lump Draven's actions were forming.

"I am taking you." Draven said without looking at me and not caring in the slightest he was getting chocolate hand prints and cookie crumbs all down his obviously expensive leather jacket. Hell, if anything he looked like he would have burnt it if the child in his lap had only asked.

"Umm, that's nice of you to offer, Draven but…"

"It's not an offer." He said and reached for another biscuit for Ella.

"Yummy Dom, Dom!" Ella shouted with glee and Libby chuckled but then said,

"Alright but last one or you will spoil your dinner." At this Draven's head whipped up and stared at her in disbelief.

"Ok Mummy." Ella said around a mouthful of crumbs.

"She is allowed no more?" Draven asked Libby clearly shocked that Ella was being denied anything. Frank laughed and slapped his hands to his knees before he got up.

"I know, it's hard to say no, right…that's why I leave it to Libs…that way she will like me more growing up." He said winking at Draven and then slapping a hand on his shoulder.

"I heard that!" Libby shouted as Frank walked to the basement door.

"I know you did honey, now let me be useful before you knee me in the nuts and get Kazzy's suitcase." At this Draven ended up shaking Ella as he threw his head back and boomed with laughter. However, his laughter was short lived as the joggling motion caused Ella to break wind and turn red faced.

"Uh…what's happening?!" Draven asked in a panic.

"Well Dominic, you are about to witness the full delights of parenthood." Libby said getting up ready to take Ella from him, but I had other ideas.

"No, no Libs, let me…Dra…Dominic why don't you help me." I said winking at Libby making her smirk.

"Hey now I'm not gonna ever say no to that offer."

"Excellent." I replied taking Ella from Draven and cocking my head to indicate him to follow. He got up looking a bit confused, which just managed to add to my amusement. I walked through to where Libby kept the changing unit in the den and the second I lay her down she started to scream.

"What's wrong with her?!" Draven asked in alarm as he watched me start to unsnap her dungarees and pull them off.

"Relax…she just filled her nappy that's all." I said giggling when he took a step back and held a hand under his nose after I whipped back the nappy.

"By the Gods…all that came out of her!?" I rolled my eyes but couldn't have held back my massive grin for all the world. I don't know why but when I thought back to when Libby was pregnant, a time when Draven and I were just starting out, I had envisioned moments like this. He and I both babysitting together or taking Ella on days out and all the while basking in the sight of Draven with my precious niece in his arms.

"Ssshh baby girl, it will be over in a minute." I soothed as she wriggled and tried everything to get from having her bum changed.

"Is it hurting her?" Draven asked after I nodded to the wipes for him to hand me.

"Of course not, she just doesn't like staying still this long… haven't you ever seen someone change a nappy before or do you call them diapers?" I asked while multitasking with holding up baby legs in one hand and cleaning the cutest little bum with the other.

"I have never…"

"Never?" I prompted when he stopped and rolled up the nappy to put in the scented bag briefly thinking a Maci's perfume counter wouldn't mask that stench!

"Been around a child before," he finished sounding slightly ashamed of the fact.

"You mean one as young?" I asked taking the fresh nappy he held out for me to take that he himself took from the stack.

"No, I mean any child." This made me let go of Ella's legs in shock and just before Ella twisted enough to escape bare butted, Draven placed a gentle hand on her belly. I looked down and noticed for once in her life she went so still at Draven's touch, as if she was too busy absorbing the feeling than trying to get away from it.

"How is that possible, Draven?" I asked dumbstruck.

"I never cared much for the life I protected…" He said looking deep in thought as he gazed down at Ella like she somehow held the very key to our existence. Then he continued,

"Or saw the beauty in such a life grow." The way he said this last part was for Ella's sake alone and it made me want to cry. It was a perfect moment and was unfortunately enough to jerk me from my unobtainable dreams and dump me back into reality.

I didn't know what to say to that so I didn't say anything at all. I just gently removed Draven's hand and continued to re-dress a squirming Ella. Once I was finished I popped her down to go toddling off back to her mum and was again left alone with Draven.

"Hey…are you alright?" He asked placing a hand on my shoulder and applying enough pressure to turn me to face him.

"Yeah, I'm fine…I gotta go pack." I added in a quiet voice and pulled from him before he could say anything more. I had to get away before I confessed as to what torture I was finding this whole day. It was the worst kind. The kind that shows you a life you always wanted to live. The kind where you lived it for a short time having a taste and finding it was a life that was the sweetest kind there was to live. But now…well, now it was a little like being out in the rain looking in the window and watching other people living that sweet life. And all that's left for you is standing in the cold with bittersweet memories hoping they will keep you warm enough to survive the winter.

I took these sombre thoughts all the way upstairs with me and all but stomped into my room. I didn't look behind me to know Draven didn't follow and somewhere deep was the disappointment when he didn't. It was buried deep in the same place where I let myself hope he wouldn't just walk out the door and me telling him I had to go pack was the last words he ever heard from me.

I didn't have long before my heart was beating faster with the realisation none of this was going to happen because Draven was now shouting my name from the floor above in my old room. I stuck my head round the door frame and shouted up,

"Down here!" I went back into my new room and slumped on the bed staring out of the window to the woods I'd become used to losing myself in.

"Why are you in here and why has your room up there not had your presence in it for a long time?" Draven asked coming to face me. When I didn't answer him, he took the hint and sat next to me on the bed close enough his thigh was flush with mine.

"I just couldn't face it…you know, after…" I said

concentrating on one of the trees outside like it would somehow help me through this.

"Ah…I see."

"Do you?!" I snapped facing him and I don't know exactly where that fiery emotion came from.

"I do…it's the very same reason I have not set foot in our…*my* bedchamber." He said looking down at his hands as though for him they had the answers written in secret across his palms.

"I'm sorry, I shouldn't have snapped. I guess I am just still finding this…"

"Hard, difficult…*excruciating."* He said finishing on a whisper.

"Yeah, all of the above." I said faking a smile as I looked at him.

"I know you don't believe me but I didn't choose things to be this way. I never…"

"Don't." I said on a plea. This was when he shifted to face me bringing his knee up on the bed making me move back to give him room.

"Please let me say this." I wanted to protest but how could I? How could I deny anyone their feelings and their choice to finally voice them? So I bit my lip and nodded for him to continue.

"When the decision was made to cut myself from your life it was in the knowledge that you would eventually go on with your life and in time…well, time is supposed to heal all wounds."

"And for you, what of the man who has eternity ahead of him, how long does it take to heal then?" I asked staring him straight on and trying not to flinch when I saw the purple pulse deeper in the depths of his eyes.

"There is no healing for that man, Keira, there are only

many lifetimes of a man who knows the full extent of great loss."

"Draven…do you think my love for you was any less than that?" I asked shaking my head.

"You don't see me in the arms of another." His reply was like a slap and I moved back as if he had in fact struck me.

"No, I just found you in the arms of an ex-lover when you led me to believe you were dead!" I said before standing from the bed and ready to take on a defensive pose which consisted of me with my hands on my hips.

"Keira, please…if you knew the reality you would be disgusted for very different reasons indeed."

"You know that makes no sense to me." At that he gave me a sad smile and said,

"I know."

"Right, well I have to pack and…"

"You need to know about this Alex, Keira…it's not safe you going off with him where I can't keep watch over you." Draven said and I made a little choked sound in the back of my throat as I couldn't believe what I was hearing.

"So you were fine walking away last year and leaving me to it but now you know I am moving on, you what exactly…? Now you want front row seats!? Oh I don't think so!" I shook my head and stormed around ready to go get my cases from Frank when he chose that moment to come lugging them in the door.

"Hey…uh…I'm not interrupting anything here am I?"

"No it's all fine and dandy Frank, we were just having a friendly chat like the best of buddies we are." I said feeling my anger bubbling up at the injustice of it all.

"O…kay." Frank said taking the hint that all wasn't well and he pretty much dropped the suitcases and ran out of the door to escape.

"Keira, just take a minute and try and be reasonable here, I am doing this for your protection." Draven said standing himself and turning to face me. I heaved a suitcase onto the bed and Draven watched it bounce before I flung open the lid.

"Bloody pig headed Alpha male crap!" I ranted as I ignored him and started grabbing random clothes out of my drawers in anger. I then proceeded to stuff them in no doubt regretting it the minute I opened the case again in Italy.

"You're so angry." Draven said stating the obvious and I rolled my eyes and snapped,

"Ya think?!"

"Look, I know this is hard for you to accept but the Nephilim are dangerous and can be unpredictable…if you would just give me more time, let me look into my different sources and then we will know more and…"

"Enough!" I shouted slamming my case down.

"Keira, just listen." He said trying for a calm voice whereas mine was getting more and more high pitched.

"No you listen. I like Alex…as in a lot and I am not going to have you screw it up for me just because you don't trust anyone."

"That's not true!" He replied haughtily and crossed his arms across his chest.

"So you're telling me if this was anyone else you would be fine with it…say for instance if it was Justin or even Jack?" In hindsight I shouldn't have said any of this and not for the reasons of jealously that I hoped for, no…it was for the very opposite.

"I was surprised it wasn't the boy Jack, at least then I would have known you were cared for, treated right and definitely not in any danger he would possess or bring to your door." On hearing this I took a step back and suddenly felt like bursting into tears. I had been a fool. Such a damn fool! I had been shown the signs and ignored them as much as I had seen signs that had never been there to see. It was now official. The only reason Draven was here at all was because he felt it his duty to see to my safety and he honestly thought Alex was a danger to that. He wasn't back because of a jealous mind that was making him rethink his past decisions. It was simple and that simple fact just happened to crush what was left of a stupid hope that I had spent these last few days fighting against.

Hope I had now lost…*again.*

"Keira?" Draven said my name after obviously seeing the hurt I could no longer mask on my face.

"Its fine…look I need to shower and finish packing, and I would appreciate it if I can do these things *alone.*" I said all this trying not to take in Draven's worried expression, so quickly turned away from him and faked looking busy.

"Keira, look at me." I didn't want to do it, I really didn't but when Draven's voice got all soft like that then I knew I just didn't have it in me to deny him, even now. So I did the stupid thing and raised my pained eyes to his.

"By the Gods Keira, you're killing me here." His reaction to me also took me back but before I got to say anything he was suddenly standing inches away from me. I sucked in a quick and startled breath just before he raised his hand to my face and cupped my cheek.

"My words hurt you little one?" I could feel my teeth instantly dig in my bottom lip and just as quick, Draven's thumb was there to pry it back from being tortured.

"I don't need your words to know the answer, your eyes tell me everything." He spoke so gently as if luring me deeper into a false sense of security. It was a dangerous place to be and I knew if I had any sense left I would take a step back and ask him to leave. But as soon as that thought entered my mind it was as if he knew and therefore made his move against my retreat. His free hand was suddenly at my hip, fingers biting in my flesh in a sign of possession. Need and want flooded my system and soon my mind was flipped once more into seeing things that weren't there.

"Have no doubt of my true feelings of jealously Keira, as I only hide them to spare you more confusion, but I will not do that if it causes you more pain." Again my breath caught in my lungs, trapped in the moment of what I was actually hearing. Was it really possible his feelings were what I had hoped for?

"What are we doing, Draven?" I bravely asked looking up at him and also braving the intensity I found there.

"For once I cannot answer you, for I am as lost as you are." He replied bringing his forehead down to mine and the instant we connected we both closed our eyes and inhaled deeply. The moment felt beautifully raw in a way that the feeling ran deep enough to touch our souls and connect with what each of us found there. In the background fog of my brain I heard the faint ringing in the distance but then Draven started to speak, and the ringing faded.

"Keira, I…"

"Kaz! It's Alex on the phone!" Libby shouted up and thus broke our sacred connection. I pulled away and heard him growl out his annoyance at being interrupted.

"Coming!" I shouted back and ran from the room, suddenly needing nothing more than to get away. I slammed the door and for a few seconds needed to calm my racing heart by leaning against the outside of it. The single panel of wood could have been a bank vault between us keeping us apart but more importantly keeping the words I was afraid to hear firmly on the other side.

"Kaz?!" Libby's voice brought me out of my mental torment and after I banged the back of my head against the door I left to go get the phone.

A short time later I found myself on the way to the airport and the weight of Draven's silence was far heavier than my packed suitcase. After I had answered the phone and confirmed meeting Alex at the departure lounge, Draven had backed off. I had turned around to find him leaning against the wall watching me on the phone and his scowl at hearing me telling Alex I was looking forward to it was now permanently fixed. After I hung up he simply gave me a head nod and walked past me to go sit in the living room. As soon as he sat down he was bombarded with,

"Dolly!" As Ella thrust a poor abused doll upside down in his lap that she usually carried round half naked by its leg. I didn't leave again until I caught Draven's hidden smile when looking down at the doll and then back up at the beautiful little face that had bestowed such a gift.

After that I had packed (A little less aggressively) and then showered ready for the day ahead. It was a lovely warm day so I decided on a summery dress in pale blue that once again Libby had lent me for the trip and added a pair of white ballet shoes and a little white hooded jacket. I wish I could have said Draven's reaction to seeing me didn't give me that little flutter in my belly but when I saw his eyes get hungry and the purple flash there, I had no hope. This was the same when he led me to his car and used a possessive hand on my hip to steer me when it clearly wasn't needed.

So that brought us to now and I was trying not to notice the way his hand kept gripping the steering wheel like it needed the warning of aggression. It seemed to get worse the closer to the airport we got and in turn the sickening feeling grew in me. It was like sitting next to a timer and dreading hearing it buzz for you knew that would then signal the end. Because realistically what was there left for us after this? These perfectly turbulent days that felt beautifully unfinished.

We started to see signs for the airport I started to fidget in my seat and pull at my sleeve cuffs nervously. One thing was for sure and that was I really wasn't looking forward to our version of goodbye.

Draven remained silent as he navigated his way through to the drop off point and immediately was out of the door as soon as he killed the engine.

"Okay then." I muttered and then jumped when my door was opened. He gave me a hand to help me out and once I was firmly on my feet it took him delayed seconds till he released me.

"Sooo…I guess this is it." I said after he lifted out my suitcase and set it down. Still he didn't say anything but just frowned down at my case like it was the cause of all this hurt between us. After silent moments that were getting harder to live through I was just about to grab my case and leave when I got my biggest surprise of all. Suddenly Draven's head snapped up and he said in a desperate voice,

"Don't go." I swallowed hard, bit my lip and felt the unshed tears pulling at me.

"Draven I…"

"And not because I'm only worried for your safety." He interrupted stepping closer making my head go back to keep eye contact.

"Then what would I be staying for, Draven?" I asked forcing the words out. He looked like he was trying to think of the right words to explain and after looking to the side away from me he seemed to come to some kind of decision. He then looked back down at me and placed his hand at my cheek.

This was it, I was sure this time he was going to kiss me and not one single cell in my body would have wanted to stop him.

Wrong or right, it no longer mattered. All questioning was rendered obsolete.

Gone in the dust of doubt and drowning in a sea of lost cares. There was only one now. Only this moment…and just before his lips reached mine he killed it with only six words when there was only three I needed…

"Because it's all I ask of you."

CHAPTER EIGHTEEN

DRAVEN

THE GIFT THAT KEEPS GROWING

Watching Keira shut down before my very eyes was a brutality I was getting used to enduring and was far worse than any tortures the Underworld's Gods could dream up. It was only in these last ten months that I started to understand the full concept of nightmares. But thinking back this would be a great lie indeed. These nightmares started the first second I laid eyes on my beautiful Chosen One. They were all the same…

Seeing, Keira and all her purity being touched by my world.

That vile creature Morgan getting his hands on her once again or the torment at knowing what he'd already done and knowing I was unable to prevent it. The nightmares she had no idea that plagued my sleep for the first time since my time began, the very ones that would replay over and over that night she told me her story.

It had haunted me then and it still did to this day, the only difference now was that I had many more nightmares added to drown my dreams in. They became black and consumed with visions of Keira being taken from me. Not only by the hands of the sick and infested mind of the human Morgan but also by Lucius, who was once my own brethren. But it didn't end there, there was also Malphas in the Temple before watching as the blade struck the killing blow to her body. Seeing all this in my short time with her and hearing the words from the Oracle were the final nails in my own coffin.

If she only knew that I had in fact chosen her over the fate of my kind, over my own blood that flowed through the vessels of my family. I had given up every chance at the great prophecy just to see her live one single full life that was always destined for more happiness than could ever be bestowed on to single living being.

But instead what did I continue to do...? Crush that soul every chance I got just because I couldn't tell her the truth. I had tried letting her go, by the Gods I had tried! I had lived and breathed my own Hell and would continue to do so if it only meant her life instead of my own.

But what now? What of the danger she was in without my protection? What could I do...ask her not to be with this damnation of the Gods and to be with one destined to end her life instead? Just what were the Fates playing at exactly? There were too many questions to ask and with the Oracle still missing absolutely no answers being given.

So what was left for me to do but watch heartbroken as those beautiful eyes shut out any light of hope that had so clearly been showing these last few days. She took a step back from me and it took everything in my power and every fibre in my vessel from reaching out and grabbing her to me. Would I have ever let go...? I wasn't so sure this time. The urge to steal her away and hide her from the world was growing inside of me like Japanese knotweed. I just needed to get away from her before it consumed me and overtook my senses. These last few days had been raw bliss stripped down and lashed across my heart every time she fucking smiled! I had almost wanted to hate her just so I didn't have to feel the pain of loving her.

So what did I do? I turned away from her. This perfect creature whose only misfortune in life was being created for me and whose only mistake in life was being fool enough to love me with an intensity that matched my own. You couldn't wish in your wildest dreams to have that type of loyalty in a heart but to witness it for yourself was something I would never forget. When I learnt of all she had gone through in the name of that love…well no other force on Earth could match it. She was more powerful than she would ever realise and made this King want to kneel and worship at her feet for the rest of eternity.

But I didn't do that. No, instead I watched her soul's light dim to a point of a soft glow as I had finally once and for all crushed her. I watched her body tense as if trying to take the blow of my rejection in an attempt at protecting her heart. I watched all this and let it be my last sight as I walked away from her. And she had no clue as to the blow on my own soul or of that on my own heart.

She had no clue at all.

I got back into my car and like the last ten months found no pleasure in its power at my hands. I revved the engine of my Maserati Granturismo and cared not for the humans who got scared at the sight. I didn't even look to see if she was watching me as I already knew the answer. That girl would make me leaving her the last sight in her life, torturing both herself and me with the knowledge. And didn't I just feel like a fucking coward for doing it!

It was at this point when I pulled over, got out of my car and destroyed every piece of metal the car possessed. I was surprised I even had enough foresight to control the minds of every human within my sight. It was only when I was left panting like a wild beast and my Demon buzzing with its small lapse in freedom did I kick some of the pieces out of my way. Then I did something I had never done before and that was to sit by the side of the road and call my brother.

"Well I must say this is a very human moment for you, Dom." Vincent said once I had explained my unusual circumstances.

"Yeah well when you see what I did to my Maserati then you won't be thinking that," I said dryly, brushing some of the dirt from my bent knee.

"I can imagine not…So you couldn't convince her to stay?" We both knew it was a stupid question and if he had been here my only response would have been to raise an eyebrow. So I was thankful when my brother got the hint and I didn't need to answer.

"Stupid question I guess." I made an aggravated sound and I could almost hear Vincent shaking his head.

"I'd better come and get you then." He said finally as a truck went past kicking up the dirt and blowing it in my face. I almost wished the pieces had been tiny shards of glass just so I could feel the pain cutting into my skin. Instead it was just an annoyance that made my Demon growl.

"That would help, yes." I said and I hung up as Vincent was still chuckling. Before I knew what I had done or got a handle on my anger I felt the pieces of my phone rain down from my palm to the roadside. I rolled my eyes and batted away the bits looking for the sim card knowing what an annoyance it was last time I had to get a new phone.

I had left it to Sophia and in an attempt to get my attention she had annoyingly renamed all the contacts to nicknames, set flowered pictures for each and set 80's pop as the individual ringtones. My reaction to this ended in needing a new phone. So in short she succeeded in getting my attention and I learned when destroying my next phone in anger to at least save the sim card.

I was just pocketing the tiny square when another truck came past but this time I threw up a hand in time to create a barrier between the debris it kicked up and myself. Unfortunately I ended up sitting here long enough to see quite a few planes leave the ground and every single one in my mind had my Keira on it. In fact I eventually lost count of the amount of times I had to heal myself after I would rip my flesh to ribbons while crushing stones in my bare hands.

I was finally glad when Vincent arrived just after I broke three fingers. This happened when punching the ground in an attempt to stop myself from releasing my wings and launching myself into the sky after the last plane.

"Thank fuck." I muttered as the heavy duty and fully kitted 4x4 pulled up with Vincent in the driving seat. I frowned at his choice of vehicles before yanking the door open with too much force, ripping the top from its heavy duty hinges.

"Don't say a word," I warned on a growl and then barely concentrated as I quickly reattached the metal work before slamming the door.

"I don't think there is much left to be said, Brother." Vincent spoke anyway and I clenched my fists in an attempt on getting a handle on my building rage. I had no reason to get angry at my brother, if anything he understood me more than anyone else on earth. He too loved Keira and even though this knowledge should have angered me, it didn't. The reason for this was I knew it was in his destiny to love her and as cruel as that sounds he would one day understand it too, for it was not my place to intervene.

"Unless you too have lost your senses Vince, I don't recall this being the way to Afterlife." I commented after quite some time of silence. He turned his head and gave me a smug look before saying,

"Well you would certainly know." I rolled my eyes at my brother's attempt at improving my foul mood and his dark humour in reference to what others would class as my job...that being sending the unruly souls back to their Afterlife.

"So are you going to tell me the reason we are soon going to be leaving this road?" I asked knowing now my brother's reasoning behind his choice of vehicle.

"I think it's time," he said cryptically. I frowned and tried to reach out and find the answers myself, but he just laughed when I felt him blocking me.

"Can't you wait for ten minutes?" I replied to his comment with an umf sound which only managed to further add to his amusement.

"I didn't ever take you for one who played into the dramatics." I commented before I recognised where we were heading.

"Oh I'm not, however I know a certain blonde beauty that found a taste for it around this time last year." As soon as he said this my back straightened and I gripped the dash so hard that I felt the material give in my hand. I then quickly scanned the area and when he pulled suddenly off the road I knew where we were headed.

"Stop the car." I warned on a growl.

"Just wait, you will understand when..." I didn't give him chance to finish as I cut the engine with enough force I blew a head gasket causing steam to bellow from the bonnet.

"Fuck, Dom!" Vincent swore as he slammed on the brakes and skidded in the narrow dirt road. But I was already ripping off the door I had not long ago fixed.

"Dom, wait!" Vincent shouted after me. I turned quickly and slammed my fist through a tree trunk splintering it like a battering ram before roaring at my brother.

"NO! You know my feelings on this, why must you persist! Do you not think I am in enough pain, enough fucking agony!" I watched as Vincent rubbed the back of his neck with his hand in frustration before taking a calming breath no doubt at the sight of my Demon panting.

"I know of your pain Brother, you know I do but what you don't know is the full depth of *hers.*" On hearing this I laughed without a shred of humour. I was just about to deny this ridiculous statement when he held up a hand to stop me.

"You are not listening to me…just stop for a second and calm yourself, I can see your Demon breaking through." I frowned and then looked down at myself to see he was right. Even my wings had erupted and I had not even felt it. I shook my head to try and bring forth the lock and key I kept that part of me controlled under.

"Now hear me Brother, for what I say now should have been said a long time ago but you were never ready…I had feared until recently you would *never* be ready.."

"And what makes you so sure I am now?" I growled.

"Because for the simple fact is you are here…you came all this way to see her the second you thought she was in trouble but more importantly…you *stayed.*" I knew he had a point as soon as he started. I had spent all this time wallowing in my own Hell and self-pity convincing myself and others that I would never see her again when it was all in vain. The second I found that not only was there another man in her life but a damned Nephilim at that and I was back at her mercy.

"Fine! You made your point so speak and get it over with!" If my brother had smiled like I knew he wanted to at that moment he would have been the next thing my fist encountered.

"It is not so much what I need to tell you but more what you need to find." As soon as he said this I watched as he released the full magnificence that were his heavenly wings. They were different to mine, not just in colour as his were a startling brilliant white but also in shape. They were larger at the top but curled round thinner at the bottom and that came past his ankles. They also skimmed the floor when they were relaxed which I always teased him about, asking if they annoyed him. His reaction was always the same as he rolled his eyes and as usual I would fend off a punch heading my way.

"What are you up to?" I asked as he stretched out readying himself to take flight.

"You know where we are going?" I nodded as I knew these woods as I knew my own vessel and what I would find opposite the cliff's edge at the end of this track.

"Then you will find out when we get there." This was the last thing he said before he launched himself into the air and I watched a brilliant flash of white disappear envying his speed. I took a moment to breathe deep readying myself for the blow I knew was coming. When I finally opened my eyes I too launched my body into the sky to catch up with my brother.

"You were always the faster one." I said as I landed on the ledge to my cave to find Vincent there waiting. He never took a step inside and I let the level of my love and appreciation for my Brother flow freely from my mind. He gave me a sad smile and then walked up to me to place his hand at my shoulder.

"Just remember, this was her only way," he said lowering his head in a sign of deep respect. He then gave my shoulder a squeeze before he left the only space that had never been tainted by another soul other than that of two people who loved each other enough to give their lives in the name of that love.

I waited until I heard him land in the distance then I lifted my eyes from the floor. I pushed all my hair back with one hand

and held it to the base of my neck as I took in her lingering presence. To feel how faint it was brought me back to earlier and being in her bedroom once more.

I first felt confused as to why nothing had been touched in so long and then the pain I saw in her eyes when she tried to explain. She didn't notice my reaction as she turned away but if she hadn't been trying to mask her own suffering then she would have seen my own.

I took in the space and was instantly transported back to that first time I brought her here. Ever since I had found out about her becoming the Maiden needed as her part in the Triple Goddess I had always known I would claim her here. In this space which was the only place that truly was my own. It had become a bit of an obsession once I knew and I couldn't help but smile when thinking back to her obvious frustrations at making her wait.

But for me, it was the last part of perfection that should have always been mine to take, to possess and to own. I had her heart that was as clear as her holding my own captive.

But then to be given the chance at being the first and last man to take her body, well something primal snapped within me and the thought was now making me murderous! I hadn't truly let myself think about it before now but what if this cretin of the earth had touched her? What if he had tasted that purity and in doing so trying to sully it with his own unworthy hands?!

"اجازه دهید که خدایان او را لعنت به جهنم!") ('Let the Gods damn him back to Hell!') I screamed out at the ceiling in my vessel's native tongue with enough rage to cause the rock to shake. I quickly had to get control enough to stop my private space from caving in on itself. It took me back to every other time this had happened and every one of them included my Keira.

This was the place I flew off to after setting her down safely in her home after first meeting her in the meadow. The same was said after making the decision to distance myself from her and lying about Celina in order to save her from another attack from Layla. Even now the name of that vile bottom feeder made me want to destroy something.

"Get a handle on it!" I shouted at myself trying not to let my emotions manifest the only way they knew how…into rage. But there were other times too. Like when I had Ava searching the skies for where Sammael had taken her. I had stood on the edge waiting until finally hearing Keira's call. In that instance I don't think Vincent had anything on that type of speed that spoke of only desperation.

But the one distinct difference between all those times and now was back then I still had her heart but now…well now I had not only trampled that heart but I had practically threw it back in her face and walked away. So no matter what Vincent thought I needed to find it wouldn't have made any difference. The Fates had decided and I could never take that chance…*ever.*

So with this dejection in mind I slumped down back on the bed letting my wings cushion my landing on the black sheets. I let my mind take me back to that night. The most precious night of my life other than the first time I felt my body join with hers. The moment our souls connected and fused together in an everlasting union that even death could not part.

My entire body shivered as the memory took hold, staring into her eyes as she found her pleasure of release from the feel of me stroking that deeper part within her. They would glaze over and go out of focus and then that would be the end of me. Seeing that was like flipping a switch to my control, rendering me utterly spellbound and powerless. Yet my goddess had no clue to the power she held in just her eyes alone.

The thought made me groan and bang my head back against the pillows.

"What's this?" My voice felt foreign due to the thundering in my chest. I turned my head and the first thing I could sense was like a kick to the gut!

"You cried for me little one." I said running my fingertips over the place I knew her tears had landed all that time ago. Was this what I was supposed to find…the evidence of what I did to her? Well if so then it was all in vain just like I knew it would be. I didn't need to scent her tears to know she had shed them!

I got up angry with myself for letting Vincent bring me here. I knew this was all I would find and what did it accomplish exactly, only more cracks to add to an unclaimed heart?

"Foolish old man!" I cursed as I heaved myself up from the floor ready to leave this place and never return! I stretched out my wings and walked to the edge to take in this sight, hopefully for the last time. No, I could never come back here. So with this in mind I turned one last time as something inside me told me just one last look. I needed to see it as it was that morning.

I had got up and stood right here as the sun rising filled the cave with the softest glow. I remember being transfixed on her skin, the way it shone like an Angel's would but somehow seeing it on a human was one of the most beautiful sights I had ever witnessed. She lay so still and so peaceful I remembered smiling knowing how I had tired her out. Her leg was tangled in the black covers and her hand held in a loose fist at her lips. And then there was her hair, like a rope of gold where she had plaited it at some point in the night so it wouldn't…

"Wait!" I shouted suddenly as I was seeing the impossible.

"It couldn't be…" I whispered as my footsteps caught jarring me forward.

"No…no…oh, Keira my darling no!" I spoke to no one as my knees hit the bed and I pulled out the golden plait I found sticking out from under the pillow. I must have disturbed its resting place for now I sat back on my haunches holding in my hands the softest most beautiful hair in the world. I couldn't believe it as much as I could. Was there ever any end to the level of love that girl had for me?

Even as I asked myself this in my mind I quickly thought to what I knew about her…about how she did things and if Keira had to say goodbye what else would she have done. This thought had me throwing the pillows wildly away until I found I was right. As there I found a small white envelope with my name written across. Only this time it wasn't Draven, it was…

Dominic.

Dominic,

I thought for a long time how to start this letter. I mean how does a letter like this even start, as I have no clue, for I only know how this letter should end.

Reading your own letters felt like hearing your voice for the very last time, which was as much beautiful as it was soul crushing. Because that's what it feels like without you. It feels like someone has taken a piece of me away and left an empty shell in which no heart needs to beat to keep alive.

The pain is unlike anything I have ever known and I think we both know I have known my fair share of pain. But this? I guess the simplest way to put it is that it fills my days with moments that are hard to breathe.

I don't know whether or not it's easier that I don't have a body to bury or even a way to say goodbye, so this was the only way I could think of. But I wanted you to know that I can no longer wait for a normal life I don't ever want to happen to come and find me. I can't choose that path to walk down because I already know my destination is you. And whether it be in this life or the next, I will stop at nothing until I join

*with you again. Because, my Dominic, I would give my life
for you and would brave going against the Fates at every
turn.*

*And do you know why? Because you are my fate and that is all
that matters. That and my everlasting love for you that I believe
with every beat of my heart, that our love is the most powerful
force in my world and yours. I believe our love can silence the
Fates and defeat any Gods that stand in our way. And I leave on
my quest to find you and prove this to you.*

*I am coming to save you and I know I will succeed because all I
need is my love for you.*

*For I will never stop and I can only pray you feel the same.
That you never give up in the only truth that matters and that is
us being together Fates be damned.*

*So I say not goodbye in this letter but only that I will see you
again soon and to trust in your love as I do mine.*

The greatest love I possess is forever yours as am I.

Your Keira.

P.s I left you a gift that only you deserve for the happiness I saw
in your eyes whenever you held it meant the world to me as did
you. Keep a piece of me safe and with you always.

"So now you finally see." Vincent's voice filled the void
and I looked up completely unashamed as my tears ran freely.

"Now I see." I finally managed to say as I stood up gripping
both pieces of my girl in my hands. I walked over to him and
looked out seeing the view in a completely different light to
before.

"And?" He prompted making me turn to look at him. I felt
as though my heart was going to burst as these new feelings
coursed around my vessel making me feel human for the first
time in all my long life. I momentarily looked down at her hair

wrapped around my fist and then to her words I held in the other.

The decision was made and there would never be any going back…not this time.

"Dom?"

"We go to Italy." I said looking at him and seeing the first real smile light his eyes since this all began.

"And the Fates?" I knew he had to ask and he knew he had to ask but now as I looked back at the sky and the sun starting to set on this day, I knew now there was a mighty difference…

"Fuck the Fates!"

CHAPTER NINETEEN

KEIRA

AND IT BEGINS

"What do you mean there is a problem?" Alex snapped at the poor receptionist who had repeated herself twice now. I placed a hand on Alex's forearm and for a second I wasn't sure he wouldn't shrug it off in anger. Thankfully he must have thought better of it because he took my hand in his and squeezed it before continuing on in a calmer tone.

"Please, if you could explain it to us again."

"I am sorry Sir, but we must have had a problem in the bookings department as it seems on the system your room has already been allocated to another guest." She looked about ready to get her head bitten off again and before this could happen, I started speaking.

"Okay, so we understand that these things happen, but can you help us in any way or even recommend another hotel?" I asked in a kind manner even when Alex scoffed when I said 'we understand' which clearly *he* didn't. I was happy to say she smiled at me and seemed more than pleased she was no longer dealing with my irate boyfriend.

"Well, we do have a sister hotel I could check for you, however it is…how do I put this…?"

"More expensive" I finished for her, obviously guessing right when she blushed.

"Yes Signora."

"Great!" Alex said with frustration making the poor girl jump.

"If you could call that would be great." I said choosing to ignore Alex and his abrupt ways. I mean yes, this was the hotel's fault but that didn't mean that this particular girl was to blame. I felt like pointing this out but I could tell it would fall on deaf ears at the moment. I was just happy when she nodded and picked up the phone.

We stood there waiting as other lucky guests came and went with their key cards in hand ready to start their holiday. I can't say I didn't envy them and not just because we were seemingly stuck in Italy with nowhere to stay. No, for me it started when I walked into the airport like a zombie thanks to Draven's abrupt dismissal. I never thought on closing my eyes I would then open them again to find Draven walking away without one word of goodbye. That was when my world went dark. It was as if someone had taken my sun and pushed me forward saying, 'now time to get on with it girl!'

So that is what I did. I turned around and walked straight into the nearest bathroom and cried for twenty minutes. It then took me a further ten minutes to sort myself out thus making me half an hour late. Needless to say Alex wasn't impressed. To be honest at the time I hadn't given a wet welly for his mood and was more than tempted to just wheel my suitcase out of there and go home. But after sensing my own mood he quickly changed his tune and was once more my sweet and attentive Alex. Now though…not so much.

"I have some good news." The receptionist brought me out of my dark place and I turned to see she looked slightly shocked at the outcome.

"Our sister hotel has agreed to give you both rooms for no extra charge and as a way of apology is sending a car over to take you there personally." My eyes widened in surprise and just as I stepped forward to thank her Alex put an arm around me and said,

"Now that's better" I couldn't help frown at his tone and hissed,

"Alex." This was something he ignored of course.

"Thank you so much for sorting that out for us and it's very kind of them to send a car." I said making the woman smile at me.

"You're welcome and once again we apologise for any inconvenience. If you would like to wait over there in that seating area a car will be with you both shortly." I smiled again at her and gripped my suitcase to wheel over to the plush chairs I was getting desperate to sit in.

It had been a long flight and one made even longer thanks to the past few days. That's the problem with flights. It gave you no other excuse than to face your problems. You can't pass the time with work or hanging out with friends. Or even throw yourself into course work and studying for exams like I had done. No, it gave you a cage the size of a seat and forced you to sit there and reflect on all the things you really didn't want to think about.

Well for me it was always the same thing and those thoughts didn't include the man who had sat next to me snoozing most of the way across the pond. It had only included one face. One

257

perfectly handsome face that had long ago become painful to look at. It was like every time I saw him it would then throw me stumbling back in the rabbit hole of wonders. It would transport me back to all those times I had touched that face, kissed those lips and simply marvelled at the sight of his smile.

Of course by the time we landed all those visions of splendour had manifested into only one sight and that was his back as he walked away. I vowed from that moment that on that the sight of him leaving was going to be the very last time. I simply couldn't do it anymore. He had broken me for the last time and I knew deep down that a man who could do that didn't love me like I had once thought. From this I then concluded that no man deserved your love when they themselves couldn't ever love you back. So that was it…

Draven and I were done. Finished. Dead.

"Well I am glad that got sorted." Alex said sitting down in the chair next to mine. I wanted to roll my eyes at his tone but managed to hold back enough of my foul mood to refrain.

"Hey, are you ok? I'm sorry I lost my cool back there but I just wanted this trip to be perfect for us," he said taking my hand and suddenly making me feel like the biggest bitch for my moodiness.

"Yeah I'm fine, just tired I guess."

"You didn't manage to sleep on the plane?" He asked giving my hand a squeeze. I just shook my head making him lift my hand to his lips and kiss it.

"Aww my poor Cathy, should we get to the hotel sooner rather than later then you should have time for a nap before our plans." He informed me looking around the corner no doubt for our transport.

"What plans?" I asked trying not to be disappointed that I wouldn't be having the early night I was hoping for.

"I wanted it to be a surprise but I guess knowing will give

you something to look forward too as well." I gave him a smile that for some reason I knew didn't reach my eyes.

"I bought us tickets to a gallery auction." As soon as he finished, I gave him a beaming smile this time I knew reflected back in my eyes and threw myself at him. He laughed as he opened his arms and hugged me back.

"Thank you, that was so thoughtful of you."

"You're welcome ma chérie." I pulled back and looked into his piercing grey blue eyes to see he looked happy. I was just in that moment about to lean in and kiss him when my name was being said from the hotel's entrance. For a brief second I thought it was Draven but then I looked up and saw it was obviously our driver.

My done, finished and dead heart still dropped.

Later on that day I found myself staring around what was to be my new home for the next two weeks in utter awe. Not only was Milan one of the most beautiful cities in the world but it seemed we were now staying in one of the most beautiful hotels in the world as well.

It had a timeless and classical elegance but with a modern twist. There was pale marble that shone like water all throughout the reception with luxurious duck egg blue velvet seating areas dotted here and there. The flower arrangement alone must have cost the same as buying a decent second hand car!

But the shocks just kept on coming when I was informed that my room was in fact a suite. I had asked if Alex would be staying in there with me but found that 'my' suite was one of the few that only had one bedroom. Alex was disappointingly staying in a room on the other side of the hotel and on the bottom floor. This also meant he literally couldn't get any further away from me considering I was on the top floor and with an amazing view of the city at that.

He didn't look happy at all but considering the fact we had been upgraded at no extra cost and were now nearer to the centre of Milan, there wasn't much to complain about. We had always planned to sleep in separate rooms anyway due to his feelings about sleeping together before marriage. But we had booked the rooms next to each other at least.

Well, I had to say that taking in all the splendour that was my hotel suite, I couldn't find myself caring much that Alex was in a different part of the hotel. I felt a little guilty about this but also couldn't supress the naughty giggle that escaped with the thought. Poor Alex, his eyes looked like they would pop out of his head when he saw my room compared to his own. I could only hope that he got over his man paddy by the time we had dinner and the gallery auction tonight.

I was getting excited for the evening ahead, even though I was dog tired from travelling. In fact the sight of the bed was looking more and more tempting. It was a huge four poster bed only it had a feminine oriental feel to it.

The curtains that hung down from the pale wood were a sheer champagne colour that matched the sheets. And then the vibrant splash of colour was crimson red added with the comforter at the bottom and two scatter pillows set diagonally at the top. This was then finished off with rectangles of material hanging in place of a headboard with delicate butterflies in shades of red and gold which were embroidered in silk thread. And it was utterly perfect.

So no longer could I supress the urge as I threw myself backwards onto the bed and landed with a little bounce.

"Mmm heaven," I hummed as I folded my arms behind my head and closed my eyes.

When I opened my eyes again, I knew instantly this time that I was dreaming. The bed I lay in was the same but only now a broken version. The sheer curtains were torn and in tatters. It also looked like someone had splatted them with black paint. I look down and saw it wasn't only the curtains that were shredded as now the covers I lay on were in pieces. It looked as though a wild beast had gone berserk in his dreams and ripped into the bed with his claws.

I sat up cautiously and held my arms around my belly as a gust of wind suddenly blew the curtains horizontal, casting them to look like the flags of a defeated side. I shivered and decided, like with most of my dreams, that I couldn't just sit here and wait for the something to happen around me. No, I knew this was always something that I would have to get up and discover, like it was some kind of test that always faced me in this damaged world.

So I shifted my body to the side and gingerly placed my feet on the floor. I felt the rough floorboards at my feet and frowned as I noticed that the floor too was also splattered with paint. I stood up and raised my eyes slowly to take in the room. It looked like the roof space in an old derelict warehouse or a large loft of some kind. The walls were slanted on one side and were made up of large glass panels that were held there by rusty iron strips. I could imagine that even in the day the windows would barely let in any light as they were so dirty they were milky and fogged.

I turned around and then quickly realised what this was as I took in all the dark passion that had been created. There were literally hundreds of canvases of all different sizes hung and placed around the room in any available space there was. It was obvious my dreams had taken me into the realm of someone's private studio. I had no idea why I was seeing this, like most things my sleeping mind would conjure but if I was to guess I would say it had something to do with tonight at the gallery.

I tried to take in every painting but there were just too many of them. However, one seemed to stand out more than the others and that was because I knew its origins. It was set amongst some of the most violent scenes, which were obviously murder victims seen from the killer's eyes. I knew this as you would see a hand holding a weapon in front of the scene in the background. The weapon was always the same in every picture. It was an elaborately carved wooden dagger whose handle was tear shaped. There were also symbols carved along the length but the only one I could make out was that of a pentagram.

But this one painting was different and not only because I knew what it was and where it was set but because it was the only one of the few that didn't hold the dagger. I slowly crept closer just to make sure my eyes weren't deceiving me but no, there it was, just as the paper had described. It was the massacred campers who had been brutally attacked. To this day the cops still didn't know what had happened and neither did I, not even with my supernatural connections.

So how on earth did something like this end up in my dreams…? What did it all mean exactly? I moved further round the long and open space until what I saw made my hands fly to my mouth so that I could keep in the gasp that escaped. Because like my last dream, I was once again not as alone as I had first thought.

A half-naked man was stood in the centre with his back to me and I had no clue how I had first missed him. He was only wearing paint splattered combats that hung low on his hips and I noticed even his feet were bare. His trousers look like bits had been added to aid in his craft. Hoops at the pockets had small painting trowels hung in them and on the other side a wide leather pocket had too many brushes to count all rammed in there. Also metal belts both thin and thick hung around his waist, wrapped around numerous times.

His bare back looked tight with muscle, but he was more of a slim athletic build. I could also see his hair was cut short at the back and sides with longer ash blonde hair on top in a messy style. Thankfully he seemed too absorbed in the painting in front of him that he was creating to be aware of my presence and giving it the raw anger which I saw was obviously his painting style.

In fact I was just walking backwards a step whist wondering these very things when I stepped into a can of paint, knocking it over with a clatter. As soon as I did this I knew no matter how absorbed an artist might be in their work, there was no missing the echo that bounced around the massive space. I cringed bringing my shoulders up and squinted my eyes as if any of this would help…of course, it didn't.

I opened my eyes just as I saw his head start to turn and I froze, being far too afraid to make any sudden movements. He kind of lifted it up as if first listening out for something as he turned his head in a very predatory manner. I watched transfixed as I was about to get my first glimpse of this disturbed artist and I could only hope that his angry brush strokes didn't reflect his social skills…dream or no dream!

The waiting felt like an eternity but in reality it was probably only seconds. Of course when he finally turned enough for me to see his features I was left with only one impulse and that was to run!

"Oh God!" I screamed out at the sight of his face. At first for the briefest time he had appeared quite handsome, with angular features, giving him a male model look about him. But that had quickly changed in a blink of an eye and at the same time the wind had pounded against the window panes making them rattle. It forced my eyes to the glass and what I saw there slammed me back into the past.

There I found words written everywhere in streaming black ink that elongated the words and in doing so made them more satanic. Words about Demons covered every panel, which in turn cast hellish shadows on the floor, like thin fingers reaching out to grab me and drag me back to where they came from. But these dripping words were the least of my problems for I was still not alone in this demonic studio.

I jumped and screamed again when I looked back at the man and now that of his side view. His skeletal face quickly became a full frontal assault on my fears. It was strange, not like a skull without skin and flesh but more like flesh and skin with bone on top. At a glance you'd have said it had been painted on especially with the black at his nose and all around his eyes.

But when he moved it gave it a translucent effect that kept flashing in and out of his human face. Whatever he was it was scary and it was definitely to be feared which was made even clearer with his all white eyes with their tiny black dot at the centres.

"Ok...time to wake up now, Keira!" I said to myself as I started walking backwards at the sight of him now crossing the loft in long strides. It was only as he got closer that I noticed just how tall he was. It was also at the same time I noticed all the paintings around the space started to shake and vibrate and the need to escape this nightmare was increasing to panic level. So before he could reach me I spun on my heel and was about to make a run for it. However, this might have worked if I hadn't ran directly into the biggest painting in the room, to a point where I had to stumble back.

I barely kept myself standing on two feet as the sight of a full-length portrait dominated any rational part of my brain, for what I was seeing was really the stuff of nightmares. Only it was one I had been seeing for months but also, until this moment not really seeing. The face that I once found so handsome I now found myself wanting to gag in revulsion. It was like a mask of breaking skin held over a void of black where his flesh should have been.

His face held skin that looked like thick parchment paper which was torn in places and curled at the edges. Around his eyes there were gaping holes which were frayed around the tears and the black emptiness circled each piercing eye…eyes I knew so well. But it was his lack of lips that really instilled me with horror.

A slash in the skin ran from under his right eye down to where his lips should have been. The flap then opened up into a large space where his mouth was but again only black nothingness was to be seen lurking like a black shadow. It was as if something was under there, ready to strike true fear in his victims. There was just something about that void that almost hurt to look at, as if it made him even less of a man without the flesh and the blood.

"For the one who carries blood in their veins, is one that can bleed and for one that can bleed, can then… *die.*" These words came from behind me but the voice didn't frighten me like I would have expected. No, if anything it was the opposite as the lulling voice soothed my fears and spoke as if he too wanted to rid the world of this creature. But that was wrong of me…

"It…it can't be…" I muttered no longer caring about the Demon at my back but more now for the painted Demon at my front…

"Alex"

CHAPTER SEVEN

KEIRA

BIDDING NOT BOUGHT THIS TIME

I woke with a start and expected that horrific face to be stood over me. It was unlike anything I had ever seen before and not something I ever wished to see again. I don't know why I had first thought the man in the picture was Alex…that was impossible, wasn't it? For one thing the Nephilim didn't have any other forms of themselves and I knew this for certain as I had got curious in the beginning. It was when Alex had explained he knew I was different and this was because he was also.

It had been a shock hearing what he was and how exactly he fit into the supernatural world, making me feel bad for him at the prejudice he faced from Draven's kind. It was the reason he said that he had shied away from that part of himself. It was not long after this that I had opened my senses to enable me to see any supernatural being in their true form. I think I was a little disappointed for reasons I couldn't explain when I found out he was really no different. If anything there was just this aura floating around him that reminded me of seeing dust floating in the air on a sunny day.

He hadn't made a big deal about who he was and over time I learned that he didn't really much like talking about it. I had hoped he would have opened up more to me in time but so far I was still waiting for it to happen. Maybe this trip would be the time for it. He definitely needed to relax and getting away from his stressful job was never going to be a bad thing. Don't get me wrong, it hadn't been like this since we met but only recently when taking on this new client. I had watched him getting more stressed for the last month and even though he never took his frustrations out on me, you could clearly see that he didn't have the same patience with everyone else.

So for these reasons I never could find it in me to give him a hard time, which only made it all the more embarrassing when Draven found me in the restaurant after Alex left but I tried not to think about that.

"Bloody Hell, Keira you are losing it!" I said out loud and shook my head. It was quite possibly one of the strangest dreams I'd had so far but instead of asking myself who was the Demon painter I was asking myself more about who was the one he painted? It just seemed like the more important question to me and as usual I had only to go with my instincts. However, I knew one thing for sure and that was it most definitely *wasn't* Alex.

I got up and stretched, now more than happy to see the bed was back to being lovely once again. But as I stretched out I kicked something and looked down to see a large black box with a massive black bow attached. I couldn't help but smile at the thoughtfulness of Alex and I jumped up to open it like an excited little girl. I bounced on my knees grinning as I pulled the ribbon that now allowed me to pull off the lid. Whatever was inside must have been expensive from the box alone.

"Oh my." I gasped and my hand flew to my mouth. I then reached out and ran my hand over the delicate black material before pulling it out and holding it up to look at. I then scooted off the bed and went to the full length mirror to hold it up against me by the shoulders. It was so beautiful but not in an overstated way.

The style of dress was an A line that cut across the breasts and came quite a few inches above the knee. It was a thick material similar to taffeta but then on top of that was a fine see through material that was edged with black ribbon. This part continued to the top and cut straight across my collarbone and slightly over my shoulders. The whole of the sheer material was then embroidered with Cornelli Lace in the shape of giant lilies, one of which bloomed over one shoulder like a star.

"Just lovely," I hummed as I lay it gently on the back of a chair. Once I knew it wouldn't slip to the floor I then went back to the box to find simple black shoes to match. However, it was the next item I found that made me blush. Surely this wasn't something Alex would have thought about considering he wouldn't get chance to see it. Well whatever the reasoning behind it I was still smiling at the thought of wearing the exquisite deep purple corset. Although I just wished he had rethought the colour as it was reminding of a certain someone's eyes too much for my liking.

I pulled it out and once again held it up to my body and instantly knew it would be a perfect fit under the dress. I ran my hand down the satin and felt the flat pearls in black that clustered thicker at the bottom and reminded me of black rain drops. It was gorgeous and I smiled at the obvious good taste Alex had for picking clothes for me. Although picking out my underwear did kind of send the wrong message about tonight…I mean was he planning to see these at some point? Especially when seeing the tiny satin shorts to match, which were also encrusted with the black flat pearls. I mean he had even remembered to buy me black gloves to match my outfit and hide my scars at the same time.

The whole outfit was incredibly sexy, and I was suddenly really looking forward to getting ready…

"Oh shit!" I shouted after that thought brought me to actually see what time it was, which was getting later by the second. I quickly whipped off my summer dress and practically ran to the magnificent bathroom at the same time trying to unhook my bra. It was far from a graceful sight, but I was barely going to make it as it was.

So after a mad dash shower where thankfully I didn't need to shave anything I was soon out and waving a hairdryer round my head like a woman possessed. It turned out that just as I was zipping up the side of my dress there was a knock on my door. This was of course after I wasted about fifthteen minutes trying to figure out my corset ties without breaking my spine.

"Coming!" I shouted. I then quickly stepped into my shoes and made sure the side bun I had put my hair into was still in place thanks to the million grips I had stuffed in there.

"Catherine, time is getting on if we're to make dinner." He reprimanded and I frowned at the door thinking he had only been stood out there not even a whole minute yet. I rolled my eyes before plastering on my smile and opening the door to find him stood there looking very dapper in his tux.

"Hello handsome." I said all chirpy and took in his half smile at seeing me in the dress he bought.

"You look breathtaking, Catherine." He told me and I stepped forward to give him a hug. Then I leant up to whisper in his ear,

"Thank you for this, I'm so looking forward to tonight."

And then I turned to kiss him. We had only a moment kissing and I felt the little pinch of disappointment when it was only brief.

"You're most welcome my dear…shall we?" He said giving me his bent arm and playing the part of the perfect gentleman.

"Certainly Mr Cain," I said as I hooked my arm in his and let him lead the way.

The rest of the evening flew by and soon we found ourselves at the gallery auction and I was in my element. Even the meal had gone by without a hitch and thankfully without an oyster in sight. I was even surprised when Alex let me order without making one suggestion as to what he thought I should try. We chatted like we used to in the beginning and I found myself falling for him all over again. In fact it made me feel a little guilty for all the negative thoughts I'd had about him over the last few days.

It wasn't his fault he was under a lot of pressure and it couldn't have been nice dealing with the added worry about my Ex being back in town. I tried to put myself in his shoes and soon realised I had been way too harsh. So now I was snuggling up to his side listening to him as he told me about each artist.

Of course this was me we were talking about so surely when something starts going well something bad is likely to happen. Well this was what I was thinking in the back of my head and I was trying hard to continue being relaxed. I don't know exactly why it was but I just had some strange feeling as though something was coming…something important. It was as if the Fates had flipped some cosmic switch and I could only hope it meant good things for me. Maybe it was Draven's final decision to walk away that had now changed the course of history. Well whatever it was I had a feeling tonight was the start of something new.

"What do you think about this piece?" Alex asked me jarring me out of my fated musings.

"Um?" I made this noise which just made him laugh at me.

"Something on your mind?" He asked and as soon as he did we both turned as there was a bit of commotion at the other end of the gallery.

"I wonder what that is all about?" I asked instead of answering him. I mean I don't know what I could have said other than a lie, which I was rubbish at doing.

"It's probably just some famous person. These types of events always attract a few A listers looking for a photo opportunity."

"I guess," I muttered more to myself.

"So?" Alex asked again and I dragged my eyes from the front entrance I could barely see for all the swarms of people all trying to get a glimpse. I then looked back at the art he was showing me and focused on the giant swirls of colours in front of me that was painted in the shape of an apple core.

"It's beautiful but I have to wonder if the artist liked apples or hated them?" I said thinking the strokes looked quite angry to me.

"You know the apple is very holy and symbolic don't you?" I turned my head and gave him a strange look.

"What, it's true." He said on a laugh and then came closer to me as if he was about to tell me some sacred secret.

"Malus domestica, family to the rose and did you know it was even said that a golden apple actually caused the Trojan War." As soon as he finished I turned round to find him smiling down at me as he knew I loved any of his historical stories. I knew, like Draven, that Alex was a lot older than he looked and also like Draven he wouldn't tell me exactly how old he was. To say it was frustrating was a massive understatement.

"Really?" I said prompting a laugh from him at seeing my enthusiasm.

"Really…ok so it began when the Greek Goddess Eris became very insulted after she wasn't invited to the wedding of Peleus and Thetis. So in retaliation she threw a golden apple into the wedding party. However, this golden apple had been inscribed with the word 'Kallisti' which means the most beautiful one." As he said this he sweetly ran a single finger down my cheek and all this in his French accent was all very appealing.

"What happened next?"

"Well now as I recall, three Goddesses all went ape shit, piled in there to claim the apple, in what I like to think of as a very pornographic sight. Then enters the stupid Paris of Troy picked to appoint a winner, only then to be easily bribed by the horny bitch Aphrodite by shoving the beauty Helen of Sparta in his face. So for once men went to war over a pretty face rather than religion but it was a Goddess from religion that started that war…go figure." The rest of the story didn't come from Alex and through most of it I think my mouth was closer to the floor than on my face! I couldn't stop my reaction as I tore myself from Alex and ran into another man's arms.

"Lucius!"

"Hello my little Keira girl." Lucius said after he caught me. I felt his strong arms encircle my body before he lifted me up and planted a kiss on my nose. I leant back to take in one of the most handsome faces on the planet and it took me back every time I saw it after he was changed that day. The fact was still astounding to know that he was now more like Draven, being both Angel and Demon. I always thought even before The Triple Goddess happened that he looked like some dark avenging Angel. Well it couldn't have been truer than in this moment.

Unlike everyone else Lucius, as usual, wasn't conforming and wearing a Tux, oh no, he was wearing a crisp white dinner jacket with black lapels and a black handkerchief in the pocket. This he combined with a black shirt that was left open at the neck with no tie and a pair of black slacks. His normally unruly hair was for once styled back and he had a sprinkling of honey coloured stubble that went surprisingly well with the look. That was if the look he was going for was Winner of Mr Universe's number one sex God!

"Well you're looking delectable as always pet…tell me, do you still kiss with a passion like the burning sun and does your blood still taste like sin?" He hummed this question and the blood he spoke of bloomed bright on my cheeks.

"Ah still shy, I am pleased." He teased again. I was about to reply with some witty remark that would have caused my brain to high five itself when Alex cleared his throat behind me. It was definitely one of those 'Oh shit' moments that I had been having a lot of lately.

"Uh…Alex, I'm sorry, I wasn't expecting to bump into an old friend," I said turning back to face him and I couldn't say I was pleased to be leaving Lucius' arms this soon.

"Hey, less of the old Sweetheart!" Lucius said placing his hand on the small of my back and leading me back over to Alex. I tried not to notice the way Alex was scowling at where Lucius' hand was and instead gave him what I hoped was a reassuring smile.

"So you're the Demon bastard that managed to ensnare our little Kiera girl um?"

"Luc!" I shouted whipping round to face him in shock.

"Its fine Catherine, I am used to this reception from *his* kind," Alex said remaining calm unlike me.

"And he's French…Jesus Pet, could you have picked anyone worse?" Lucius said laughing and I quickly wasn't feeling all fuzzy about seeing my friend again.

"Stop it!" I hissed stepping away from him and back to Alex's side.

"No wonder the big guy has got his wings in a twist." He said laughing and I opened my mouth ready to give him a piece of my mind again but he beat me to it carrying on,

"So Nephilim tell me, how long exactly have you wished to die?"

"Right that's enough! Lucius, not so great seeing you again!" I snapped as I grabbed Alex and started dragging him off in the opposite direction.

"I must say, I am *not* loving your choice of friends, Catherine." Alex said as we could still hear Lucius laughing.

"See you soon Pet… no doubt when I will be saving your biteable ass yet again!" Lucius shouted not caring in the slightest that people were staring.

"What was he doing here, did you tell anyone about tonight?" Alex asked in an accusing manner.

"No! I didn't tell anyone! It's not like I have a bloody party's worth of friends here Alex. Hell I don't even have one!"

"Fine! Look let's just forget this and move on and hope that no more of your 'friends' turn up out of the blue." The way he said this was so filled with bitterness I was surprised he wasn't spitting venom. I frowned at him, but he ignored me and just walked me further round to a different section of the gallery where another artist's work was being displayed.

Well this night certainly couldn't get any worse I thought pulling up my gloves.

"So that golden apple story…was that really how it ended?" I asked thinking of the only safe way to break the tension.

"Well yes, only your vulgar friend there told it with a lot

less romance." Alex remarked haughtily. He then looked down at me and released a big sigh hopefully when he realised what a moody plonker he was acting.

"I'm sorry, Catherine, I am letting that blood sucking cretin get to me."

"Uh, I know he was rude but I'm not ok with you calling him that." I remarked folding my arms.

"And were you ok with him calling me a Demon bastard?!" He snapped back.

"You know full well I was not or I wouldn't have shouted at him now would I?" After saying this I wanted to stomp away, which turned out to be precisely what I did.

"I think you need time to calm down, feel free to find me when that happens!" I said looking back over my shoulder as my parting line. Then I proceeded to let my anger and frustrations lead me to another part of the gallery.

"Argh!" I shouted stamping my foot in annoyance.

"Nope, still adorable." I growled at hearing his voice and said,

"Yeah well let's see how adorable it is when I put my foot up your ass!"

"Mmm feisty still, just the way I always liked it." This time instead of growling I groaned and then turned to face the troublemaker.

"What do you want Lucius, don't you think you have caused enough damage?" I said seeing him leaning casually on the far wall with his ankles crossed and looking at his nails.

"Does the Nephilim still live?" I frowned and shook my head in confusion before replying,

"Yes of course he does!"

"Then the answer to your question is no, I haven't yet done enough damage." His answer was likely turning me an unattractive rage red but I didn't care.

"How dare you!" I said hitting back and took what I hoped was a threatening step forward. However, when he just pushed off the wall and came right up to me I knew I had been about as threatening as a mouse in a bow tie! This was further proven when he tapped me under the chin and gave me that cocky, bad ass grin of his.

"Chill out Doll, you're the one playing with fire here, I'm just here on orders."

"What?! By who?" At this question Lucius burst out laughing.

"Really?! You wanna ask me who…that bun your hair's in wrapped too tight?" This was when I hit my limit and walked up to him where he now stood and smacked him on the arm.

"Look you big Vampire bully, I asked you who?!"

"Ok fine you wanna play dumb I'll still find it cute, but just so long as you know, you hit like a girl" He said finally losing his smirk.

"That's because I am a girl dipshit, now spill it!" I shouted hitting him again only this time on the other arm.

"Fine Keira *girl*, I am here on orders from the big man himself…there, happy now little miss 'I wanna ignore the obvious'!"

"What!" I shouted as I stared at the unbelievable.

"Wow, he must really have done a number on you." Lucius commented dryly and I couldn't help my response.

"He faked his own death to get away from me." This came out in a quiet voice that sounded as broken as the words would suggest. This was when Lucius' eyes turned soft but thankfully all he said was,

"Yeah I forgot, that sure would do it."

"Yeah, would and did…so Draven really sent you here?" Lucius was once again grinning at the question and I wondered what it was he saw in my face enough to grin about.

"That he did and he is less than happy about the Nephilim situation, Keira but seriously though, what were you thinking, don't you know how dangerous they are?" This question once again had me frowning.

"Alex isn't dangerous…I mean he's an architect for Christ sake, what's he gonna do, draw a building falling down on me?!" I asked sarcastically this time making Lucius roll his eyes.

"Do you not know anything about the Nephilim?"

"I know all I need to know not to make unfair judgements… after all every single person on the planet is able to murder someone if they choose to." I said thinking I was making a good point.

"Yes but not everyone would do so for fun and could with a simple flip of their wrist." Lucius all but snarled back at me.

"Look I am done arguing this point with you, why would Draven give a shit about me being here?"

"Are you being serious right now, I mean we are taking about the same obsessed King of the Supernatural world who has found his Electus?" Ok so it was obvious I wasn't the only one who could do sarcastic.

"Yeah well he made his choice and it couldn't have been clearer when he gave me his back to say goodbye to, so excuse me for being a tad confused right now!"

"Ok look, I never claimed the dude was sane or even that he made the right decisions by you but it is beside the point, as I am in fact here and in me being here clearly shows he still cares for you." Lucius said but this time in a softer tone which instantly caused me to drop the attitude.

"Well I have no idea." I said releasing all my pent up anger and frustrations in a big sigh.

"My guess, and I'm no scholar here, but I would say it's called a Nephilim."

"Yeah it's a good guess." I muttered dejectedly. This was because of two reasons. One was that it was now even more blindingly obvious Draven only landed back in my life because of Alex and two… he was now getting other people doing his dirty work for him!

"So where's my favourite Imp these days?" I asked trying to change the subject to one definitely more colourful.

"Trying to take over the world in the form of planning her own birthday party." Lucius remarked sardonically. I had to laugh at the picture he painted and soon was in fits when he said,

"It's true, you should see what she has poor Percy doing, I think he is rethinking his life as a recluse."

"Poor Percy…how is he these days?" I asked thinking fondly of my little friend.

"Faithful and loyal…oh and of course being Pip's new life size doll he is often wearing street wear and resembling Ruto's relation more each day." This made me smile knowing that he had found the family which he had always wanted and I couldn't have chosen a better one for him other than what was once my own at Afterlife.

"I'm happy to hear that."

"Of course you are." He said smirking and looking at me from the side. I rolled my eyes making him laugh and we quickly fell into a comfortable silence as we stood side by side taking in the world of art around us.

"That's so beautiful." I said as we came to stand in front of one piece that was the epitome of love. It was a painting that almost popped out of the canvas to the point that you felt you could reach out and touch it. It was almost like the artist had actually made what he or she wanted to paint just so they would have something more lifelike to work from.

"I must agree, very striking indeed, given its nature." At Lucius's scepticism I had to laugh again.

"You don't believe in love? Or in the one being made and born to this world just for you alone?" I asked feeling sorry for anyone who didn't believe in love.

"Well now, that's quite a question, considering whose lips it came from."

"That's not an answer, Luc." I replied giving him a look.

"You were such as one born to a single being and yet if you're not the master of your own fates then what is the point but only to taste an addiction before it had chance to take hold?" His answer turned out to be one I didn't care for after all but subtle wasn't in Lucius' nature.

"Well I won't give up on love." I said turning back to the very proof it existed in the world, for if not, where did such beauty really come from. Surely you had to first know love inside you to really recognise it when it hit you. Or was it something you learned with time and mistakes? And if so, what of these two phantom people who were displaying it so freely. What of their story?

The painting was two wired faces of both man and woman that looked as though a cast was made and then the wire was its thickest where they kissed. Only what made the picture so truly captivating was not that they were actually kissing but the way they were kissing. The woman was lay down and the man was kissing her from above only from the opposite angle, so his nose was at her chin and hers at his. Their lips were open but only just whispering their touch against each other. It was as sensual as it was raw but both made for a stunning combination. And I wanted it. In fact I wanted it like I hadn't wanted any other painting before.

"I'm going to buy this."

"Really? Now that will be interesting to watch, if I

remember correctly the last auction you were at you didn't get chance to bid on anything…a little tied up if I recall."

"Ha, ha," I said nudging my arm into his and once again feeling bad for the amount of money he'd had to cough up for me.

"Ha ha indeed, I couldn't even claim on my tax for that one." Now at that I burst out laughing causing a couple next to us to jump.

"Catherine?" I abruptly cut my laughter at the sound of Alex's voice.

"I guess this is goodbye, Lucius." I said leaning up on the tip of my shoes to kiss his cheek.

"Oh it's never goodbye Pet, with you it's only ever until next time." And then he winked at me and after giving Alex a scowl he turned and left with his usual masterful air.

"The Auction has begun." Alex said and held out his hand for me to take. There was no apology but there was no mention of me being found with Lucius either so I focused on that aspect as I walked to him. After a small smile my way he led me to the large open space that had been filled with rows of seats that were filling up. They were white just like the walls and I guessed this was so no other colour got in the way, with the art letting it speak for itself.

Alex grabbed a paddle as they were being given out and I smiled seeing it was the number 77. I could only hope it would be my lucky number considering it was my birthday, the 7th of July.

"You seem very keen, have you seen something you wish to buy?" Alex asked me and I nodded excitedly. However, it was to be short lived as soon my lot was up and it turned out I only managed to afford one bid. I don't know what I had been thinking but there was no way I could afford over four thousand for it and the price was now at forty thousand. I tapped the paddle on my knee in frustration knowing at heart I didn't want anyone else to own the picture.

"I only wish I had the money, ma Cherie." Alex whispered in my ear and I turned to kiss him on the cheek for being sweet. Then there was a load of commotion coming from the back of the room.

"Do we have a new bidder on this piece?" The auctioneer shouted. I shifted in my seat like most people did but I was the only one that gasped out loud. For there was my nightmare and wildest dream combined stood like the master of the universe in a black tux.

"Draven?" I said as a stupid question to my own mind and I think if it could have slapped me it would have also said, 'Yeah no shit, keep up bitch'. I shook my head like this would help and when I refocused on the man in question that was when I also noticed Lucius standing next to him. He first nodded to the picture then said something to Draven leaning in with that damn smirk of his. Lucius then pulled back, found my eyes in the crowd and winked at me before slapping Draven on the back as he left.

This was when everything happened at once. Draven's paddle went up, he then shouted a number I missed and the auctioneer shouted,

"Sold to the highest bidder of the night, paddle number seven."

I numbly turned back to face Alex to see his furious face and made it even worse when I asked,

"How much?" The look he shot me was disbelief mixed with hatred but still he answered and therefore letting me know the reasons behind this look.

"Seventy-seven thousand."

CHAPTER
TWENTY-ONE

KEIRA

PAINTED DEMONS

I couldn't believe it. No, actually there were levels to what I was seeing and couldn't believe. Level one would have been sending Lucius here in the first place. What did he think exactly, that in the hour he wasn't here something might have happened? Then there was level two which included that fact that the man who had only yesterday stormed out of my life was now in fact here and now evidently doing his own dirty work again. But then there was level three and this was the one I was stuck on the most…

Why buy that damn painting?!

Was he making a statement and if so, what was it exactly? All of these thoughts bombarded my mind in the seconds it took for the auctioneer to write down his number and move on to the next lot. However, in these turbulent seconds my mind had to process, it took Draven the same time to find me in the crowd.

This was when I stood up making a bit of a ruckus ready to storm over to him and demand what he was playing at exactly.

"Ah the lady in the black dress, your number Miss?" My eyes locked with Draven and the bastard had the audacity to raise an eyebrow and grin at me. I think he must have seen the panic drain my face of all colour and in this he found something to amuse him! I made sure to give him my best 'I am going to kill you Mister' look before turning sheepish eyes back to the auctioneer.

"Uh...sorry, I was...uh..." Think Keira damn it! The loo... yes, say the loo!

"She was coming to me." Draven spoke up and it was one of those voices that just dared anyone to not only deny his claim but brave speaking against it. I was not surprised when no one said a word.

"I will be right back." I said between clenched teeth and started to sidewalk past all the people sat down to get out and thus proving just how ungraceful this Scouser can really be.

"Sorry...oh...sorry again." I said all the way along until finally I was free. All the while Draven stood there casually waiting and with a hand failing to hide half a smirk behind his fingers. I was surprised I didn't snap my heels with the force of angry stomping I was doing.

"Come with me!" I hissed as I grabbed his forearm roughly and I was thankful when he let me drag him away. I kept looking round for a place that was void of any people as I didn't need an audience for verbally kicking demon butt!

"You know if you want to get me truly alone it can quickly be arranged." Draven said in a tone that left me dumbstruck. So much so that I let him go and leaned forward to whisper in disbelief,

"Are you flirting with me?" To which he laughed.

"I must certainly be losing my touch if you need to ask that." He replied and once again he was actually flirting!

"I'm sorry but I must know…*have you lost your ever-loving mind?!"* I asked once again leaning forward like this would somehow help in getting my point across. He too leaned forward but when he did it, he had to dip his head to get to my level. Once there he too whispered,

"I believe a better term is, losing my ever-loving *heart."* At this I reacted the only way my body and heart knew how to…*I gasped.*

"Is this some cruel joke?" I asked after a minute of being locked by his eyes and trying in vain to find my answers there. As soon as I said it his eyes got soft and then he looked truly regretful.

"No, it most certainly is *not."* He replied after a pause I knew helped to get his emotions in check.

"You bought my painting." I said pointing out the obvious.

"It's a beautiful painting." Hearing the way he said this made me bite my lip to keep it from quivering.

"It's love." I added for no particular reason.

"It is and I remember what it tasted like." Draven said which ignited the thundering in my heart to start its heavy base. Also his comment reminded me of what Lucius had said about love. Something about what was the point of tasting an addiction before it's given the chance to really begin.

"I…" I didn't know what I was going to say exactly but Draven beat me to it.

"About yesterday…"

"It's fine, let's just forget about it." I said interrupting him and not at all comfortable with where this was going.

"Hurting you is never fine with me."

"Then you came all this way to say sorry?" I asked and this

time I was trying my best to keep my voice from cracking and giving away exactly what his words meant to me.

"You know I didn't," he said, and I sighed letting him know I was getting tired of his rollercoaster ride.

"I know you didn't, Draven but unfortunately I also know why you did." That got me a raised eyebrow but before he could comment Alex was by my side making Draven snarl.

"I would say what a coincidence at seeing you here, but I think we all know that would be a lie." Alex said wrapping his arm around my waist and suddenly Draven looked as though he was three breaths away from committing murder.

"Yeah okay, I am so not doing this again!" I snapped pulling from Alex and stepping away from the both of them. One of the main reasons for doing this was because I could no longer stand to see Draven's eyes locked to where Alex was touching me, and I wasn't cruel enough a person to let him see me like that. So I turned my back to them both and started walking away.

"Catherine?!"

"Keira?!" They both shouted at the same time, but I just flipped them both the bird without looking back. I was so sick of this! I just wanted both of them to decide what it was they wanted and let me get the Hell on with my life! First Alex with his mood swings and blaming me for shit Lucius said to him. But mainly it was Draven. Bloody Draven and his cryptic bullshit! Well I had already decided when I saw him walk away for the last time yesterday that it would be it for me and now this was me walking away proving it.

I kept walking round and down the corridors until the main part of the pictures on display for the auction started to thin out. Also the lighting in this part wasn't as bright which made me stop and turn, knowing I had gone too far from the main event. I was just about to start on back, hoping that I wouldn't be returning to body parts and Draven stood amongst the remains of my boyfriend when a noise stopped me.

"A piano?" I muttered to myself as I turned back to face the music. It was another one of those situations that I really knew I should be bitch slapping my curiosity into submission and marching my behind back to safety. But did I do that, of course not. What I did do was follow the haunting sound further down the corridor and right to the closed door at the end. It was much darker here now so you would have thought with the eerie music combined it would have been enough to make me realise this wasn't a good idea.

So why was I reaching out for the door handle? Because it was like something was pulling me and it wasn't just my curiosity this time. No it was something much more than that and the word 'need' was tightly knitted to that reason. I knew it was an irrational feeling, even as my hand started to pull the handle down and I felt the door give.

I quickly had one last look behind me to make sure no one was there and I half expected someone to coming shouting at me in Italian at any minute. However, when I saw it was all clear I knew there was no other reason to back out now, so I went on inside.

It turned out that this room was some type of storage room or small warehouse for where they obviously stored the art. I still heard the piano playing somewhere so I knew I wasn't alone. The thought should have scared me but strangely enough it didn't.

"I know you're in here, girl." A voice said and I tried to place it, almost like I had heard it in my past from some time I couldn't place.

"Uh…yeah, sorry I was just looking for…"

"I know what you're looking for." The male voice said cutting me off. I frowned in the dim lighting and said,

STEPHANIE HUDSON

"And what's that?"

"You're looking for answers," he said quite offhandedly.

"I am?" I replied with a nervous laugh.

"Yes, but you won't find any, not until you start asking the right questions." This time I actually groaned out loud, no longer caring if the voice thought me rude.

"Yeah right, give me a break."

"You like Demons, little girl?" The voice asked and the amusement could easily be detected in his voice.

"I...I don't know what you mean." I said only stumbling verbally in the beginning. The voice didn't answer me but instead I heard the sound of a large switch being flipped before the section I was stood in lit up. There was a few hanging lantern shaped lights that hung from the high ceiling but I could tell not all of them were turned on. So I turned to the wall as there was obviously something he wanted me to see.

"Oh my," I said holding my hand to my face as I took in the painting before me. It was nothing like I had ever seen before and was a combination of a black and white photograph, paint and words crudely scratched into the finished canvas. In fact, if the words hadn't gone with the piece so well, I would have said it had been vandalized.

The black and white picture was of two lovers embraced and entwined in peaceful sleep. The bed in which they lay had an ocean painted beneath it which looked so serene and calm. Yet it was the faces of the people that had been painted over in such a way you could see both how they looked before and how they would have looked as demons.

There were slanted slashes in their eyes, mouth and nose and the writing was reflected on the sheets that covered them. It bounced off the wall behind their bed where it had been scratched into the actual canvas. And it read...

*'Monsters don't sleep under your bed,
But they sleep happy inside your head.'*

I shuddered at the thought but more like the memories of so many nightmares I had witnessed in my life, this was something I knew to be true. I was about to speak when another switch was flipped, and I stepped further into the room to see the next painting. It too was in the same style as the one before it, only this time it was a picture of two lovers on their knees holding one another in a tight hug. It had also been taken in the form of an x ray so only their bones were showing. The background was a hospital room and behind them showed the same picture on a lit white board. Only unlike the main picture of the two, all the bones were broken in the background with the bloody words…

*'Sometimes I wrestle with my demons,
Sometimes we just snuggle.'*

"Ok, so I am seeing a trend here," I said thinking the one Draven bought was the crowning jewel compared to all these morbid tales of woe. As soon as I said this the piano playing stopped and it was in a way as if he had just placed both his palms down on as many keys at once.

"Demons come in many forms but sometimes it takes others to push people into *really* seeing them and the unknown pain they inflict." The voice said and suddenly I wasn't feeling so great about my little exploring.

"So you're a demonic artist?" I asked hoping that question could go either way in case I was talking to a human.

"Amongst many things." He said and I heard the sound of a chair being pushed back against the stone floor.

"Ok…well…uh…it was nice chatting to you I guess but I'd better go…people will be looking for me." I added this last part in the hope that this wouldn't turn into one of those slasher movies and any minute a knife was gonna come bursting out of one of those paintings. Well that would certainly make me the stupid blonde who ended up getting chased and knowing me the clichéd tripping over would definitely happen.

"Until you're ready to be pushed, Girl" The mystery man said and this time it was so much closer to me that I screamed out,

"Ahhh!" Then I spun round and ran straight into someone.

"Hey?!"

"Alex?" I said out of breath from fright and as soon as I said his name all the lights in the storeroom came on with a loud bang. I actually thought it sounded like a fuse had blown but all the lights were still on. I turned slowly now in Alex's arms and gasped. There must have been hundreds of paintings all like the two I had been shown, meaning Alex and I were now surrounded by hundreds of Demons.

"Oh God!" I said in shock. I stepped further back into Alex and his grip tightened on the top of my arms until it was almost painful.

"Who was in here with you?!" Alex suddenly demanded angrily.

"Uh...I..."

"WHO?" He roared from behind me and at the sound of him getting so angry I tore myself from him. I turned to face him and the rage I found there was so out of character I took a step back. This was a side of Alex I had never seen before and it twisted his features into something ugly.

"No one! I was in here alone." I snapped back and for once it didn't sound like a lie. It was more like a determination to protect someone I didn't know but more importantly I had no idea why? I couldn't help but feel like it was the right thing to do, which only left me feeling more confused about this weird situation I had put myself in.

"You're sure?" He asked, this time a bit calmer but the damage had already been done, so when he took a step towards me I took one back. A flash of anger made him frown but then he quickly masked it by then turning regretful.

"Catherine I am sorry, I didn't mean to snap at you like that, only I was worried. I couldn't find you and when I found you here you looked so terrified, I was angry at the thought of someone scaring you that's all." He said and he seemed so sincere that I now took a step closer to him.

"Its fine, you just scared me when you shouted and with all these paintings..." I didn't need to say more as Alex took me in his arms and whispered the rest of his apologies in my ear. Then he said the only words I needed to hear right then,

"Let's go." I smiled and nodded by his shoulder. He then reached down and took my hand to lead me from the room. I looked back one last time and tried not to react to what I was seeing. My mouth dropped in the face of the man now standing at the far end of the room stood in front of one of his biggest paintings.

His face was half hidden with a hood that was covered in straps hanging down. His trousers were the same as before, but the tight long-sleeved top was black with the same straps crisscrossing his torso that were hanging from the hood. He was looking down at the floor and my eyes followed to see words in shadow were stretching out at me like fingers.

> *'See him, See me,*
> *See the Devil, See all three.'*

My eyes snapped back up to him and I saw he was now looking at me smiling. I then watched as he raised his hand to his lips and placed a single finger over his mouth to indicate my silence. This all played out in slow motion as I was still being dragged away and I nodded to the man who I had now seen for the second time that day. Once in life and once in my dreams, only he wasn't the only reassurance to happen to me this day.

I was just about to be pulled from this place through the door when the man nodded once and moved from in front of the painting. I had to put my fist to my mouth to bite down on to stop from crying out as I took in its horror for the second time…

My Demon Alex.

CHAPTER TWENTY-TWO

KEIRA

SEVENTY SEVEN REASONS

I let Alex pull me from the room and as soon as the door closed behind us I let myself believe it was all in my head. Had that guy even really been there? And if so, then what was going on in my mind? Why was I dreaming about this guy and what was he talking about me really seeing? There were once again just too many questions and not enough answers to deal with.

"You're sure you were alone in there?" Alex asked again looking back at me and it was starting to look like he was a bit paranoid. Only was it still classed as paranoia if in fact he had been right in thinking I hadn't been alone? Well whatever the answer, it still didn't change mine.

"I'm sure." He looked at me as if assessing the truth for a second and then nodded once. I must have been getting better at this lying business I thought wryly as we made it to the end of the corridor.

"I think I'm good now, Alex." I said nodding down to where he still had his hand gripping the top of my arm.

"Oh," was his response and it was as if he hadn't realised until then that he was still holding on to me.

"I'm sorry, I guess finding you alone and frightened is just playing on my mind." I smiled at him and peeled away his fingers hoping there wouldn't be a bruise tomorrow as that was the last thing I needed a certain someone to see.

"Its fine, I was silly wandering off."

"Yes you were, but I understand your frustrations…you weren't expecting him were you?" Alex asked and I could tell he was trying not to let that question sound accusing.

"Of course not," I said and in turn trying not to let my answer sound like snapping.

"Right."

"And what is that supposed to mean?" I asked folding my arms and unable to resist the urge to cock out my hip to one side.

"Nothing…look, let's just get out of here, I think this night has been ruined enough for us, don't you?"

"Fine!" This time I didn't care about snapping and just walked past him knowing that he followed. I didn't see Draven as I was making my way to the entrance and for once I was happy about it. I didn't want to give him the satisfaction that it was obvious Alex and I were fighting. After all, there would have been little doubt as to why or more like *who* we were arguing over.

When we both reached the street I left it up to Alex to shout a taxi over and after a few tries we finally got one. I was just bending down to get in when I noticed a blacked-out Rolls Royce that looked very similar to the Phantom we drove in that one time. It didn't take a genius to know who that held inside and as I scooted over to the other side I watched as it went past slowly. I quickly sucked in a breath when the passenger window started coming down and Draven's worried expression was all I could see. He then went out of sight and by the time Alex got in beside me I still had my eyes closed.

"Still angry?" I resisted the urge to roll my eyes and instead turned to look at him. What could I say? I mean the guy had tried everything tonight to give me something special and because of my past it had been one thing after another. He had bought me this dress, shoes and all what lay beneath it. He had taken me for a beautiful and romantic dinner and then to a gallery simply because he knew how much I loved art. In theory it should have been the perfect evening. So surely the guy could be forgiven for getting a little pissed off when my past shows up to bite us both in the ass…right?

"Only with myself." I found myself saying.

"Why?"

"Because it was the people from my past who turned up tonight that ruined it for you but for what it's worth, I still had fun." And that was the truth, however I just didn't want to delve too deeply as to why. For starters I would then have to fully admit the pounding of my heart when seeing Draven again or what his words had meant to me, no matter how confusing.

"Then that makes me happy to hear."

———

The rest of the journey back to our fancy new hotel was mainly taken in silence but at least now we had cleared the air it was comfortable. It didn't take us that long and soon we were seeing one of the most beautiful sights I believed in all of Italy. The Duomo, Cathedral of Milan.

"It's stunning," I said on a sigh and Alex chuckled next to me before saying,

"It has a haunting beauty at night I think." Of course, he was right, it did have a haunting beauty. It dominated the open square and with its many spires looked as though it was reaching to the sky and trying to touch Heaven. The lights surrounding it illuminated it in such a way that it almost looked painted against the black canvas of the night.

"Can we go see it tomorrow?" I asked as the car came to a stop not far past the centre.

"We will have to see, I was supposed to being in a meeting tomorrow regarding this new account."

"Oh." I said feeling dejected.

"Maybe another time or you're welcome to explore on your own." Oh goodie I felt like saying but instead I said,

"Yeah, I should do that." Then I got out of the car hoping he missed my sarcasm.

"What's wrong?" Ok, so maybe he *didn't* miss it.

"Nothing," I muttered and as we walked through the lavish reception I had an idea.

"Come with me." I whispered and pulled Alex along to the elevators.

"But I am on this floor."

"I know, just trust me, I wanna have some fun." I said giving him a playful wink. I dragged him in the lift and pressed the floor to go down.

"Catherine, down there is the gym and spa." Again I gave him a cheeky grin and said,

"Yeah, I know." And down we went.

"You know it's going to be closed at this time of night." I ignored Alex's worries and waited excitedly until the lift came to a stop. I then had to pull him out and I looked up to see the marble archway that had a metal sign in script writing,

'Spa Sensuale'

"Spa Sensual" Alex read the sign and my first thought was…perfect! So I pulled him through the arch with an exaggerated tug and looked round to find it empty.

"See it is closed, let's go." I laughed and ran away from him, thanking the fact that there was at least some light still on. You couldn't see much but enough to know the large open space held what I had been looking for. So I reached round and unzipped my dress, letting it fall to my feet.

"Catherine! What are you doing?" Alex hissed as if I was committing the biggest crime this side of Italy.

"What does it look like I'm doing?" I said hoping to sound seductive enough to get him to at least play along. After all, this was supposed to be a romantic trip away and so far all we had done was bicker.

"It looks like you're doing something stupid." He reprimanded and this made me turn to see he was in fact scowling at me. I frowned pulling down my gloves and kicking off my shoes before thinking my new favourite saying, 'oh to Hell with it!' Then I said,

"No, I am about to do something fun!" And then took a running jump and did a cannon ball into the pool. I couldn't help but smile under the water at the fact it was heated but when I rose to the surface, I soon lost my smile.

"I refuse to deal with this!" Alex was saying as he walked away.

"Alex! Where are you going?!" I shouted after him but he just continued on until he was out of sight.

"Fine! You were a killjoy anyway!" I shouted knowing he couldn't hear me but at least it made me feel better. I mean what was his problem? It wasn't as if they would chuck us out of the hotel, the worst I would surely get would be someone coming in here telling me it's closed. Jesus but it was sometimes like dating a choir boy!

I just shrugged my shoulders and turned my back on the lit entrance. It would have been nice to have seen all the room as the water looked quite eerie and black without enough lighting, but I was in here now, so I was going to make the most of it. Of course, I was going to look a little obvious trying to get back to my room with ringing wet hair but thankfully I had spotted a large amount of towels as we came in so at least there was that.

I had to say swimming in a corset was definitely a first for me and not the easiest feat at that. But there was also something very sexy about the way it clung even tighter to my skin when wet. I swam over to the side and decided to pull the pins from my head to free my hair from its confining side bun. I was just glad my feet could touch the bottom at this end as there were so many pins I would have probably have got cramp from treading water for that long.

Once my hair was down I swam back into the middle and dived under the water. Then something bad happened. I had been busted! It was when I was still underwater that someone had suddenly flipped the lights on and I could now see the soft glow lit all around the pool. If I hadn't needed to breathe I would have both said 'Oh Shit' and stayed under there hiding. But of course I was human so, I had little choice.

"Hello Love."

"Draven!" I shouted in utter shock at seeing him here.

"Keira." He said my name with a grin he didn't try and hide, unlike me when I couldn't stop my arms from crossing over my breasts that were nearly spilling over my underwear.

"What are you doing here?!" I screeched moving further away from where he stood casually against one of the marble pillars. He was still wearing his tux and the last time I had seen one on him was when he took my virginity, making me shudder with the intense memory.

"I must say sweetheart that you have developed quite the knack for breaking and entering…tell me Love, is this a new hobby of yours?" He teased ignoring my question and pulling his bow tie free.

"I hardly think this constitutes as breaking and entering, Draven, it's an open archway not Fort Knox." I said frowning.

"That's true… no warehouse fire escapes to pull down, no ivy ladders to scale, no fences to climb or villas to scope out… I think you see where I am going with this." He said after taking off his suit jacket and now he was undoing the buttons of his shirt. I thought he was going to stop at the neck but oh no, he wanted to try and give me heart failure and carried on going.

"Er…what are you doing?" I said as his cufflinks dropped to the floor without him touching them. His shirt quickly followed, and I watched open mouthed as he threw it casually on top of his jacket. I tried not to notice all those lickable muscles but one thing I couldn't ignore was the two bands of leather that I knew covered the scars that he always kept hidden.

"Isn't it obvious?" He asked smirking and I snapped my mouth shut just so that I could swallow the pebble sized lump that went down like hot coal. I shook my head letting the wet strands part and one stuck to my cheek. This made his smirk deepen to a one sided grin as his hand went to the fastening on his trousers.

"I'm becoming an accomplice." He finished at the same time as unsnapping his pants.

"Ohh my…oh dear…ok, ok…umm…" I started making all these noises in response to seeing him getting naked and I had to quickly turn around before I passed out and drowned. I heard his deep laughter behind me before I heard the splash. I needed to get out of here…like in a big friggin way!

I started to make my way to the other side, wading through the water to get there quicker but was stopped when an arm quickly wrapped around me from behind.

"Hey you, where do you think you're trying to swim off too… um?" He said all this with his lips at my ear and the feel of his rippled muscles at my back had me close to drooling.

"Uhh…" Was the only sound my brain could muster up my body into making. I looked around the room trying to focus on anything other than the desire blooming within me, pushing against the barriers I had put into place. Of course, one look at the room and I knew I was in trouble. Let's just say there was a reason it was called Spa Sensual!

The large room was made to feel so intimate with its low ceilings and ambient lighting in blues and muted orange and pinks. All the lights were directed at the walls and some twisted iron artwork that also doubled as a water feature. The sound of water trickling along different materials like metal and glass added that gentle sound in the background that was needed to cover the pounding of my heart. Then there was the marble loungers running along one wall and the whole place reminded me of some kind of harem, as I could just see naked beauties spread out seductively, trying everything to entice the King at my back. But wait…where did that vision just come from? It was so real, like a flash of the future.

"Well at least breaking into here I didn't have to worry about you breaking this pretty little neck." He hummed as he tantalisingly ran his fingertips up and down the length of it. This was the point that a moan escaped, and he growled behind me quickly making me forget any vision. Luckily it was also the moment that I came to my senses and tried to pull myself from him. Although this was Draven we were talking about, so it didn't exactly go to plan, as in, not at all. No, instead of me getting my own way his arms tightened across me and the fingertips that were exploring became a full hand at my neck, holding me immobile.

"Tut tut Keira, I think you know by now how I feel about you leaving my arms." This made me frown and find my anger through the heavy weight of lust that was also infecting my mind.

"Actually I know exactly how you feel about leaving *me* as you have done it often enough."

"Ah there she is." He said ignoring my pissed off tone altogether.

"Let me go, Draven." I demanded and I felt him sigh behind me before he granted me my wish. I pushed away and turned to find both his arms outstretched as if making a show of letting me go.

"You can't just do this whenever you feel like it."

"Do what exactly?" He asked raising an eyebrow and folding his arms across his naked chest. The action caused his biceps to bulge and now there was no material hiding them I felt my mouth go dry at the sight. There was that delicious line from the rounded and defined muscle of his massive shoulders that cut into the powerful force of his arms. It shamefully made me want to lick the length of it.

"You can't just come flying back into my life when it suits you, then walk away, leaving me with nothing but a load of cryptic shit to deal with and a messed up hea…head afterwards." I said and thankfully caught myself before I said the word heart instead of head.

"I'm not going anywhere this time, Keira." I couldn't help but laugh at this.

"Yeah right…whatever! Look you wanna be friends then that's fine, it won't be easy but I think I can do it, but we will never be anything more, not again, do you understand?" I asked trying to sound firm, but it was getting harder when he kept stalking closer to me. I hadn't even really realised it until now, but I had been moving backwards. So how I was shocked when my back hit the side of the pool I didn't know.

"Uh…so…do you…understand that is?" I asked as he came at me to the point where I had to tip my head right back to say this. Both his arms came to rest either side of me, gripping the edge of the pool and I knew this was Draven's way of saying you're not going anywhere and effectively caging me in.

"You want to be friends then that's what we will be." He said this in a way that sounded far too friendly to be classed in the same realm of 'Just friends'.

"Well, alright then." I said filling the void with something that didn't need to be said but helped mask my nervousness anyway. Well ok, given the look Draven just gave me he knew I wasn't masking diddly squat but thankfully he didn't have to say anything other than with his cocky grin.

"I must say *friend*, if I thought you looked exquisite in your dress earlier then now I think you look like Heavenly sin in the rain." Draven said and I had to bite my lip to stop myself from saying something stupid or more like… *dangerous.* However, Draven took this silence as an advantage to continue with whatever game he was playing with me as he first leant forward and said,

"You're blushing Keira, any reason for that?" So I did the only thing I could and that was escape. I quickly ducked under his arm going under the water and swam away to the deeper end. I was left trying to stand up on my tiptoes before I knew I would be treading water.

"I don't think you have had many girlfriends…I mean… girls that are friends that is…you know what I mean…like before." I said stumbling around the words.

"Are you suggesting that I don't know how to behave?" He asked and I knew it was another tease.

"Oh I *know* you don't know how to behave, that's my point." I said in reply laughing and once again watching as he stalked me through the water.

"Then educate me."

"Yeah right, isn't that like teaching an old dog new tricks?" I said now teasing him back and not being able to help the compulsion.

"Well this old dog responds well to petting if that helps." At this I burst into a fit of giggles and threw my head back.

"I'm starting to think you might have a behaviour disorder, Draven" I said but finished it with a little yelp when I saw how close he now was again.

"What me?" He said and before I could register what he was doing by leaning to one side, I just felt a hand shackle my ankle and pull. I went under the water with a gasp and came back up immediately when he gripped my waist and lifted me back to the surface.

"Oh no, now you have gone and done it!" I said after pushing the hair from my face and then launching myself at him trying to take him down. I wasn't sure whether it was all my weight being thrown against him in my surprise attack or whether he in fact just let me take him down but we both went under, with me on top of him. I didn't miss the way he kept his eyes open under the water as I did or the way he was smiling in a way that mirrored my own daft grin.

We both came back up for air but I knew only one of us needed it.

"And you think I have behaviour problems." He said pushing all his wet hair back with one large hand. I was just thankful I didn't start spluttering at the sight. In fact all he was missing was a waterfall and him throwing his head back to some cheesy nineties track…I had something like Mysterious Girl by the endearing Peter Andre in mind.

"Keira, you're chuckling again and I have no clue why." On hearing this I stopped and bit the bottom part of my smile.

"And now she blushes…I have no hope." When he said this I couldn't resist and put both my hands together and pushed water in his face, splashing him. I ended up giggling again when his hair flopped down in front of his face and I could just see as he lifted an eyebrow at me. This was when I started moving backwards again smirking.

"Now, now Draven, play nice." I warned in vain.

"Just remember sweetheart, you started this war." And this was my only warning before he was at me and lifting my body in the air to then throw me back into the water. I went under like a sack and came up gasping to find him laughing.

"Oh you are so going down!" I warned pushing my hair back like he had done, and the play fight began. I wasn't sure how long this went on for but it only stopped when I was gasping for air from both laughter and exertion.

"Ok, ok! You win…you win." I said as he had my wrists gripped tightly in his hands.

"Of course I do," he said being cocky. I rolled my eyes and tried to pull my hands from his hold, but he wouldn't let me. I gave him my wide eyes in question as he walked us both backwards into the deeper end.

"I can't stand up here." I said now relying solely on Draven to keep me afloat. He leant his face closer to mind and whispered,

"Oh, I know."

I was left treading water but after our 'fight' my legs felt like jelly and really weren't up for the task. I think Draven must have felt me flagging because he started holding up all my weight with his hands.

"I think somebody could do with a little pick me up." He said and for one shocked moment I thought he meant his blood.

However, this panic only lasted for a second before it was consumed with another one. He suddenly let go of my wrists but before I could go under he had both my thighs in his hands and he spread my legs at the same time moving flush in between them. Then he wrapped my legs around his waist and my instincts kicked in to grab onto his shoulders.

"Much better." He commented looking intently down at me.

"Uh…I think at least one of us should point this out as I don't think you will but…"

"But?" Draven said getting closer to my lips.

"But…this isn't exactly being *friendly.*" I whispered the last word as I continued to trace his movements as they got even closer. It was only when his own lips hovered over my own did he respond with,

"I disagree…I believe this is me being *very friendly.*" And with that he only had barely a centimetre to go when…

"Mi scusi, non puoi essere qui!" I felt Draven's growl vibrate up his chest and he looked far too reluctant to turn his head from mine. It was as if our eyes locked in some silent battle and it was only when I saw the flames of Hell staring back at me did it pull me back from his hold. Draven growled low again and then turned his head to face the security guard who had a flashlight on us.

Then the bulb popped and went out, which I knew Draven had done. The guard jumped at the sound and after hitting the end of it a few times promptly gave up.

"Il centro benessere è chiuso Signore, tu e tua moglie ha bisogno di lasciare" The guard said, and I whispered to Draven,

"What did he say?"

"That we need to leave" Draven sounded about ready to commit murder and even more so when I started to struggle to get off him.

"Lasciaci!" ('Leave us' in Italian) Draven barked and the guard stepped closer as if to get a good look at him.

"Mr Draven! Oh, me sorry Signore, I not know." I pulled my face away further to see Draven grimace as if he had been caught out, which of course he had.

"And why would he know you exactly?" I asked folding my arms but Draven still had hold of my legs around his waist. He let out a sigh before saying,

"Go, now!" To which the guard quickly nodded his head and almost ran out of the room. Then Draven walked us through the water and when we got to the edge he hoisted me up and onto the side with little to no effort. I got to my feet at the same time Draven lifted himself from the pool. If I wasn't so angrily preparing myself for what I was about to hear, then I would have definitely taken the time to admire the lust worthy sight.

"So?" I said after Draven remained silent. I watched as he walked over to grab two big white bath towels and came back to me to wrap my body up in one before he answered,

"I own the hotel."

"What!?" I shouted making him for once look contrite.

"You own the hotel...this hotel?!"

"Yes."

"Of course you do...Jesus I am so stupid! I should have known they wouldn't have just upgraded us like that!" I ranted turning my back to him, walking away and then storming back again. I wrapped the towel so tight and tucked it in around the top of my breasts before carrying on.

"So you planned all this?"

"I wanted you close, yes." At his answer I shook my head and then as a thought entered my head I had to ask quickly,

"How close?"

"I have the suite next door to yours."

"Oh…My…God…oh my god! Oh my god, Draven!" I shouted and then added,

"Does your level of crazy know no limits?" To which the bastard actually laughed.

"Keira, come now, are you really so surprised?"

"That you would pull this kinda crap, no! That you would even bother too…then yeah I am!" I said being honest and I hated myself for loving the way his eyes got soft when I would reveal my true feelings.

"Look just forget it! I'm going back to my room now or should I say *your* room Mr I Own The Damn Hotel!"

"Keira, don't be like this." He said and once again after I had stormed past his arms were around me from behind not letting me leave.

"You're making this a habit." I said in response to being captured again.

"And it will continue to be one if you are insistent that you want to leave."

"Let me go." I asked only now being this close and feeling his arms around me I could feel myself losing the fight.

"I will but not in the way you think." He said in my ear.

"And what is that supposed to mean?"

"You will find out soon but first, let me dry you so you can put your pretty dress back on." Damn him but I hated when he used logic against me.

"Fine!" I snapped and I tried not to wince at how childish I sounded. However Draven just chuckled and before I could come up with a witty response I felt his hands start to rub along my arms before dropping down to my sides. I started to feel the warmth he created and in no time at all I found myself dry. Even my hair was back to how it was before I had put it up for the evening.

"There now." He muttered and then peeled away my towel

307

leaving me standing there in just the corset and underwear. I hadn't been self-conscious before when my anger was in full flow. However having him standing there in just his tight underpants that clung wet to him and the obvious bulge that he shamelessly didn't even try to hide on full view I felt like I might self-combust.

"Like what you see?" He asked on a laugh and I mentally scolded myself for openly gawking.

"That was never the issue." I threw back and turned to pick up my dress but couldn't find it.

"Looking for this?" I snatched it off him and annoyingly made him chuckle again.

"Allow me." He said when I started to fumble with my zip.

"It's alright, I can do it."

"Yes you can, but I will be doing so for my pleasure." He then knocked my hands away gently and with one hand holding my hip the other slowly zipped me back up. Once finished his hands then came to rest on my shoulders.

"I saw this dress and knew I had to see you in it but when I saw the underwear I just knew I had to see you without the dress." Draven said seductively and I sucked in a shocked breath as his words hit home.

"You bought it for me?!" I hissed not truly wanting to believe it.

"I bought it for you and for me."

"Oh God…you really are crazy," was my only response,

"Crazy for something, yes." His response made me close my eyes and my head fell back onto Draven's chest.

"This is insane." I muttered mainly to myself, giving my mind a few seconds to play catch up with my heart. When it did I pulled myself from Draven and said,

"I have to go…thank you for the dress."

"I will walk you to your door." He said taking a step towards me.

"No, no, it's fine...please don't." And then I turned and practically ran out of there as if being chased by my Demons. It was only when I was in the lift, rising back up to the top floor that I finally let myself lose it. I mean what was all of that?! The whole evening was messing with me but it was back down in the pool that really played with my heart. All the flirting and the playing was something I could put down to natural between us I guess but what about all the hidden meanings to the things he said...what of those? Or what if what was really going on was Draven was so obsessed with keeping me safe that he was now down to playing his last card?

The door opened and it was only when they started to close again that my hand shot out to stop it. I numbly slipped passed the door and as I walked to my door I couldn't help but think I might be on to something with Draven's new behaviour. What if he was trying to get me once again to fall for him. Playing this whole thing a new angle just to get me away from Alex and promising me something he knew I still wanted...*him.*

Would that then mean as soon as Alex was out of the picture or as soon as I had blown my chances with him that Draven would then destroy me once again by leaving? Could he even do that to me? I didn't want to believe it but then again I would have never believed it the first time and look what happened. No it was the only explanation to all this. Because I knew one thing for sure, if the Fates had changed and we could now be together, then all Draven needed to get me back was the truth... something I wasn't entirely sure he was capable of revealing.

I came to my door and my conclusion both at the same time unfortunately like most things to do with Draven as soon as I opened the door I was once again thrown into the deep end. For there, now hanging in place of the butterflies behind the bed was the very same painting I had bid on. The very same one Draven had bought and now I knew had in fact bought for me. I walked in slowly with my mouth hanging open and not even bothering to close the door. I just walked straight over to it and after my eyes took in its beauty they then took in something else as well.

The note.

It was simple and it simply tore my heart apart before fusing it back together in seconds. It read...

'Seventy seven reasons to say I am sorry, Keira.'

CHAPTER TWENTY-THREE

DRAVEN

ALL OR NOTHING

"So you have resorted to stalking now?" Vincent's voice came from the shadows of my suite just as I was walking onto the balcony.

"How do you know I am not just enjoying the night air?" I asked with what I knew was a mischievous glint in my eye.

"Because like me you are far too old for such sentiments… and besides, ever since you finally made the decision to take back what is yours, you have been like a man possessed." Well he wasn't wrong there. As soon as I left the cave with her gift wrapped around my fist and her words in the other hand I had started putting my plan into place. I had demanded to find out every aspect of their trip and had most of the details by the time I boarded my private jet.

"And you wouldn't be the same?" I asked with my back still to him, only looking back over my shoulder.

"I would have probably killed the Nephilim by now." At this I couldn't help but laugh. No one on first meeting my Angelic brother would think him capable of such deadly intent but they would be dangerously wrong in their assumption. Vincent was as lethal as I was but on some level even more so, because facing me in battle you expected death to come at you head on. But with Vincent it was a different matter entirely. He would lure you first into a false sense of security and then lash out like a cobra at all sides. You would find yourself defeated before you even registered the first strike. Oh yes, he was deadly indeed, so his comment on the Nephilim scum didn't surprise me.

"Leave the half breed to me, he won't be a problem for long." I said walking through the doors knowing he would follow me. We both came to stand side by side and looked out at the sleeping city.

"You know it's been quite some time since Lucius played assassin." I huffed a short laugh at that.

"As much as I doubt Luc losing his touch in that department I have not ordered the hit."

"You haven't?" Vincent seemed genuinely taken back with my reply.

"I think you have been spending too much time around our blood thirsty sister, Vince."

"Speaking of whom, she will be here shortly…oh now don't look at me like that Dom, you knew it would not take her long, no matter how you asked Zagan to distract her." I knew this to be true indeed but I didn't know what I was least looking forward to. It was a toss up between the ruckus she would no doubt kick up at being left out or the interference that would most definitely follow in her wake.

"Hey, look on the bright side, her meddling helped the first time, who knows, it might be once again be on your side." At this I gave him a wry look to the side which made him laugh.

"So Lucius?" I knew what he was asking and I gripped the railing to the point before my strength could dent it. I was still uneasy with my past lieutenant, but I understood his reasons to a point. However, what I knew without a shadow of Hell's doubts that he cared deeply for Keira and like my brother, only I knew the reasons why. And like my brother it was not my place to say or more importantly to interfere. But I was not above using this knowledge to my advantage in any way that would first protect my girl and then aid me in getting her back to where she belonged.

"Lucius is a master at finding the truth, he will find out about this Alex I am assured of this."

"Well its certain he is hiding something. You don't go to great lengths at hiding your past as he has unless there is something you don't wish people to know." I nodded at this, knowing exactly what my brother was saying. His past was far too clean for one as old as he. Although his documentation only went back to the mid 1800's I could sense an old soul when faced with one.

But there was something else that also bothered me. It was as if there was something sour in the air every time I was near him and I didn't trust it. Not one bit. It was like tonight at the gallery when Keira had run off. I had taken a step forward and the second he could see I was searching for something, I saw the brief panic in his eyes. Then after a threat from me about hurting one single hair on her head and he would know what it felt like to become the next play thing in Hell, he promptly left.

"Did he say anything before his abrupt departure?" Vincent asked obviously being able to pick up on my thoughts.

"Just some generic nonsense he thought sounded good at the time"

"About?" Vincent asked not wanting to let it go.

"He asked me why I couldn't I see what I was doing and how I was hurting her by being here."

"And once again you didn't snap his neck why?" Again Vincent made me laugh with his easily concealed violent nature.

"And here I was thinking I was the one with anger issues."

"Ha, I just hide it better, brother." Vincent said slapping me on the back before turning to leave.

"I will leave you to your murderous musings and obsessive stalking for the night."

"And for that I thank you, Vincent." I replied sarcastically making the last thing I heard from my brother was his laughter as he shut the door. I then looked left and saw her balcony awaiting me. She had been so angry with me on finding out I owned the hotel, putting two and two together with how I manipulated the situation.

On my flight over here and while she was still in the air I was putting my plan into place. The start of that plan being to put her somewhere I could control. I needed her close and him far away. Hell I would have had him dropped in the Pacific Ocean, preferably shark infested waters, if I could have but the first floor was as far as I could push it. Or more like push her. I always knew she would eventually figure out I was the reason behind their little 'mix up' but I must confess I didn't think it would be quite this soon.

I walked to where my own balcony ended and threw myself over the side to then push my body off from where one hand clung to the railing. I made the short distance of ten feet to the other side and grabbed hold of her balcony before swinging myself up until my feet where now that step closer to her. I felt almost giddy at the idea of seeing her again, even though she would be asleep. I waited outside the door and extended my senses until I could pick up her even breathing I knew meant she had fallen under to find her private dreamland, one I could only pray was a peaceful one.

I had too many memories of Keira lost to her nightmares and the weight of my guilt she knew nothing about was immeasurable. She saw my kind since being a child and all because of her destiny of being mine. Like a cosmic test she had no clue she was taking but every day passed with the kind of strength only the finest warriors could hope to conquer. She was a marvel in my eyes and in many ways far stronger than I.

I mentally unlocked her door and walked through soundlessly transporting me back to the beginning. The starting point of my first, last and only obsession. It was very much like it was now, where I couldn't even stand being without her presence for mere moments. She never fully believed the level in which this inflicted me with hours of suffering. Every single time I had to be without her I would find my own personal Hell and one I continued to suffer to this day.

She had no idea the power she held not only over my heart but my very soul. I knew there was a reason that every time we touched and when that love would bloom again between us I would find the demon I became when locked to Tartarus. I would see myself as him writhing in anger at being kept the furthest point I could away from her. It's one of the reasons I chose a prison so deep and so far. If the Titans couldn't escape then neither could who my demon became down in the pits.

But these thoughts were far too dark for the presence of one who was all light. A light that filled me so fully, that every single time it simply took my breath away. It stole it like an Angelic thief who had no clue as to what they were doing. The thought made me smile but the sight of Keira fast asleep made me *really* smile. The type of smile you felt from your toes and didn't give one damn that the sentiment sounded soft.

But that's what I learnt from the very start, all the different things love made you do. The new feelings that coursed through you were like an assault on your once sound mind. It bombarded you with emotions that you didn't know how to deal with. I don't think I had ever felt as human as I did that day when first finding her. Even now my heart thundered its classical beat beneath my chest to the point where my ribs would ache. Yet she had no clue to any of this and the thought made me clench my fists just to stop myself from doing something foolish. Like wake her up and demand she listen until she finally understood the levels of my love.

But one day. One day I vowed she would know, just as I had discovered the levels of her own love for me. Now all I needed was a sign it was still there. It might have been buried deep under a mountain of doubt I myself had placed there but if it was there at all, then there was cause for hope…wasn't there?

I slowly approached the bed and the second I saw her I was captivated by her immense beauty. It still astounded me how she wasn't a vain creature as she certainly had the right to be. Yet if anything it seemed to be the other way, finding herself plain and ordinary if that could be believed! The very thought was insanity to me. I also took note of the new painting I had bought for her and hung over her bed. I wondered what she had thought when storming in here earlier and seeing it there for the first time.

It was a beautiful piece so I wasn't surprised when Lucius came up and told me how she had been bidding on it. He also informed me how she had tried to convince him about the obvious love in the world if such a piece could have been created. I had tried not to smirk when his last words uttered to me were,

"I would take this as a good sign, my friend," before walking away to start his mission. I looked down now and hoped with everything that was in me that my old friend was right.

She lay half covered with only a sheet and I realised she must have been too warm because the part of her on display was tantalisingly naked. I wanted badly to pull the sheet down, if only enough to give me a glimpse of her perfect breasts. However I knew, no matter how my Demon roared at me to do just that, I knew even what I was doing now was crossing a line. Anything more would have been unforgivable and I had to remember I was trying to win her back, not push her away with my adolescent behaviour.

I had to supress the urge to laugh at these thoughts, taking me back to earlier. 'Did I have a behaviour problem' had been her question in the pool. Ha, that was a joke in itself considering I had supressed every natural urge I possessed just to refrain from taking her there and then. How easy it would have been to slip into her when her legs were wrapped around my waist. To just lower her onto me, my constant hardened state of arousal whenever she was around.

I had caught her looking a few times and as before I just couldn't resist the need to tease her about it, feeding on her blushes. Her shy behaviour about sex had always brought out the alpha in me, the beast wanting to claim his prize. It made me want to take her for hours just to prolong the pleasure I got in not only the act itself but mainly the bliss I would witness in her eyes as she chased her pleasure. It made me want to be cruel and withhold it from her just that bit longer, knowing the intensity that would coil tighter within her.

I knew her body better than even she did and looking at it now was like being reunited with an old friend. Now this was true torture. Seeing all that splendour spread out before me like the greatest mouth-watering feast and this starving man couldn't even take one bite. Yes, it was cruel indeed.

I decided to take pity on myself and lower the temperature in the room to what I knew her body needed. Then I pulled the sheet over her body so that she would find the comfort I knew she liked. And as expected she curled her body tighter into it and I cannot tell you the elevation to my heart at seeing her smile in her sleep.

This I knew was a rare treat, as I had sometimes spent hours watching her sleep before. Normally she would frown or mutter something I couldn't quite make out. But on the good nights... on the best nights, I would sometimes get not only a smile but also a little laugh. These moments you have found at the very roots of my happiness, along with a million other things at my core that she did on a daily basis.

Yes, I needed that hope. I needed that sign or anything. A smile, a laugh or the Gods be willing even my name uttered from her lips...lips I had come so close to kissing tonight. So I would wait and stand watch all night if I had to but I needed this sign. I needed it as the last puzzle piece to know I was doing the right thing and finally, the right thing by her. Because no matter how much I hated that Nephilim scum, I still couldn't shake what he had said tonight.

I had made out to Vincent it was nothing of circumstance but in actual fact what he said had hit a nerve and shamefully, a big one at that. The thought that I was hurting her even more with my presence wasn't something I knew how to deal with. No, I needed to be sure. I could deal with the half breed in other ways and one way or another he wouldn't be in Keira's life for much longer, that I could be damn sure about.

So I soundlessly sat on the bed and waited. I waited for I know not how long but when it finally came, when I found the proof I had been needing to see, I could barely believe it. I had been moving a piece of her hair back from her face that I could see was tickling her nose in her sleep. It was making it do that ridiculously cute wrinkle thing it does when I saw she was gripping something in her fist that she also held to her heart.

I knew the only way to enable me to see it would be to do something that also constituted crossing a line but this time I felt that I had no choice. This time it was all or nothing.

So I opened up her mind and using her vulnerable state as my own weapon, I delved in there and took control.

"What are you protecting, sweetheart?" I whispered in her ear, letting my voice roll over her senses in waves. It was a little like using a drug and something I was a little ashamed to be doing…that was until she uncurled her fingers.

And there it was…

My beacon of hope.

CHAPTER TWENTY-FOUR

KEIRA

CATCHING THE RIGHT WORDS

I woke feeling refreshed as the morning light filtered through the curtains and I stretched out as I usually did like a big cat. I think I would even have purred in that moment if I could, I just felt that good. I looked down seeing I was still naked and last night flashed back into my mind. I felt my cheeks get hot as I thought of the pool. Draven had been so playful and flirty it had been like seventh heaven for a time. However it had played havoc later on with my mind and wondering what exactly was he up to?

I looked up and saw my beautiful new artwork hung over my bed from upside down and I smiled thinking, it even works looking at it like this. Then I looked down and saw the piece of paper I had purposely gone to sleep holding to my heart last night. The words that had meant so much to me and words that I also felt change something deep within me.

'Seventy seven reasons to say I am sorry, Keira', I read it out loud still feeling the weight of those words settle against my chest. It was a soothing balm to my battered heart and even though it wouldn't fully heal it, it most certainly helped.

I decided today would be a day of exploring considering Alex had to work. It was an annoying factor about our trip but after last night and him storming off, I was starting to think we needed the distance. So with that in mind I jumped enthusiastically out of bed and straight into the bathroom to start getting ready for the day. The shower felt amazing as jets pounded my skin from all different angles and because of this I ended up being in there for a lot longer than I thought I would.

It was only when I was out and wrapping a towel round myself that I heard a knocking at the door.

"Coming… just a second!" I shouted also grabbing the robe from behind the bathroom door and I had just finished tying it when I opened the door.

"Uh…" Ok so it wasn't the best opening line when faced with a gorgeous man, but I added that it was still early yet to my list of excuses.

"Well, aren't you going to invite me in?"

"Uh…do I have to?" I said still obviously functioning on that level of stupid.

"Well I believe it is customary between humans when finding old friends at your door," he said laughing.

"And you *are* old…or so I hear." I teased unable to help myself and thankfully kicked my brain into the next gear…I think it was happily labelled 'witty'.

"Careful with the compliments sweetheart, you will give this Angel a big head."

"Oh so you're an Angel today are you?" I asked folding my arms and leaning against the door which prevented him coming in.

"I am when I'm bringing you breakfast." He replied with a wink and held up a brown paper bag, which had a grease patch coming through. Oh and didn't it just smell divine!

"Oh you're good." I remarked narrowing my eyes and making him laugh.

"A guy can only try." When he said this, he shrugged his shoulders and it was such a human moment that one could forget who I was actually talking to.

"So you gonna let me in?" He asked waving the bag and tempting me with its delicious smells.

"Well now that all depends…hey!" I finished with a yelp as Draven swooped on in there, circled my waist with one arm and lifted me out of the way. He then kicked the door closed before setting me back down and walking over to the little sitting area.

"Nice room." He said like an everyday Joe would and not like the Barbarian who had just manhandled me before forcing his way into my room.

"Yeah whatever caveman, it's not like you haven't been in here before," I said nodding to my new favourite possession hanging above the bed. At this he sat down and winked at me saying,

"Yeah, but not in the daylight." And then opened up the brown bag. He first laid some napkins on the table and then proceeded to take out what I thought of as breakfast of the gods…

"Pastries!" I shouted and raced over to the opposite seat.

"But of course." He said smirking and then handed one over.

"To start a cheese and ham croissant and then a…" He rummaged deeper until he pulled out a smaller bag and then pulled out the contents making me shout,

"A Pain au Chocolat!" In obvious excitement causing him give me a soft smile.

"Gimmey gimmey!" I said taking it off him and making him chuckle.

"I thought you would save it for dessert."

"Oh I am but I don't trust you, I remember the last time when you kept taking massive man bites out of mine." I said defending my greed and possessiveness over the still warm pastry.

"Ah yes, I remember now...the morning after St Valentine's." He said making me blush as I remembered that eventful night of the kinkier side of love making. He noticed my blush, then took a bite of his own croissant and winked at me for the second time in minutes all with a trademark bad boy grin.

"So apart from establishing your new role as room service provider, you still haven't told me why you're here?"

"Ha, and you know I was so close to wearing the uniform as well." He said after he swallowed and looked down at his casual clothes. In fact, it was surprising to see him looking so... well so *normal.* In fact he could have easily passed for a tourist as he was only missing the camera around his neck and map in one hand.

He had on a pair of navy blue cut off combat style trousers with a metal belt buckle that had a car etched on the front. This was combined with a light grey, long sleeved T shirt that had some old faded white car logo on the front that looked cracked with age. I had to smile wondering if it was one of his favourites which had been worn that much or if it was all part of the design. Either way he looked hot and had hit a whole new level of summer cool...one I didn't even know was on the scale!

He even had a pair of Aviator sunglasses hanging from the neck and a pair of brown leather flip-flops.

"Sooo...?" I said with a mouthful of buttery genius.

"I'm spending the day with you." On hearing this I chewed a little faster so I could swallow quicker before saying,

"Excuse me?"

"We are spending the day together." Again I shook my head.

"Er…doing what exactly?"

"The whole tourist thing," he said taking another bite, which I knew was his way of steamrolling me into something but acting all casual at the same time, he was sneaky that way.

"Hence the outfit…" I said waving my hand up and down indicating his amazing body that was unfortunately covered… uh, I mean, his clothes!

"Hence me wearing clothes, yes." I frowned when he laughed at me.

"So breakfast was a bribe?" I asked taking the last mouthful before my next course.

"I have my tricks."

"Oh don't I know it after last night." I commented drily.

"When needs must."

"You know I have no idea once again what you're talking about, so I have decided to just pretend you're not speaking." I said feeling cocky with the awesomeness of my come back.

"You can pretend all you want darling it just means I will have to up my game."

"Ha! So this is a game?!" I demanded trying to hold in any reaction that gave away how much I hated the idea.

"Not in the sense you think, no." This made me frown.

"You know if there was a prize for the most confusing man ever then you would be wearing the ribbon right now, you know that?!" I knew he could detect the frustration in my voice, but he chose to ignore it and gave me a warm look that just made me throw my hands up at the same time making a 'Grrr' sound.

"Bloody supernatural men!" I said then snatched my

chocolate goodness off the table and stormed back to the bathroom.

"Where are you going?" Draven asked laughing at my dramatic behaviour.

"To eat, get changed and sulk and not necessarily in that order, caveman!" I shouted before slamming the door to the magical sound of his laughter.

"So what do you want to see first?" Draven asked as we walked through the hotel lobby with his hand at the small of my back.

"How about the Cathedral?" I asked turning to look up at him. I caught his eyes alight with mirth and just before he slipped his sunglasses on he said,

"Good choice, sweetheart," and then he took my hand in his and led me out of the door. I would have been lying if I said I wasn't excited but I also couldn't help the guilt I felt. I had spoken to Alex this morning on the phone in my room after getting ready. I was just thankful that I had reached the phone before Draven but that didn't mean I didn't have to hold my hand over his mouth at one point to stop him from asking who it was.

Alex had said he was sorry about the way he left abruptly but he said it was because dressed like that I had been too tempting for him to stay. I wasn't sure I fully believed his reasons but there was nothing for me to do but accept what he was telling me. So after telling me he had to work all day and for me to have a good time sightseeing I hung up. It was only when Draven bit me playfully on the finger did I realise I still had my hand over his mouth. Then after a simple but tummy fluttering moment of him saying,

"Let's go, Beautiful," we were off out of the door to start our day.

Which brought us to now and walking through the expensive and exquisite shopping mall with its domes of glass and shops like Prada.

"This place is amazing." Draven looked down at me and smiled before informing me,

"It is called Galleria Vittorio Emanuele II and it is one of the world's oldest shopping malls." I couldn't help the little hum of pleasure that seemed to ripple through me at hearing Draven speaking Italian.

"It looks old." I said and I quickly looked to the side to roll my eyes at how dense I just sounded.

"It is. The Galleria is named after Vittorio Emanuele II, the first king of what was known as the Kingdom of Italy." He said speaking quietly down at me.

"Really... So when was it built?" I asked feeding my history addiction.

"I believe it was designed some time in 1861 but was only built between 1865 and 1877. I am also trying to recall the human's name." At this I giggled and I could tell even through his glasses that he just raised one eyebrow at me.

"Something funny?"

"Only that there is something in history that you have forgotten," I said feeling smug at being able to tease him.

"Umm we will see...I think this old dog is just distracted." At this I tried to think of a good comeback but when he lifted his shades to give me a heated look, all thoughts fled me. In fact it made me feel naked instead of the denim shorts, summery mellow yellow t-shirt and the thin material, white zip up hooded top, that I only wore to cover my scars.

"In fact I don't know what is more distracting, you teasing

me or your blushing skin." Well in response to that statement I know which distraction he received.

"Ah Giuseppe Mengoni! I knew I would remember." Draven said startling me as we neared the massive archway onto the Paizza del Duomo.

"Congratulations, you have officially hit elephant status on the memory front." I remarked but once again spoilt it by giggling at my own joke. I was still laughing when I noticed he had stopped walking alongside me and I turned to see that bad boy grin come out to play, telling me I was in trouble.

"Elephant status?" He asked.

"Uh…" Was the only intelligent thing my brain came up with as I watched him stalk towards me.

"Draven behave," I warned on a whisper and I looked round at all the people, hoping we weren't causing a scene. But in the end I had no hope so decided 'oh to Hell with it!' I turned around and ran out of the massive archway laughing like a maniac until I felt arms grab me from behind.

"Gotya!" He said with his lips to the top of my head and I was left panting in his hold, which wasn't only down to exertion. It was the feeling I got whenever I was in Draven's arms that was hard to describe. Of course, being hugged by Alex was also nice but there was just something else about being in these particular arms that felt…*more.* The word 'more' was the only word I could use. It was more strength, more warmth, more affection and most of all I was always left wanting more.

"Look up." Draven murmured into the back of my hair as I was still looking down at my feet being shy. I did as I was told and for a second the sun blinded me but then Draven's hand came up and shielded it for me to see.

"Oh my!" I said in total awe. The shopping mall opened up

right onto the square and facing me now was the utter breathtaking view of the Duomo, Cathedral of Milan.

"You like it?" Draven asked me softly and the shiver that wriggled up my spine wasn't only due to the imposing beauty before me but the way his hand brushed some of my hair back from my neck.

"It's incredible," I said and it truly was. In fact I doubted there were any words known to man that would have been able to do it justice. But what was the most profound truth about this imposing sight was that it just proved that some beauty in the world was man made and that in itself was a beautiful thing to know. To see something that human hands had crafted in sight and faith of their God was a feeling that warmed my heart in a way I couldn't explain. But the one thought that kept repeating was what escaped my lips,

"I think that anytime the Gods looked down at this they would simply smile." I felt myself being turned and I looked up to find Draven smiling himself down at me.

"I think you're right…Shall we go inside?" Draven then asked and I nodded enthusiastically making him smile once again.

As we walked up to the pure white marble Cathedral I was trying to take in just how many spires and columns made up the Gothic building. But it wasn't just the multitude of these mighty structures surrounding the building like protective soldiers standing guard. It was the large arched windows, the flying buttresses and the extravagant sculptural decoration that almost consumed every square foot of the place that had your mouth hanging open in awe. It was also the overabundance of statues and as Draven informed me as we got closer that it had not only 135 spires but each and every one all supported a figure of the saints.

I had to smile as he reeled off all the structural facts which made me turn to him and say,

"You seem to know a lot about this place."

"I called Milan home for a time." I stopped walking as I thought about this. It was such a strange thought for me to contemplate and I wasn't really sure why. Thinking about it there must have been so many places that Draven had called home in his many lifetimes I don't know why I was so surprised. If anything it just made the probability of us meeting in the first place seem like fate. Which I guess all things considered it was the Fates that had thrown us in each other's paths. But this in itself just made what happened even more confusing. Why would they have bothered if we were only ever meant to be friends?

Was it that one day there was something more in store for us or just that we had had our time, no matter how brief but no less precious. Was that all that was in our fates? Whatever the answer was it was a depressing thought.

"Keira?" Draven calling my name shook me out of my thoughts and I managed a fake smile.

"Sorry, it's nothing."

"I very much doubt that." He said holding his hand out to me to take, which of course I didn't think twice about doing.

"So how long ago did you live here?" I asked ignoring his questioning looks.

"Um, let me think…see those doors there, well they were still wood when I was here but they were damaged in the 1943 bombing of Milan, then they were replaced with ones made of bronze."

"Oh God, but the thought of any of it being damaged is a horrible one." I said looking at the dark greenish doors that were highly decorated and looked as if they had always been there.

"Well now, that's the great thing about humans..."

"And that is?" I asked when he didn't carry on and I knew when I looked at him that is what he had been waiting for, he wanted my eyes.

"Their strength in fighting for what they believe in...*for in what they love.*" Upon hearing these words, I had to swallow the lump it caused but it just wasn't the words that affected me, no, it was the complete sincerity in which they were spoken.

"And um… when exactly did you realise this?" I asked my voice thick and uneven.

"I believe since I first met a certain human girl that touched my heart deeply enough it changed the way it beat within my chest…"

"Oh God," I whispered feeling the tears clog my throat before they reached my eyes. Then he made it beautifully worse with his next statement.

"However, I didn't really understand the full extent and power of those words until ten months ago." I bit my lip and raised myself up on my tiptoes. I then pulled off his glasses and cupped his face with one hand before thanking him with a kiss on his cheek. I felt his arm come around me and for a moment it felt like he was locking me in place.

"Keira, I need…" I never got to hear what he was going to say because a flash of light cut into our moment with cruel reality. It was one of those guys who obviously took pictures of tourists in the hope of selling his photos and lived his life through a camera lens. In that moment I envied him as I couldn't help but wonder what he saw when taking that picture. A happy couple caught in a loving embrace on holiday together? Well that was certainly a prettier picture painted than the one that reflected the pains in our life together.

"Excuse me." Draven said and walked over to the man. At first I thought Draven's temper at being interrupted would come out but I was pleasantly surprised when I saw him paying the man. Then he waited for the picture to be printed from the portable printer the guy carried with him.

"Souvenir?" I asked as he walked back over to me, obviously being admired if the backward glances from the female population was anything to go by.

"One to add to my collection." Was his cryptic answer.

"Collection?"

"Let go inside" He said ignoring my question and instead taking my hand again.

"I can't believe this place." I said after being far too absorbed in its glory and splendour for the first ten minutes. Walking inside was like being transported into a different time and one where we as a race still took the time and expense to create places like this for the world to witness a nation's triumph. The years, the manpower and the endless hours of craftsmanship that went into building this place were incomprehensible.

"It is quite magnificent isn't it?" Draven said by my side as we walked first along the left side.

"Just look at the stained-glass windows and the way the sun is casting rainbows of colour on everything." I said feeling giddy in a way only an artist gets when finding something they want to paint.

"Oh wow, Draven look at this one!" I said grabbing his hand and pulling him over to one of the side windows that was definitely different from all the rest. I heard him chuckle at my obvious enthusiasm.

"Well this is definitely more your scene." I said laughing and looking up at the most vivid scene of Heaven battling Hell. It was cut into two sections and at the bottom Demonic figures were raising their tridents and spears to the onslaught above. At the centre was a creature with what looked like at least five serpent heads and a horned Demon that was being held back by emerald green chains wrapped around his limbs. Then my eyes took in what everyone would depict as the 'good guys', as Heavenly figures rain down their gold tipped arrows to the monsters below. There was even a white horse draped in an emerald robe with its rider the saintly warrior ready to strike.

"I can assure you a battle between Heaven and Hell is far more gruesome than the likes of this painted glass."

"Oh trust you to bring blood and gore into it." I teased nudging his arm to which he just gave me a coy smile in return.

We continued round and it was like having my own personal guide. He would tell me about the history of each Altar statue, sarcophagi, and plaque we came to which were situated under each big window along the sides. The centre was dominated by row after row of pews and there was a forest of pillars that dominated the inside. I looked up and even though the arched ceilings were plain it worked well so as not to distract from the top of the pillars. Each one was enriched by a large number of statues of saints and martyrs that encircled the tops of every pillar, causing your eyes to dance between each one.

"I think I could spend hours here."

"Wait until you see the roof." On hearing this I gasped in excitement.

"We can go up on the roof?!" He laughed at me as we cut across, what Draven informed me was called the Transept. Then of course he had to explain that a Transept was the shortest arm of the church that is shaped like a Latin cross. So basically it's an aisle cutting across the length of the room.

"Yes, it is an unusual feature I agree, but on a clear day the views seen from up there are spectacular." He said referring back to the roof. We walked to the south side passing tourists as we went and even though I was sure they weren't allowed to take pictures, I couldn't say I could fully blame them. It was just one of those places that made you want to take those picture memories away with you so that you could impress your friends when you got back home.

"I can't wait to see it…oh…that's…that's…" I said coming to a dead stop at the statue that was now in front of me.

"That's St Bartholomew." Draven said obviously amused by my reaction to seeing it.

"Uh…What's wrong with his skin?" I asked wrinkling my nose.

"He's wearing it like a piece of cloth."

"Eww!" I said but even as I made the noise there was just something about it that drew you in. It was a masterpiece there was no two ways about that, but it was as gruesome as it was stunning. The man stood almost proud with a book in one hand that rested open on the top of his thigh. His skin had been completely removed and on closer inspection his face rested at his back, his hand was next to his boned hand and the same with one of his feet. It was incredible as even the marble that had been used had a blue running through it that gave the appearance of veins on the muscle.

"Who was he?" I asked but Draven started to lead me away.

"Just someone who studied anatomy. Come, the lift is this way." I frowned behind Draven as it was the way he said it that I knew there was more he wasn't telling me. I looked back one last time and for a split second I could have sworn I had seen him move.

But wait…Hadn't that book been open before?

———

334

Once on the roof I found yet another astonishing sight, only this time it most definitely wasn't man made. Although the roof to the Cathedral was in itself a masterpiece, allowing you to see the spires and statues up close. But Draven had been right, the view was incredible. The snow-capped Alps ran along one side and looked almost too surreal to be actually there. Almost like the snow on top could be low floating clouds or the mythological stories of Mount Olympus also came to mind.

"You can see the whole city from up here." I said and then had to look around for Draven as it seemed I was talking to myself.

"Draven?"

"Right here, love." He spoke in my ear at the same time his arms came round me, which they had been doing a lot lately. Didn't he understand what it did to me every time I would feel his arms around me, holding me to him like he never wanted to let me go?

"Hey, relax…I've got you." He said when he felt me tense in his arms as these thoughts of confusion filled me to the point where I wanted to pull away. It was beautiful cruelty and I was just about to tell him as much when he spoke again,

"This has always been one of my favourite places in the world and I think the words of Alfred Tennyson best describe its beauty…would you like to hear it?"

"Uhm…yes please" I said after first needing to clear my throat.

"Very well, let me just engage my elephant memory," he teased first and gave me an affectionate squeeze as I laughed.

"Don't give yourself a headache now," I replied back and found my hand going to his at my front to hold onto where he automatically entwined his long fingers with mine.

"Since when did you get so cheeky little one?" He asked into my hair.

"Since I met a big Alpha male who needs keeping on his toes and bringing down a peg or two."

"And that is something you certainly do well, sweetheart." He finished and walked us forward just a few steps until we came right up against the marble arches that ran the full length of the roof like a medieval fence caging us in. The one hand that wasn't linked with mine then lent against the arch in front of us, which created a little private space for us that felt far too intimate for friends. This was proved even more so when he started reciting the poem in a soft, luring voice that instantly made me give him more of my weight to hold.

"I climb'd the roofs at break of day;
Sun-smitten Alps before me lay.
I stood among the silent statues,
And statued pinnacles, mute as they.

How faintly-flush's, how phantom fair,
Was Monte Rosa, hanging there
A thousand shadowy-pencill'd valleys
And snowy dells in a golden air."

"That was lovely," I said feeling breathy and swallowing hard at what this moment was meaning to me.

"It was made even lovelier saying it with you in my arms." Draven responded with his lips at my ear. My head went back on his chest and I couldn't hold it in any longer. He was cracking my walls and seeping his way in once again. I just hoped I could hold it together just a little bit longer…I only needed a little longer.

"Draven, I can't do this again." I said on a plea, turning my head to the side and I felt his hand leave the marble arch to cup my face.

"Can't do what again, Keira, *tell me?*" He asked and I turned in his arms and looked up at him with pleading eyes before I finally whispered the truth of my heart,

"I'm falling for you again." I braved saying but getting this off my chest wasn't what lifted my heart and made my breath catch. No, it was what Draven said in response to my bravery, to my honesty and to my greatest wish in all the world.

It was the gift of bravery, honestly and a single wish that he gave back to me, with five words that would change the world...

"Then let me catch you."

CHAPTER TWENTY-FIVE

KEIRA

ASK ME ANYTHING

The rest of the day went by where I remained in some hypnotic fog of confusion and bliss. After our moment on the roof we had both just held each other and I knew that if I had only looked up he would have kissed me. And this knowledge was an internal battle that raged on within me, tempting me into sin and placing me on the line I knew I should never cross. Because as easy as it would be to simply step over that line, to do so still meant putting myself out there and under his mercy to once again crush me. No, not just crush me but this time something a lot worse because this time I just don't think I would have survived it again.

So I ran scared. I pulled myself away and one look at his face said he knew it too. I was even a little surprised that he allowed me to withdraw from him. All he had done was run the back of two fingers down my cheek and said,

"Hey, it's okay," then he smiled, took my hand and we left the magical rooftop to continue our day. After that we continued our day like tourists, with Draven taking me to his favourite places in the city and explaining all of its history to me. I would allow myself at my weakest moments to be weaved deeper into his spell and because of this most of the day was spent hand in hand.

We would jump on and off the busy trams which Draven used as an opportunity to wrap a protective arm around my waist and one hand on the bar above to hold me steady. He would point out different buildings through the window I faced but in reality in these moments I rarely took anything in other than the feel of him at my back, holding me close.

At one point I had Draven pulling my hand back and pulling me in to this old traditional ice cream parlour that the Italians called gelato. There were so many flavours I was stood there umming and ahhing for a small age. Draven just laughed at me and picked his own flavour of Grand Marnier, which I teased was such a posh choice. I ended up being torn between three flavours, so in the end Draven just ordered me all of them, chocolate, mint choc chip and for something a little different, toffee with amaretto.

"I hope you're planning on helping me finish these?" I had asked at the time which was precisely what he did. We sat at a window seat together watching the Italian world walk by and I regaled him with funny stories about working at the library. He showed no restraint in telling me how he didn't care for the way my boss had spoken to me that day, making me smile.

We had then moved on and it was me being the one to drag Draven into the next place. It was a big souvenir shop that had a dressing up section at the back. I made a bee line for it and started picking up wigs and trying them on.

"Oh no…no, you don't!" Draven had said backing up and

putting his hands in the air to fend me off. I giggled harder and continued to come at him with the Elvis wig, complete with sideburns.

"Oh come on, you know you will look hot with any of these wigs…you're not scared of looking foolish are you, oh mighty King?" I said in a way that clearly taunted him. This was when he raised a single eyebrow at me and crossed his arms as if thinking about it.

"Ok, I will play but you have to wear the ones I pick." I gave him a beaming grin and held out my hand.

"Deal."

"You should be careful who you make a deal with, darling." He said winking.

"I am not afraid of you, now put this on and play a different type of King." I said going up on my tiptoes and placing it on his head. I stepped back and burst into a fit of laughter. Of course it was made even worse when he started trying to do the Elvis's famous leg move, saying 'Huhuh', causing my laughter to hurt my ribs as I bent over double.

He pulled the wig off laughing with me and then went to pick out my own. He came back to me smirking and I knew it was going to be funny. He placed it on my head and then turned me by the shoulders to face the mirror. It turned out to be a massive black Mohawk so I started playing on my air guitar, using my leg at one point making Draven, like me, bend over double laughing.

We ended up being the shop for ages and thanks to Draven's powers of persuasion no one took any notice of us. So after a blonde mullet, monk's bald head, black afro and the Mohawk I made him wear, I was forced through the clown's rainbow wig, red plaits, pink bob and of course not to be left out, the blonde mullet!

After laughing and giggling at each other like loons and me

using feather boas and Draven putting on giant glasses we finally left the shop with two matching key rings to remember the shop by. I think my cheeks were still aching the rest of the way round Milan from smiling so much. It was just turning out to be the most perfect day ever and I found myself never wanting it to end. I think if I could have picked my Groundhog Day then this would have been it.

In fact I was just thinking about asking what Draven had planned for dinner as we were making our way back up in the lift to our suites when he beat me to speaking.

"So I have something I have been meaning to ask you."

"Ok, go for it." I replied as we came to my door and I bent sideways to pull my key card out of my back pocket.

"I wanted to know if you would come with…" Draven was abruptly cut off when my door was suddenly opened.

"Alex?!" I said in shock at seeing who the intruder was.

"Catherine…oh and look, how surprising to see who you're with!" He snapped and I felt like I had been caught with my hand in the preverbal cookie jar!

"Draven I will see you later." I said pushing Alex back and storming into my room.

"Oh I just bet you will!" Alex snapped but I ignored it and instead had to give Draven a small shake of my head as he looked to be holding back his Demon's wrath from finding his hands around Alex's neck.

"What are you doing in my room?" I asked turning the emphasis back on him and wondering what in fact he *was* doing in my room. I slammed the door and stood with my arms folded waiting.

"Well, I was obviously just about to interrupt something between you two, that's what!" Was his sharp retort.

"Oh don't be ridiculous, we are just friends."

"Yeah sure you are…is that why he followed you all the

way to Italy!? Don't be so naive and foolish Cathy." He said rolling his eyes.

"Don't be so dramatic, we spent the day together because he didn't like the idea of me spending it alone in a city I didn't know." I said knowing this was actually part of the reason because he told me so himself.

"It's Milan Catherine, not the Middle East for fuck's sake!"

"Yeah well at least he cares enough. So far all you have done is take me for one meal and then gave me a night of you acting stroppy!"

"Stroppy?!"

"Yeah stroppy, you know… moody, bad tempered, irritable or my personal favourite being a basic sulky asshole…so pick one!" I said stomping past him.

"Well you didn't have to deal with my asshole friends turning up and getting in your face!" Ok so he did have a point with that one.

"That's true but either way if I did, I certainly wouldn't have been a bitch to *you* about it!" I said thinking I was making a valid point, however his face told me otherwise.

"Oh right because this is you we are talking about and little Kazzy can do no wrong." At this my mouth dropped open and I made a strangled noise in the back of my throat at the audacity or what he just said.

"How dare you!"

DRAVEN

"I will kill him!" I simply stated as I walked to the door ready to tear it from its hinges to get to spill his blood quicker.

"Dom stop! You need to think about this." Vincent said holding me back by my shoulders from behind.

"Oh trust me brother, don't doubt the hours that I have *thought about this!"* I said letting a part of my demon speak for me.

"No, I mean that anytime that they spend arguing is only to be seen as a good thing…you need to calm and let *him* do the damage, not *you* and your interference right now would only be doing that…*damage."* I growled, not only because he was preventing me from feeling the Nephilim's organs rupture in my hands, but also because he was right.

"Besides just listen to her giving him what for, I almost feel sorry for you Dom, she has a sharp tongue our girl, Keira." Sophia said walking from one of my suite's bedrooms with what I could smell was a strawberry daiquiri in hand.

"She arrived this afternoon." Vincent informed me with a shrug of his shoulders.

"You're damn right I did!" She said coming over to me and slapping me across the face without spilling a single drop. My head snapped to the side and I growled low down at the floor in response.

"That was for keeping something this damn important from me you big bastard!" She said getting on her tiptoes to get in my face before she then sweetly kissed the cheek she had inflicted her wrath upon.

"Now let's get back to our entertainment shall we…listen, she is about to tell him to leave." I quickly forgot about my sister's disrespect and turned my head to hear my girl giving the half breed what for.

"Will you just drop it now! The picture was a gift because he obviously knew how much I wanted it…it's not like I asked him for it Alex!" No she hadn't but once I learnt from Lucius

how much it meant to her then no force on earth could have prevented me from getting it for her.

"Oh yeah and are you going to give it back to him?" I wanted to roar at the thought and even took a few steps forward in my reaction.

"Whoa there brother, get a lid on it." Vince said now putting a hand to my chest and using an abundance of strength to hold me back.

"No, I am not going to take it back! That would be rude and cruel." I heard Keira say and only then did I stop pushing on Vincent's strength.

"That's my girl." I said out loud causing Vincent and Sophia to share a knowing grin.

"Oh of course you're not! So you think it's acceptable to not only spend the day with your ex-boyfriend, who I will remind you left you obviously heartbroken but also to accept gifts off him? ... Think Catherine, do you not see the only reason he is lavishing all this attention on you now is because I am in the picture."

"I will destroy him!"

"I think you need to leave." Hearing Keira saying this quickly changed my thoughts of a vicious death to ones of pride instead.

"Look, let's just talk about this, we came here to get away to be together not be torn apart by your psychotic ex."

"Oh he will soon understand the true meaning of psychotic." I said making Sophia laugh and add,

"Oh go on Vince, let him go and introduce him to our own brand of psycho."

"Not helping Sophia!" Vince complained but only receiving a casual shrug in return from our blood thirsty sister.

"Ssshh both of you!" I snapped as I missed the first part of Keira's response,

"...So far it was lucky he was here or I would just have ended up spending all my time alone...which reminds me, I think that is exactly what I would prefer to be doing right now!"

"Booya! You go Kazzy girl!" Sophia said and high fived Vincent making him laugh, she then turned to me and held out her hand for me to do the same. I raised a single eyebrow at her and she rolled her eyes before lowering her hand. You would have thought by now she would have got the hint that ever since that ridiculous gesture came into circulation in the seventies I was not one to conform to such things.

"Fine!" We all heard before the door slammed and found extreme relief in the sound of the parasite leaving.

"Fine!" She shouted back and then you heard the distinct thud of something being thrown at the door he had just walked out of.

"That's my cue." I said walking towards my own door when suddenly I found an Angelic arm thrown around my neck and a tiny Demon stood with her hands at my chest pushing me back.

"Oh no you don't!" I looked down at my beautiful sister and snarled, showing her my elongating fangs and thus the extent of my anger.

"She's right brother, you can't go storming in there now."

"Why not!? She needs me, she is upset." I disputed.

"Yeah she is, but she's angry upset and right now a pissed off Keira is a good thing just so long as it's not directed at you." Sophia said finishing to the sound of something else hitting the door from the next room.

"She will not be angry with me."

"You're kidding right, cause in there, right at this moment is a scorned female who hates *all* men! Trust me on this, I may not be human but if a man pisses me off, then *all* men piss me off." I frowned at this silly logic but after hearing another frustrated scream from the other room I took it as a sign that maybe my sister was right. So I told her so and stopped fighting my siblings.

"Maybe you're right."

"You think?!" She said on a laugh when we heard yet another bang come from my little spitfire along with the only confirmation I needed to know Sophia was right.

"I do," I replied on a wince.

KEIRA

"AHHH! Bloody men!" I screamed out after throwing yet another shoe at the door. I now had a nice pile gathered there. I was just so angry! This was by far the worst argument we had ever had and I had come so close to ending it before he left. But the only reason I hadn't was because I never wanted to be one of those people who truly ended a relationship on the basis of a fight.

Of course, the annoying thing was that a lot of my anger was also aimed at myself. Alex had been right in some of the things he had said about Draven. For one it was obvious the only reason he was back in my life was because of Alex and I hated this thought more than most! And in effect I hated myself for being sucked into Draven's warped sense of duty.

I knew he wasn't doing this to hurt me and you could tell that none of the time he spent with me being his usual affectionate self was faked. It could have never been possible between us to fake that type of connection. It was never going to change the truth of the matter and that was Draven and I could never be just friends…not really.

I knew this, he knew this and yet we still played the game just so we could continue to spend time together. Yes the thought made me angry at myself but it was like a drug you just couldn't give up, no matter what it does to your soul in the long run. So when I cursed men, I included Draven in this as Alex was right, he had left me heartbroken and now he was back again no doubt to put me through the same damn thing. So what did I do…I got angry and the little anthill by the door of sandals and dress shoes was the evidence of that anger.

But I knew what I needed to make this right, so I stomped over to the phone and picked it up pressing the only number I needed.

"Room service?"

Hours later I must have passed out from a junk food coma because the next thing I knew I was being woken up by a tapping noise. I lifted my head and felt the line of unattractive drool string from the corner of my mouth. I then lifted my head and the first thing I was faced with was the half-eaten pizza that I shamefully thought still looked quite appetising. I remember feeling the dead weight of disappointment when opening the door to room service and not seeing Draven stood there with the tray.

Which brought me back to the tapping sound that had woken me in the first place. I turned my head and looked towards the balcony doors and ended up letting out a shriek at the figure I saw stood there.

"Draven?!" I shouted getting up quickly and ungraciously knocking the pizza to the floor in my haste to get there quicker.

"Have many midnight callers do you?" Draven asked smiling as I opened the door for him to come in. I stuck my head out and asked,

"You jumped?" His only response was to laugh at me,

which would have been fine if he hadn't then plucked some sort of food from my hair and sniffed at it.

"Pepperoni?" He asked and I went the colour of said meat product before he grinned and popped it in his mouth to chew.

"Tasty?" I asked thinking this situation couldn't get any weirder if it tried.

"Of course." He replied with a cocky wink and then walked past me as if he owned the suite, which I guess he did being that he owned the damn hotel.

"So you're sleeping with your food now?" He asked raising a single eyebrow at the pizza on the floor.

"Well what can I say, a girl has gotta get her kicks somehow." I said giggling at my own joke as I walked past him to pick it up and place it back on the plate. I turned round to find Draven lifting the other silver domes on the tray to find half eaten pasta, garlic bread and what was the remains of a chocolate dessert that felt at the time it was sent to me from the Gods.

"Did you lick the bowl?" He asked laughing picking up the bowl to show me, which I snatched off him and said,

"No, give me a little credit... I used my finger." I added because it did in fact look as though I had licked the bowl like a hungry dog. I replaced the bowl on the tray and turned to Draven crossing my arms over my chest.

"So I gather you didn't jump over to my balcony to discuss my room service pig out."

"No, but I'm certainly sorry I missed the show."

"Ha, ha...now confess." I said trying not to let his handsome face or infectious smile deter me from my 'What's going on in Draven's crazy mind' fact finding mission. I was actually surprised to find that Draven for once seemed to look unsure. He frowned down at the floor and I noticed he kept clenching his hands at his sides into fists.

"Are you nervous?" I blurted out without thinking. His head snapped up and he looked shocked by my question.

"I…uh…no, why?" Ok so his answer didn't really back him up at not being nervous but I just smiled and unfolded my arms. I walked over to him and for a moment he looked unsure as to what I was about to do. Then I stepped into him and wrapped my arms around him and said,

"I had a wonderful day, thank you for giving that to me." He released a big sigh and I felt him relax instantly.

"You're welcome and it was my pleasure." He said to the top of my head. I then pulled my head back a bit and looked up at him.

"Now are you going to tell me why you came here because I doubt it was to pick food out of my hair for a midnight snack?" I said on a laugh.

"You would definitely be my first choice for a midnight snack." He teased and I pulled myself out of his arms and smacked him lightly on the arm.

"Oi, behave you or I will have to call hotel security on you." At this he laughed.

"I doubt they would be very effective in this case considering I could have them fired but very well, I did come to ask you something." I had rolled my eyes at the point he mentioned about firing anyone but quickly became focused on the last part.

"Is it what you were going to ask me earlier? You know, before we were interrupted?"

"Yes it was."

"Ok, do you want to sit down?" I asked then feeling foolish when he grinned at me.

"What, I am being polite okay." I defended sitting down anyway but just as I was about to Draven grabbed onto my hands and pulled me to him. He then kept hold of my hands, looking down at them as if deep in thought for a moment before raising his dark eyes to mine.

"There is this Masked ball my kind host every ten years and due to my position, I always attend."

"Okay, so what you're telling me is that you're going to be gone for a bit?" At this he smirked at me and shook his head slightly as if I was missing something.

"Then…?"

"It's in Venice."

"Right, so in that case you *will* be gone for…" He never let me finished but placed his fingers over my lips to silence me and asked me something that made me suck in a breath and made my heart soar to new heights…

"I want you to be my date."

CHAPTER TWENTY-SIX

KEIRA

ALEX AND ANSWERS

After Draven had dropped that bombshell on me he left shortly after that, giving me the time needed to think about it. I think he could tell with the utter shock on my face that I needed time to process. It wasn't long ago that I had been convincing myself we couldn't really be friends but that didn't mean I still didn't find this a shock. I even asked him if he meant as friends and the look alone could have told me what his lips did anyway,

"No, most definitely not." After that he bid me goodnight, literally saying,

"I will bid you goodnight," and then kissed me on the cheek before walking out of my door. Of course, he first looked down at my mountain of shoes and smirked at me as if he knew exactly the reason for them being there.

"I uh…thought that was a better place for them." I added sheepishly making him smile before saying,

"I agree." And then he left shaking his head to himself as if highly amused at stepping over my shoe collection.

So I spent the rest of the night tossing and turning over what to do. In one corner I had an obviously failing relationship with Alex who still managed to have a point in some of the things he'd said. And then in the other corner there was the man I loved with everything that was in me, but he had taken that love and crushed it to heart-breaking proportions. So in truth when someone you love like that could do that to you once then in theory they could also do it again. The only thing I knew for sure was that having it happen a second time I would not survive it or most certainly not come out of it the way I had again.

I would have liked to have said that waking up after these chaotic thoughts rolling around in my head most of the night, I had now found my answers but that would have been a lie. I was still just as clueless as to what to do.

In fact, I had just finished getting ready for a day that I didn't know what it had in store for me when my door was knocked. I almost wanted to roll my eyes at the idea of who it was going to be this time. Either way I had to rather ready myself for a fight if it was Alex or ready myself for the onslaught of feelings if it was Draven.

In the end though this was a wasted effort as it was neither of them.

"Uh…they're lovely but I think you have the wrong room." I said as I stared at the huge bouquet of flowers that was covering half the man dressed in a hotel uniform.

"Your name is Catherine, is it not Signora?"

"Oh, then I guess they are for me." I said letting myself feel a bit of excitement at the prospect of who they could be from.

Oh who was I kidding, I knew who I wanted them to be from and it wasn't Alex, which unfortunately was exactly who it turned out to be.

> *To my beautiful Catherine,*
> *I cannot express fully with words how*
> *Sorry I truly am, so I hope the colours in these flowers*
> *Show you the colours you bring to my heart.*
> *Yours faithfully*
> *Alex.*

I had the guy set them down on the table near the balcony and after trying to give him a tip, one he wouldn't accept, he promptly left. So now here I was, staring at the massive arrangement of peach roses, pink carnations, yellow chrysanthemums, orange lilies and little purple flowers that I didn't know the name of. This was all surrounded with palm leaves and ferns in a crystal vase. It was beautiful but along with the message written it just didn't feel right somehow.

In fact, I was staring at them so long that when the phone rang I jumped and ended up answering it with my heart still racing.

"Hello?"

"Catherine, did you get the flowers?" Alex asked and I had to hold back my sigh, once again in disappointment that it wasn't someone else on the other end.

"Yes, thank you they were stunning." I replied giving my voice the umph it needed right then.

"Not as stunning as their new owner." On hearing that I gave him a warm laugh and soon we were arranging to meet up for lunch.

I was just on my way out to meet Alex, closing my door when I stopped and could do nothing but stare at Draven's door.

I wanted to knock, hell I even took two steps towards it to do just that but in the end I chickened out. For starters I still didn't know what I was going to tell him. It wasn't really a question of whether or not I wanted to go, because that would have made things easier. There was nothing I would want more than to be Draven's date, especially after he told me it definitely wasn't as friends. But was it right? I wasn't so sure. I just knew one thing and that was I needed to guard my heart and protect myself above all other things.

So I didn't knock. No, instead I turned away from his door with a shake of my head and walked myself to the lifts without looking back. I even let my hand hover over the call button for a few seconds before pushing it angrily. It was just so damn frustrating!

By the time I got down to the lobby and met Alex I was in a foul mood and it was one I had to hide. I couldn't really understand it but tried to put it down to the argument last night that was still slightly stewing in the back of my brain. I knew that things with Alex should end because with me having these obvious feelings for Draven it wasn't fair on Alex. But what held me back? Well in the back of my mind I knew that one as well and it was an ugly realisation because it made me a horrible person. But no matter how I tried to ignore it, I couldn't. I was still with Alex because I was terrified that if I ended things with him then it would have been mission accomplished for Draven and therefore he would simply get up and leave again.

I knew this logic was warped into the shape of something ugly, I really did but I couldn't hide the truth from myself. What I really needed to do was be thinking more along the lines of… well if Draven could leave me a second time then surely I am better off without him? I wanted to believe this and put him to the test but the simple matter of it all was I was petrified.

I didn't want to lose Draven all over again…*I just couldn't.*

"Catherine, you're looking radiant." Alex said and I automatically looked down at myself to see what he was seeing. I had on a light blue, white and maroon coloured check skirt that kicked out just above my knees and to this I'd added a cute navy blue T-shirt that had all the same colours the skirt had, in the shape of a messy heart on my chest. It was a V-shape neck so for once I was showing a good amount of cleavage, but I liked to think not too much. I'd also slipped on my light cotton zip up hoodie that was white and thankfully went with everything to hide my scars. To finish off my hair was simply plaited to the side.

"Thank you," was my shy reply making him smile.

"I thought we could get an early lunch?" He said motioning to the hotel's main entrance. I nodded and said,

"Well I skipped breakfast, so I could eat."

We both walked out of the hotel and as I passed the bellhop I thought there was something funny about the way he looked at us both but I decided just to ignore it. For starters if it was Draven taking over someone's body then there was nothing I could have done about it. However, this thought still didn't prevent me from looking back over my shoulder at him.

Once we found somewhere to eat and a spare table to sit at outside Alex started talking.

"I am so sorry about last night."

"Me too." I said because I knew there were in fact things I was sorry for.

"I guess I just let my jealously get the better of me." This I could understand and the instant I thought it I was bombarded with painful images of Aurora. It left a bitter taste in my mouth and I started looking around for our waiter, now almost desperate for something to drink.

"Catherine?"

"Um...? Oh yeah, I can understand that." I said trying to focus on our conversation.

"Are you alright? You seem a bit distracted." Alex asked and I whipped back round from trying to find the waiter too fast and knocked over one of our empty wine glasses at the same time as I said,

"I'm fine reall…" The clatter quickly shut me up but thankfully our waiter finally made his appearance. We ordered drinks but because I was feeling agitated, I picked up the menu and ordered the first thing I saw which happened to be wild mushroom risotto.

"Oh, you want to order now?" Alex asked fumbling with his menu and trying to scan it quickly.

"I really am hungry." Was my answer and the waiter smiled down at me.

Alex ordered some fish dish and I once again shocked him by ordering a large glass of white wine.

"Catherine!" Alex scolded after I downed half the glass.

"What is wrong with you?" He hissed looking around like he was embarrassed to be seen with me.

"Sorry, I guess I am a little jittery is all."

The rest of the meal was stilted but I managed to get through it faking I was tired whenever I would seem unresponsive.

"So tonight? Do you want to go to that concert at the Castello Sforzesco?"

"Uh, yeah I think so." I said feeling like it was the wrong thing to say but honestly there was just something about Alex I couldn't break away from. I wasn't entirely sure I had come here today to break things off with him but I knew something inside me told me I wasn't ready. Was it really the level I would go to keep Draven around? Was this the desperate person I had become?

"You don't sound so sure?" I laughed and for the tenth time told him I was just tired and didn't sleep well from our argument. Well it was almost the truth I just missed out the bit where I obsessed over Draven most of the night after he popped up like some stalker.

"So I will come to your door, do you want dinner before we go?" He asked pulling me to him at the waist and looking down at me.

"I think I will still be full from today's lunch."

"Well you did wolf it down." At this I frowned making him laugh.

"You know that's not a very flattering thing to say to a woman, right?"

"I like how you enjoy your food." Again I gave him a disbelieving look but then let it go.

"So maybe we should just grab something afterwards if we are hungry, there are plenty of places open till late."

"Then that sounds like a plan. I will see you later ma cherie." Alex said before leaning down to kiss me gently on the lips. Then he walked away leaving me by the lifts. A part of me wanted to call him back and tell him I couldn't do this anymore but something stopped me but I couldn't fully explain what it was. It was like having your mind clouded to the truth. Almost like believing what you wanted to believe and ignoring the facts staring you in the face.

I gave myself a mental shake thinking I had been doing that a lot lately. I waited for the lift and numbly got in wondering how on earth I was going to go through with what I needed to do next. I walked to my door and added on those few extra steps that took me to Draven's suite. Then I stared at his door until I mustered up the guts to actually knock on it. It opened just as my hand was coming down and my fist ended up landing on Vincent's chest.

"Is that anyway to say hi to an old friend?" He teased before I shouted,

"Vincent!" And then threw my arms around him causing him to go back a step.

"Whoa! Happy to see me by any chance?" He said smirking and I was just about to reply when I heard a voice from behind me say,

"I hope I get the same welcome."

"Sophia!?" I then left Vincent for his sister and ran into Sophia's arms, making us both giggle.

"I didn't know you were both here as well?" I said pulling from Sophia to give her some breathing space.

"Yes, well once again someone wasn't prepared to share." Sophia said making a growl come from one of the bedrooms behind her. I was only just now starting to notice that Draven's suite was considerably bigger than mine but looked more like an apartment. It had a full sized living room, dining table that could seat at least ten people and even had a bloody piano! I mean why did hotels do this? Did they really think that was a priority when coming on holiday? And if they didn't have one, did the hotel get complaints like…'well my little Rupert here wanted to play piano before being served his fois gras and caviar'.

"I never felt inclined to share what belongs to me." Draven said as he walked from the bedroom in a way that made me want to drool. In fact, I think a little moan came from my lips at seeing him in nothing but a towel wrapped low around his hips. In fact, I tried not to focus on his face as I could feel my cheeks hitting level nuclear meltdown. However, this turned out to be a bad plan because I just ended up watching each droplet travel down the ridges in his eight pack with nothing short of envy.

"I think we should leave them be, Sophia." Vincent said grinning as though he knew exactly where my thoughts lay.

"But this is going to be so entertaining." Sophia complained as she was being ushered out of the room. I even heard the door close but still couldn't force myself to look away.

"Keira?" Draven asked on a laugh and my eyes shot to his as if he had snapped his fingers. I had to clear my throat before speaking, blurting out the first thing that came to mind…which was never a wise move for me.

"I can't be your date." I watched his eyes smile and go soft before he walked closer to me. I automatically put up my hand to stop him.

"Uh, no please…um…can you like, I don't know…give a girl a break and put some clothes on or something…or a robe… surely you have one of those, here let me get it for you…" I said going to walk past him.

"No!" He suddenly shouted in panic and I was stopped when he stepped in front of me.

"Ooo…kay." I said wondering what all that was about.

"It's a mess." He said and I raised my eyebrow at him knowing this was a lie. I folded my arms across my chest which was all the look he needed to know he had been caught out.

"Ok, so it's not a mess but just trust me on this one okay?" I read the sincerity in his eyes and decided to drop it.

"Alright, so back to me not coming…I appreciate the gesture in being asked but…"

"The gesture?" He asked obviously amused at my choice of words.

"Okay, whatever. I just came here to tell you I can't go and…and…uh…" Suddenly I was cut off when Draven started walking me backwards. I made it all the way to one of the walls without bumping into anything, thanks to Draven's hand at my hip, leading me. Then when I went to open my mouth again he placed a hand over it, silencing me in a very effective way.

"Let me stop you right there, sweetheart. This is what is going to happen. You are going to give it some more thought as to what you want and I mean *really think about what you want* and I will be waiting in the lobby for you until 8 o'clock tonight. Then I will leave and hope with an intensity I only know when having you in mind that your hand will be in mine when I do. Now do you understand?" I could only stare into his deep eyes in amazement.

"Keira, say yes to me and do it now." I took note of the obvious need coating his words and gave him what he asked.

"Yes." As soon as my answer passed my lips, he visibly relaxed and planted a soft kiss on my forehead. Then whispered,

"Good girl"

"Good girl…good girl…*Good girl?*" I kept repeating this back to myself over and over again once back in my room. I walked the length of the suite that much I was surprised there wasn't track marks left in the carpet. I was so stupid!

"Stupid, Keira!" I said smacking my forehead and remembering that kiss placed softly there. I obviously couldn't be trusted to make these types of decisions on my own, not when a half-naked God stood before me…I mean he was dripping wet for Christ sake!

"Oh come on!" I shouted up at the Fates, now remembering the sight. I looked at the clock on the wall that kept taunting me that time was getting on. I knew I needed to be ready for Alex by 8:30 but I cared little for getting ready. I was just trying to think about the ten minutes I had until Draven didn't find my hand in his. What would it mean? What would it *truly mean?* Would that be it for us?

"Oh God!" I said thinking if I asked hard enough in my head then someone would take this decision from me. I couldn't do this, it was too much.

"It's too much." I said repeating my mind out loud. Nine minutes…oh no, now eight minutes. After staring at the clock for nearly another minute I then jumped when the phone rang. Oh God, was it him?

"Hello?" I said on a whisper too scared to know.

"Catherine it's me, I am so sorry to have to do this to you but…"

"You're cancelling?" I asked quickly interrupting.

"Yes, I am sorry but work came up and…" He never got to finish. I looked up at the clock seeing I had seven minutes. This was it. This was my sign. So I dropped the phone mid Alex explaining, no longer caring about anything but those seven minutes.

I just ran out of the door with nothing but my heart pounding.

"At least it still beats." I said to no-one but myself knowing this was the truest thing I had said out loud. Because that was my answer. My heart was still beating, and it wasn't for the man on the phone but for the man waiting for me.

The man waiting for my hand.

"Oh come on you stupid son of a bit…" I never finished because I saw the lift was stuck on 3 and I was running out of time.

"Oh sod it!" I then saw the sign for the stairs and ran. I shot through the door as if I was being chased and jumped the last steps every time there was a landing. I used the railing to swing my body round quicker hoping I could get there in time.

"Seven minutes." I said as I saw the numbers to the floors going down but not quick enough.

"Five"

"Four"

"Three"

"Shit!"

"One, finally!" I shouted as I burst through the door. I ran blindly around a corner until the lobby opened up in front of me. I was panting, I was a mess and I felt like crying because I couldn't see Draven anywhere...

"No." I whispered feeling the pain of crushing disappointment start to invade my senses. Then I heard it, the most amazing name in all the world just because hearing it meant the beautiful flower of hope could now bloom.

"Keira?" I turned around and saw the most perfect man stood there. He didn't need to say anything else. Not one thing. Not one single thing.

Because right now actions spoke louder than any words ever could have.

He held out his hand to me and I...

Took it.

CHAPTER TWENTY-SEVEN

KEIRA

I MISS YOUR WINGS

"Oh Hell no! No, no way…not doing that again!" I said shaking my head enough that my plait snaked around me like a rope.

"Keira, come now, it's not that bad." Draven tried to reason with me but I just kept shaking my head.

"This coming from the man with wings… yeah right, give me a break!" There was no way, absolutely no way I was getting on a helicopter again, no matter how shiny, sleek and expensive it looked. I heard Vincent laugh behind me and my head shot round to give him the evil eye. He held up his hands in surrender but did so still laughing, the gorgeous bastard!

"Keira it takes three hours to get from Milan to Venice by car but only just over an hour by chopper." I growled at this and then said,

"Fine I will take the train and meet you there." Then I

turned to walk away only I didn't get far. Draven grabbed me from behind and started laughing in my hair.

"Come with me, I need the company." He teased.

"You have Vincent and Sophia for that, I am sure they can keep you entertained." I said trying not to let the feel of his arms around me keep me from being strong on this matter.

"Now, now, little bird, you know there is only one divine creature I want entertaining me on a flight." Ok so now not only did I have his arms around me to contend with but now I had the sexy lure of his voice whispering in my ear. Damn men!

"I am not getting on that thing." I said as sternly as I could with Draven now rubbing my belly in soothing circles.

"You are."

"Why, did your dad call and tell you it's snowing in Hell?" At this he burst out laughing and I felt his head fall back.

"Alright my Keira, you are going to listen to me now and hear the depth of my words when I tell you this…" He leaned down further and this time I felt his lips graze my neck before they touched my ear. I knew what he was doing and damn him it was working but when he spoke next, it went from working to bloody worked!

"…do you think I would let anything happen to you? Do you think you would be in any danger nestled safely in my arms because that is where you will be and that is where you will stay…*I won't let you go.*"

"You'd better not let me go." I said vulnerably repeating his words.

"I won't let you go…*ever.*" He said and his words sounded thick with emotion. He also said this at the same time as giving my body a protective squeeze as if proving his words with actions. I wanted so badly to believe that there was a deeper meaning to the way he said that but I wouldn't fully let my mind travel that path of hope quite yet.

"Okay." I said softly and as soon as I did I yelped in surprise when Draven scooped me up into his arms and carried me to the waiting helicopter.

"I didn't mean like right from this second." I said laughing nervously the closer we got.

"I did." He said grinning.

"Oh God." I moaned as he walked us across the heli pad and ducked us both under the fast-moving blades to the open door. I tried not to notice the details, but I found myself scanning the body of the thing, suddenly wishing I was an engineer and able to detect problems on sight.

"Well there looks to be no leaks, that's a good sign at least." I said using humour to hide my nerves. I wasn't surprised that Draven could hear me over the loud noise of the engine.

"Trust me, sweetheart." Draven said stepping up effortlessly into the small cabin. It only had four seats, two that faced each other, and Vincent and Sophia were already sat next to each other across from us.

"Oh dear, she looks a little pale." Sophia said looking worried.

"Actually, I think I might be sick!" I shouted and started struggling in Draven's hold.

"Calm yourself, you won't be sick." He said placing one hand over my stomach and the other over the column of my throat. I don't know what he was doing exactly but the tingles that started tickling my skin and the warmth that spread out under his palm started to make me feel less nauseous.

"There, do you feel better?" I nodded the little I could with still being held immobile in his hold. It was as if he let go of me for a second then I would bolt out of the door.

"She will have to be strapped in a seat before we take off." One of the pilots said before closing the door making Draven growl.

"As you can see she is now seated." Vincent said moving a hand in front of the pilot's face reminding me of a Jedi.

"Oh, my mistake." He said before slamming the door.

"I can't do this!" I shouted but Draven just pulled me closer and cooed in my ear.

"Ssshh, love, I have got you." I settled but only slightly because I kept jolting in his hold with all the different noises that were going on around us.

"Come here." Draven ordered softly but he was obviously getting agitated at seeing me so scared. He cradled the back of my head and pulled my face to his neck, keeping me there.

"Right, now I want you to listen carefully to my voice, are you listening Keira?" He asked, his voice becoming a gentle hum, lulling me deeper and deeper into his care.

"Yes." I murmured into his neck.

"Good girl…now close your eyes."

"Draven?"

"Close. Your. Eyes." He said more firmly this time making me do what I was told.

"Now the noises around you are going to fade into something else."

"Something else?" I asked quietly.

"Yes sweetheart, they are going to sound like the rain hitting your bedroom window. You're sat at home on your bed with a book in hand and it's your favourite one, Jane Eyre."

"You know that?" I asked surprised and I heard Sophia giggle at the fact that I obviously wasn't playing Draven's game properly.

"I do. Now concentrate on where I am taking you, Keira."

"Sorry…AHHH!" I shouted out when I felt the movement of us lifting.

"It's not working, I can feel her fear." Vincent said and I wanted to shout 'Well durr genius I'm terrified!', however I was too busy with *being* terrified to do anything but shake in Draven's hold.

"Yes thank you Vince, I gathered as much." Draven snapped.

"Please, can I get out now?" I asked whimpering the higher we went.

"No love, just listen…"

"It's not working." Sophia said interrupting her brother making him growl again.

"Right! Keira, you are going to let me into your mind."

"No, I can't, I…"

"Now Keira!" He shouted and I caved. I instantly let down my guards and felt him swoop on in there. He entered my mind in such a way, it was like trying to fend off a stampede of wild horses. It made me feel fuzzy as if drunk for a few seconds before I heard Draven whisper sweetly,

"Open your eyes." I did as he asked, happy that he no longer shouted at me. I opened my eyes and saw my old bedroom as it first was at Libby's. The bedroom where I first fell under Draven's spell and was now back to doing so once again.

I was being carried over to my bed and the sight hit me like a memory shaped sledgehammer. I remembered the nights like this and the times when I believed my life couldn't be or ever get any more perfect. Because being in the arms of the man that you love and feeling that same love projected back at you was like nothing else in the world. Being carried to the bed knowing that love would only spread out like wildfire the second our bodies connected was the stuff dreams were really made of.

Draven lay me down so gently it was almost as if he was worried I would crumble away like dust.

"Are you going to sleep for me, my precious girl?" He asked and looking up into his eyes was like finding the meaning of life written there. It was like finding your purpose for being born. Like finding out that nothing else mattered but having those eyes looking down at me now. So of course I said,

"I will do anything for you." This made those perfect dark eyes glow before he had to close them, as if savouring a deeper feeling within him my words had put there.

"Then sleep and find peace in my arms…I will protect you, *always.*"

"Yes." I mumbled already feeling the weight of exhaustion seep into me, coming at me from what seemed like nowhere. But it wasn't coming at me from nowhere at all, it was all Draven. So before I could let this moment pass, I placed a limp hand at the back of his neck and used the last of my strength to pull his head closer to mine. He came to me willingly and there I gave him the unguarded truth with four words,

"I miss your wings."

I woke up not in my own bed like my mind was prepared for but in another lavish hotel room. I looked around the masculine space and rubbed the sleep from my eyes. I was surrounded by solid wood furniture that was dark and very Draven, which quickly informed me I hadn't been put in my own room. This thought had me squirming under the satin plum coloured sheet that had been placed over me. In fact the more I looked around the less and less this actually looked like a hotel but more like an actual home.

"Oh dear." I said out loud thinking I was in so much trouble, as once again being back in Draven's bed, what other words were there.

"You're awake." My eyes quickly found my trouble at the door grinning at me. I must have looked dwarfed in the space, sat up in another one of his monster sized beds. And what was it with four posters for him anyway…probably an old-fashioned thing.

"Old fashioned uh?" He said causing my mouth to drop.

"You have woken an open book, sweetheart." He informed me with a small smile that at least looked somewhat coy.

"Well I guess I should thank your mumbo jumbo this time." I said stretching my arms out and yawning.

"You know you really do have the most flattering ways of describing my talents." He teased making me grin.

"Yep, that's me!" I said in reply and bounced out of bed. Then I walked up to him, reached on my tiptoes and kissed his cheek before saying,

"Thanks for making me pass out handsome, but can you feed me now?" To which he laughed.

"I think I could do that…" He said but then leaned down closer to my face and finished with,

"…but only because I like you." Which he had no idea, but in cartoon land my toes would have curled up like the witch from Wizard of Oz. However he caught my blush no problem. So with half his lip tipped up to one side he took my hand and led me through the house.

"Oh wow!"

"You like it?" He asked and I could hear the pride in his voice, one I could understand why.

"It's stunning and very you." At this he laughed but still gave me a look that silently meant he wanted me to explain that comment.

"It looks like a palace." And boy didn't it just! It was all highly polished marble floors, pale walls that had heavenly figures painted into what looked like the plaster and elaborately carved wooden ceilings. The furniture all looked pristine as though it had been plucked right out of the past. Even the glass chandeliers sparkled as if they had only been cleaned no more than hours ago.

"I have had this place since the 16ᵗʰ century and it is one of the most impressive Grand Canal palazzi in Venice…if I do say so myself." He added smirking down at me.

"Palazzi?" I asked.

"It is Italian for a large splendid residence or public building, such as a palace." He winked at me for this last bit.

"It's strange thinking about you living anywhere else but Afterlife." I said being honest.

"And why is that?" He asked in that smooth voice of his that was bordering on teasing and seduction.

"I don't know why, maybe just because I love Afterlife so much, that's the only place I want to see you." The words were out before I thought about what it would mean to Draven to have me saying this.

"By the Gods woman, you are killing me!" He said stopping me and pulling me solidly into his embrace.

"I… am?" I asked in a shy, unsure voice that wavered. I couldn't look him in the eyes as I asked so he tipped my chin up with his fingers curled so I had no other choice.

"Yes, *you are.*" He said and there was not one thing in his look I could fool myself into saying was anything other than lust. The purple ring intensified and just as his head lowered they quickly transformed into a blazing inferno.

"Draven?" Upon hearing his name, he ceased his descent to my lips and closed his eyes tight as if in pain.

"What is it…why does that keep happening?" I asked but when he stepped away from me I knew I had lost him. It was obvious he took a few seconds to calm himself enough that when he opened them again, they were back to black.

"You must be hungry, come and let me feed you." This wasn't snapped at me but there was something that wasn't right with Draven. It was the same as when someone puts on a fake smile when inside you know they are freaking out about something important. So instead of pushing, which I had every right to do, I decided to do what was best for Draven and that was to smile back and nod my head.

———

After that strange moment we shared in the grand looking hallway I soon found myself sat in a less formal kitchen nook. But even then it still looked as if it had just jumped from the pages of a rustic homes magazine. All thick butcher's block counter tops and hand carved cabinets, with panels and wrought iron hinges. There was a big island in the middle with a massive black slab of marble which broke up all the wood in the room.

Draven had led me into the kitchen and before I spoke a word on its beauty he had picked me up by the waist and sat me on top of the island like I was its new centre piece. My legs just dangled from the ground making me feel tiny.

"How hungry are you?" I looked out of the window and noticed it was only now just going dark, so I knew I must have slept a few hours.

"Snack hungry."

"Right, baguette, cheeses and meats it is then." He said turning to open the huge stainless steel fridge door.

"Sounds perfect." I said still finding this action from Draven an odd one. Then he started to get out packets of sliced meats, quarters of cheese, olives, butter and some baby tomatoes. Then with his arms full he carried them to a table by a bay window, where a half moon shaped bench was carved from the stone wall.

"I must say you look very domesticated right now." I said once I was sat in this little nook. This was of course after he had stepped up to me and hooked me with one arm around my waist, brought me down from the counter before sitting me in said nook. Now he was walking back over to take his own seat with the baguette in one hand and bottle of wine in the other.

"Well I don't cook as you know, but I can raid a full fridge with the best of them." He said as he popped the cork and poured me a glass.

"So I see, does this mean your next Christmas present from me should be a frilly pink apron?"

"I don't know, do you like getting spanked?" He asked over his glass before he took a drink. I on the other hand nearly choked on a cherry tomato!

"So this ball…you know I was in a bit of a rush and well…I didn't have time to bring anything with me, not that I had a ball gown stashed in my case or anything…" I said talking none stop to try and hide exactly what his last question had done to my girly parts.

"It's fine."

"It's fine?" I repeated as a question.

"You don't need anything whist your here and tomorrow evening has been taken care of." He replied tearing into the bread with his hands and handing me a piece first.

"Taken care of how?" I asked but then thought it odd when I saw Draven roll his eyes as if listening to something else and that something else wasn't me.

"You're about to find out." And after less than a second the doors burst open and he wasn't wrong.

I found out and I found out in the best way ever…

"Tootie cake!"

CHAPTER TWENTY-EIGHT

KEIRA

GIRL MADNESS

"Pip!" I screamed and launched myself at her, which wasn't an easy feat, as shimmying out of a nook is never a graceful thing. But I didn't care and why would I? This was Pip we were talking about. I think I would have belly flopped over hot coals to get to my Pip.

"Whoa Tootie pants, you miss me or what?!" Pip said as I grabbed her tiny frame and yanked her to me for a fierce hug.

"You're really here!" I said stating the obvious making her laugh.

"Well it's not every day an Imp gets the royal invitation." She replied winking at me but wait, it wasn't at me at all, it was at Draven. I turned my head to watch as he unfolded himself out of his seat and only had eyes for me.

"You did this?"

"I did." Was his simple reply.

"You did this for me?" I asked again only this time clarifying the specifics. This time he only nodded and that was all it took. I left Pip's arms and ran at Draven. I registered his shocked face for a split second before he caught me, and I started raining little kisses all over his face for what he had done. He seemed to keep himself immobile for my assault as if he was afraid any sudden movements would cause me to stop. So he just let me show him my appreciation.

"Aww, well isn't that just the cutest sight you did see baby pop, pop?" I heard Pip say, smacking her lips at the 'pop, pop' bit. I pulled back to find Draven grinning as big as I had felt it with my lips pecking at him.

"You've made me so happy!" I told him.

"Then it's definitely worth all the extra noise and colour invading my home for that very reason alone." This answer made me smile big and I looked back round to Pip to find her being held from behind by the handsome Adam. Then I turned back to Draven and whispered over his cheek,

"Thank you for inviting a rainbow into my life." And then I kissed him where I had spoken.

"You're welcome, Love."

"Alrighty, alrighty, enough of the mushy shit, I wanna drink!" Pip said light-heartedly making me laugh. Draven let me go and I walked back over to my personal rainbow, as I hadn't been lying when I said that to Draven. Pip was literally wearing a rainbow!

She wore a chiffon halter neck dress in the brightest colours of the rainbow, with a massive double layered bell shaped skirt. To this she added a skull and cross bone hello kitty brooch at her cleavage and neon green tights with a monster pattern. She also had on round mirrored sunglasses that reminded me of John Lennon and I was only just now noticing the panda bears she had painted on her nails.

"My Lord." Adam said bowing to Draven before coming over to me and giving me a warm embrace.

"Hello little troublemaker." Adam said to me with a smile in his voice.

"You are so gonna be glad I'm here for tomorrow night, it's gonna be a blast and we are gonna have so much…"

"Winifred." Adam warned letting me go and crossing his arms across his chest.

"It's fine Adam." Draven said obviously knowing what she was being scolded for and for a minute I thought it was because she was about to blurt out something she shouldn't have.

"What?! What did I do this time, cause you know you already punished me for what I did on the plane, and I told you my teeth wouldn't get in the way but oh no, you just couldn't keep still, you had to move and jerk around and I told you that would happen, but would you listen…would he listen…" She repeated again to me making Adam frown down at her.

"Winifred." He warned again.

"What...? Oh…that." She said turning back to face Draven and bowing like Adam, only holding out her skirt creating the perfect curtsy.

"My Lordie Boss Man." She said then looked my way and winked at me making me giggle. Draven just nodded with his lips twitching and Adam rolled his eyes to the ceiling.

"Everyone happy now…um let's see, punished on plane, check, super happy fun time reunion, check, Royal bullshit taken care of, check, watching Boss man and his little woman practically hump, check! Now let's get shitfaced!" Pip shouted in a way I think she was expecting everyone else to cheer…of course they didn't. But I did give her a little,

"Yay."

So the rest of the evening was spent as a little reunion party and even though the room next to the kitchen was as posh as a palace, none of us really acted like we belonged there. We laughed, we joked and we drank like wine was going out of fashion and we had to get rid of a cellar full before the next season! But I soon learnt that even when you had hundred year old furniture that sloppy wine stains weren't an issue when you had Draven Mumbo Jumbo.

And this was a good thing because at one point me, Pip and Sophia were all up dancing on the large coffee table in the centre. I even thought it was pretty cool how Draven had offered me his hand to help me step up, the same as Adam and Zagan had done for their girls.

Of course I knew I was drunk when I started shouting for Dolly Parton's 9 to 5 to come on. Thankfully Draven had the foresight to save me from singing like a banshee by putting his shoulder to my waist and folding me over his shoulder.

"Time for water I think, my little diva queen." He had said making me giggle.

"Aww, no fair...we lost our human." Pip complained to Sophia who was swinging her hips without losing a single drop of her pink Cosmo. I smiled as I was manoeuvred into Draven's lap and handed a bottle of ice cold water. But it wasn't the water that made me smile, or unbelievably even being in Draven's lap, although that was always something to smile at.

No, it was none of these things but what it was, was one of the most beautiful things in the world and that was watching my family. The family I thought I had heartbreakingly lost. It was watching the love surrounding me in so many different forms but each holding a powerful place in my heart.

It was also the way the husbands in the room looked at their wives like the sun rose and set with them. Like the only reason the stars came out at all was to see their girls. Zagan kept looking at Sophia like he was fighting a secret grin that spoke of private things she would soon discover later from his thoughts. Adam looked like he was just fighting the urge to grab his wife and run, looking for the nearest building to climb like King Kong taking his prize possession away from the world. Although both tried to act the perfect vision of calm, I knew better.

It almost felt like I was absorbing all the love in the room and it was making me feel lightheaded it was that powerful.

"Isn't love grand." I said relaxing back to Draven's chest and sighing when his arms encircled me from behind.

"It should be the only true reason for living." Draven's response surprised me. I turned my head to look up at him from the side.

"You sound like you've only just discovered this philosophy?" I asked on a laugh. His eyes turned soft and his hand came to cup my cheek.

"I never knew what it was like. I watched my sister find it and those around me, but I never understood the level of power held there…" He paused and leant further into me before saying,

"…until there was you."

———

I don't know what happened after that but one thing was obvious…I was wasted! I was in that state where you are semi-conscious to all around you and it's like living in one of your dreams. Well at least it was for me right now because I was pretty sure I was in Draven's arms once again being carried towards a bed.

"The water didn't work." I heard Pip say.

"Well that is what happens when you add vodka to it."

Draven almost growled this and I shivered but that then ended on a hiccup.

"You okay, sweetheart?" Draven's voice changed dramatically when he started talking to me and not Pip. I felt him push some of my hair back as he lay me down.

"Umm mmm…fink so." I said wondering if it sounded as blurred to them as it did to me?

"You need to leave, I must get her comfortable."

"You mean naked is what you mean!" Pip said and without fully seeing straight I knew she had her hands on her hips.

"Leave Imp!" Draven snarled making me moan,

"Fight…no."

"Great, see what you did, now she's turned into Yoda!" Pip argued making me giggle and hiccup again.

"What is a Yoda?" Draven asked as he pulled off my shoes.

"Not what, who and don't you go worrying your little royal head over midget green, big eared Jedi masters…you worry about me mister if you ever hurt my girl again, well then I would scratch off your balls and stuff em up…"

"Mrs Ambrogetti…I think that's quite enough for our King to visualise." Adam's gentle voice filled the room and I only managed to see a shadowy silhouette stood with arms crossed at the door.

"Ooops, boy am I sooo in trouble now, thanks boss man… laters! Oh and take loving care of our girl now!"

"I live and breathe to do nothing else." Was Draven's soft response when I heard the door close.

I woke the next morning with the intense feeling that some small rodent had taken up residency in my mouth during the night and then died some horrible death! Yes I truly felt that bad. Bad enough in fact my first noise of the day was a groan.

"Feeling rough perchance?"

"I'm not sure, is my head really cracked wide open and shameful moments of last night are pouring out, or does it just feel that way?" At this the bed started shaking with Draven's raucous laughter.

"Here, let me check." He said finally when he controlled his humour. I felt his hands at my head, and it felt kind of magic what he was doing there, rubbing gentle circles at my temples.

"Oh that's good." I moaned still all the while keeping my eyes closed.

"You know I hear the light won't actually burn your retinas from just a hangover."

"Ha, ha, and since when did you turn into such a funny man?" I asked sarcastically.

"Since I met some beauty in the woods who taught me how to laugh." Oh god, but that was such a beautiful thing to say, it took me a moment to be able to reply.

"You're smooth I will give you that." I said but Draven knew with the thick emotion in my voice that there was no malice in my response.

"I do try, Love." He whispered making me finally open my eyes. The room wasn't as bright as I first thought it would be thanks to the thick curtains that were pulled across the sight of Venice.

"Ah there she is…good morning my little drunkard." I couldn't help but fail at supressing my grin on hearing my new pet name.

"Morning my sober knight in khaki pants." I replied making him laugh and say,

"Well not anymore." I looked over to him to see only his

bottom half covered with the sheet and found he was right, now he wasn't wearing anything.

"Draven!" I shouted.

"What? Do I look like a pyjama man to you?" At this I laughed as well.

"No, I couldn't see you in blue and white stripes."

"Then naked it is, count yourself lucky your little Imp guardian was around to put me in my place last night or you would find yourself the same." He said nodding to me. I looked down at myself to see I was wearing the same T-shirt that Draven had on last night.

"Umm…and was my little green haired guardian the one to put me in your T-shirt?" And there it was, my answer all wrapped up in a bad boy grin.

"I will take that as a no."

"Would you believe I closed my eyes?" He asked resting his head up on his hand having his bent elbow to the bed.

"Not if the Pope himself told me so." I replied, to which the bed was once again bouncing with Draven's laughter.

"See I told you they're up…Pip bomb!" Pip suddenly shouted running into the room and leaping onto the bed to then start jumping like a five year old. She was of course wearing a Sonic the Hedgehog onesie.

"Get up, get up! It's Christmas, mum and dad!" She yelled then burst into a fit of Pip giggles.

"Calm down Squeak, it's too early and I have the mother of all hangovers!" I said holding my head like this would help. Sophia followed in through the door, now answering my silent question as to who Pip was talking to before she burst into the room. Sophia walked over to the curtains and pulled them both back letting the light come pouring in. My instinct kicked in and before I could stop myself I rolled into Draven and buried my head into the little nook by his shoulder.

"Ahhh!" I complained and Draven's other hand came to the back of my head to hold me to him.

"Well it's not early, and this you see here is afternoon light. So chop, chop, lots to do, lots to be done." Sophia said coming to stand by one of the bed's thick wooden posts.

"Yeah, this is totally dress dolly human day! It's like one of my favourite days and actually, I think it should be a national holiday!" On hearing this I groaned into Draven's skin making him chuckle. I then turned back to face my girls to find Sophia smiling softly at the sight of me and Draven in bed together.

"You know I have become quite good at dressing myself these days, in fact let me show you later…yeah?" I said and tried to ignore the slither of tingles up my spine with having Draven's hand making its way down to rest at my bare hip where his T-shirt had ridden up around my waist.

"Oh no, not this time Kazzy, your ass is ours!" Sophia said and Pip who was still standing at the bottom of the bed added,

"That's right Whoopie Toot, your ass has been sold to us chickiedees!" Then after giving Sophia a high five, she then smacked her own ass a few times as if this would help get her point across better. I then looked up to Draven and after a smile he looked like he was concentrating on something in the distance. I was about to ask him about it but before I could he spoke.

"Alright ladies, fun time is over, you can wait for my… *your* doll outside." Draven said and his fingers dug into my flesh after his little slip up.

"Oh no fair King dude! We wanna play now!"

"Turtle Dove!" Adam shouted as he made it to the door frame from what looked like a dead run. His plaid shirt had several tears slashed across the chest and around the muscles of his arms, like he had been straining and ripped his shirt.

"Oh dear not again." I muttered when I followed his arms

down to see thick chains hanging with broken links from his wrists.

"Pipper, you didn't." I said making her shrug her shoulders before winking at me and turning to her frantic looking husband.

"My bad hubby pot pie."

"Excuse me my Lord, my wife forgot her kiss this morning." Adam said straightening up and stormed into the room like he only had one purpose in life. He then reached that purpose and bent her bodily over his shoulder, taking her right off the bed with one turn.

"One of these days, Winnie you will be the death of me." Adam said with a naughty Imp hanging over his shoulder.

"Well technically dear I already killed you once." She replied sweetly receiving a swift smack to her ass that made a cracking sound. After wincing she then lifted half her body up and gave us all the gnarly sign with both her hands as she was carried from the room.

"Well Brother it looks like you have your wish after all because our little Imp will be getting punished for a few hours at least." Draven grinned at his sister and then nodded his head. She laughed and blew him a kiss before leaving us alone once more.

"Poor Adam, Well at least that was lucky he broke free." I said making Draven laugh.

"Who do you think helped free him?" I pulled back and raised an eyebrow at him.

"You did?"

"I did."

"Well other than the obvious reasons at him being held captive by walking, talking, breathing trouble, why?"

"The most obvious is for what I have held in my arms right

now and it is not something I am ready to give up." I blushed at Draven's answer and even more so with the look he gave me.

"Keira there is something we need to talk about…something I have been trying to say and something you need to know about my hea…" At this moment he got cut off by Vincent bursting into the room and Draven closed his eyes in frustration.

"Dom, you need to come now!" On hearing the panic in his brother's voice Draven sat up still holding me to his chest, as though I was his main point of concern.

"What is it?" He asked and suddenly I was transported back in time to a night of both horror and salvation.

"It's Takeshi, he…well he has had another vision and Dom…" Vincent said only this time the difference was that Draven was the one to finish it…

"He is again near death from it."

CHAPTER
TWENTY-NINE

KEIRA

SAY THAT AGAIN

"I must say I am loving the hair." I said at the sight of Pip sat cross legged in a Buddha pose on the couch. Her hair was braided tight on either side of her skull in multiple rows, creating a green and blue tipped Mohawk. It was mesmerizing the way it swayed with every move she made and even more so because she had corkscrew curls stuck up in every direction. This was so Pip, to choose to have a mad riot of curls instead of straight hair you would normally find on a Mohawk.

Of course just looking at her dungaree shorts in the material of a patchwork quilt, with a Miss Piggy faded T-shirt underneath was enough to put a smile on anyone's face. This included Sophia also, as when she had walked in the room with that 'I just got me some' swagger, Sophia with her perfect timing had Maroon 5's 'Moves like Jagger' bursting from the hidden speakers in the room. And Pip being Pip started doing a moon walk backwards whilst punching at the air in front of her in some cute 'Hell yeah' dance.

"Why thank you Tootie whoopie pie." She replied to my compliment making me laugh.

"Whoopie pie?"

"She's going through her baking phase again." Sophia answered shaking her head as if she remembered the first time she went through this phase.

"Hey, let's just say it wasn't Sweeney Todd's lovely Mrs. Lovett who first came up with the recipe for 'meat pies'." Pip said with a huff at the end. I swallowed hard and gave her a disbelieving look...one I was really hoping wasn't going to be followed by shocking disgust.

"What! Don't look at me like that Toots, they were already dead and people needed to eat back then, shit girl do you know how expensive a cow was back then...? We didn't all have some magic beans like the stupid Jack to trade with...poor Betsy." I shot Sophia the crazy look instead of aiming at the ranting Pip and mouthed the word,

"Betsy?"

"Her favourite cow." Sophia whispered back to me and then shook her head telling me to drop the 'Betsy topic'.

"So, tonight, what am I to expect?" I asked trying to change the subject to one I thought was safer than random farm animals. However, I didn't miss the look exchanged between Sophia and Pip making me frown.

"Ok, come on guys, fess up!" I said folding my arms so they knew I meant business. I think after the cryptic way Draven had left me that morning I had hit my limit on secrets or being the human left in the dark. I mean it was clear that something big was going down if Takeshi was having visions so damaging to him but one look from Draven and I knew there was no point even asking. So after Sophia had come to get me I knew it was her job to entertain 'The human' whilst the big boys dealt with the Supernatural shit. It was frustrating but I was no longer in a position to demand anything from Draven, let alone badger him with loads of questions.

"Don't worry Kaz, it's just some stuffy Ball we all attend every ten years."

"Yeah, it's no biggy, Toot Pop, just one big party with masks and mini crab cakes." Pip added shrugging her shoulders making her curls bounce.

"Crab cakes?" I decided this question was safer than the five hundred that I wanted to ask.

"Oh shit yeah! Do you remember them? They came with that little dip that I swear I wanted to bathe in! Do you think it had lime in it...? I tried to get the staff to give me the recipe, but the bitches were as tight lipped as Caspian's asshole...poor Liessa." She said shaking her head. I burst out laughing and Sophia just rolled her eyes before getting up and pulling on a big cord attached to the ceiling, which I gathered was her calling for someone. This was confirmed when she said,

"All this talk of food is making me peckish and Dom would as usual be angry if I forgot to feed you."

"Well Adam already fed me!" Pip said with a wink and I covered my ears and said,

"LA, LA, LA, LA!" making her laugh.

I started shaking my head and instead focused on the most girly and elaborate chintzy room I think I had ever seen, knowing instantly it was Sophia's sitting room as soon as she brought me in here. For starters the room was pink and the kind of pink that would make men like Draven bleed from their eyes if they were forced to spend any longer than a minute in its space. The ceiling was nothing short of incredible and the only way to describe it was like being under a giant white and gold umbrella.

From the centre hung a hot pink crystal chandelier and each section of the ceiling that fanned out was painted with gold filigree. But the ceiling continued half way down the walls and every other point was a tear drop shape with a mirror at its centre. It was beautiful in a fairy tale way but completely ostentatious and totally over the top in every way possible.

"Oh goodie!" Pip said jumping off her couch and bouncing on her feet as three servants walked in carrying trays and three tiered cake stands.

"I love afternoon tea!" She shouted clapping.

"I know you do."

"I know you do." Sophia and I both said at the same time making us all burst out laughing.

The rest of the afternoon consisted of us nibbling on delicious pastries, dainty sandwiches and scrumptious cakes that Pip declared she would try baking them all for us again. I didn't miss the way Sophia winced and made a mental note never to try anything Pip cooked in the future if I could help it.

Now we had reached that part of the day where we had started on the champagne. Because let's face it, this was Sophia we were talking about and I was now being used as a large doll. Although I had to say, I accepted it a lot better than I used to considering the time spent playing dress up with these two. To be honest I was just happy being around them once again.

"So will Lucius be there tonight?" I asked as I thought it was odd that Pip hadn't yet mentioned him.

"Yeah I think so, I mean he has gone on some secret ass assignment looking into some scum bag half…"

"Pip! Come and look at this one, I think this would be the perfect head dress for tonight." Sophia interrupted quickly and it was obvious the look she gave her was for my benefit. What didn't she want her to tell me? And did it have something to do with Alex? I knew one thing and that was my new mission was getting Pip alone at some point before tonight! Sophia wasn't an easy nut to crack when having information she knew her brother didn't want me to know but Pip…well Pip was like a peanut shell, she was sometimes just begging to be cracked!

Just then a bell sounded and once again Pip was clapping and rolling back on her heels in excitement.

"It's finally here! Mega cool beans!" She shouted then raced to hold the door open as a woman in her early fifties strolled in followed by two girls rolling in a clothes rail. You could tell the older lady was Italian, but you could also tell she was a designer judging by the professional air in which she carried herself. She was perfectly styled and groomed, with not one single hair out of place. Oh and she was beautiful.

"Ah Concetta Collini my dear, how lovely to see you." Sophia said warmly as she was followed further into the room by the two girls that looked so similar they could have been clones. In fact, I don't think they were people at all but really fashion robots in sharp cut black wigs.

"Miss Draven, it is a pleasure as always. I spoke to the head of your house, Mr Draven and he approves of my designs for his lady friend." She said and I wanted to giggle at being called his lady friend.

"Fidanzata." ('Fiancee' in Italian.) Sophia said this one Italian word like she was informing her of something very important and if the designer's look was to go by then it was also shocking.

"Capisco" ('I see' in Italian.) She said nodding her head and then walking over to me.

"I am very pleased to make your acquaintance, Signorina." She said leaning into me and kissing me on both cheeks.

"Uh…It's nice to meet you too." I replied wondering what it was exactly that Sophia had said to her. She then gave me a single head nod and I knew this was her way of accepting me… I just wish I knew exactly to what she was accepting me.

"Ok enough of the smushy whushy let's see the dresses!" Pip shouted making Concetta Collini turn a scowl Pip's way I didn't care for. She scanned her from head to foot and frowned.

"Why you insist on wearing such things Winifred I have no idea." She said turning her nose up at her and I quickly began not to like Concetta Collini. So I took a side step next to Pip and said,

"Actually, I really like Pip's sense of unique style. Come to think of it, I think Pip is so special a person that every day, conventional clothes just aren't good enough for her because she is such a beautiful colourful painting, she needs an equally colourful frame to show off such beauty." I said folding my arms and adding,

"Don't you agree, Sophia?" without needing to look at her to know she had my back, which was proven when she said without hesitation,

"Yes, I completely agree."

"Well…I guess so…but…" Concetta Collini started to say but was completely ignored when Pip shouted,

"OMG! Oh my giddy! You…that…you! Aww you guys! You really think so, that's like the nicest thing anyone but hubby pants has ever said to me! I love you guys! Come 'ere!" She said flinging her arms around me for a huge and bone jarring hug that was surprising considering how tiny she was. I laughed until I had no air left and then Sophia had to come and place a warning hand on her shoulder before saying,

"Let go Squeak, she can't breathe."

"Oops, my bad Toots!" She said letting me go and I coughed once, dragging in much needed air.

"Ahem." Concetta Collini made a noise of impatience in front of us and then said,

"Would you like to see your gowns now ladies?" To which all three of us burst out laughing but nodded our heads all the same…however it was only Pip that said,

"Do donkeys eat cherries?!"

"I can't wear this." I whispered to Sophia in panic making her smile in a way that wasn't taking a blind bit of notice in how serious I sounded.

"Why ever not, it's stunning on you and my brother will of course think so too." She said circling me as I stood in front of the massive mirror and butchered my lip in worry.

"But it's as big as a wedding dress!" Sophia laughed and responded,

"It's a masked ball Keira, what did you think people wore?"

"Ok, ok so I get that it's a big deal, but this dress…*it's not me.*" I said looking down trying to hide the vulnerability in my voice.

"Yes it is and do you know why?" She said lifting my head up with her gloved hand. She didn't wait for my response before she continued,

"Because it is only a dress but when someone as beautiful as you wears it, it then becomes what it was always made to be, spectacular! Now wear it how it was always meant to be worn."

"And how's that?" I asked and she turned me back round to face the mirror and whispered fiercely,

"With the same pride my brother will feel having you on his arm."

"Oh Sophia." I said touching her arm and then pulling her in for a hug, or at least as much as I could do in this tight, corseted dress.

"I will give you a minute." She said after pulling away and seeing the tears in my eyes. I nodded knowing that I needed it, so as not to disturb my carefully applied makeup that Sophia and Pip had spent an age fussing over. They had made my eyes sparkling white with the black mascara making my eyes look huge and what they thought was Angelic. But it wasn't my makeup that was making me try and swallow down the nervous lump that seemed lodged in my throat.

No, it was the dress.

What Sophia said was heart felt and touching but she was also wrong. Because with this dress it was going to be beautiful no matter who wore it over their skin. In fact it was the idea of what Draven would think when he saw it that was making my palms sweat under the black velvet gloves that I was pulling up my arms nervously. I then ran my hands down the fitted bodice gently as it was completely covered with, what Concetta Collini informed me were black Swarovski crystals. It was at its thickest all around the top of my breasts in the sweetheart neckline and spanned out like the tail of a shooting star all the way down to the over skirt.

The dress was mainly a taffeta material in a light grey colour that ruched across the bodice and down to my hip on one side. It then gathered in sections held there by clusters of the black glittering crystals that too burst outwards like stars. This part swooped right round and reached the floor in a small train. But it was the rich material of the under skirt that really got my attention and I wouldn't fully understand why until later.

It was a thick luxurious material in silver grey with a paisley patterned brocade in black velvet and it's what gave the dress most of its weight. But it hung beautifully as the underskirt and made you wanted to lift it up and twirl like a little girl dreaming of her wedding day. I think that was what it was about the dress that made my heart flutter. It was more about the ideals it held. The possibilities that let your mind go flying off to dangerous lands of hopes and dreams. Dreams that you knew couldn't come true but did nothing to crush the feeling of soaring high for what you desired most in the world. And for me, that dream would always be the same…

"To be Mrs Dominic Draven." I whispered to myself and then froze as I felt the air around me start to electrify. And with this feeling I knew I wasn't alone. Oh no, I was far from alone and I knew this when I heard a voice speak from behind me. But even if I hadn't heard his voice, I had his handsome reflection now staring back at me from the mirror. Shock wasn't the only emotion I could read on his face as there were too many to digest in those short moments. I was the deer caught in headlights. The girl in the mirror caught in an intense black gaze that kept me prisoner as he searched for the truth in the words he had just heard.

And then he spoke and as I knew Draven would, it was a demand he needed…

"Say that again."

CHAPTER THIRTY

KEIRA

SAY SOMETHING

"Draven I uh…"

"Say it again." Draven demanded again and I felt my cheeks flame. Jesus but the raw intensity coming from him was like a weapon of power he possessed. It was like being caught in a net.

"Draven *please…*" I begged knowing I couldn't repeat those words, but he cared little for my pleading and I knew this when he stormed across the room and stood at my back. He gripped hold of the top of my arms tight enough for me to know it would have been a foolish attempt to pull away, not that I wanted to. He stared at me in the mirror easily with being a full head above me in height, even with my heels.

I gasped suddenly when he pulled me back into him until our bodies were flush with one another. Then one arm left mine and snaked across my front up to grasp my bare neck, holding the last part of me to him.

"I want to feel that name under my hand when it is spoken from your lips…Now…*say it again."* I let the rest of my head go slack and fall back into his chest on a sigh he felt on his palm. I had closed my eyes and was taking in the feel of his heavy breathing at my back and I knew he was hitting his limit of waiting for something that was obviously very important to him. It was elevating to my heart to know that he wanted to hear it again. And it was this thought that made me open my eyes as I started saying,

*"To be Mrs Dom…*Draven!?" I shouted cutting it short as I noticed Draven's eyes staring back at me, or more like burning back at me through the mirror. It was pure fire and Hell staring back through his eyes and it looked almost like it was trying to consume his soul. As though I was looking through a portal to the other side and that's when his hands started to get hot.

"Draven!" I shouted again making him tear away from me before his touch would have no doubt burnt me, if it had been given the time. Luckily it only left slight warmth from where his hands had been.

"Draven? You have to tell me what's happening?!" I asked turning around to face him and only just now taking in his appearance.

"I am sorry…did I…by the Gods but did I hurt you?" He asked taking a step closer to me and reaching out his fingertips to touch my neck.

"It's fine."

"It's not fine!" He shouted ripping his hand away and fisting it by his side as if disgusted with himself.

"I could have hurt you!"

"But you didn't." I said softly taking the tentative steps needed to bring me directly in front of him.

"Keira, if I hurt you, I…well, I just couldn't…"

"I know but just stop." I said interrupting his tortured thoughts as I couldn't stand hearing them any longer.

"You have to give me some answers here Draven, what's going on?" I asked softly. His hand came up to cup my cheek and it pained me to watch as he hesitated before touching me.

"I can't give you answers yet, because I don't know them myself, but I promise…*I promise you…*" He said this leaning into me and touching his forehead to mine before continuing,

"…I will not rest until I find out, for nothing will ever stop me from touching you." I sucked in a quick breath at hearing his confession and closed my eyes as the emotions swept over me.

"Isn't she breathtaking?" Sophia said walking into the dressing room and we broke away from each other as the moment was stolen from us. It was one of those times when I wanted to scream for it back. I wanted to rewind time and make every second count in a way that was filled with the words I needed to hear. But no matter how supernatural my secret world was it still didn't have the ability to change the past and turn back time.

However, it was now that I got my first real look at Draven and what he was wearing, causing me to blurt out,

"We match?!"

"Impeccable timing as always, Sophia." Draven snapped as he walked past her out of the room and out of sight. To be honest I couldn't say I fully blamed him for his sudden foul mood. It seemed every time we were having a moment it seemed to be robbed from us before it had chance to develop into something more. I knew there was something Draven was trying to tell me and the only thing that stopped me from pinning him down and demanding to know was my ultimate fear. One that would mean the end.

What if he was really trying to find a way to tell me once and for all this could never happen? But surely if that was truly the case then what about all the flirting? What about all the times he had referred to the past and how he felt? Did he still feel the same or were these the subtle hints something he wanted me to see a deeper meaning into?

Oh God it was just so frustrating not knowing but instead of voicing any of my fears the only thing I found myself saying was just a repeat,

"Why do we match?" to which Sophia burst out laughing and did nothing to provide me with an answer. No, instead I just followed her out of the dressing room and out through a series of rooms which were obviously in her side of the house. It was only when she opened the last set of double doors that I knew we were back into the main part of the house as the décor changed back from girly style to classical 16th Century Renaissance.

And there stood Draven in all his masterful glory.

In fact the room was full of everyone ready for this ball but my eyes took in only one man. I hadn't been lying minutes ago saying we matched but obviously not in the sense that Draven had lost the supernatural plot and was now wearing a dress. No but what he was wearing made me want to sink to the floor and drool whilst begging him to take me to some forbidden island where no one would ever find us.

He wore a black and silver double breasted waistcoat that was the exact same material of my under skirt. To this he'd added a deep purple cravat and a black shirt with billowing sleeves that reminded me of a time long past. The same silver buttons on his waistcoat matched his cufflinks that held his family crest. His black trousers were tighter than his usual tailored suits but this was so he could wear the thick leather boots that came up to just below his knees and they reminded me of Jane Austin's time.

He reminded me of some sexy buccaneer with the cutlass sword he had hanging at his side. Hence this was why the first thing out of my mouth when seeing him was blurted out without a filter.

"I like your sword." Hearing this made him smirk down at me.

"Oh do you now?" He said taking the last step to me and scanning my body like a hungry lion would a defenceless gazelle. I laughed at his rude thoughts and found myself just happy he no longer looked as angry as when we were interrupted moments ago.

"Behave." I said first having to clear my throat, so it didn't sound quite as breathy.

"With how enchanting you look tonight, I know behaving just won't be possible." He replied before taking my hand and kissing the back of it as he bowed slightly at the waist. I blushed and gave him a little nod in thanks not knowing what else to say. But in the end no words were needed as we merely shared a heated look that said it all. There was more passion and fire in that simple touching of hands to leave no doubts that we hadn't lost one shred of desire for each other. No, if anything that fire just burned brighter, only now it seemed that I was the one who could get burnt from it.

"Wit'a woo Tottie Toots, look at you looking all hot and shit!" Pip said bouncing over to us with Adam in tow. Actually it was hard to say if it was Pip or the new owner of the Little Shop of Horrors!

"Wow Pip, that's...well that's..." I said trying desperately to find the right words to explain the utter outrageousness that was Pip's dress.

"I know right! Isn't it just amazeboozyballs?" She said

twirling around and under Adam's arm that he held up for her. I had to smile at the adoring way he looked down at her and her crazy dress. Although crazy was kind of an understatement as it looked as though she had robbed some gothic flower shop!

It started with a bodice that was made from strips of black see-through organza that crossed over her small breasts, which showed her little pierced nipples. Then over her shoulders like a shrug was some kind of long black grass that hung down almost like pointed fur. But it was the skirt that was the real showstopper. It started at her waist with a belt of real black dahlias and then from there started with a row of black violas that each had a hint of purple and a touch of bright yellow at their centres. After that it was a full ball gown skirt of raining black flowers all hanging down and layered by their stalks.

"Well it's definitely you Pip, that's for sure…although I must say it's the first time I have seen you all in black." I added noticing the only colour on her was from her tattooed skin and bright hair.

"I know right, but well this is an official snotty nosed business affair and with being a shadow Imp and all, then we chickidees normally are seen wearing black…I uh…" She leant closer after pausing which managed to pull Adam's arm straight out from behind her as she hadn't let go of his hand. But of course he didn't seem to mind.

"…I'm kind of not like others of my kind and well…those bitches don't like me." She said looking a little sad which made me frown. However, the deep belly growl came from the man at her back and I could tell it was more Abaddon responding than the more placid Adam.

"Oh that's ok baby cupcakes, those meanie bo beanies can't say shit to me the boring bastards! Anyway back to the pure awesomeness that is my dress, we have lilies, Irises, Tulips, Hollyhocks, roses…oh and loads of other shit in there but isn't it pretty and don't I smell incredadooble? Here smell my pits Toots!" She said lifting her arm up and thrusting her Pip pit in my face.

"That's enough my little garden Winnie, we don't want to be late if we are to get you first chance at those crab cakes." On hearing her husband reminding her of this important fact, she gave me a big toothy grin making her black rose lip ring wilt down before blowing me a smacker of a kiss.

"See ya there Tootie doll!"

"Well it looks like I won't be the only flower at the ball." Sophia said coming from around the corner with two velvet boxes in her hand. She was also referring to her own stunning dress that was a deep crimson colour and the material had been so cleverly cut and sewn that the skirt looked like the petals of a blooming rose. Almost like she had stepped into the centre of a giant rose and then let the petals fall delicately around her.

"Sophia you look so beautiful!" I said only seeing her dress for the first time as before when she led me in here she had on a long covering cloak.

"Thank you but I believe all eyes will be on a new crowning jewel tonight." She said cryptically. This was when Draven nodded to the table and then made a motion with his head cocked to the side like he wanted her to leave. She placed the boxes down and then bowed her head before leaving the room with a massive grin on her face.

"Am I missing something?" I asked looking round the now empty room where I was pretty sure Zagan and Vincent had also been.

"May I?" Draven said holding out his hand for me to take. I didn't hesitate in doing so and he led me over to the table where the two boxes awaited.

"Draven?" I said nervously as I could very well guess what he was about to give me, especially since my neck was bare.

"I have had this in my possession for a while now." He said looking down at the box and running his fingers over the top of it.

"I was going to wait but when you agreed to stand by my side tonight I knew the time had finally come... birthday or not." He had continued to speak to the box until this very last part. I sucked in an emotional breath at his confession and his eyes shot to mine.

"This was my birthday present?" I asked clearly shocked.

"It was." He answered and it was easy to see there was pain in his eyes with the memory he no doubt associated with my day.

"I can't express just how sorry I am that I wasn't there for you and I know this doesn't make up for it, but I wanted you to know that you still had my heart that day."

"Oh God!" I said on a whoosh of air that escaped me as he finished this passionate admission when opening the box.

"Do you like it?" He asked after I just stared at the most beautiful necklace I had ever seen, other than the one I had torn off that awful day at the lake.

"It's...it's..." I mumbled making him laugh and I couldn't seem to be able to move my hand from in front of my lips in awe.

"May I?" He asked lifting it from its case and holding it out to me. I could only nod my head as all words escaped me. I felt the few curls that hung down from my pinned hairstyle being brushed gently to one side and he must have felt my shiver.

"Such a beautiful neck needs not only to be framed in the treasures of the earth but to also display the heart she captured long ago." He added verbally as he placed the heavy weight to my neck before he turned me to face the gold gilded mirror on the wall.

"I give you my heart, Keira." He whispered in my ear

making a single tear fall. I followed its path all the way down my cheek, the side of my chin and then my neck until it reached the large purple heart that lay close to my own. It was stunning and up until that moment I didn't even know you could get diamonds that colour. It hung by a string of white gleaming diamonds which were flawless themselves, but this wasn't what held my attention. It wasn't even the heart shape in which the main diamond was cut. No it was what was holding the precious stone either side and it was what my shaky fingertips were reaching up to touch now.

"You told me that you missed my wings, so I added them for you." He said from my back and my watery eyes sought his in the mirror. Because he hadn't just given me his heart, he had given me it encased in his wings. This was the exact moment I closed my eyes letting my tears fall and the power they held was the crashing of the waves against my guarded walls. It brought every single last one of them down into the sea of hope with a thunderous roar and I was left with only one thing I needed to hear.

"I need the words." I said trying to force the sentence past my lips without my voice shaking like my body was. Then without a single second of hesitation he turned me around and said the most beautiful words in the world,

"I still love you."

And then he kissed me.

CHAPTER THIRTY-ONE

KEIRA

A ROYAL APPEARANCE

The kiss.

That kiss.

It was simply the kiss I had been waiting what felt like a lifetime for. It was a mind consuming kiss that stole my senses and electrified them. It was as if Draven had taken every last part of me and was trying to fuse our lost souls together so they would never be alone ever again.

It was the second he placed both his hands on my cheeks and pulled me to meet his lips his touch seared my skin with those delicious tingles. I had almost forgotten what they felt like. In fact, I started to shake from the overload of emotions they caused, and this was when he decided he too wanted more. He tilted my head to the side and one hand left my cheek to grip the back of my neck. I sucked in a breath and he took this opportunity to deepen the kiss, taking it to a dangerously sexual level. I knew this when he suddenly wrapped an arm around my waist and lifted me up so we were the same height.

Then he consumed me totally with an even deeper kiss.

It was raw power in the way he mastered my mouth. The way he tasted me and searched me out like he needed to remember. It rendered me weak and barely able to hold on. I could feel my cheeks were wet from tears that couldn't be held back. It was all too much and yet because our bodies craved each other it wasn't enough. It was like two extreme forces of nature coming together as one and you could just feel the dangerous power underneath the surface begging to be released. I felt his hand slide from my neck to my cheek and wipe away the tears there I had silently cried.

"Draven." I didn't know why I whispered his name I just knew that I had to.

"Don't worry, I have you…" He said placing me gently down on the table.

"…and this time, I won't *ever* let you go." He finished before his lips once again claimed mine. And he was right…

He didn't let me go, not once.

DRAVEN

By the Gods I could barely believe I finally had her in my arms and was kissing her. It felt as if every cell in my host was coming alive for the first time again since the day all that time ago when my soul first entered it. My body hummed and almost shook with the force of it. In fact, I wasn't the only one with the compulsion to do so as I felt the beauty in my arms start to vibrate with the sheer force of our lips reuniting once again.

This was where she belonged, right here in my arms and it felt like nothing else in, not only this world but the next!

But she had no idea how hard an emotion like this was for a man like me. The concentration needed to not hurt her by the overwhelming urge to crush her body to mine in a way that could somehow fuse our very souls together. It was like succumbing to the most dangerous drug and I was hopelessly and undeniably addicted. She was my beating heart, my life and my every breath that was needed for my body to function. But not only that, as it went far beyond the realms of the physical world. It was everything in my very creation as not only a man but as a child of the Gods. It was what I believed in my heart and not the organ that beat but the very core of your soul.

The essence of who you were.

And at my core, at my heart and what made up my essence, was Keira.

KEIRA

"Do you mean that?" I asked pulling back the tiny amount he would let me.

"That I will never leave you again?" I nodded not trusting myself to speak.

"Leaving you the first time tore my soul apart but leaving you the second would destroy every last part of it. I cannot, I will not and more importantly I outright refuse to leave you ever again, not even for one single day…do you hear me?" He said putting his forehead to mine.

"I…I can't believe it…I just…I can't stop shaking." I said after laughing nervously at the end and he took my hands in his and held them to his heart between us.

"I know I haven't always been truthful with you Keira and I will explain the reasons why…I will explain everything…"

"Okay." I said waiting to hear it but Draven shook his head gently.

"But not now."

"But why?" I said thinking nothing could be more important than the truth.

"Because sweetheart, as per usual these days, time is not on our side. But I promise you, I will explain after the Ball." He said pushing back a stray curl behind my ear.

"Do we have to go?" I said fully admitting that I sounded desperate. He laughed without humour before saying,

"By the Gods you have no idea how much I wish we didn't." He said suddenly pulling me hard to him and kissing me once more. It ended as quickly as it had begun and he whispered down to me,

"All I want to do right now is pick you up and fly to the top of St Mark's Campanile to re-join our bodies by making love to you."

"Oh God!" I said before grabbing his face with both hands and then being the one to force my kiss upon him. It took all of about two breaths taken before he took control of the kiss and soon our hands were all over each other.

"We have to go." He said tearing his lips from mine before coming right back at me. I kissed him back and then pulled away myself saying,

"I know but…"

"Just one more kiss." He said finishing off for me and finding my willing lips again. It was as though now our minds had finally let go of all the barriers we ourselves had put there, then now there was nothing stopping our bodies from celebrating the fact.

"Have…to…go…" He said as he now took to kissing my

neck and my head fell back to look up at the ceiling in a dreamy haze.

"I know…uh, actually I don't…why do we have to go again?" I asked and he pulled away from me to laugh.

"The Ball won't start without me."

"Seriously?!" I said and he shrugged before responding awkwardly,

"I'm their King."

"Oh shit, then we really *do* have to go." This made him laugh out the word,

"Yeah."

"Okay then, let's go." I said pulling away from him but I found my hand quickly captured and as I was pulled back I fell into him.

"Not yet."

"Draven?" I asked as he tilted my body backwards and just before he took what he wanted from me Draven said something very out of character but amazingly hot all the same.

"Let them fucking wait!"

And then he *really* kissed me.

"Can you run?" Draven asked and I shot him a cheeky grin before lifting up the front of my skirt with both hands.

"I don't know, can you keep up old man?!" I said winking before turning round and running down the long gallery with a Demon King close on my heels laughing. Not surprisingly it didn't take him long to catch up and he grabbed my hand as he went past, pulling me along with him. He looked back at me grinning and I wondered if the picture we painted was one of two lovers from the past on the run from the world?

"You guys are so late." Sophia said shaking her head as we ran round the last corner together and down the steps. I went to answer her by stepping forward when Draven suddenly whipped me around and with a hand at the back of my head he kissed me in front of a speed boat full of his family and council. Then he let my lips go and pulled me towards the boat in a daze.

"We don't care." Draven said as he passed Sophia before nodding to the guy at the wheel. She then turned to me and couldn't hide the shocked grin from lighting up her face. Only then did she really take in my appearance and turned an accusing look to her brother with hands on hips.

"Look at her hair, her makeup...what did you do to her, ravish her?!"

"Well it's about damn time." Vincent said making Draven step up to him and clasp his shoulder before agreeing,

"Yes, it certainly is."

Sophia rolled her eyes at me, but the smile didn't match her pretend frustrations. Not only that but I think my own beaming grin was enough to show I cared little for my messy hair and smudged makeup.

"Come here and let me fix you." She said and pretty soon with the Draven's own brand of Mojo I was back to how I looked pre-Draven and the beautiful confession.

"There, beautiful again." She said standing back and obviously admiring her handy work. Draven walked up to me and pulled me into him like it was the most natural thing in the world once again. I wondered in fact if he had any clue what this was doing to me or my neglected nether regions?

"She's always beautiful." He said before kissing me like it was once again his given right. In fact, it was slightly worrying at how much of a dream this felt. It was almost like stepping on thin ice and waiting to hear the crack beneath your feet. Because once you heard it you then knew you had no chance of reaching the other side and if I looked up I would only ever see one man that I needed to reach.

"Are you alright?" He asked me tilting my face up, no doubt to get a read on my expression.

"Yes." I said and with one raised eyebrow I knew he didn't believe me. I was however thankful when he said,

"Alright, Keira, I will give you this evening, but you have to promise me something." I just started to pull at my bottom lip with my teeth and nodded. He gave me a small smile before using his thumb to free up my self-inflicted torture.

"I want you to promise me that you're not going to run scared from me." We both knew why he said this because one look in my eyes and that was all he needed to know…I was terrified.

I nodded but it wasn't enough for him.

"I'm going to need words, Keira."

"I promise." I said quietly making him smile.

"Good girl, now look, we are almost there." He said turning me and pointing an outstretched arm towards a line of gondolas. The canal opened up into what almost looked like a lake and I could see the tallest buildings that we were heading towards.

"St Mark's Square is where our Ball is held every ten years." Draven told me after shifting me to stand with my back to his front.

"Did you go to anything like this last year?" I couldn't help but ask. I heard him sigh behind me and I gave him the minute he needed. Actually, it felt so long to wait for my answer that I was surprised when he spoke.

"Yes I did."

"Oh."

"Keira." He said my name in response to my dejected 'oh' and I felt him pull me closer to him as the boat steered its way closer to the side.

"Its fine, I understand life doesn't just stop because we broke up." On hearing me saying this he started laughing. I

413

frowned and turned to face him, no longer caring about the spectacular view. However, it was only when I saw his face that I realised it was a laugh of the bitter variety.

"But that's where you're wrong sweetheart, my life did stop. Yes, I had to continue in my duty to my people. I had to continue in my ruling and maintaining the balance in my world, but I did this a shell of a man. I did this as a dead man walking. Which included coming to events like this and trying not to show my world their dead King."

"Oh Draven!" I said before throwing my arms around him and this time holding him to me. I reached up my hand and placed it on his cheek before saying,

"I had no idea."

"And for that I am thankful. The pain I inflicted on you was great enough."

"Draven I…" I started to say I wasn't exactly sure what but I didn't get that far.

"Hush now." Draven said before taking my face in his hands and kissing me silent.

"Uh, I hate to be the one to tear away reunited lovers, but we are here." Sophia said giggling passing us as she then made her way off the boat. I felt the start of Draven's growl in his kiss before he let me go.

"It's moments like this I don't care for duty." I laughed making him smile down at me.

"You're stunning." He said taking me back and making me blush.

"Thank you." I replied shyly before letting him take my hand and lead me off the boat. It was only when we were on the street that he stopped me from going any further.

"It is why I am both thankful and regretful in giving you this." He said confusing me. He then produced the other box that had been on the table, one that I had forgotten about until now. Before I had time to ask he opened the box and it all started to make sense.

"My mask?" He nodded and lifted the delicate lace from the box. I didn't see any ribbon so I wondered how he would get it to stay on my face.

"You'll see." He said answering my unasked question.

"This will tingle." And this was my only warning before he lifted it to my face. He gave me a wink before placing it on my nose first and with his thumbs he pressed the lace down on either side first over my cheeks and then over the top of my eyes. He was right, it did tingle but more in the way your body shivers when something emotional captures you and it's your body's way of expressing it.

"There and now time for my matching crown." He said after he finished placing it on my face, making it stay there in a strange way. It was almost as if I couldn't even feel it. He held out his hand and Sophia who was now also wearing a mask handed Draven his own.

It was matte black and a very masculine shape with two silver filigree embellishments under the side of the eyes. This then matched the silver wings at each side that started the silver crown. It wasn't big and in anyway ostentatious but looking at both Vincent's and Sophia's matching masks you could see Draven's was slightly bigger, showing who was in charge between the three of them.

It held their family crest at the centre along with that strange symbol I still didn't know anything about, despite having it on my skin as a birthmark. I was so close to asking but what he did next took my mind from it. He held onto the top of the mask and snapped off the crown part so it was now in his hand in one piece.

"Draven what are you…?"

"I wanted you to have mine." Was his strange answer and I

could see this obviously meant something to him. Then he lifted the crown to the top of my lace mask and held it there, staring at it as if concentrating. I felt something start to move, almost like the lace was growing around it and after a few seconds he nodded.

"Perfect." He said and placed his own mask on his face, holding it there where his too automatically stayed in place without aid.

"It's growing?!" I said fascinated as I watched in awe a new crown exactly the same as before start to rise from the top of the mask. He smiled at me and gave my chin a little hold as if he found my excited ways endearing.

"Time to go, Princess." He said and took my gloved hand in his and I stared up at him as I watched something black darken the skin under the mask like makeup seeping through his pores.

"Your eyes?"

"It adds to the theatrics." Was his only explanation before leading me along a beautiful arched building.

"Where are all the people?" I asked knowing that St Mark's Square was the biggest tourist attraction in Venice since my parents had come here for a weekend getaway once. My mum had told me all about it and how romantic everything was and now looking around I had to agree with her.

"Your kind?" I nodded to his question.

"For this night only none of your kind will be interested in seeing the square. The businesses will have closed and for one night it will be like this never happened."

"Wow, you can do that?!" I said shocked at the level of power needed to control so many people all at once.

"It's a combined strength but yes."

"Dominic." Vincent called his brother and Draven nodded to his silent question.

"Stay close to me, no matter what…do you understand?"

"Draven?" I didn't like the sound of this but it was too late as we walked around the corner and I gasped at the sight. The sun had already started to set before we left so now it left the sky an unusual electric night blue colour that made for an effective backdrop for the illuminated buildings of the square. I had seen pictures of the place before as photography was one of my dad's favourite hobbies, so I knew the place had been transformed for the event. It was as though every single light bulb in every single arched window had been swapped for a red bulb, creating a crimson glow all around us.

But this wasn't the most startling part or the sight that had my heart pounding.

"Draven I can't do this!" I hissed in a panic grabbing onto his arm like it would save me.

"Just breathe." He said down at me and gave my arm a squeeze before walking me forward into the parted ocean of people. There seemed to be thousands of masked faces all looking at us as we walked down the centre of the great crowd. I looked frantically behind me to see Vincent first and then Sophia with Zagan behind her. I wish I could say the wink Vincent gave me helped or the thumbs up Sophia thought I needed.

"Breathe again, Keira." Draven said and I hadn't even realised until that moment that I had been holding my breath. I looked down at the red carpet we walked down not being able to look at all those faceless masks and studying eyes staring at me.

"Eyes up." I heard from next to me just as we walked past a group of people dressed as demonic goats with horns on their masks.

"I can't look at them."

"Then let's rectify that should we and give you something else to look at." He said confidently and just before I was about to ask. He held up his hand and stopped, which effectively stopped the procession behind us, one I only just now realised was most of the people I remembered from the VIP.

"Draven what are you…" I started to whisper but was cut short when I was suddenly swooped up into his arms making me cry out.

"Draven!" My startled shout was drowned out by the great wave of shocked gasps from the endless crowd. However, Draven didn't seem to notice, or he did but he just didn't care.

"Now eyes on me, my love." He commanded and I gladly did what I was told.

"I don't think I have ever seen a brighter blush on you." He said laughing at my obvious outrage.

"This hasn't helped in making them stare less." I said frowning at his huge grin.

"But that wasn't my goal." He replied as he strode purposely to the other side of the square where I could now see an awaiting throne had been set up.

"So what was exactly?"

"Well for one you're breathing again." I rolled my eyes and couldn't help but laugh at the sight of his smile.

"And the other?" I braved asking as we came to the end of the red carpet. I expected him to put me down before answering but he didn't. No, instead he mounted the steps up to the higher platform. One that was covered in what looked like black wired petals sewn together in a pattern of the same symbol we both wore. Then he let my legs go till I was standing.

"To make a long overdue statement to my world." He said and before I had chance to fully process what he meant to do next, he lifted my arm up, faced me to the crowd and boomed out the words that floored me…

"I give you all your Queen!"

CHAPTER THIRTY-TWO

KEIRA

IT'S ALL ABOUT THE MASKS

I didn't really have much time to react to this grand gesture before I was spun round, bent over his arm and kissed in front of Draven's kingdom. Deafening cheers erupted from the vast crowd and Draven let me go only to smile down at me.

"You are in so much trouble for this." I warned unconvincingly. I knew this thanks to the wink and bad boy grin he gave me before lifting me so I was once again upright and facing Draven's people.

"Che la festa cominci!" Draven shouted which I gathered meant to get the party started in Italian because the crowd went crazy. I watched Vincent walk up the steps and smirk at me before taking a seat next to his brother's centre chair. Next was Sophia who rolled her eyes at Draven's brazen behaviour, but her smile was easy to read. She walked over to the other side of Draven's throne and bowed her head gracefully to the crowd before sitting in her own grand chair.

"Should I just…" I nodded my head to the side where there were more chairs which were being filled up with the rest of his Council.

"Oh don't worry sweetheart, I have just the place for you." He said walking me backwards until I had no other option than for my legs to fold into his seat. Then he came down leaning into me with his hands on the arms of the chair until coming to my face level.

"Now be a good girl and stay right here, I will be back in a moment." He finished this by kissing my forehead and then pushing off the arms. I watched him walked over to the side to speak to a man wearing an elaborate violin mask and a tux. I decided not to look like I was being nosy so I turned my head away and tried not to focus on the massive supernatural crowd. Of course, I was also trying not to be the most obvious human in St Mark's Square but sat up here it wasn't exactly as if I could blend in.

Maybe if I was wearing more of a hidden costume like the sea of colour in front of me. It was an incredible sight and there was so much to take in, it was hard not to openly stare. The masks were like sculptured pieces of art that were being worn and with the costumes added they each told a story. There were horned gods and mythological creatures like the Centaurs. One woman's mask was combined with a wig and even had snakes all entwined in the shape of a 16th century wig that looked like Medusa on a night out.

There was everything from the usual jesters and harlequin clowns to double sided masks that showed both happy and sad faces. Or even bright gold suns, blue moons and tear shaped landscape painted masks that really should be hanging in some gallery somewhere. There was one woman who walked past dressed like some forest pixie and had a beautiful mask made from gold leaves all layered on top of each other.

However, these were definitely the tame ones, as there were those that made me want to gag they were so disturbing to look at. One couple that walked past were obviously lovers as the woman walking in front of the guy had a hand covering one breast possessively. This would have been fine as I had seen far worse since my time entering Draven's world. But the disgusting part was the fact that her mask was her actual face that had been sliced all the way round so blood dripped down her neck. Then huge fishhooks had been put through her chin, cheeks and forehead and attached to thin chains that her partner's other hand held wrapped around his fist almost like a sadistic puppet master.

There were others, like the woman's mask that looked like she was looking in one of those crazy house fairground mirrors that made your features look tiny and pulled your eyes, nose and mouth into the centre of your face. I lost count of the number of monsters and decided to look away when one of them looked like it was eating itself, puss filled boils and all.

"A lot to take in isn't it?" Vincent said leaning over the arm of his chair.

"You can say that again."

"Would you believe me if I told you that one day this is will all seem normal to you." I couldn't help but laugh at this.

"Not really no, but I wouldn't take offense, I have been seeing Demons since I was seven years old and I'm still not used to it." At this he gave me a gentle smile before saying,

"Well you have a lot of years ahead of you, so give it time and you can become immune to most things."

"Like loving someone?" I asked and I wanted to bite my tongue off for saying it. His eyes widened for a second before I watched him slip on a new mask, only this time it was of the emotional sense, not like the crackled cream and gold one he was wearing. It was the same design as his brother's along with the waistcoat they both wore only his was like his mask, in cream and gold. And this, unlike Draven, he wore under a fitted black suit.

"Unfortunately, if it is real love then time heals nothing, or so I have seen for myself." He said nodding towards Draven who was walking back this way.

"Vincent, I didn't mean…" I tried to explain but he held up his hand to stop me.

"I know what you meant, Beautiful." He said giving me a small smile and then he lowered his head in a respectful bow. I wanted to say more but I felt Draven come to stand over me.

"Catherine *Keira* Williams…" Draven said my full name and smirked when he changed my middle name from one less boyish. Then he asked a question that I had been dreading,

"Will you do me the great honour of dancing with me?" Then he bent at the waist and held out his hand.

"Uh…"

"I will take that as a yes." He said taking my hand and pulling me into his arms causing me to land on his chest.

"I don't know…" I started to say looking down at the crowd to see not a single couple was dancing.

"Hey, do you trust me?" Draven asked gently as he placed a hand at my cheek.

"Yes." My quick answer made him smile and my happiness came at seeing his own lighting up his eyes.

"Then let me take care of you." He said leaning down to kiss my forehead. Then before I knew what was happening, he turned and clapped twice making a booming sound resonate throughout the crowd. He obviously didn't need to say the words as this was no doubt the way it was done every time they held this Ball. Because now like some practiced dance group the crowd parted perfectly and created a circular dance floor.

Draven looked to the side and nodded at someone. Within seconds the sound of a piano being played was being pumped through hidden speakers, filling the entire square with the most beautiful music. Draven led me down the steps and into the centre surrounded by a wall of people.

"Trust me." He said in response as my panicked eyes scanned the crowd.

"Give me your eyes Keira, no one else...*just me.*" As soon as my eyes looked up at his he pulled me in with a hand at my waist and the other clasped tightly in mine. Then the most perfect words started to sing around us in a heavenly voice.

"I chose this song for you." He told me and as soon as I started to listen to the lyrics I had to hold back the tears. It was as though the first verse was from Draven's point of view and the second was definitely from mine.

'You are the avalanche, one world away
My make believing, while I'm wide awake
Just a trick of light, to bring me back around again
Those wild eyes, a psychedelic silhouette
I never meant to fall for you but I
Was buried underneath and
And all I could see was white
My salvation'

'You are the snowstorm,
I'm purified
The darkest fairytale
In the dead of night

Let the band play out
As I'm making my way home again
Glorious we transcend
Into a psychedelic silhouette.
I never meant to fall for you but I
Was buried underneath and
And all I could see was white
My salvation'

"You're *my* salvation, Keira." Draven said fiercely after spinning me around the open space. I clung on tighter upon hearing his declaration of love and let the rest of the world simply fade away. I didn't need to look around to know they weren't there anymore. It was just me and Draven dancing in an empty square, somewhere on this earth where only we existed. Where only we existed to be together. I knew that now. I knew that ever since either of us took our first breaths in this world that we were destined for each other. Gods or no Gods, Fates or no Fates!

"You are *my* salvation, Dominic." I said looking up and with that he stopped us moving. His eyes flashed purple and this time there was no Hell in sight. Then without another word between us he took my face in his hands and kissed me with enough passion I felt his essence start to flow back into me for the first time since that day at the lake.

It was like lighting up my heart.

The kiss and the song came to an end at the same time making everything about it one of the most perfect moments of my life. It was beautiful in every way and even though the rest of Draven's world started to come back into view I no longer cared. Because I was here, right here in their King's arms and this time I trusted that I wasn't going anywhere without him ever again.

It was only the sound of the echoing applause that brought us back to reality from our secret moment. Draven gave me a gentle smile and with my hand still in his he walked me back up to his awaiting throne. I looked behind me to see the space was quickly being filled with new dancing couples and the music started to play something more upbeat.

I turned back just as I felt Draven lean down to once again pick me up into his arms and before I could protest he had already sat down with me positioned in his lap.

"Uh…don't you think this is a little…?"

"A little?" He said smugly pulling me tighter to him and it was impossible to miss the massive erection pressing into me from behind.

"…inappropriate for royalty?" I managed to force out even though my voice felt thick with lust.

"Well that's the best part about being King, sweetheart, I get to make my own rules." I turned my head to the side and rolled my eyes at him making him laugh. Then he put his nose to my cheek and whispered,

"I can't wait to get you alone." Making me shiver with anticipation and fail to hold back the moan that escaped.

"Ah the happy couple! I must say Dom, it's finally nice to see you dancing at one of these things with someone other than your sister."

"Lucius!" I shouted as I heard the voice I would know anywhere. I was about to get up, forgetting myself, when I felt bands of steel hold me still. So instead I was left to watch as his powerful frame mounted the steps wearing a double-breasted military jacket made in a steampunk fashion. His mask was a cream porcelain skull that fit over his entire face. It was creepy but also had an amusing side as it was wearing steampunk googles. He flipped it up to rest on the top of his head before nodding to me.

425

"Keira girl." Lucius said with his handsome yet sadistic grin firmly in place.

"Back so soon?" Draven said in a serious tone that sounded like it had a hidden meaning.

"Well as you know I usually try and miss these things but alas, this year it was not meant to be." Lucius said and then winked at me.

"You have what I need?" Draven asked making me frown back at him, one he ignored being too focused on Lucius.

"I am here for that sole purpose."

"Keira, you will have to excuse us a moment." Draven said shifting me gently off him and to my feet.

"Something I should know?" I asked *knowing* it was definitely something I should know but all I needed was the *what, why, how and who is trying to kill us this time?*

"Nothing you need to worry about, love." He said gripping my chin and giving it an affectionate shake. It was nice but a little chin shake is never gonna stop this girl from worrying, not considering what we had been through.

"Yeah right, when have I *not* heard that one before!?" I said with a hand on my hip.

"Nice to know that when you do finally pick em, you at least ended up with a feisty one." Lucius said slapping Draven on the back making him turn his head to growl, which only made Lucius laugh harder.

"Well I am as ever here to bail you out before she drags your king ass to counselling, as I brought reinforcements." Lucius finished his little 'I am so the dude' speech and nodded to the stairs.

"Percy!" I shouted and this time flung myself at my little friend who was just lifting up his mask. I put both my hands on his scarred cheeks and pulled him into me for a joyous hug.

"My...fffri...end." He stammered and I pulled back to first

426

kiss his skin puckered cheeks and then look into his beautiful sea green eyes.

"How are you?" I asked as I took in his appearance. He was wearing tight leather trousers and red and white striped braces over a leather suit jacket, one cut short at the front and complete with tails at the back. His mask had been of two demon hands held over his eyes as if playing the kid's game peek'a boo.

"I. Am…Gggood." He said trying to say it slowly and I could tell he had been practicing with controlling his stammer. I felt Draven come up behind me and place a hand at my lower back.

"I will have to leave you now but I won't be long. Percy, it is good to see you again." He said and nodded to my friend.

"Mmmy Lllord…ththe pleasure issth mine." He said bowing and I supressed a smile when his mask fell forward causing him to giggle nervously. Draven gave him a small smile back and then gave me a wink before he left with Lucius. But I had to wonder what Draven meant by seeing Percy again? This was definitely something I would be adding to the mounting pile of answers needed from Draven later.

"Doesn't he look so punktastically dashing! I dressed him of course!" Pip informed me as she bounced her gothic garden dress up the steps with a mouthful of crab cakes. I knew it was that because poor Adam walked behind her not holding on to a tray of them himself but the next best thing.

"Isn't he good holding onto that waiter for me…stingy little bugger won't be running off now will he?" She said swiping another crab cake from his tray making him cower. I had to laugh as now she was in full costume and unlike everyone else she had gone for something a little more daring in the mask department. In short there was no other way to describe it than as a PVC sex bondage mask combined with a blue and green Mexican wrestler's mask. It only covered half of her face but fit snug over her head like a swimming cap, only had a gap for her hair, which she wore in a high ponytail. And it was all Pip!

"Nice mask." I said making her grin and Percy was still blushing so he put his mask back down making me giggle.

"Oh you like…I was gonna go for a full face one in rubber but that's a bitchy ass to get on and besides, I wanted my mouth free for you know…" She then pretended she had a penis in her hand and put her tongue to her cheek like she was giving oral sex. She laughed when I rolled my eyes in response to her wagging her eyebrows.

"You definitely have your hands full, Adam." I said looking round at him making him smile.

"I am a lucky man indeed." Adam said smiling at his wife and catching the imaginary kiss she threw at him.

"Are we getting a fucking drink or what!?" Caspian said dressed as a massive wolf coming up behind Adam but gently holding onto his partner Liessa who was dressed like a gothic red riding hood. I waved at Liessa getting one in return and I was even surprised when I received a curt head nod from the big scary Caspian himself.

"I bet Ruto and Hakan are already doing shots by the bar, the bastards! Come on honey pot, I wanna slippery nipple! Laters lady dudette!" I laughed and then winked at Percy after saying,

"I will see you later." To which I could have sworn I could see a big grin from behind his mask. Then they all left me and I was in two minds whether or not to follow them but I knew Draven would be looking for me. So instead I decided to go and see if he had finished with Lucius. I saw that Sophia was now out of her seat and when she saw me walking to the side to where Draven had gone she quickly stopped me.

"Hey, where are you going? Come and tell me about how

Percy is doing." She said and I could tell by her voice something was off.

"Uh yeah, I will in just a second, I just want to see if…"

"He's not, so just come and wait over here yeah." The panic in her eyes was clear to see and I turned my head towards where he'd walked and frowned. What could be so bad it would have Sophia panicking? Well it was time to find out!

"Okay." I said giving her a false smile which she was too relieved to notice wasn't real. She nodded over to where Zagan and Vincent were discussing something, and I made out like I was walking her way. Then as soon as she turned her head back to the group I made my move. I looked to the other end of the throne platform and knew he was on that side but more importantly, he was on that side hiding something from me. So I just went for it. I didn't care if every supernatural being in the square was looking at me as I just picked up my skirts and ran.

"Keira no!" I heard Sophia cry from behind me but by that time I had already become lost in the crowd. I ran into sadistic laughing jesters that seemed to mock me and long beaked, feathered birds that followed me curiously as I pushed my way past.

"Sorry…sorry." I would mumble as I made my way through and I felt lucky when some recognised who I was and stepped out of the way for me. Well that luck continued right up until I spotted Draven from behind and ended very abruptly when I saw who he was stood with. I came to a crashing halt and the crowd took their time to take in my presence but once they did they started to slowly back away from me. This happened at the same time I heard the soul crushing words coming from Draven that were being spoken to someone other than me.

"I need you…"

"Keira?" Draven was interrupted by the woman he was speaking with, as she could now see me when the last of the crowd slipped away. I watched as Draven's back stiffened at hearing my name and then he turned his head slowly my way looking over his shoulder. His regretful eyes hit mine and flashed purple when they took in the unshed tears held suspended in my own.

Then I hissed the name I truly loathed…

"Aurora."

CHAPTER THIRTY-THREE

KEIRA

WHEN THE APPLE FALLS

"*K*eira don't" Draven growled knowing what was coming next because let's face it, it was what I always did.

I turned and ran.

"Keira!" Draven shouted from behind me as I bolted through the crowd once more, only this time in the opposite direction. I just couldn't face this, not again. It was like catapulting me back over ten months ago. Back to the day my heart discovered true pain. The day it shattered and became lost like my soul, wandering around in the bitter space of a hopeless abyss. And all this time together had been like the net, reaching out and slowly but surely piecing together what I had once lost. And with that dance, with that kiss, with every moment I felt his touch it had done the impossible. It had made me whole again only to have it implode with three words,

"I need you." I had heard him say to her. Was it really possible that all this time I had been lied to? Had I been played? I couldn't believe it! But was that because I just didn't want to believe it…I mean this man had faked his own death and fed me the cruellest lie of all. Could the only man I ever loved do that to me again?

These thoughts plagued me as I forced my way through the joyous crowd that were all oblivious to the crumbling life that ran pushing past them. There was just too many of them! The sound of their laughter was like fingernails raking down my skin and leaving bloody track marks in my flesh. It was pulling me in and becoming too much for me to cope with. I covered my ears with my hands and looked around feeling dizzy. The faces! All those faces, all too colourful, all too frightening… *all too real!*

"Stop it…" I whispered in a weak voice as they all seemed to be sniggering at me. I don't know what was happening, but it was like they were closing in on me, suffocating me with their cruel mocking. I spun round and round trying to block out their horrific faces that just seem to warp and twist into uglier versions of their masks.

It was almost like being on a demonic merry go round. One second I would see the mask of an animal or just some feathered pretty mask held on a stick. But then the world would change and the animals would be dead and decomposing. The pretty masks would change from black velvet to human skin and bare bloody flesh would be the only thing left when the crude mask was pulled back. Skulls would bleed, horns would twist into deadly shards and eyes would turn black into endless pits of despair.

"Stop it!" I shouted louder this time as I held my head and sank down into the middle of the spinning crowd. The weight of them all getting faster and faster until blurring into an uncontrollable force of evil around me. I needed to block them all out, I needed to…

"STOP IT!" I screamed as loud as I could and stood. The force of me pushing my hands out knocked everyone around me backwards. But the worst part was that just before everyone went forcefully hurtling backwards, no-one had even been too close to me. There hadn't been anyone laughing at me, pointing at me, not even taking any real notice of me. But now they stared, because I had just given them something real to stare at.

"Keira!" I heard Draven calling me over the crowd as he searched and before I let myself be found I threw up every mental guard I had. It was so strong it felt like an invisible layer covering my skin, not only my mind this time. It felt like a fortress around me and flowing with some new energy. I hadn't felt this strong in a long time and I knew why.

"The kiss." I whispered to myself touching my lips briefly as I ran. I kept going only looking behind me to check Draven wasn't following.

"KEIRA!" I just saw him roaring in the crowd looking all around for me. If anything, seeing him this way was just like going back and reliving that night even more. I almost felt bad watching him panic, my dark knight in a sea of colour but then I thought back to those words and who they were spoken to…

So then I ran harder. I ran faster. I ran scared.

I jumped as I dodged a masked fire eater blowing flames into the air and the people around him clapped.

"Sorry…I'm sorry." I muttered as I backed up into another one of the entertainers, only this time it was a creepy skinny guy dressed in what looked like jet-black skin with arms down to the floor. He wore a startling white mask that had a thin beak dripping with blood that came from the centre of where his eyes should have been.

"Oh!" I said as he walked on his hands and turned his head

to look at me like an owl would, listening out for prey. I started backing away now that I had finally crossed the mass of people and found the other side. I turned and walked straight into another body.

"I'm sorry…wait, what are you…?!" I never got to finish as the mystery man started manhandling me away from the rest of the crowd. Suddenly running from Draven instead of confronting him was not looking like one of my best ideas.

"Get off me!" I shouted and tried to twist my body from his painful grasp.

"Be quiet!" A grating and harsh demonic voice spat from behind a sculptured white mask that looked like a handsome but evil man smirking. The eyes were black voids of nothingness and two single tears of blood dripped down the stark white plaster of his mask on one side.

"DRA…!" I started to scream but then a hand was clamped tight over my mouth. My first thought after the panic was, 'Jesus, not again!' but as soon as the thought entered my mind I felt something.

At first, I wondered if it was the same energy that knocked all those people back moments ago and I hung on to hope until I realised it wasn't. No, it might have started in the same way but it ran along my skin like when your body shivers for no reason other than an overload of some emotion you can't always place. This feeling rippled from the ends of my limbs and crawled along my nerves to the centre of my heart.

I sucked in a heavy, harsh breath as I felt the weight invade my organ as if someone had sent some supernatural charge to my core. As soon as I released the sharp gust of air from my burning lungs it all shot straight from my chest through to my back and straight up my spine, ending at the base of my neck, where my birthmark was. The feeling made my body arch and bow backwards, making it now impossible for my captor to keep a hold of me with the force of my sudden movements.

"No!" He growled trying to restrain my body back to under his control, but it felt like my bones were made from steel and my flesh from granite. I was unmoveable and the feeling was like taking an intoxicating drug that flooded my system with a calming and euphoric presence. It was as though I was an invincible force and with my head still thrown back looking at the night sky I felt like someone up there was also looking back down at me.

"Seth!" He hissed the name and I angled my head, still looking up enough to see him staring above me towards St Mark's Basilica. There at the Cathedral above its central arch stood a man against one of the four bronze horses. He wore a long jacket that was split at the back and both sides were blowing around from being up so high. I could tell he was wearing a mask, but I couldn't make out enough of the details, only that it looked like stiff material wind swept to one side. It almost gave him the appearance of some Cathedral phantom standing watch.

Well whatever the case the man who tried to take me knew who he was and what was happening. It was enough to give the guy second thoughts at least as he let go of me and fled into the oblivious crowd. The instant he let go I was released from this extraordinary power and my body slumped forward as if exhausted. I placed my hands on my knees as I bent forward trying to compose myself, dragging in air and suddenly feeling constricted in such a tight dress.

I then looked up one last time to see the man who seemed to have saved me. He gave me a salute with his hand from his temple and this was combined with a nod before turning to leave. I then watched as he jumped down to somewhere out of sight but not before I noticed the artist's utility belt at his waist where his jacket split.

"Seth." I uttered his name, testing it from my lips as the name of my new saviour. I had no clue as to whom either of these men were or more importantly what they wanted with me, but I knew one thing…now wasn't going to be the time to find out. So I stuck to my original plan and that was to get the hell out of this freakish masquerade.

I looked around trying to make my way out of this labyrinth of bodies and looked up at the giant tower that stood next to the Cathedral. I remembered it from when I came in so I started to make my way across the square and as far from that wannabe kidnapper as I could get. I didn't actually know how I hadn't yet crumpled to the floor in a mess of mixed emotions, I just knew that I couldn't yet afford to. So instead I did the only thing that I could do and that was to keep running.

It seemed like a small eternity when I finally broke free of the crowd and I felt as though I could finally breathe for the first time. By this time my hair was half tumbling down and my beautiful dress had torn in a few places. I had no idea where I was going but one rarely did when they didn't even have a destination in mind.

I wanted to scream at the sky in frustration, but I think I had caused quite enough of a scene since the chase began. In fact I knew I needed to act quickly before Draven caught up with me, shields or no shields. But this thought quickly had me thinking back to the power that affected me just at the right moment, one that obviously had something to do with Seth. So if this was the case then how could he have broken through when someone as powerful at Draven couldn't?

I shook my head knowing now was not the time to bombard myself with more questions I wouldn't be finding the answers to anytime soon. So with this in mind I walked quickly along, still looking over my shoulder but at least finding it easier now I was away from the main event. I looked around and saw a massive building on my left that had an Arabian palace look to it, with its elaborate arches and a long row of columns holding up a pathway you could walk under. Above this were the same miniature arches that made up a balcony that was lit and would have made a great view to see the party from.

I decided it was smarter to walk under the balcony than being out in the open, so I started heading left without really looking where I was going.

"Look out!" I heard being yelled but as I turned, I knew it would be too late as I saw what looked like giant mechanical demonic horses charging my way. In the split second before they would have ploughed straight into me, no doubt killing me instantly, I thought about Draven and him finding me this way. It was a morbid thought but one driven solely by guilt for running. But more so for realising that my last act on this earth would in fact be my broken promise to the man I loved.

I closed my eyes tight and waited for the impact but holding on to the image of Draven when we danced together.

"My salvation" I said then felt myself being held tight by what felt like many arms and I started to float away. It seemed like time was slowing down and I wondered if this was what really happened when you died? Was this the other side's way of giving you that last shred of time before taking everything you have ever known from you. Was it like the last supper for a man on death row before going to Hell or like relishing the last touch from a loved one before reaching Heaven?

"Lille øjesten?" I frowned when I heard this thinking it an odd thing to hear when first making it to the other side. Was my mind playing tricks on me? Well there was only one way to find out for sure and that was to brave opening my eyes.

"Ragnar?" I said looking down and screamed when I saw

what looked like a smoky serpent wrapped tight around my body, wound round and round until its face was just in front of my own.

"Uh! And that's the thanks I get!" I heard that gruff pissed off voice and the sound filled me which pure bliss.

"Sigurd!" I shouted no longer frightened of his manifested powers and I spun round to throw myself at his huge bulk as his serpent evaporated. I then hugged him and gripped onto his hooded jacket as my arms wouldn't meet in the middle of his back. I felt him hold me back and I took a moment to bask in the knowledge of feeling safe for the first time since I ran from Draven.

I heard him breathe me in as if it was a secret he needed to feed with just the scent of me. I held on and silently let him keep his secret for instead he gave me something else in return.

And this particular something was the meaning to a name that touched my heart and made me family…

"Hello, my little Apple."

CHAPTER
THIRTY-FOUR

KEIRA

RUNNING FROM THE TRUTH

I t was the first time I had heard him call me what Lille øjesten actually meant and it warmed my heart.

"You saved me." I said telling him something he obviously knew already, and I heard him huff in response.

"Yeah it seems like it's a requirement when being your friend." I rolled my eyes to myself before pulling back to look up at his shadowed face.

"So where were you running off to before the entertainment almost killed you?" I turned to look back at what in fact was the start of a new act making its way through the now parting crowd. I could just make out the giant steam horses that were made from crudely hammered metal sheets riveted together. These four horses that no doubt represented the four on the Cathedral were pulling along a gothic chariot that was like a hellish prison combined. Twisted black lava stalagmites rose from the base of

439

the chariot until all the tips met at the top. Inside of this enclosed rock cage were people dressed as demonic Spartans who looked as though they had each been dipped in a live volcano. The costumes they wore were equally incredible as they were horrifying.

"What are they?" I found myself quietly asking.

"They represent the Titans." Sigurd said and the disgusted way he said it made me look back up at him.

"As in the imprisoned Greek Gods?" I asked and for a moment he just seemed transfixed by the sight of them.

"Sigurd?" I said his name to try and prompt him into responding, which eventually worked after the second time.

"I gather the only reason you're out here alone is because you did a runner?" I felt myself blush, but he just rolled his eyes at my silent answer.

"Come on, I know a place." He took my hand in his, engulfing it and pulled me across to the opposite side. I noticed that for some reason people got out of the way for us now a lot quicker than when I was flying solo. It was also a reason I didn't think was just down to his colossal size and the clues were the whispers and stares from everyone he passed. Some even cowered backwards as if trying to get away unnoticed.

"Uh...everyone seems pretty scared of you?" I said as a question to which my only answer was a frown I could only barely see from under his hood. One could only see as I had to look up so far he was that tall.

It didn't take us long to come to the huge red brick bell tower that stood what must have been hundreds of feet tall. I stopped dead and just let my head fall back to look up and up and up.

"Yeah, yeah, big fucking tower, I get it...but sometime before another one of these bullshit shindigs, øjesten." Sigurd said marching back from the black double doors he had been stood at to then grip the top of my arm and pull me back with him. It was surprising how gentle such an enormous guy could be I thought as I was calmingly manhandled up some steps. Of course, the poor doors ahead of us didn't receive such a luxury, when he suddenly reared back his foot and crashed it through the panels.

"Uh…I hate to point this out but isn't someone gonna like notice this, say some poor mortals that have to deal with why their tower was broken into?"

"Yeah do I look like I give a shit, besides what do you think the level of damage that all them lot are gonna cause by the end of the night?" He said retaking my hand and pulling me into the dark space.

"Oh…well I guess I didn't think of it that way." I admitted now wondering what did happen at the end of the night. Thankfully after an eye roll from my giant friend, he was kind enough to inform me.

"Well lucky for all those simple mortals…"

"Hey!" I said interrupting him and not surprisingly getting ignored.

"…the square the next day will be like this night never even happened, which I am sure will include this door."

"Oh… I guess that's ok then."

"Great, well now that I have eased your conscience enough to live with yourself for another day, can we get on." He said trying to keep the teasing smirk from his lips.

"That's a lot of steps." I said looking up.

"Yeah but we aint takin em." He said and before I could say anything, he grabbed me around the waist and my Hell ride really began. I briefly had time to blink and in that split second all I could see was his shadows reaching out its long tentacles and we were off. I suddenly knew how poor Mary Jane had felt when dating Spiderman and I will tell you now, that web shooting ride looks way more fun on telly!

It didn't take long to get to the top and that was my one consolation. By the time my feet touched the floor I felt like my stomach had been for a bungee jump without the rest of me!

"Jesus are you insane!? A warning might have been nice, not even a bloody, 'Don't look down'!" I said mimicking his voice in a ridiculously deep way making him cross his arms.

"I do not sound like that." He said and I threw my hands up saying to myself,

"And of course, that's the bit he focuses on!"

"And besides, if you'd had this warning would you have still let me do it…um?"

"Oh, Hell no! I would have taken the stairs and met you up here in say an hour…" I paused and looked down the stairs and added,

"…maybe two…but that is beside the point, I would have done it without the chance of a heart attack or feeling like a bloody pebble in a slingshot!"

"I dunno, you don't look as fit to me as the last time I saw you." He said and then laughed when I hit him on the arm.

"Yeah, just what I thought, turned into a weakling." He said pretending to flick some lint off the arm I hit.

"Don't make me push you off this bell tower and wave at you all the way down!" To which he laughed.

"Yeah let's see how far you get with that one, Honey." He said walking over to the lattice of bars across each rounded arch. Then he waved his hand out and I watched fascinated as the tattooed skin on his hands started to spin. The Ouroboros almost looked like they were vibrating just beneath the surface and the quicker they moved the closer together they got until his hand was consumed by black ink.

I sucked in a quick breath as the shadows seeped out of him

and broke off into streams of smoke that each wrapped themselves around the bars. This all happened in less than a minute and I don't know how they did it but when the smoke started to disappear there were bars no more.

"It makes a better view." Sigurd said nodding for me to step closer to see for myself.

"Wow, that's amazing." I said taking in not only the sight of the party below but mainly the incredible view of Venice's lights twinkling like fallen stars against the night.

"So you gonna tell me why you were running like that dog Cerberus was yapping at your heels?" Sigurd said coming over to stand next to me and leaning his forearms on the ledge.

"You do know me and him are kind of friends…right?" At this he laughed and pushed his hood from his face. The sight had me instantly biting my lip just so I wouldn't gasp at how beautiful he was. You would have expected such a hard and gigantic man to be rough and rugged in all his features and I suppose some aspects of him were. But it was also combined with a classical sculpted look that artists would weep at the chance to paint. The high cheek bones and the square jaw that was always speckled with tawny stubble. But really it was all down to his eyes.

They were the eyes any girl could get lost in after making love and finding themselves almost drunk with delight, but they were also the eyes that could burn like the sun, telling you he could destroy you with little effort.

"So no mask for you then?" I said looking sideways at his perfect profile.

"Yeah, fuck no! I don't go in for all that dramatic bollocks…no offense." He said with a smirk.

"So talk to me øjesten." He said softly after we silently looked out at a supernatural world he obviously didn't want to accept. In that way we weren't so very different. Two people

443

struggling with something we always considered a curse. So did that mean all he needed was to find his girl and take that last step as I had done? I often thought about that young girl on the plane I met that day. I wondered what the Fates had in store for her and what the man next to me would one day mean to her.

"I must say, I'm not bitchin' here but I don't think I have ever heard you this quiet…shit girl but I remember you saying more when I had to save your ass in that alleyway." I had to smile at this, and I shook my head as he grinned at me.

"Yeah well I wasn't a weakling back then and still held my bad ass badge." I said dryly making him throw his head back and laugh.

"Ok I will give you that, you did know how to kick ass back then…for a chick that is." He added with a wink making me groan and him laugh again.

"Right, now spill it." He said turning a hip to the side and looking at me head on. I looked out at the party knowing Draven was down there somewhere looking for me and knowing him, probably going frantic. I tried not to feel guilty and knowing the reason I ran it helped in some sense, but it was that damn promise I had made!

"Let's just say I saw and heard something I didn't like." I said bringing my head forward on a sigh and resting it on my gloved hands. I knew he was looking at me with that raised eyebrow of his.

"Okay, so this something you didn't like, were his reasons for it not something you could trust in?"

"Uh…"

"You ran before giving him chance to explain, didn't you?" He asked sounding exasperated and started rubbing his forehead and closing his eyes.

"Yeah, I did but you don't understand."

"And now neither do you." He said on a huffed breath.

"Look honey, I get it, I do but don't you think you have had enough of running when shit gets serious? So he fucked up, then you stand your ground and demand your answers. You scream at him and prove I'm wrong and that you've not gone soft, whatever but you stand there and face it like the bad ass I know is still inside you…" He paused and then stepped closer to me to softly run a finger over my bare shoulder brushing a long escaping curl back. Then he got close to my ear and whispered,

"And, sweetheart, don't ever be the type of girl to run from the truth because of fear." He finished his advice by giving my shoulder an affectionate squeeze and then took a step away from me. Then we found ourselves both leaning against the ledge and finding that comfortable silence you only ever really find with great friends.

"You're not really friends with that prick Cerberus, are you?" He said after a time and I burst out laughing before saying,

"What can I say other than I must have a soft spot of difficult, hard-headed bad ass men." And then I nudged him making him smile down at me.

"Well I am taking that as a compliment." And just like that I knew he was right and more importantly, I also knew the right thing to do.

But first I gave my friend my honesty by saying,

"And so you should because I love my hard headed, bad ass friends."

DRAVEN

"Did you find her?!" I said storming down the corridor of my Venice home wanting nothing more than to spend my time tearing it down by its watery foundations!

"No my Lord but…"

"And why not? Am I not right in saying she ran into a crowd full of our kind? Are you telling me that no one, not ONE OF MY KINGDOM SAW HER!?" I let my Demon take over in my rage as he needed the small release I would allow him. Having her finally in my arms these last few days was the calmest I had felt him for a while and if I didn't get her back soon, I didn't know if I could contain his rage and mine combined for long.

"But…but…"

"Spit it out!" I snapped at one of my generals who was in charge of the security at events like this one. I opened the door at the end and tried to take care in not ripping it off its hinges. I walked into my office and slammed the door behind my nervous subject.

"My Lord, other than some strange occurrence that no one can explain she has gone unnoticed since…"

"What occurrence?!"

"There was a crowd of people that felt a strange presence of power but could see no one. They say it got stronger and stronger until…" He paused and my patience snapped. I grabbed him by his costume instead of giving in to the urge to grab his neck and brought him closer to me.

"Until what *exactly?*" I said letting my eyes change with my voice.

"Until the power exploded enough to force everyone back." He said trying not to show fear and the instant I got my answer I let him go as shock registered.

"Go!" I said turning to hide the pain of the news from being witnessed.

"My Lord." He said respectfully and then he followed my order. As soon as the door closed, I picked up the nearest thing to hand.

"AHHH!" I roared and threw the object at the door, making a palm sized hole due to the paperweight that I heard smashing at the other end of the hallway. I then let my body fall back a step and put my unsteady hand out on the side of my desk as my body leant against it in defeat. I had looked everywhere for her but those damn shields of hers were growing. Hell, not just growing but literally exploding into new levels of power. I always knew she would eventually develop the gifts into which she had been born but I had no clue to the strength I would find myself facing.

"Damn foolish girl!" I said angrily looking at the floor shaking my head. Did she not know of the dangers that surrounded her, despite being able to hide herself to my kind? Anything could happen! The worry and guilt of being forced into yet another position like this was almost crippling.

"Ah, I gather our little bird has not yet returned?" Lucius said after picking a shard of wood from the hole in the door and flicking it to the side.

"I want her found!" I commanded slamming my other hand down on the desk making it crack under my palm.

"As do I which is why I have my council doing the same as you, but you do realise the level of power in which we're dealing with here?" I frowned at my once right hand man and growled,

"You think I don't!"

"You left her so no, I don't." He snarled back and for a moment losing that famous control of his.

"Careful old friend, you tread on broken skin this night." I warned pushing away from the desk.

"Your love for the girl blinds you and you know it does. What I say is merely a truth you don't wish to face."

"Oh make no mistake, I fucking face it! Every damn day I was faced with it and meanwhile what is she doing but being kidnapped and being auctioned off like damn cattle by my enemies! So don't you talk to me about love making you blind when I was the one to rip out my own fucking eyes in the Gods be damned first place!" I said letting my rage lose enough to flip my desk and make it crash into the wall hard enough to shatter like glass. Lucius didn't even flinch but instead just crossed his arms and gave me a look I would have liked nothing better than to tear from his skull.

"You are forgetting one very important fact my friend."

"And what's that!?" I forced out whilst trying to calm my breathing enough to keep my wings from erupting.

"She came back to you."

"She ran from me!" I reminded him making him laugh once without humour.

"And what of it, that's what she does when she doesn't want to face what she believes is the truth. But like a moth to the flame, she comes back to what she sees as her light in the dark." I shook my head and said more calmly this time,

"And what if she doesn't, she could be out there right now getting attacked, getting…" I stopped when Lucius actually did start laughing,

"I think out of us all our little bird is one of the safest people alive right now, after all you maybe her light, but the rest of us are *her* moths." I thought about that for a moment and realised he was right.

To think some of the most powerful beings of my kind, each a King in their own right and each one putty in her mortal hands. All of them willing to risk their very vessels on this earth just to protect something they didn't fully understand but knew nothing else mattered. Everyone was drawn to her and each had played a part in her journey in keeping her safe and each I knew would still act as such. Which begged the question, did this all have something to do with the prophecy?

"Ah, now I can see you're finally asking yourself the right question." Lucius said looking as if this was something he had been waiting for all along.

"You thought the same thing, didn't you?" I said losing the last of my anger as my focus was centred on something far greater.

"Just think about it, think about what she has gained since knowing you? But then think more of what she has achieved since she lost you. She has done what none of us would have ever been able to do, something if I recall we ourselves tried to accomplish with little success." The more Lucius spoke the clearer the picture became. He was right, there was a time when the plan was to reunite all the most powerful beings the Gods had given life to. To join forces, ready for the one day we knew would come…*Judgement Day.*

"You really think it could be possible?"

"If you would have asked me that question before meeting your Chosen, then I would still be trying to kill you but now… well, now I owe her not only my life but also for a life I never knew I *could* have." I let Lucius' words sink in deep and held them there until they became completely ingrained.

"So you need to ask yourself, what is the one and only thing that the Fates would need in making you leave?"

"Her death." I released my biggest fears on a tortured breath.

"And in doing so she sets out on this prompted journey by the Oracle herself. The sole vessel of the Fates themselves is sent to your girl and guides her. Not only that but also binds her to the broken shadowed King of the Ouroboros and draws her a map straight to the bitter Cerberus, that he even took her to a place he vowed never to return."

"By the Gods! I have been so blind!" I said knowing now in the depths of my soul it to be all true.

"I think my friend you will find in today's terminology they call that 'being played'."

"The Fates set it all up!" I bellowed feeling the outrage build.

"It would seem so but don't beat yourself up to much, as like I said, love can blind us all, it just so happens that after she left me to find you I had the time to see things clearly and do a little digging."

"What do you mean?" I asked after running a frustrated hand through my hair and only just realising my mask was still firmly in place.

"I spent some time retracing the footsteps before she reached me. I found out what each of her unlikely guardians had done for her and then I waited. Once she came home after not finding the outcome she hoped for, I put my people on her from afar and do you know what I found?" I growled at knowing he had his men watching her but decided quickly learning the truth was the most important thing right now.

"Tell me."

"I found that your own men weren't the only ones keeping a watchful eye on her. That in fact, it would seem there are players in this game we didn't even know about, that are making it their mission to protect who they clearly consider their Queen." Hearing this filled me with equal amounts of dread and relief.

"Cerberus and Ragnar's son?"

"Both of which had their own men watching her."

"And another you say?" Lucius nodded slowly and I knew him long enough to know the concealed rage at this knowledge that only showed in his eyes.

"I have tried to track him down, but the power of manipulation and manifestation is even greater than my own. His mind is near impossible to get a hold of and up until this point I did not think there was a being alive that had the power to defeat me." I almost laughed and probably would have if the circumstances hadn't been upon me, for I knew how painful that must have been for one such as Lucius to admit.

"I think I saw him in the library where Keira works and I agree, the power I felt was unlike anything I ever felt before." I thought for a moment and then asked the hardest question,

"Do you think he wishes to harm her?"

"Well that is the odd thing."

"What?" I asked getting impatient as I watched Lucius casually take a seat.

"He only appeared months later, after she had been home a while."

"Then something happened, something too…*Cain.*" I said as it all clicked into place.

"To the very day." Lucius confirmed.

"So this Nephilim turns up and all of a sudden Keira has a new protector, is that what you're saying?"

"It would seem so, because make no mistake, even with the hidden army she has protecting her, the power this one possesses would have no issues in taking them down as easily as you or I and simply taking her."

"This thought doesn't comfort me." I confessed.

"Well if I was you I would choose to overlook the dangers and look at it as our girl simply drawing in a new moth. You do remember the prophecy words, don't you…?" At this my head shot up and I frowned down at him.

"But that was never proven…"

"It was also never disproved My Lord." Lucius said knowing that by once again calling me his Lord that it was a clear sign we were back on the same side once and for all.

"And I saw when the Lamb opened one of the seals, and I heard, as it were the noise of thunder, one of the four beasts saying, come and see. And I saw, and behold a white horse: and he that sat on him had a bow; and a crown was given unto him: and he went forth conquering, and to conquer" Lucius said reciting the Book of Revelation or better known as simply The Apocalypse.

"The Seven seals." I said out loud feeling as if the wind had been knocked right out of me.

"There is of course no proof other than time will tell. But at the very least now you know the reason the Fates have been using you and your Chosen as pawns in a game you didn't even know you were playing." Put like that I had to agree with him, although he was forgetting one very important rule,

"But you know the Fates can't lie." I reminded him.

"No, this is indeed a fundamental truth we as our kind have been born into. However, they are not without their skills at both exploiting their importance and implicating a lie hidden within a truth." This made sense, so much so I said,

"You're talking about slight of hand in the form of words."

"It is easily done preying on someone's fears but when it is their greatest fear, well up until Keira you had none. But then whisper the chance of the loss of your greatest love and your mind will hold onto that fear and not let go." Lucius said all this and then I lost the serious advisor I used to have as my right hand when he said,

"I mean, look how they fucked me over giving me you as a friend!"

And there he was… *the cocky bastard was back.*

Before Lucius left, he assured me Keira would be safe and soon found, to which I could only hope my confidence in him wasn't misplaced. I decided to get out of these clothes and then go in search of her once again myself as the mounting time away from her felt like a razorblade to my nerves. For not only was she out there alone but she was also out there thinking the worst of me.

I slumped on the end of the bed and held my head in my hands. I felt the mask still there and feeling it only reminded me of her own mask and how dangerous it was for people to know what it meant.

Claiming her as my Queen tonight had been a bold move but one I only made with the intention of never letting her out of my sight. But then seeing Lucius and knowing what had happened in Sophia's dressing room, well that was enough to know what needed to be done. I could not have her hurt by my touch and there was only one person who would know what was to be done about it and that was the person who had put it there.

"AHH!" I made a sound of frustrated rage and ripped off my mask throwing it across the floor towards the door. If only she had just heard the rest of what I was going to say then she would…

"I tried to do that with mine, but it wouldn't work."

"Keira!" I shouted her name in shock and she shrugged her shoulders. Then told me the only words I needed to hear…

"I promised you I wouldn't run."

CHAPTER THIRTY-FIVE

KEIRA

DONE WAITING

I watched as Draven lifted his head and he said my name as if he had just battled the greatest of wars and come out of it far from the victor. He looked like a man lost and unsure of what his next step should be. In fact, the sight took the breath from me in a whoosh that forced my hand to my chest.

"I promised you I wouldn't run." I said knowing these were the only words that needed to be said right now. Because the words I had come here with had left me in sight of the man I loved looking worried and broken. No, this wasn't the picture of a man who had been in the throes of passion with his ex or even someone who had even ever considered it.

No, this was nothing short of a man in despair.

Suddenly he stood quickly and before I had chance to say a word, he stormed over to me like a man on a mission. I swear my heartbeat fell into a rhythm that matched each of his determined steps. He came right up to me breathing heavy and I watched in silence as his chest rose and fell with his mounting tension.

"Draven?" I whispered but his next movement stole my question as he took my face in his hands and said,

"I'm done waiting!" And then he pushed me back against the door and ripped my own mask from me. He threw it to the floor to join his own and kissed me like he was trying to imprint his soul onto mine. I briefly heard the crunch of his own mask that he must have stepped on to get closer to me. Well he obviously didn't care one bit considering he didn't stop. No, instead he took me further. He took me deeper under his spell and one that was labelled the past.

I felt the kiss fire my nerves and he must have felt the same as I could feel him shuddering against me. His hands found mine and he linked his fingers with my smaller ones before lifting them above my head and pinning me there. I could barely believe this was actually happening. It was like so many cruel dreams of mine all coming together and taking it to a whole new level. It made me want to cry out to the Gods and beg for this to be real, for them to just let us be together. It made me want to battle his world and mine just for the right to hold on to this moment and keep it where it belonged. I just wanted him with every staggered breath I took and every lit cell in my body.

"Draven" I said breathlessly as his lips tore from mine just long enough to allow me the needed air. He transferred both my hands into one of his to continue to hold me to the door. It was as if he feared I would get away from him if he gave me the chance. Of course, this action also freed up one of his hands.

"You won't need this for the rest of the night." He said as he first ran his fingertips across my collarbone and then along the

456

stunning necklace he'd given me. I drew in a shocked breath as he snapped it from my neck, but he didn't give me time to worry about it being broken as he fixed the links before dropping it to the floor.

He ran his fingertips slowly down my cheek as his kiss softened slightly, teasing my lips and biting gently. Then I moaned in his mouth and that gentle hand suddenly gripped my neck tightly forcing my head back to the door. It was such an aggressive move I was surprised that it didn't hurt but the shock of it made my clit pulse in response.

"You're my girl," he growled low into my cheek after using his thumb on my chin to turn my head to the side. Then he opened his mouth as if he just wanted to bite me but thought better of his instincts and kissed me instead. His lips kissed their way up my jaw line and up to my ear.

"Say it." He ordered making me moan again and close my eyes.

"Say it, Keira...say it now!" I didn't need to ask what it was that he needed to hear as I felt it coming from him in waves of possessiveness. I let my head fall back further onto the door glad that I was being held up by one strong arm above me. Then I let my mouth fall open on first a blissful sigh before speaking the truthful words he needed to hear,

"I'm yours." As soon as I uttered what felt like a confession his hands left me. I opened my eyes in shock and for an awful moment I thought this was my rejection. I was just about to protest when one look at the animalistic lust in his purple eyes and I knew it was far from over...no, now it was only the beginning. This was proven when he grabbed handfuls of material at the top of my dress and in one swift action completely tore it in two until it barely hung limp from my hips.

I must have looked like some nobleman's daughter being ravished by some powerful land owner, considering he too was still in costume. I watched as his hungry gaze mentally caressed every naked inch of my torso as there had been little room for underwear in this dress. And boy did he look happy about it, if the bulge in his pants was anything to go by.

He suddenly picked me up and the rest of the dress fell to the floor leaving me in just a pair of black lace briefs. I got the hint of a grin when he looked down at them like he was thinking about what they would feel like when shredded in his hand. I was then carried to the bed and with each step he took his own clothes started to deteriorate as if we were stepping rapidly through time.

By the time he lay me down at the bed's centre he too was naked. He followed me down and lay out on top of the length of me but holding most of his weight from crushing me. It was just enough to feel trapped and this, along with everything else that was Draven, made my thighs wet with the evidence of my need.

Before his hands went to either side of my head he reached down and proved that I had been right moments before. He ripped the lace from me that covered my sex and it tugged me to the side forcefully making me moan with greater need.

Then with his hands back to my face, his fingers inched their way into my hair as he stared down at me. This was when time seemed to slow down and that raw intensity that was our attraction seemed to soar to a new level of intimacy. It was in that next second that something passed through his features and if I had to guess what it was, I would have to say it was as though he was looking back on all the painful times he had missed this sight. It was no doubt the sight of me under him and looking up with eyes heavy with my own lust.

The thought made me blush as there was nothing else in that moment that his eyes were telling me. It was as if we didn't need words to explain what we had both been through. We just needed our silent bodies to communicate for us. And as my legs fell open it was all the communicating Draven needed. So with his eyes still locked to mine and keeping me captured by the power of emotion, he surged into me, filling me on a cry deep to the core.

My body arched with the feeling of being stretched in the most beautiful way and he held me immobile and encased in his arms as I adjusted to his size. I vaguely heard him whispering words of encouragement in my ear, calling me his good girl for taking all of him and giving him what he needed.

After a few seconds more he started to move so slowly it felt like he was lighting up all the nerves inside me. It was like my body needed to move, it needed to groan and show its pleasure, but I was still being held down in Draven's hold.

"I need…I need…"

"Only *I* know what you need." He growled in my ear before tipping his head down and biting into my neck, making me cry out when at the same time he thrust back in. He sucked at the broken skin at my neck, drinking me down. With each pull at my blood he thrust mimicking the action like playing a fine tuned instrument. Well as far as I was concerned he could play me till his fingers bled and until there was nothing left of me to sound out.

"Look at me." He ordered softly and it was only the sound of his voice that made me realise I had indeed closed my eyes. I felt like my lids were begging me to stay closed as if the emotion I was feeling was too much for them to bear.

"There she is." He said when I finally managed to look up at him. He still had my head held in his hands as he started to once again move so excruciatingly slow.

"Faster." I managed to mutter but knowing he would hear me all the same.

"Not yet, *I want to savour you.*" He said coming down and whispering above my lips with his nose to mine. He then pulled back again and used the pad of his thumb to gently run under my eye then circle along my cheek.

"Please." I shamefully asked and I felt his other hand fist in my hair drawing a sharp breath from me. He quickened his pace but still he held himself back.

"Please Draven." I said again adding his name and this time I cried out as his teeth found my nipple. He feasted on my breast and once again at the same time increased his movements.

"Yes." I said on a moan and when I arched my body in the little space he had created, I managed to force my nipple deeper into his mouth, making it vibrate as he groaned around it.

"Ahhh." I said as his teeth dug in further and he started to roll my nipple between his painful hold. It felt incredible and was like a direct line to my pulsating clit.

"More?" He asked releasing my breast and I nodded my head not being able to find the words as I felt myself building.

"I like your words, sweetheart." He said before kissing the side of my lips.

"Please." I said again and after one, two, three hard thrusts that had me gasping he said,

"After you give me what I want." He said and sucked at my neck again where he had left it raw this time. The sting of pain made me clench around his length and the hurt soon sank under a pool of pleasure, flooding my system with endorphins.

"Anything…" I told him in an almost pained voice given how close I was. It was as though he wouldn't let me come but wanted to keep me right on the edge of this heavenly chasm. He growled and this time it was mainly his demon side, which only managed to send another spasm of me rippling around him as his thrusts became that little bit quicker. He kissed his way up the side of my breasts and over my lips where he told me exactly what he wanted from me,

"Then beg for me my Electus. Give me your eyes and beg for me to give you what you need."

"Please…Dominic…please." As soon as I finished saying his name, he kissed me at the same time driving into me and managing to use my cry to his advantage as he plundered my mouth with his tongue. Then he started to pound into me at such a speed all I could do was hold on and I cried into his mouth with unspeakable pleasure.

"Oh…oh…oh yes!" I shouted as I felt it coming closer and closer until coiling round like something needed to be released or my body would shatter. Then my body started to quake in his arms, and he put his forehead to mine.

"Are you going to fall with me?" He asked and I could only nod as I was desperate for him to just let me come. It was like climbing a mountain and reaching out for that next handhold. You're so close and you're reaching, so close, too close but you just can't make it. So I forgot about any of that and decided to let myself fall and hold on to the only thing that mattered. My hands reached up and locked around Draven's neck where I managed to just pull myself up enough to whisper,

"Are you going to catch me?" I watched fascinated as his eyes grew darker before he replied with,

"Always." And then as if to prove his point he erupted into his other self and his wings engulfed the bed and cast us both in shadow. It was like making love under a canopy of feathers and each one was coursing with what looked like a purple flame. Draven's motions got even faster now that his wings were adding in his movements and propelling him forward to charge into me. I wrapped my legs further up his back and held on for what felt like my life as it was starting to crumble around him.

Then I opened my eyes and saw the start of Hell's fire start to invade the man I loved, and I knew I couldn't let him lose that side of himself. I couldn't stop what was happening and he seemed so lost in what we both knew was a divine moment that he hadn't yet realised it. I took in his strong features transformed by pleasure and that was when I started to notice the glowing coming from his arms. I sucked in a startled breath at the sight of his raw scars that was thankfully masked by the increased power of him taking me harder.

I could see the moment he started to really fall and in the end I knew it was up to me this time to catch him. So I did what I hoped wasn't a stupid thing and I braved facing that hidden side of him. I let go of the grip I had around his neck and then placed my hands over his forearms. I felt the burn but instead of pulling away I concentrated on using all of my shields and transferring them to one place. I had no idea if it could be done but I knew one thing and that was if I let Draven stop now, he would never touch me again from fear of hurting me. I knew I was taking a risk, but I also knew that in this moment, right now and in this time, there was nothing stronger than the two of us joined as one.

And I was right. Without Draven even realising what I was doing I felt my strange power shield me from his other self and it almost felt like taming a hidden beast you knew was there in the shadows. I gripped tightly onto his arms once more now that the burn had fled his skin and then regained my hold around his neck. I watched as the last of the fire left his eyes and the darker purple was dominant once more. Then I let myself soar…

"Now come with me!" Draven roared in his demonic voice and I screamed out as I felt him finally let me erupt around him. He continued just inches from my face maintaining the eye contact the whole time, holding onto my hair until my neck was arched back. My release seemed to spiral out of control and I actually felt like I was falling. It felt like I was close to passing out from the sheer intensity of it all.

"Oh no you don't!" Draven said turning my head to the side

and he deliciously punished me with each last motion before he himself exploded inside me. He threw his head back and I watched through half lids as his fangs extended before then seeing them coming at me at a dizzying speed.

"AHHH!" I screamed as he sank them in to my neck for the last time and sucked hard making me come once more. There was a blinding light that detonated behind my eyes just as I felt him pulsate inside me as he emptied himself. My back bowed coming off the bed and I felt his arms go under me, holding me steady as I quivered uncontrollable.

"You're ok, you're ok… I've got you…I got you my Angel." He cooed in my ear and he gently lowered me back onto the bed. It felt like I was coming down from the biggest high of my life and that combined with training for the Olympics marathon, well it had me in pieces.

"Let's sort out the mess I made." He said as I lay there panting and gasping for air. He groaned when I continued to spasm around where he still lay hard and embedded inside me. I felt him lean down and seal my neck, licking away any evidence before coming back to look at me. Then he put his forehead to mine and said the only words I now needed to hear,

"I love you."

CHAPTER THIRTY-SIX

KEIRA

THE TRUTH FINALLY COMES OUT

I don't really remember what happened after Draven told me he loved me, but it was like the last thing my body needed to hear before I could give in to sleep. I knew without a doubt I needed it, but I also knew it wasn't just physically but almost mentally that I needed the rest. It was as if all the worry, heartbreak and frustrations over the last year had finally come to fruition in this one moment. And the knowledge in that was like my mind taking a big sigh and only needing one thing…

Peace.

I had no clue how long this had lasted as I stretched out my limbs expecting to feel sore. Then I clued into the fact that I was obviously once again benefiting from Draven's essence and would heal very quickly. Well it certainly came in handy being with a sexually dominant partner and considering how rough

465

Draven could sometimes be when he let himself go. Not that he ever really hurt me, and I relished in the knowledge that I could do that to him and his control. But it also meant that waking the next morning or in this case still the night that I wasn't going to be walking like John Wayne had lost his horse.

I rubbed some of the sleep from my eyes and looked towards where Draven was still resting. I was surprised I hadn't woken him with my movements as he was on his side with his arms around me. Seeing him look so peaceful made me smile and I gently pushed back a piece of hair that had fallen over his forehead. I drank in the sight of the man I loved with the soft moonlight filtering through the windows and casting shadows on his skin. I think I could have stared at him for the rest of the night, but my restless mind wouldn't give me the calming thoughts to do such time real justice.

So with this in mind I shifted gently from his hold taking the added care in not waking him. Once I was free, I pulled off the top sheet and wrapped it around myself before rising from the bed. The first thing I noticed was that Draven must have cleaned me of any trace of him after our time making love and after I had obviously passed out on him. This thought made me both blush and smile to myself at the thought of him taking care of me in the most intimate way a man could to the woman he loved.

I walked over to the windows and saw the glass doors in the middle that led out onto a balcony. I looked back at the bed to see Draven still in the land of King nod and decided it wouldn't wake him, so I opened the doors. The cool night air felt wonderful on my blushed skin and I closed my eyes taking it in. I stepped out into the night and wondered what time it must be.

But wondering the time didn't keep my mind occupied enough not to find it overloaded by all the questions I now had. It was like being in a room full of towering files and all I needed was one last question to be added to the top for them all to come toppling down over me. I felt buried under the weight as it was and that was ever since I knew he had lied all that time ago. I had tried to fool myself by believing I had moved on or no longer cared enough thanks to the hurt but it had all been a way of coping with my loss.

"I must say, I am not a fan of waking up without you in my bed, Keira." Draven's voice startled me to a jump, but he soon put his arms around me from behind and pulled me back to him.

"And I have been forced without the pleasure for far too long." He said leaning down to kiss my bare shoulder after slipping the sheet from my skin. I shuddered in his hold and I felt his satisfied grin smile against me.

"I guess I couldn't sleep anymore." I said looking out onto the canal and watching the still water reflecting the night sky.

"Are you alright?" He asked losing that playful tone now it was replaced with concern.

"I'm fine, not even an ache." I smiled up at him from the side.

"Good." He leant down and kissed my nose, laughing when I felt it wrinkle out of habit.

"I gather it is an ache of the mind given the amount of questions you must have." He said pushing back some of my loose hair from my face. My response was to turn fully and plant my face in his chest where I then groaned making him chuckle.

"I understand. There are things between us, things that have gone left unsaid for far too long. I would be a fool not to understand this and the obvious frustrations you must be feeling but if you are ready, then so am I." I looked up at him when he finished and said all I needed to say,

"I'm ready."

"Then come, it's going to be a long night and I want you

467

comfortable." He said taking my hand and leading me over to a sitting area that comprised of a two person sofa in a soft grey and two matching arm chairs all positioned around a chunky wooden coffee table. He let go of my hand and I sat on the sofa pulling the sheet closer around myself, getting comfortable as Draven suggested. Then some of the lamps around the room started to glow so it was enough for us to see each other.

Draven gave me a small smile before taking the armchair closest to me and I finally noticed Draven had put on some soft looking pyjama bottoms in a dark grey colour that hung low on his hips. The sight of his naked torso and hard muscles on show nearly made me say to hell with questions let's go for round two instead. Then he spoke and that thought took a nosedive.

"I was giving her an order." Draven blurted out after a moment of silence had fallen between us.

"Okay, you know you are going to have to explain that to me." I said calmly trying not to wince at him even talking about her.

"I needed her to find out why I could hurt you whenever I touched you." He said as he reached out to touch me, then thought better of it and fisted his hand instead.

"Alright, I know I don't really want to ask this, but I have no choice…why would she know that?" I said closing my eyes and bracing myself.

"Ahh!" I shouted in shock when I suddenly felt Draven's arms around me and picking me up to sit astride him.

"Ssshh…" He cooed holding me to him.

"I just needed to feel you in my arms, to feel that you're safe." He said and the relief was easy to hear in his gruff voice. It was as though he had just suddenly had a flash back to this evening and me running from him.

"And to make sure I don't run again." I said on a laugh trying to ease the tension I could feel in his hold. It was like he was wound up so tight, as if he was trying to hold himself back from something.

"Well there is that." He replied to the top of my hair as he held my head to his chest.

"You can't do that again, my heart won't survive it." He said pulling me back after placing his hands at my shoulders.

"I…"

"I mean it Keira, do you realise the danger you could have been in?" He said bending his head to look me in the eyes.

"Oh I know…" I muttered thinking back to earlier and then wanted to follow it up with an 'Oh shit' as I realised what I just said.

"What do you mean!?" He demanded raising his voice a notch with a new worry. I knew that at some point I would have to have told him but I had been hoping to at least get my own answers first.

"Ok so something happened but it was all fine and I'm all good yeah?" I said trying to placate him.

"Keira." He said my name as a warning, and I could see he was about to lose it in a big way. I shifted on his lap and pulled back to take in his darkening eyes that spoke of rage if I didn't word this right.

"Ok so I ran and then something weird started happening where it was like all these masked faces were laughing at me and getting closer and closer and I got freaked so I…I don't know, it just happened and something I couldn't see pushed them all back, but it was like it was coming from me…but that's impossible right?" I said in a rush and I watched him sigh.

"I heard about that. Did it hurt you in anyway?" I frowned at his question as I thought back to it.

"No, it just…well it kind of felt like an overload of emotion and then…well then it just… *exploded."* I said shrugging. I saw his shoulders relax and at that point I knew I had made a mistake telling him the easiest thing first.

"It's alright we can deal with this, just as long as you're safe and…"

"There's something else." I blurted out before I lost my nerve. I winced when his hands on my hips gripped me tighter, but it wasn't from pain, it was from the worry.

"Okay, so running from you was a bad idea, I admit that now and I…"

"Keira, have pity on my nerves and tell me." He said after placing four fingers across my lips to silence my nervous rambling.

"Someone tried to take me." I announced in a rush and watched as the rage swept through his features in slow motion. Suddenly I found myself being lifted off him, landing on the couch with a whoosh and he was stood up and raking his hands in his hair.

"Draven its ok, I am…"

"I wouldn't finish that sentence if I was you." Draven growled knowing I was about to say 'I am fine'. The feisty side of me wanted to snap back but I knew he needed this moment to calm, not have me making it worse with throwing him attitude. So I gave him the time.

"Explain." He managed to hiss out the word and I tried not to take it to heart that he was angry at me but knowing him, more at himself for letting this happen. Of course, if we were to point fingers and blame it would be me first for running and the man trying to take me second. But I knew he wouldn't see it like this, so I just gave him what he needed and answered him.

"I was running one minute and the next was grabbed from behind. He tried to pull me from the crowd when my body started fighting back. It was like…well, I don't know how to explain it but my body became immobile so he couldn't move me." Draven finally turned back to me and asked,

"Was it the same as when you block out my kind?" I would have liked to have told him yes to the question, just so I knew he would find the little comfort that I had defeated this new enemy on my own…but that would have been a lie.

"No…I…I had help."

"Keira, my patience…" I didn't let him finish before I butted in with,

"It was someone called Seth…who saved me I mean. Well anyway, he was stood by the four horses on the Cathedral. The man who had hold of me looked up and said his name like he knew he was there to help me."

"Did he hurt you?!" Draven snapped at the thought.

"No, he just let me go and then the power I had left me like he had snapped his fingers…then he kind of waved and left."

"Another moth." Draven muttered to himself and I frowned.

"What do you mean?"

"Nothing… so what did you do then?" I decided to let the cryptic moth comment go and continue with my foolish adventure.

"Then I ran some more and bumped into Sigurd." I said deciding it was a good idea to leave out the fact I was nearly ploughed down by the night's entertainment.

"Gods be damned, Keira!" Draven roared and then hit out at the bedpost he was stood by, snapping it nearly in two, so it now bent at an angle. He had twisted his body as he lashed out and now stood with his back to me.

"Draven!" I shouted back, standing up and watching as his tensed muscles heaved with his heavy breathing. He didn't say anything, but he did put a hand out to the bed post and without touching it the wood started to fold back together until right again.

471

"Damn interfering Snake-eye!" Draven said to himself with venomous spite making me angry.

"Actually that damn interfering Snake-eye is the one who convinced me to stop running and acting foolish. He is also the one who made sure I got back here, back to *you* safely!" I said letting my irritation seep into my words and help in getting my point across. On hearing this Draven turned back to me and the disbelief was easy to read in his eyes.

"Truth?" He asked making me frown and fold my arms across my sheeted chest.

"Of course it is!" I snapped.

"You really are a beacon of light, aren't you?" He said more calmly and I shook my head not knowing what he meant.

"I'm sorry?" I asked, as hearing this shocked me. But then I watched as all the tension fell from his shoulders. Then without answering me, he walked straight to me and lifted both my hands to his lips and kissed them sweetly.

"Are you alright?" He asked looking down at me over my hands that he still held to his lips. I nodded in response making him wrap his arms around me and hold me to him in a much needed hug.

"I was so worried." Draven said before kissing the top of my head and it felt like he never wanted to let me go.

"I'm sorry I ran from you." I told him back, as I truly was. I realised how stupid it had been and that I should have trusted him to explain, which brought us right back to the beginning and all we still needed to discuss. And that was why I said,

"We need to talk."

"I know." He replied in a deflated tone that spoke volumes to how much he really wished we didn't have to have this conversation. I felt his arms loosen around me and soon we were once again sat next to each other on the couch, only this time I could only hope there were no more Draven explosions of temper…my own however I couldn't yet vouch for.

"Okay so back to my original question. Why is she the only one who would know why you could burn me?" I asked knowing there was no way of asking that in a delicate way.

"Alright Keira, I will explain everything but first for you to really understand I will have to go back to the beginning and well…"

"Well…?" I prompted when he dragged a frustrated hand down his face this time.

"It's painful." I closed my eyes briefly and absorbed what he was telling me. He was about to tell me everything. I knew this but what I needed was to be sure that I was ready to accept it. Because this question was the only one, above all others that I needed answered the most and the one I had asked myself from the very beginning and what had inevitably sent me on a journey that had changed my life.

And that question was simple…

"Why?"

CHAPTER THIRTY-SEVEN

KEIRA

TRUTH

I looked at Draven and waited as my simple sounding question grew into a million answers that needed to be told. You could tell he was trying to think of where the best place to start was and like he himself had said, there was only the beginning. So that's where I started.

"What happened that day you left?" I asked thinking back to that moment outside my house and replaying the same torturous words he had left me with, ones I didn't trust in after I found out his greatest lie.

"I love you, keeper of my heart."

I shook these words from my thoughts and turned back to Draven. He was bent over with his elbows to his knees and his head in his hands. I put my hand on his shoulder and said,

"Hey, I get it…I mean I don't know exactly why but I know it must have been something bad, so bad in fact that…"

"She told me I would kill you." Draven blurted out quickly and it felt like someone had kicked me in the gut. My hand dropped from his shoulder and I felt the shock penetrate deep inside me like my veins were being flushed through with ice water. I couldn't believe it! I just couldn't. It was as if everything I had ever known was crumbling down around me and I couldn't even find the strength to care enough to put my arms up as protection.

In fact…

It was like my whole world had just ended.

"Keira come back to me." Draven said reaching out to me and I couldn't help my flinch. The look of hurt I saw there wasn't something I could ever take back but I could at least explain it.

"I don't believe it." I whispered as if first testing my voice.

"Keira."

"I don't believe it!" I said this time louder after he said my name, trying no doubt to sooth me.

"Keira you need to listen to me."

"I DON'T FUCKING BELIEVE IT!" I then screamed losing it in a big way. I shot out of the chair and after walking a few steps away I stormed back to shout over to him.

"You believed this shit?!" I accused making him wince.

"The Fates themselves told me this and they can't lie, Keira." Draven explained but I was beyond any reason that wanted to take me to a calm place.

"Oh yes they fucking can!" I bellowed not caring one bit that I was swearing, in fact I was just letting the foul word fuel my rage and give it greater depth.

"I need you to calm down." Draven said standing and reaching out for me. I spun away from him and said,

"Calm down, calm down…you tell me about the biggest load of bullshit the Fates ever told you and that you believed it enough to fake your own death and you want me to calm down…have I got that right!?" I ranted wanting nothing more than to hit something. I knew I was taking this out on him but part of me was utterly devastated that he would have believed something like this from the very beginning.

"I need to explain." He tried saying, coming an extra step closer to me.

"Actually, I don't think you do, in fact I have a bloody good idea who exactly does need to explain, the Oracle that's who!" I said folding my arms and he took this opportunity to make his move. Before I could utter a shocked yelp, I was trapped in his arms and struggling became useless.

"Calm down and I will explain everything. I know you are upset…please, just let me continue…" He said when I tried to speak silencing me before carrying on.

"I left you that day with no knowledge that I wouldn't be coming back to you. Pythia really did go missing, only what I didn't know at the time was that it was planned. They needed to get me away from you and keep me that way and unfortunately for us both, they succeeded."

"But why would you believe them?" I asked in a quieter but no less whiny voice.

"Because I had no choice but *to* believe in them. The Fates cannot lie, and I mean that in the sense that Pythia would literally die and be exiled from Heaven if such a thing happened. So you see, I had no choice but to believe in what she told me." I shook my head and felt the anger turn quickly to a bitter devastation.

"So what are we to do? I mean did they at least tell you how or give you a date?" I asked and Draven laughed once only it wasn't because he found the situation funny.

"Come and sit back down and I will explain everything." I nodded knowing that every feature on my face showed my despair.

"Trust me, it is not now as dire as it seems." Draven tried to assure me as he walked me back over to the sofa that it felt like we had both being playing jack in the box with this evening. We sat down and I listened as Draven began the real truth of the matter.

"Around the time my contact with you stopped was when I finally found the Oracle. I ended up finding her exactly where I first found her all those years ago in Mount Parnassus in Greece and at the now hidden Temple of Apollo. It was as though they knew they needed to get me as far away as possible from you before they could contend with my rage. I couldn't believe it and was very much like you to begin with. I couldn't understand why they would finally send me my Electus and then so quickly take her away from me again." I shook my head not understanding it either and he gave me a sad smile before carrying on.

"They explained how this is the way of the Fates and the prophecy must be fulfilled at all costs. I demanded to know details but other than telling me how I would bring forth the death of the one I love and gifted with my life's blood, this was enough for me to make that soul destroying decision." I still couldn't believe it as it just seemed too cruel to believe.

"But why didn't you just leave me…why have me believe you had died?" I asked feeling hurt and the evidence of this ran down my cheeks and dripped onto the sheet.

"I was told there was no other way you would have let me go. They needed you to live they said, as you were still important to their plans. But they needed you to continue along your chosen path and if you knew I had simply left you then that path would never have taken place. I never understood it, but I just wanted you to live. I wanted you to have the full life that they spoke of, telling me of how your life's plan was set and in the future they saw only happiness..." He paused long enough to pull my body back to him and then say,

"...and I so wanted that for you Keira, I needed that for you. For if I couldn't be with you, if I couldn't give that to you myself, then I needed to know at the very least there was happiness waiting for you." I held him back and started sobbing on his shoulder. It was the hardest words to hear and yet I needed every single one of them he gave me.

"But then after I saw you, after I heard how the Fates had not only intervened in my life but in yours also, I was furious! I knew they had set you out on this journey and that was the path they spoke of. They had said things to you and spun their little webs of twisted truths until they got what they wanted, only I just didn't figure it all out until now." Hearing this and the bitter edge that laced his voice I lifted up my head.

"What do you mean?" I asked wiping away my tears.

"I was so blinded by my self-pity and self-loathing for what I had put you through that I couldn't see the smoke for the flames. It's ironic then that it was my once enemy who made me see the truth."

"Lucius?" I said his name in shock and Draven nodded in response.

"And what was the truth?" I was almost too scared to ask but it was like Sigurd had told me, '*Don't ever be the type of girl to run from the truth because of fear*'.

"We have both been played from the very beginning."

"I...I...don't know what to say." And this *was* the truth.

"Now I don't know exactly how they have twisted what they told me to make me believe I would end your life but the only certainty I have is that they did."

"But why?!" I shouted throwing my hands up in the air as my anger came back at me.

"Because they needed you to do what no one else could do." He said taking one of my fists and uncurling it gently to then run his fingertips down the length of my hand.

"And what's that?"

"It's simple. They just needed you to be yourself." He looked up and saw my confused face and in that moment, I don't think I have ever seen him looking so proud.

"You have no idea how my kind is drawn to you. Even from your childhood they never shied away from you. I never understood it when we first met, just saw it as an annoyance in a selfish greed to have you all to myself and I suppose I still possess these traits but at least now I am more understanding of why."

"Draven you're not making much sense to me." I complained making him smile.

"It's your gift, Keira. It's the power of your heart and how you open yourself up to people, my kind, them all, to the idea of knowing such a heart. You let them in and they instantly see the gift you have given them. But not only do they take this gift, but they treasure it, they believe in it and they will stop at nothing to protect it." I shook my head and was about to tell him he had it all wrong, that it was impossible, that I was only one girl...just one mortal girl. But he didn't let me. Instead he took my head in his hands to cease my shaking and said,

"Yes. That is your greatest gift as the Chosen One. You are the one they all follow and that is why for the prophecy to ever happen they needed to send you on your journey to find me."

"But I still don't understand why!? I mean, what did they gain other than me discovering the truth?"

"Think about it. Think about your time in a different light. It wasn't the goal they wanted you to reach but all the important points along the way. Sigurd your guardian and chosen King of the Ouroboros, one who refuses to take his position in our world." Draven held out his finger as if crossing them off a list.

"Then there is the Alpha of Hellhounds, Cerberus, another King of a different kind yet one too bitter and lost in his grief to take the last steps to the throne. And even your little friend Percy, who braved the wrath of the hand that gave him his greatest fear but all for you. I can even go as far as meeting my own father in a level of Hell that no mere mortal would ever survive. Yet you did. So ask yourself again, why…why does it take one single heart of such purity and strength to change and challenge the frozen hearts of men who for centuries have said no and denied who they truly are." When Draven had finished I was left dumbstruck, but with only one thing that came to mind,

"But I'm from Liverpool." To which he threw his head back and laughed.

"Maybe the fates are a fan of the Beatles." Draven teased making me too burst out laughing. I think this was something we both needed after such an intense conversation. It was as if I was about to believe all that Draven had told me because let's face it…who would? But some of it at least made sense after all, if this great prophecy meant it needed Sigurd and Jared in the picture then I could certainly see how the Fates could have used me to get their way.

"So what about these?" I asked as I looked down at his bare forearms and saw the raw scarred flesh that I could now see was in the shape of a Pentagram. Only it was strange and made up from a series of smaller symbols I had never seen before. There was also a circle around each one and these too held their own symbols. Draven lifted his arm and looked down in disgust.

"Do you remember me ever coming to you in your dreams, Keira?" I knew the instant he said it what this was about.

"You're of course talking about the night with…uh…"

"My brother, yes." He said looking down at his scars and clenching his fists. I thought back to that night that up until now I thought was only a dream.

"Back then I lived in the shadow of your absence, going through the daily motions barely living a life but I still managed to preserve my control. Oh don't get me wrong, there were many times, too many to count when I would fight within myself to take back what was rightfully mine. However, I always replayed those despised words of warning back to myself and I would resist. But then the nights came, and it was where I found I was at my weakest."

"What do you mean?" I asked softly placing my hand over his where he held one over his forearm, as if hiding that part of himself.

"I guess it's simple really, my mind and body would crave you to the point I would project myself to where you were, and I would wake hating myself even more for doing that to you."

"Oh…I see." I said not really knowing what else to say.

"But it was when I took control of my own Brother to get closer to you. I knew then that it was no longer safe for me to be free at night." This was when it all started to really click into place, and I said the name I had been hearing for the last year,

"Tartarus."

And his simple reply,

"Yes, Tartarus indeed."

The rest of the night I sat and listened to the tortured tale of a grief-stricken king who was forced to give up who he believed was his queen. And by the end of his story I had cried for, not only what I had been through but now also what he had been through as well.

He explained about Tartarus being a prison in the deepest bowels of Hell but first he had to tell me about why such a prison was created. So he began to tell me about the Titans. Before the Earth knew mortal men it was said there was a great battle of Immortals. For many years they were a peaceful race until they first discovered that they could kill one another, branding them immortals no more. It was the greed for gain in power that started the War of the Heavens and was led by an immortal called Cronus.

It was also said that day that the skies rained with blood, sinking into the Earth and giving its first life to mortal men. Adam being the first and Eve soon thereafter. Now in regards to the victors they declared themselves Gods and vanquished the fallen enemy into Mount Tartarus and imprisoned them there, renaming them the Titans. Cronus became the King of Titans and in history it is known that Zeus forgave him his sins and made him ruler of Elysium.

Of course I wanted to know what Elysium was, thinking it would probably be some pretty bad place if this Cronus had been made ruler over it. Well I couldn't have been more wrong when finding out it was actually an Afterlife for Gods and their relations to go when their time was at an end. I think at this point I was close to getting a headache, so Draven put an end to my confusion and said,

"We do not believe Cronus has ever been ruler of Elysium nor do we believe he is even hidden there but we do know that he exists and still to this day is the biggest threat to releasing the Titans."

"And that would be bad…right?" I said making him reply simply and to the point,

"Extremely."

After that Draven went on to explain that the possibility of anyone, let alone Cronus ever releasing the Titans was near impossible as to do this they would need the blood of one of the first. And the bloodline of the Titans had long ago become too diluted to ever hold any power as the human race bloomed into its own unstoppable force. And Cronus' punishment by Zeus was actually that the power in his blood was stripped, so even as one of the original Titans, he had no power to free his brothers or sisters.

I had then asked Draven about Tartarus and he told me it was located in the deepest levels of Hell and where the most dangerous of his kind was still to this day imprisoned. The Titans are said to be held at the belly of this mountain surrounded by a flowing river of lava and their bodies infused within its hardened rock that the lava can't touch. It is said that this rock that covers their bodies is to prevent any of their blood from touching the chains in which they are bound. Chains that were part of the mountain itself.

This was all fascinating and I told him so making him smile but then he soon lost this smile when I asked the most important part,

"So what does this have to do with Aurora?"

This was where the story really began.

He started telling me about someone called Eos, who was known as the Goddess of Dawn, but she was also classed as a Titaness. Now a Titaness is what is referred to as a female Titan. In the first generation of Titans there were twelve of them. The males were Oceanus, Hyperion, Coeus, Cronus, Crius, and Iapetus Draven told me listing them off at an impressive speed. Then there were the females, the Titanesses and they were named Mnemosyne, Tethys, Theia, Phoebe, Rhea, and Themis. I nodded at this point thinking I was never going to remember those names other than Cronus as the main baddy.

But then Draven informed me there was in fact a second generation and in this second generation was Hyperion's children Helios, Selene and Eos.

"So this Goddess of the Dawn was one of the original Titan's daughters?" I asked and when his expression looked sad I knew the next part I wasn't going to like and I was right.

"Eos in Latin is Aurora."

"What!?" I shouted in both annoyance and shock.

"So she really is a Goddess." I said laughing without humour and feeling my shoulders slump.

"Yes, in a sense but she is also a Titaness, and this believe me, is not a good thing." Draven said lifting my chin up and rubbing a thumb over my bottom lip that I held in my teeth.

"Well I guess that's something." I said sulking at this new information.

"So this was the only reason you saw her like you did that day." I frowned across at him and asked him what he meant. He went on to explain that the only place he knew of that would contain that weakened side of him and therefore force himself under control was Tartarus. The only problem was that he needed his demon side to be tied to a place physically or it would simply override his control and break free. That was where Aurora came into it.

With her being a second-generation Titan she was the only one with the gifts to bind Draven's demon for the night, until he was once again in control. He told me how he had gone without sleep to begin with but his vessel still needed the rest to function.

So in the end he found this was the only way. He had a special bed made, that journeyed everywhere with him and this bed would also be his travelling prison. It was made with the same mountain rock that was in Tartarus as its headboard so that his arms would be locked and encased there making it impossible for him to move. Then as his demon side would be sent down to the deepest depths of Hell, his Vessel and Angel side would remain asleep until Aurora came to free him in the morning.

I thought back to that night and he agreed with me how it must have looked but looking back I knew he spoke the truth. Once again Sigurd's advice came back to me and I knew I shouldn't have run even then. But saying that, I doubt I would have received my answers as I was doing this night.

"So how long did this have to happen for?" I asked although the question pained me. The very last thing I wanted to do right then was think back to the amount of times Draven had to be straddled naked by his ex!

"Up until the point you tore off your necklace." He said looking pained by the memory, but his answer surprised me. He then went on to explain that it was in that moment that his demon finally recognised that I was no longer theirs. After that there was no longer any pull that couldn't be controlled and his time in Tartarus was no more.

Well all this certainly explained all the dreams of him in Hell that I had been having over the last year. And it also explained why people often referred to Draven as being in Hell, along with the Oracle herself. She hadn't lied but she also hadn't told me the truth either. I was starting to think back and realise that what Draven had said about the Fates was most likely right.

"So now you know the truth." He said finishing the conversation just as the sun had started to rise. We had been up for hours but the importance of hearing everything he had said was like living through something monumental. It all made sense and even though I would never agree with Draven's decision, I couldn't honestly say what I would have done differently if the roles had been reversed. After all, I had literally gone to Hell and back just to try and save him. He had died in a sense and imprisoned a part of himself in Hell just to save me.

"Come, I think it is time we put that busy mind to rest, don't you?" He said picking me up off the couch I had slumped down on to get comfier and then he walked me over to the bed. He lay me down and the instant he did I could feel my eyes start to give in.

"Wait! One more question?" I said forcing my eyes back open and alert making him laugh. He rolled his own eyes in good humour and lay back next to me, pulling my body into his arms.

"Why am I not surprised?"

"Can you blame me?" I asked and he gave me a soft grin before saying,

"I never would, now tell me your question and then you can sleep."

"I just wanted to know if Takeshi was alright as I didn't see him at the Ball tonight." I said remembering this was a question that had been coming in and out of my head all day.

"He is fine, he just needed to rest."

"What is it that happens to him?" I said trying to sit up but Draven shook his head and pulled me back down so my head was resting on his shoulder.

"Takeshi has a very talented gift that I will explain in detail at a later time, but for now all you need to understand is that he has what is known as a 'Second sight'. His gifts allow him to home into certain beings and channel their memories. I guess the best way to explain it would be like picking out pieces of a puzzle at random and trying to discover the picture. The closer the beings the more puzzle pieces there are to grab."

"So what happened?" I asked referring of course to the

same thing that must have happened all that time ago after my kidnapping by Morgan.

"The puzzle pieces all showed the same thing." I frowned and asked the question I thought was a safe one to ask, but I soon discovered I was wrong...

"A wooden dagger with a Pentagram."

CHAPTER THIRTY-EIGHT

KEIRA

SECRET SYMBOLS

"Keira! Keira wake up!" I woke with a start and bolted upright in bed panting at what I had just seen. Draven was holding me and gently pushed my wet hair that had become drenched with sweat back from my face.

"It's okay, it's alright now, I have you my girl. It was just a bad dream that's all." He said soothing my jittering nerves as he put my head to his chest. I took the long moments I needed to feel Draven around me and the safety he provided.

"Do you want to tell me about it?" He asked after my breathing had calmed. I thought about that question and knew that after last night, there were still things I needed to tell him. And having this nightmare only reinforced that decision that the time was now.

I let my mind go back to that frightening place and it was as if I could even smell the blood that saturated the ground. The only difference this time was that in the meadow of death there was no Draven and the sky was raining with blood. Even I knew that this change in my nightmare reflected on the facts that Draven told me that night and I remember looking up in the dream expecting to find the Gods fighting a war above me.

The skies were filled with dark stormy clouds and the ground was foggy in the distance. It was as though all my dream wanted me to see was what was directly in front of me and that was pieces of a Pentagram. I looked down at my own skin that was quickly getting soaked and was at least thankful to realise it must only have been raining blood inside the circle of the star. Everything on the outside was simply wet and that included me, but so long as I wasn't covered in blood I didn't care.

In my dream I bravely took a step further and came stupidly close to the Pentagram, stopping at the first body part that had been crudely hacked from some poor soul's body. I could only pray that these people had all been dead when this had happened. That thought alone made me want to heave but I had already done that once in this dream. No, now was the time for me to be brave and really see what the dream wanted me to. I could only hope it would give me some answers as to why this had happened and more importantly, who had done this?

Was it the man in the painting with the wooden dagger or even worse, the man that was shown to me at the end, the one I thought I had trusted? Could it be? I stepped closer and looked down to see my feet couldn't get any closer without crossing the gruesome line. Then that's when I heard it. The sickening sound of meat being butchered and when I saw a shadowy figure of a man throwing chunks and pieces away behind him, I knew I could no longer be naive.

The figure stood up from being hunched over the slaughtered body with what looked like an arm held in his hand by the bone that protruded from the top. Then he turned, keeping his hooded head down and placed the arm at a diagonal on the grass, creating the last sections of the symbol.

This was all so horrifying and sick and twisted that I would have liked nothing more than to take that wooden dagger and drive it into the chest of the man. The man that I now thought was Alex. But this was when something started to dawn on me…where was the dagger?

This man wasn't holding a dagger in his hand but something that looked more like a lengthened machete. And it was when the figure started to rise up and finally take notice of me that it all started to make sense. Everyone had it all wrong. It wasn't Alex who was the bad guy here.

Not at all.

It had all just been made out that way with his connection to me. I knew the truth now. I knew it all…now it was just time to have it confirmed and that happened when the figure pushed back his blood splattered hood.

I knew I was right but no amount of knowing can change the shock you experience when you're proven right in the worst way. I took in those piercing white eyes with a tiny black dot in the middle that I could barely see. His skeletal face which had seemed to be transferred onto his original handsome features was now even more painful to look at. And then he said the same words to me that he did that day at the Auction.

"Until you're ready to be pushed, Girl"

———

It was at this point that I had awakened, only this time Draven had been there to hold me.

"It was Seth, he was the one to murder all those hikers, it was him all along." I said making Draven frown and this was

491

when I started to explain everything to him. I told him about my dream at his studio and also when I actually encountered him at the Auction in the storeroom. Of course I then had to explain why I hadn't told him all this before, to which my lame answer of,

"I kinda forgot," was one he didn't care for.

"This has certainly changed things." Draven said and when he started to get up I knew he would soon be leaving me to deal with this new information.

"But now we know that should make things easier right?" I asked pulling the covers up in front of me and sitting up to watch Draven as he dressed. He walked into what I presumed was a walk in wardrobe and came back out a few moments later wearing jeans and pulling down a vintage black T shirt that had some racing car logo on the front in faded white. I also notice he had put back on his leather cuffs that hid the Tartarus markings beneath.

I had asked him when we had been chatting last night how long before they healed or left his skin but he didn't have any answers as he didn't know. Not that I was bothered because let's face it, I came with enough of my own scars. I think it was more the reminder that bothered me as I felt that they stood for a past I never wanted to look back on.

He came to stand at the end of the bed, and he looked down as he did up his belt buckle, which looked like hammered metal with some kind of engine emblem on the front.

"Another gift from Vincent?" I asked nodding to his belt.

"Well I am predictable when it comes to gifts, but now it's time for my favourite gift." I was about to ask what when I felt my ankle being shackled and suddenly, I was being pulled down the bed, covers and all.

"What are you…?!" I started but was cut off when Draven whipped the covers off me and bent over me at the end of the bed where my legs were now left dangling. Once there he then kissed my question right out of my brain, and I arched up to him trying to get as much of him as I could get before he left.

"Mmm, I like eager morning Keira." He said over my lips and I turned my head to moan into his neck.

"Then maybe you should stay and see just how eager morning Keira can get." I said before sucking and kissing up his neck making him groan.

"And my Vixen is back and right where she should be." He replied before turning his head also to retake my lips in a demanding kiss. The kiss lasted a while and we managed to get so caught up in the moment that I was surprised when he pulled back.

"By the Gods but temptation isn't a word great enough to describe what you do to my control." I gave him a coy smile before lifting my hips to meet the hard length of him I could feel pushing against his jeans. I smiled even more when it made him growl down at me.

"Then give in to temptation." I suggested but one look at his pained expression and I knew his duty to protect me would come above all else. This was proven when he pushed off me and raked a frustrated hand through his hair as was his habit.

"Its fine, I know you have to go and deal with all this." I said sitting up and covering my nakedness.

"I won't be long."

"I know and the sooner you go, the sooner you can come back and finish what you started." I said winking at him making him groan again.

"You winking at me whilst sat on my bed half-naked and looking all wanton is quickly testing my control, *again.*" He informed me, growling the 'again' part and I laughed.

"Well it's lucky then that you're a King and therefore have

the natural born ability to delegate." I said smirking and got my meaning across loud and clear.

"I like the way my Vixen thinks." He said leaning in once more and kissing me, only briefer this time considering what usually happened once we got started.

"I will send someone in with breakfast, you must be famished?" He added and as soon as he said it my stomach felt like it had given up and started munching on itself.

"Uh…I could eat."

After Draven left, I decided to get a much-needed shower as my hair was starting to look greasy after a night of sex, tales and nightmares. I didn't want to be too long as I knew precious food would be here any minute, so I did what needed to be done and I did it quickly. Once I was out I then had the dilemma of possessing no clothes as I had left everything I brought with me at the hotel in Milan. So the only thing I could think of was maybe Draven had a shirt I could wear that might pass as a dress given our height difference.

I walked through the same door Draven had not long before and I quickly entered déjà vu territory. Where I had been expecting a miniature version of what he had at Afterlife the fact that it was the same size wasn't what shocked me. But what did was the fact that the opposite side was filled to the brim with all summer clothes that I would have worn. I didn't really know why I should have been shocked exactly seeing as this was Draven we were talking about but I still looked through the vast selection shaking my head.

In the end I picked out a pair of denim shorts that came with a braided tan leather belt, a duck egg blue vest top and a denim shirt that had pearl popper buttons. I was just tying the ends of the shirt into a knot at the front as I kicked on some flip flops when the door was knocked.

I think my stomach actually high fived the nearest organ it was that happy about the prospect of food.

"Come in." I said as the door opened and a man in some sort of uniform stepped inside carrying a tray. He put down his burden on the coffee table at the seating area and then looked up at me, making me shout his name,

"Alex?"

"Hello Catherine." He said calmly with those piercing grey blue eyes of his taking everything in.

"What are you doing here?" I said in a panic thinking if Draven found him, I didn't know what he would do, but of course I had ideas alright and what worried me was that they all included blood.

"I'm here to save you." He replied closing the door and coming towards me.

"What do you mean?" I asked trying to resist the urge to take a cautious step back.

"I understand why you left me and it's alright, it was always meant to be this way." I started to shake my head, so he carried on.

"My main reason for being with you was to keep you safe."

"Safe from what?" I frowned not liking that our relationship was all a lie but knowing from the very beginning that it wasn't ever going to turn into more than what we had.

"My job was to keep you safe for the prophecy and protect you from Seth." He told me this time coming to me and taking my hands in his to hold.

"Seth?"

"Yes. He and others who are out there are also trying to take you." I looked into his eyes and tried to find the lie there, but I couldn't see one.

"What do they want with me?"

"To keep you from reuniting with their King."

"Draven?" He nodded and this was where I started frowning at him and pulled my hands from his to take a step back.

"If that is the case then why did you yourself try everything in your power to keep us apart? I mean at the time I understood it because you were my boyfriend but if what you say is true then why not tell me this from the very beginning?" I saw him take in a deep breath as if trying to compose his frustration at answering such a question.

"I knew if I dated you eventually the Lord would allow jealously to override any logical thought he was convinced was right. I was sent to set you two back into motion and played the part of a loving boyfriend to…well to basically rub his nose in it." I listened to him speak and it all started to make sense. Which made me wonder what would have happened if Alex had in fact not been on the scene…the answer was a crippling one to realise as I knew it would have meant nothing. Draven wouldn't have come back to me if he hadn't considered Alex a threat. I knew that deep down.

"That's why you kept standing me up isn't it? Because you knew every time Draven would be there and it would force us closer together?" I asked and for a moment he looked sheepish.

"It was the only way. I needed you two back together."

"You did?" I asked frowning at the odd way he put that.

"The Fates did and therefore so did I as that was the reason I was sent to you." Ok so put like that I suppose it made sense.

"So who is Seth?"

"He is the leader of a cult whose sole purpose is to put a stop to the prophecy and release the Titans."

"What?!" I shouted knowing the depth of bad shit this would be for the world if this was to ever happen.

"We must leave." He said trying to take my hand, but I pulled back.

"Why and where?"

"We need to find the King and tell him all I have learnt, as I fear Seth and his men are getting closer to making their move." Ok so I liked the idea of finding Draven more than going somewhere without him and I thought it was best to let Draven decide what was best to do right now, so I agreed.

"Alright, let's go."

DRAVEN

After painfully leaving Keira I walked back into my office and knew it was Vincent that I had to thank for restoring the room back to the way it was before my temper had got the best of me.

"I contacted Lucius as I knew this news would include him." Vincent said as soon as I closed the door. I looked around the room and saw my brother was leant by my desk with his feet crossed at the ankles, whereas my sister was lounging on the red leather chesterfield chair looking at her nails. I had mentally sent them both a brief idea of what was happening on the way here, so I didn't have to waste my time in explaining.

"Where is he?" I asked, only my response came from the man himself.

"He is on a plane." Lucius said over the hidden speakers in my office. I frowned at hearing this until my brother elaborated.

"He is following a new lead on this Seth character."

"Good. There has been a development as now Keira thinks he isn't as he appears." By the Gods but even saying her name had my gut twisting in need just to get back to her.

"How so?" Sophia asked frowning in concern at the part that I had not yet explained.

"She dreamt of him and believes he might be the one behind the massacred hikers in Evergreen Falls." I informed her causing her to shake her head before she said,

"But it was only a dream."

"Yes, and I am not taking any chances, not again. Besides, how many times have we known Keira's dreams to be wrong?" I repressed the urge to shudder at the thought knowing what she had been through.

"I am already looking into that but found some useful information from an unlikely source." Lucius said on the other end of the phone.

"Explain."

"Well it seems your least favourite Viking investigated the slaughtered scene before the humans could get involved." I growled low at just the mention of that big disrespectful bastard!

"And what did he discover?" It was Vincent who asked this as one look at my face and he knew I wasn't this minute up to the simple task.

"Well that's the interesting part…"

"Trust you to find a massacre interesting." Sophia said interrupting him and I shot her an irritable look making her hold up her hands in mock innocence as Lucius merely laughed.

"Continue." I snapped feeling my control slipping the longer I was kept from my girl.

"We are looking at two separate events that happened within hours of each other." Lucius said pausing to what sounded like speaking with the pilot.

"Does that mean there are two working together and one tried to clear the scene?" Vincent asked.

"Quite the opposite actually. Sigurd told me that he found

evidence of two supernatural beings. The first was the one to cause the initial slayings and there seems to be very little reasoning other than maybe it was a diversion of some kind. However, the second, well…"

"Well what?!" I demanded stepping closer and I think if he had been in the room fists would have flown for how much he was dragging this out.

"The bodies had all been dismembered and their limbs had been placed in a symbolic way, then used in a ritual. However, it was one even Sigurd had not seen before." Upon hearing this news my eyes closed and I held the bridge of my nose with my thumb and forefinger as if trying to ease the pressure that was building along with my mounting rage.

"Needless to say, he did his duty to our kind and rearranged the bodies in an attempt of hiding the truth and making it more believable that it could have been an animal attack." Lucius added making Vincent nod at the importance of keeping our kind hidden from the mortal world. I, on the other hand, cared little for the matter considering this meant Keira could again still be a target.

"Find out what you can, I gather we are to stay here for the time being?" Vincent said looking to me.

"Indeed." I answered no doubt sounding strained as I was closing in on my limit to hearing anything more before I fled to room to go in search of her. The compulsion to simply hold her was one I was fighting every second the longer I was having this meeting.

"So what about the Nephilim scum?" Sophia asked raising a good point.

"For the time being he has vanished." Lucius informed me causing my spine to tighten.

"What do you mean?!"

"I do believe he went missing from the hotel in Milan a few

hours before the Ball. I still have my men looking for him…" Lucius said but was cut off when Vincent also added his confession,

"As do we but our men also have found nothing." Then he turned guilty eyes to me.

"You knew of this?" I accused but it was our sister that came to his aid,

"You have been a little busy, Dom." To which I knew I had no excuse.

"I knew the importance that last night meant to you so took matters into my own hands in dealing with a situation to which you would have dealt with no differently." Vincent said and I knew he was right.

"As touching as all this sounds, can we please get back to the matter at hand. There is something you should all be aware of." Lucius said sarcastically which was not surprising.

"Which is?" I asked irritably.

"When my men searched his room, they found the same ritual symbol under his bed in his hotel room."

"Damn it!" I roared wondering how this could get any worse…of course still being on the phone with my personal bearer of bad news I quickly learnt how in fact it could get so much worse.

"There is more." Lucius took a breath and sighed as we waited before finally putting us out of our misery just before I lost my temper completely.

"I had my men check Keira's room also, just to be sure what I already suspected."

"Tell me they didn't find anything?" I growled and felt my brother's arm rest against my shoulder as if holding me back.

"They found the start of the same symbol but luckily it seems he must have been disturbed halfway through completing it."

"By the wrath of Hell, I will destroy him!" I bellowed until the windows rattled in their metal casing. Before Lucius had even finished, I knew what he was going to say from looking back on that day we found him in her room. I should have known he was up to something even then, but I just couldn't get a read on him. It was as if he had been blocking me, hell blocking us all since the very beginning, as even one such as Lucius couldn't get a read on him. It was almost like a part of him was being hidden from all of my kind but that type of power didn't exist...unless... could it be...

"What was the symbol at the massacre and under the beds?" My voice almost shook as I asked the most important question of all. However, I didn't wait for the answer before I bolted out of the door, suddenly having the worst feeling of loss drop to the pit of my stomach.

I was running down the hallway and the last thing I heard from Lucius was my worst fears confirmed...

"A Pentagram."

CHAPTER THIRTY-NINE

KEIRA

EVELEEN

I looked around confused as to why we were even in this room as I doubted very much that Draven conducted his important business at the kitchen table over a cuppa. I watched as Alex walked over to a bolted door and started pulling them back one at a time. I wanted to ask outright what he was doing and why we were in this part of the house but if my suspicions were right then I needed to be clever. So instead of asking the obvious, that being are you in fact a raving psychopath that kinda has a demonic side...I went with,

"So you say the Fates sent you, does that mean you were visited by the Oracle?" And I asked this in such way that it sounded more excited than suspicious. He looked back at me and nodded. It was almost as if he didn't trust himself to speak, so I carried on.

"She's lovely, isn't she? I remember when she first came to me, I thought she was the most beautiful and angelic looking creature. And with her golden hair, I remember wondering what she would think if I asked for tips on how to get mine so shiny." I said on a laugh. He gave me a soft smile as he walked back over to me and I knew I had him when he said,

"I remember thinking her hair beautiful myself." That's the moment I backed up and dropped the pretence.

"The Oracle is a seven-year-old black girl with black curls." The moment I informed him of this I started to see the change. His eyes turned darker, colder and more sinister and his grin cocked up to the side as if all of a sudden, he liked this game.

I laughed once and then knocked over a chair putting a barrier between us as I turned and ran. I didn't get very far before I was wrenched backwards on a scream as he grabbed my hair from behind. He pulled me backwards and I had no place else to go but move with him as the pain increased on my head.

"Ahh! GET OFF ME!" I shouted hoping someone would hear me. He brought me over to the kitchen island at the centre of the room and pulled me up in front of it. Then he yanked my head back and laughed once before snarling,

"Oh, Keira...you really are one dumb bitch!" And then he slammed my head into the counter hard enough that everything went black.

My last thought was...

I hope Draven knows I was wrong.

DRAVEN

It could not be believed. Less than twenty four hours back safe again in my arms and now I found that she had been taken right from under my nose and in my very house! I had made it back to the bedroom and had prayed to every God I knew that possessed enough power to aid me that she would be there safe. But I should have known better than anyone that the Gods would not interfere in such matters, not unless it conflicted with their fucking precious Prophecy!

Once back in the room I had to be careful not to tear it apart as I shook with the beast raging inside me. I took in hers and my combined essence as I knew she had showered, then I followed it into the closet and saw the towel she had left there when changing. By the Gods but I had even been looking forward to the scolding I would have received upon me coming back here after she found I had yet again filled another side of the closet with clothes I knew she would like.

"Dom!" Vincent shouted my name and a few angry steps took me back to the main room. I found Vincent looking down at the untouched tray of food on the low table. Sophia ran through the door and one look at that tray told us all we needed to know.

"I'm on it!" Sophia said taking off once more. I don't think at that moment I had ever been more thankful of the sibling link we shared. It was understandably needed at this point in time when my rage dare not let me speak, so having my brother and sister both know what was needed of them was a blessing I would later relish.

Now however, I only wanted blood.

"We will find her." Vincent said as always so sure of himself and in what he believed.

"Do you think it was the Nephilim?" He asked as I walked

over to stand opposite the sofa we had shared last night. The same one where I had held her in my arms and told her the truth she had always deserved to know. And what had she done? What she always did. She accepted every word I told her and absorbed it with such strength it nearly brought this king to his knees just before begging her to become my wife. But then had not been the time and now time had been stolen from me.

It was these thoughts that unleashed my demon's rage.

"I WILL DESTROY HIM!" I roared out and there wasn't one shred of my angel there to calm him. I let him feel his pain and I let him lash out even if it was only at swiping the table free of the tray that held food I knew she would have enjoyed. Danish pastries flew across the room along with small ceramic jars filled with butter and jam. A one person tea set smashed, with its pieces bouncing across the floor like porcelain shrapnel.

"Dom." Vincent called my name but it was like someone shouting across a field during a storm. It was just a noise I could hear in the distance as I mentally and physically fell to the ground on my knees and roared up at the sky cursing the same Gods I had moments ago been praying to.

"Dominic!" Vincent tried again but I was too consumed by fury to rein my demon back in. It was as though for the first time he was getting a small taste of what it felt like to be in control and like those nights he used to take us back to Keira, now he was trying to do the same.

"Allow me." This was all I heard before I felt just enough pain to bring me back with the shock of it. I shook my head and looked up dazed and when my focus finally did come back, I found my sister was stood over me with a bronze statue of the Egyptian god Horus in her hand. I winced and put out a hand to brace myself as I got up.

"Now cut out the demon shit and focus, Vincent found a

note." She snapped and dropped the statue with a crack as it landed on the tiled floor.

"Well not a note as such, but a piece of parchment paper with nothing written on it." Vincent said lifting it up for me to see. I stood up straight and patted my little sister on her head,

"Thank you." To which she replied,

"Any time," and smirked.

"Did you find anything?" I asked her as I walked over to Vincent to take the note he handed me.

"Uh…" I looked back at her and it didn't take the fact that we were triplets to know there was something in their shared look they didn't want to tell me. I growled when I saw Vincent nod at her but decided to let it go as there were more important matters at hand.

"Well I tracked her down to the kitchen and I can believe that due to the lack of essence of another that it must be this Nephilim we are looking for who was with her."

"She couldn't have gone down on her own?" I asked hoping that by some miracle we had it all wrong and she had in fact done something stupid instead and left in search of something she thought she needed.

"Well at first that's what I thought, that was until…"

"Speak!" I demanded as she hesitated.

"Well the service door had been unlocked and was left open."

"Well that could mean…" I started to say when the next words she interrupted me with were like being speared in the heart with an icy shard.

"Blood. What I found was some of her blood."

"Where?" I asked shaking in an attempt not to let myself be taken by my demon again. I needed to be in control if I was to be any help to Keira. She needed me now and I was no good to her letting my demon make all the decisions. No, if anything I

would have only succeeded in tearing down this old house and burying it beneath the water upon which it sat.

"It was on the counter, as if she had hit her head or was knocked out. There was also a broken chair, so my guess is that she tried to run before he took her." As Sophia gave me all this information, I examined the note but only after being sure I wouldn't damage it in my attempt at cooling my temper. The level of restraint felt almost like my greatest test and this was one I knew I needed to pass for Keira's sake.

"He obviously needs her alive and my guess is that he's going to use her as bait." Vincent said making me frown.

"Bait for what though?" Sophia asked before I could voice the same question.

"Well isn't that just the right question?" Said a small voice I would have known anywhere that came through the door. And the reason I would know had to do with the fact that I had been searching for her for the last ten months!

"Pythia." I hissed her name as one I had come to loathe considering all she now represented. There had once been a time when I had felt protective over her and the need to keep her safe wasn't only for duty's sake. But now when I took in her childlike appearance all I felt was anger for the unforgivable pain she had caused.

"Now, now, don't take that tone with me." She snapped with hands on her hips. I growled low feeling it building up and Vincent came to my aid by putting a restraining hand on my shoulder.

"Not now brother." He told me quietly and I nodded in agreement.

"Much obliged to you Angel." She replied smiling sweetly as if she wasn't the cause of all that had happened.

"Why are you here?!" I barked and she rolled her eyes before responding.

"To read that…" She nodded to the parchment I held and then continued,

"…and to help your stubborn ass save your girl." I felt my lip curl at the distrust I now felt but walked over to her all the same. I looked down at her tiny frame and handed her the paper saying,

"I only hand you my trust right now because I have little choice, so make no mistake it's not because you have earned it." This made her frown up at me and in turn I scowled down at her. If anyone who hadn't know our past or who exactly the Oracle was had walked in right now to see a grown man having a showdown with a small child they would no doubt have found this comical. And for that reason alone, it made me glad Lucius wasn't here.

"Whatever!" She said throwing up her hands in defeat, but I could tell her little act was hiding the hurt I had inflicted with my words.

"Sophia." Pythia said nodding to my sister and Sophia's response was very much like my own, that of being unable to curb her tongue.

"Home wrecker."

"Fine I get it! I had to tell you shit that you didn't want to hear but I only did what was needed, from both sides. And one day you will all understand why because what do you think would happen to, not just you, but everything this Earth has ever known, and those you care for calling it home if the prophecy never happened…um? Oh you'll all see and then I will just make you all buy me cake! Yes, the biggest darndest cake I ever saw, with the words 'sorry, I guess you we're right after all' written all over the damn thing! Now can we all just stop pointing fingers and get back to saving the Chosen One!" She finished her little speech with a foot stomp making her black riot of curls bounce around her head. I simply folded my arms across my chest and said,

"Fine." Then she turned her gaze to Sophia who stood with her arms folded also and said her own,

"Fine!" It was only my brother who said,

"I think that would be best," in his usual calming manner.

"Right, good, so now that's all done and dusted and the royal trio have been reprimanded let's begin should we?" This time is was Sophia's turn to growl, however Pythia just ignored her and lifted up the paper to examine it.

"Umm…"

"What is it?" I asked getting impatient.

"You have taken Keira's blood recently." This wasn't a question as the Oracle rarely needed to ask anything of anyone. I nodded all the same.

"Then come here." She ordered and I stepped back up to her and stared down into her chocolate eyes that matched her perfect youthful skin.

"Bite." She said motioning to my own hand and I now knew what she recognised the paper needed. So I raised my own hand and bit into the flesh feeling little pain. I fisted my hand to get the blood pumping and dripped it over the paper she held out. It didn't take long before she was proven right.

She held it up to the sun beaming through the windows and we all watched as our combined blood, Keira's and mine, dripped down the page. Then one word started to shine through like the paper was almost burning with the name.

"Impossible." Vincent said behind me as I was left speechless.

"It can't be…can it?" Sophia asked looking from each of us until finally my lips formed a name I had not heard in centuries.

"Eveleen."

"Yep, looks like the past really does like to bite you in the ass!" I ignored Pythia and turned to Vincent and asked him the only question I needed to know as I now knew where the Nephilim had taken her.

"Where was Lucius heading?" The answer I got back was the right one…

"Afterlife."

CHAPTER FOURTY

KEIRA

THE APPLE DOESN'T FALL FAR FROM THE TREE

I woke up to the sound of pained whispering voices all around me. I winced as though I had hit my head and that's when everything started to come rushing back to me.

Alex.

I shook my head at how blind I had been. All this time people had warned me against him, and I had been too damn stubborn to see it. Well this time I had my eyes wide open and the blinkers were off as I prepared myself for the fight ahead. So what did I see when I first opened my eyes. I saw the broken pieces of a storm beneath my body and when turning my head to the side one image of something mighty was all it took for me to know where I was.

"Finally, you're awake. I had feared I hit your head too hard and you would be waking an even dumber shit than before."

Alex sneered as he walked from behind the colossal fossilised tree at the centre of this crypt I knew lay at the heart of Afterlife. Alex had brought me home and I could only guess why.

I lifted myself up and felt my head where there was no doubt it had been split open from my attack. However, I was at least grateful to know that thanks to Draven's essence back in my system, my skin had healed. Unfortunately for me though, it still left me a bit wobbly on my feet.

"Me dumb? You're the dipshit who brought us to somewhere Draven will know I have returned the second you crossed the threshold. And what do you think he's going to do, shake your hand and thank you?!" I snapped back straightening my body with fake confidence that this was true.

"You just don't get it yet do you, Keira? This…" He turned around the huge room that was like a miniature football stadium and held out his arms as if he commanded the space.

"… has all been planned down to the very last thread. Every single thing was planned and executed perfectly. So you see, I am not only hoping he will come, I am expecting nothing less and when he does, he will do every last thing I command of him." He finished raising his head and looking down his nose as if he was the royalty in the room and soon everyone would be on their knees at his feet.

"You're insane!" I spat the insult at him with my nose wrinkling in disgust. However, it mattered not what I said as he just started laughing at me and the sound was like a cheese grater along my skin.

"Let's see shall we…now get over there and open the fucking door!" He ordered motioning to the one wall that wasn't covered floor to ceiling with coffin sized holes carved out of the stone. I remember thinking back to that night and how the place reminded me of some supernatural morgue.

"Now!" He shouted and I jumped as his bellow echoed around the room, making it sound as though there were ten of him.

"Not a chance but you go right ahead, that is if you think you have what it takes." I said knowing that considering he was a half breed there was no way the vine covered door would grant him entrance. His response was to snarl at me which curled his lips back in an ugly grimace.

"You want to play this game...oh then *I will play*...but..." He said dropping his once cool demeanour and now bat shit crazy was setting in. He started skipping backwards like some freaky jester who now spent his days in a mental hospital. Then he held up one finger and his creepy jogging backwards started going back around the tree. I frowned at what he was up to and wondered how I had missed this level of insanity all those months we had been together.

I decided to follow him around the Jurassic stone tree where I heard him laughing in a way that sounded more like high pitched hiccups.

"...but to play our game I think we need more players, don't you?" He continued as I came round the tree to his side and I gasped at what I saw.

"LET HER GO!" I screamed as the sight made my heart drop.

"Uh huh...I think not, I think my new plaything likes my apple tree dagger, don't you dearie...? Umm, I know!" He had bent his knees, staying on his feet next to the frightened body of a quivering girl I knew. He put one arm around her tied body, and she whimpered and struggled in vain. I watched in horror as he pulled the same dagger I had seen in all the pictures out from the waistband of his black trousers and pulled it to hold at the front of her.

"I think we should see if this little apple has a rotten core." He said smiling and holding the point to her chest.

"NO!"

"Or maybe let's peel her first and see how sweet her flesh is." He carried on, this time bringing the blade to her outstretched tied arms like he was going to take a slice of her skin off.

"Stop! Please! Jesus Christ just stop, and I will do it!" I shouted letting my shoulders slump in defeat.

"Of course you will. Now get fucking doing it!" He lost it at the end making the body he held captive shake and sob even harder. I looked into her terrified eyes and tried to convey with one look that everything was going to be alright. But the truth was that I had no clue if everything was going to be alright, I only knew that I had to get him as far away from my friend and doing that meant letting him into the one place I knew he needed access to.

"I'm sorry RJ." I said letting a tear overflow down my cheek before turning around and walking towards the dead vines that protected the door lay hidden beneath.

"Mhha!" My head snapped round and I shouted,

"RJ!" I started to run back to her when I saw her body slump sideways.

"Get back to it, your Goth bitch still lives...*for now.*" He added the threat and I breathed a sigh of relief that at least with her now being knocked out she wouldn't be sat there against the tree terrified. I watched as Alex stood up and threw his dagger around before shaking it back at the entrance towards the Temple. So I did as I was told, wishing I could just use the powers I knew were locked inside me, all I needed was the key.

The closer I got to the stone vines the more I was drawn back into the past and what happened that night.

"Yes...reach for us...touch our souls...yes...do it." The

same whispers I heard when waking and also back all that time ago started to filter around the room as if trying to pinpoint me. They seemed to come from everywhere all at once and even Alex looked around as if he hadn't expected it.

"Do it!" Alex barked from only a few metres behind me as I took my last steps towards the huge wall. I looked up at the twisted and entwined network of what looked like stone snakes that were guarding this place for good reason. I couldn't say that I was looking forward to this next bit, so naturally hesitated as my hand reached out to what looked like the exact same place as last time.

"Yes…yes…free us…let us live again…touch… touch…touch…"

"Now!" I closed my eyes tight as I thrust my hand forward and waited for the sting.

"Ahhh!" I hissed as the vine I touched uncurled from its brothers and wrapped itself around my wrist. Then I felt it tug me closer and it penetrated my palm over and over, almost as if tiny pins were branding me, which I guess was exactly what it was doing. It was all over after a few seconds and as soon as my hand was released, I stumbled backwards passing Alex who was staring up at it in demented awe. He watched as the vine that had ensnared me in its trap started to pulsate and turn a lush green colour, like my blood had just breathed life into it.

"Why isn't it opening?" He snapped at me looking back over his shoulder. I looked down at the hand I was now clutching and after wiping the blood across my denim shorts, I saw the same mark that represented the Prophecy.

"Give it time, asshole." I said letting my hate seep into my tone and just before he could respond, the vines started to move. And like last time they writhed around as if trying desperately to escape the 'infected' one and pretty soon the doors beneath were revealed.

"Ah! Perfect and just how I imagined!" Alex said clapping in crazed glee.

"Yeah, it's just peachy." I muttered sarcastically and started walking back over to the passed-out RJ and leaving him to it.

"Where do you think you're going!?" Alex said chuckling when I screamed out because he had once again pulled back my head by my hair. Then he turned us and propelled me forward but thankfully at least letting go of me.

"I can't help you in there!" I said trying to reason with him, but that in itself would have made me laugh if I wasn't faced with my dire situation.

"Oh trust me, I think you can." He replied and gripped the top of my arm as he went past, dragging me to the now opening doors and into the blinding light. I closed my eyes against the power of it and let myself be pulled through the tunnel of light that was like walking into Heaven itself. Although with this half breed crackpot next to me I doubt they would have answered the door!

"You know it makes me wonder just what else you would have done if I had succeeded in my first choice of hostages." He said as he pulled me through the brightest part at the end. Coming out the other side was like that fuzzy blurred feeling you get after staring at the sun.

"What do you mean?" I almost hated myself for feeding into his sick game, but I had to ask.

"That old fucking Viking Ragnar, the big bastard was sent to ruin my fun by protecting your sister, her thick headed husband and the brat…now the look on your face seeing them tied up and screaming would have made the sweetest sight, don't you think?" On hearing this and having the worst image alive planted in my mind I lost all reasoning but one…*attack*.

"YOU SICK FUCK!" I screamed turning around and lashing out at his face, trying to grab his head to bring down to my knee. Unfortunately, he ducked backwards so it was only the tips of my fingers that came into contact with his face. I was however, glad to see I had inflicted some damage as I looked at the three bloody lines my nails had caused.

"You bitch!" He said backhanding me to the side and I flipped with the strength he possessed. The landing was so painful it knocked the wind out of me, and I clutched my side as I gasped for air.

"Now get up!" He said dragging me up and I grimaced when I felt his own nails bite into my arm. The only thing I could hold onto as we made our way through the first section of the prison was to thank both Heaven and Hell for creating such a man as Draven, knowing how he had protected my family from this mad man. One I myself had welcomed in their home was one I would never forget, however it was one I would also never forgive in regards to my own stupidity.

"I don't get it, why are you even doing this?" I asked thinking if I could first understand why, then maybe I would discover a way of stopping it.

"Do you remember when I told you about the apple?" I frowned up at him at the same thinking that there went my hope in getting any sense from him.

"Ah but I know you do. Well let me tell you another story." He said whispering this last part in my ear making me cringe away from him in disgust.

"So where are we in time…um, well why don't we start from the very beginning of time, or mortal time at least. Back to a time when the skies rained with blood of dead immortals and therefore gave birth to their weaker offspring…you mere mortals." I actually rolled my eyes at this point and couldn't refrain from saying,

"Yeah, I already heard this story, dickhead!" His response to this was to push my cheek into the side of the tunnel we were walking down, and I felt the dripping wet stone pressing painfully into my face. Then I felt him get really close behind me and his voice dipped to one that filled me with more fear. This was Alex's other side coming out.

"Adam and Eve were the first pure bloodlines to the mighty Titans and therefore the key to their release. So a serpent found its way into the garden that was meant to protect them and keep them safe from the traitorous world all around them. Only someone discovered a way in…and do you know why?" He asked getting closer until he was pretty much speaking over the cheek that wasn't being squashed into the stone.

"It wasn't for eating the forbidden fruit at all…it was for *becoming* the forbidden fruit."

"You make no sense, you crazy shit!" I snarled back at him only my voice was pained despite my bravery.

"The serpent wasn't there to convince her to eat some fucking fruit! He was there to impregnate her with his seed, planting her with a truth. He came to her a creature of trust and then transformed into a man with the knowledge of sin. He couldn't have her corrupted and the bloodline weakened. There were others out there that were being born to the Earth. Mortals that had already started to water down their precious blood. But in this garden they had remained safe as was Satan's will…" He let go of my head and spun me around to face him as if he needed my eyes as audience.

"But powerful beings were getting restless. And one in particular wanted his key intact. So whilst innocently eating an apple she was taken against her will, forced to sin and destroyed the garden along with their safe sanctuary. Did you know if you cut an apple a certain way it forms a Pentagram? Did you know that Keira? Did you know that a Pentagram can be seen from two angles? Did you know that?!" He said getting louder with each time he asked me this.

"No." I said looking away only to have my chin wrenched back.

"And did you know that one view is all the good and purity taken and the other is the devil from Heaven that took it away and fucked it!"

"Get off me!" I tried to move my head after he sickened me further by licking up the length of my face.

"It's all about the seeds, that and what was born from those seeds. Oh how I did love my mother." He said making me gasp at the impossible.

"It can't be! No!"

"Oh I am not the original, but like him I did murder my brother." He said laughing.

"Now come on, enough stop and chit chat…soon it will be time for the main event!" He yanked me away from the wall and started to once again pull me down another tunnel.

"But I don't understand…you said."

"Oh but I see I will get nothing done unless I explain to the stupid blonde." He laughed at his own unfunny joke. We were just coming through the last door and I knew the light at the end was the Temple.

"My mother was Eveleen, and like many before her she was the last pureblood to be reincarnated into the same body. It's the Titan's blood you see, once it finds the same resurrected soul the body would relive again. So along comes the serpent to try and plant his next seed but it doesn't work after the first time… that was until the last time. I like to think Eveleen was his favourite…she deserved that I think."

"Oh God! That means…"

"I am the last in my bloodline after my mother was dispatched for good this time." He said smiling but I could see the anger rooted under the surface and it wouldn't let him go.

"You're…"

"The last Cain and the only key to releasing Hell on Earth and you know, I really, really want to." The way he said this I knew it wasn't some frenzied uncontrolled plan, but one fuelled by hatred and crippling determination. This wasn't just about me or even some quest for power. This was about changing the whole world because of revenge, because of…Oh God…I just figured it out.

"Draven killed your mother…*didn't he?*" Alex turned back to me and he became a shadow with the light behind him, making his presence even more menacing now I knew his plan, but more importantly, where his plan had grown its roots from.

Then those roots grew deeper with one truth…

"And my father."

CHAPTER FOURTY-ONE

LUCIUS

CALIBURNUS

I could barely believe I was back in this town let alone stood outside the one place I vowed I would never set my eyes on again. Well, not unless I had a sword in my hand and was about to face my enemy but oh, how things had changed and all in the name of one troublesome little blonde.

And speaking of troublesome little blondes I knew any minute I would be receiving yet another panicked call from my once King and someone I had pledged my loyalty to. So how I found myself back here after the part he played in my demise was down to one core point...*The Electus.*

Of course I was rational enough to know the reasons why he did what he did in keeping the spear tip from me but still bitter enough not to give a fuck. Or at least this was what I told myself and also at least finding comfort in the knowledge that Draven had also been fucked over by the Fates just as I had.

"Ah just as predicted." I said to myself as my phone started blasting out Rage Against the Machine's, 'Killing In The Name', which I found very apt for my current mission. I rolled my eyes to the Heavens I still loathed before swiping across the name Dickhead that I had Dom stored as a contact in my phone.

"I am standing outside Afterlife." I said in answer to what I knew would be yet another demand as to my location.

"Any signs of her yet?" Dom barked at me from the other side.

"I have tracked them to this point but as you know I will not be granted access into the Temple…unless…?" I left the question unasked and I smirked when I heard the frustrated growl coming from a being I knew was close to the edge of losing his famous temper. I would have thought for a Being as old as he was that he would have learnt the level of control needed with both great power and position.

"There is a way in." He finally said after a few contemplative moments and this time the bastard in me grinned.

"But of course."

"Facing the building walk down the right-hand side and you will see an access door, to the right of that is a hidden door above you, get there and call me back." Dom said petulantly and then hung up.

"Charming as always." I said looking at my phone screen and now seeing the new Lamborghini Veneno I had on order. I looked back up at the building and even in the dark I noted how much time the ivy had had to take over the pale stone. I expected to see the mortal line of bodies waiting to get inside and unbeknown to their simple minds a feast for the council I was once a part of. However, this late into the night more souls were resting than not.

Oh those were the days. Having the essence just walk right up to your door and literally beg for entrance. Although my distaste for the race helped fuel the power that was enforced upon me, I couldn't help but feel compelled to aid in their survival. This sense of duty was of course renewed since the Fates intervened forcing me to see myself differently and finding that image was mirrored back in the eyes of one blue eyed girl. One mortal girl created to change the course of impending doom. But on a more personal level the one girl who managed to bring me back from the dead sands of time and forced me into the light of the living sea.

She had done the impossible and given me a peace I hadn't wanted to have ever admitted I was searching for.

"Sneaky…very sneaky, my little Keira girl." I said to myself as I shook my head smiling at the thought of my people's Chosen One. The possibility of the fate of the world resting on the shoulders of one feisty little blonde from Liverpool was a thought that always had me shaking my head with a knowing smile on my face.

I could just imagine what it must have been like for her back in those naive days of innocence. The first time she had taken these steps back when she had no clue of the hunters closing in on her heels. Two Kings that each wanted separate things but in the end they had become one and the same. It hadn't taken me long to begin my obsession with the girl and soon that started to override one that had been with me since my rebirth. Because in the end the Fates had decided that my destiny was to follow one path and for a long time I had believed it to be my king but now I knew the truth.

It was his Chosen One.

And now it was once again time to save the little bird before someone clipped her wings. So with this new mission in mind I walked to where Dom had told me and with each step I took going back to a time. One that was tainted with bad blood now made pure with the Spear of Longinus embedded beneath my new wings. And it was these wings that I now used to fly up to a small balcony that unbeknown to Dom I already knew about. What I didn't know however was the words needed to gain access to the building I had once been welcomed into.

"Call Dickhead." I commanded to my phone knowing it would be picked up after the first ring.

"You found the door?" I rolled my eyes at his absurd question and didn't dignify it with the wasted breath on an answer.

"To gain entrance it is 'Persian heat' in Latin. There is a door at the end of the passageway and level to the top iron hinge is a protruding stone, press it and a direct tunnel will lead you down to the Temple."

"I think we still have the small matter of banishment to contend with old friend." I reminded him with satisfaction.

"The tunnel's end brings you out…" He hesitated and then cursed before continuing,

"By the Gods I can't believe I am trusting you with this…" He said now cursing himself with the decision he knew he had no choice in making.

"Tick, tick Dom, time is getting on for our little bird and I doubt your Viking will be able to handle this Viper alone." I reminded him in a cool voice I was only maintaining through one clenched fist. Really I wanted to roar out at him in my own rage and frustration at knowing someone had her in their grasp.

"Fuck! Okay it brings you out into the main treasury and there you will find an old friend. I think you will remember what you did last time, so do the same here and it will open a direct route to the Temple. If they are in there, then you might be able to get her out and away from danger before dealing with him." The tone of his voice told me all I needed to know about Dom trying not only to keep control of his Demon side but also the panicking side of his Angel.

I never understood just how conflicting it was living with the two forces converged inside you. It was like trying to keep two tyrant dictators from going to war with their armies ready at the border.

"I would have thought you would have been here by now." I knew a low growl would be the first thing I would hear before he answered me and I didn't bother to supress the grin that would arise at every opportunity taken to rile my old friend and enemy.

"NOW LISTEN TO…" Dom's voice was cut off as his calmer brother must have intervened given the King's mounting rage.

"We encountered a new development and therefore had to make a stop at Dublin to visit…"

"Belphegor." I said interrupting the most powerful Angel I knew.

"Yes." Vincent said and even he couldn't keep the same disgust from his voice as I had let coat the name.

"And what did that vile cretin have to offer?" I asked frowning up at the building and letting my irritation grow that I wasn't yet inside breaking one Nephilim's fucking neck.

"He told us of Eveleen's sons."

"And let me guess, Alex Cain by any chance." I said voicing what now seemed like a blindingly obvious discovery, one that angered me to my core at not unearthing it sooner. The compulsion at the time when seeing him next to my Keira girl was to follow through with one swift and brutal act that would have solved all our current problems. But foolishly Dom thought it best to investigate the asshole first. Well I bet my ordered Veneno that he was beating himself up for that idiotic decision.

If it had been me there would have been no hesitation in reminding him of some of the more effective ways of torture.

Ah but those were the old days. Like the Brazen Bull for example. The size of real bull made of bronze and hollow ready for the victim to be placed inside and once there they were then cooked slowly from the fire blazing beneath them. Oh yes, then even a Nephilim would beg and sing out his secrets in cries of pain.

I was so deep into my bloody torturing days that I hadn't realised Vincent was still on the phone until he started speaking again,

"As we know Belphegor was the one recruited to find the Eve descendants and inform…"

"Yes I know." I said interrupting him impatiently as I could easily piece together the rest of the family affair without wasting time.

"So you know what this means?"

"Yes, I know what this fucking means." I said letting my irritation known.

"We will be landing in about an hour's time…" I heard Dom retake the phone and the last thing he told me was the one thing I had vowed to do till my death,

"Protect her at all costs."

"Always." Was my curt reply before I hung up the phone. I then placed it back in my pocket and cracked my fists as a way to relieve the mounting tension before turning back to face the door.

"Persae Calorem" I repeated the Latin for Persian Heat and didn't have to wait long before the door opened. I folded back my wings drawing them into my body before walking down the narrow passageway. Trust Dom to have a place like this, for I knew it wasn't just for reasons of another entrance into his home. No, this was purely for spying. I grinned in satisfaction knowing that his paranoia no doubt increased after our little encounter…oh who was I bullshitting, I could have torn the asshole apart that day!

After following the instructions that even a child could have executed, I found myself pushing open a hidden door and the first sight that greeted me made me want to try and kill the bastard all over again.

"Son of Angel Bitch!" I said as I walked around an old friend indeed. The room I remembered as Dom's treasury, but I ignored the large holes carved out of the bare stone which held artefacts that didn't interest me. No, the only thing that did was what was once mine and was in fact taken from me. Of course, I had my suspicions back then but now having it confirmed made my control slip enough to smash the glass case with one pounding of my fist.

It shattered around me but by the time the last of the shards skidded to a stop my anger was back under tight control.

"Caliburnus." I said its name again like one would speak to a lover and caressed the stone hand with pretty much the same affection. The black blood that constantly flowed down her delicate hand made me frown at the reminder of what it represented or more like *who.*

"It's alright pet, I am back to claim what is mine." I said taking hold of the sword's handle and Dom was right, it was like being reunited with an old friend. As soon as it felt its rightful owner take hold once more the Lady of the Lake let go of her charge and the steel blade slid from the deep grooves it had made in her stone flesh. The blood that symbolised my own stopped flowing and I braced knowing what was coming…*the test.*

The deceivingly unthreatening hand quickly forgot about the treasure I had reclaimed and snatched out to sink its fingertips into my flesh, drawing now fresh blood. I barely registered the pain as a result of what happens over centuries of living in a brutal world. No, instead of flinching I just let it happen and allowed my blood to travel down to the pool of dark liquid on the floor. Once the first drop hit the rest, the stone fingers peeled themselves back one by one and I was free to pull my arm away from her grasp. I then took a step back feeling my heavy boots crunching on the glass and wanting nothing more than for it to be one Alex Cain's bones.

I lifted up the sword to the ceiling so my face was mirrored back in the blade and kissed my own crest forged there.

"Now let us reunite in the best way old friend and kiss your fine steel in the heart of Nephilim scum." I said as the Lady of the Lake slid to the side and hidden steps appeared from beneath. And one thought entered my sadistic mind as I took the steps down...

Lucius the Assassin had come home.

CHAPTER FOURTY-TWO

KEIRA

SCREAM BLOODY MURDER AND RAISE THE DEAD

"You're insane if you think this plan of yours will actually work!" I said just wishing I had Frank's baseball bat in my hand so that when he turned around, I had something to back that statement up with. Oh I had no doubt someone would be coming to rescue me but this time thanks to what Alex had said, I was just wishing for anyone but Draven.

"Insanity only fuels the imagination." Alex said laughing as he continued spreading jar after jar of what looked like congealed blood around the altar at the top of the Temple. Unfortunately for me though I hadn't been left to wander round looking for my escape whilst evil villain of the year here had been busy playing lead role in One Flew Over the Cuckoo's Nest. No, in fact it seems he was sane enough to remember to tie my hands behind my back and then to tie the end to one of the pillars closest to

531

where he was working on redecorating the place. Maybe he was going for the Jack the Ripper crime scene look.

"Well in that case you must be tanked up by now." I said pulling at the rope and feeling it only twist further and burn against my skin. I quickly gave up and looked around the room taking in the grandeur of the place that was being decimated with old blood by Mr Shits and Giggles mental case over there. It was a huge space that had the shiniest marble floor I had ever seen. It mirrored the sky painted on the ceiling above making the floor almost look like a glass sheet lay on the surface of a lake.

I followed the flame painted pillars around the room and took in the story scenes painted between them, that I now knew were actually not just a war between Heaven and Hell as I originally thought. No, this time I knew it as the War of the Immortals.

It was funny what knowledge could do to how you viewed the world around you and being thrust deeper into Draven's world with every breath I took was forever an eye opener. So when I took in the winged Demons fighting Angels on horseback I couldn't honestly now tell you who were the good guys and who were the bad guys.

But one thing I did know for sure and that was I could definitely say the last time I was here was considerably better than the first. But having my first dance with Draven to Etta James' 'At last' was better than thinking he was Lucius in a black robe at the time trying to kill me. Which made it totally ironic then that he was the person I was actually seeing right now, sneaking in through a hidden door to no doubt save me...*again.* And what was with the massive sword looking like Braveheart?

I saw him do a full body scan before he winked at me and

held a finger to his lips to indicate my silence. If it hadn't been doing the exact opposite of what he asked I would have shouted, 'Duh, you think?!' Which I didn't do for obvious loud reasons. I couldn't help but notice when he first saw me, the moment of relief I saw in his eyes when he saw I was uninjured. I looked back at Alex to see he was still preoccupied with his little bloody project and it was only now that I could see it was a star inside of a circle, one I now knew was an important Pentagram symbol.

I jumped when I suddenly felt a hand at my mouth but luckily, I managed not to make a noise. I knew it was Lucius at my back and that was true in more ways than one. I felt the slack of my restraints as he untied the rope from first the pillar and then I felt lips at my ear.

"Now pretty girl, hold still so I don't cut you." Lucius whispered and then after a few seconds I started to feel the pressure disappear completely from around my sore wrists. I wanted to hiss in pain as I felt the raw skin being disturbed but bit my lip instead. After one last look at the crazy guy to make sure he was still busy doing crazy things, I turned back to Lucius. He didn't say anything but nodded behind him for me to follow and we headed to the hidden doorway I'd seen him emerge from. It looked like one that could only be opened from one side as he had propped it open so that we could escape that same way.

Keeping behind the pillars and out of sight we made our way to the door as quickly as we could and just as Lucius was stepping through behind me that's when Alex Cain finally caught on.

"NO!" He bellowed racing towards us, and Lucius merely gave him the middle finger as a salute before slamming the door.

"Won't he just be able to follow us?" I asked making sure and Lucius' bad ass grin was answer enough.

"I must say if you wanted my attention then you should have just asked me on a date." He said winking at me and grabbing my hand as he passed to pull me along after him.

"To where, the Devil's ring?" I said sarcastically referring back to Jared's private fight club.

"Umm…not your worst idea pet, we could get you wrestling Angels naked in the mud." I rolled my eyes but couldn't help but laugh, mentally thanking him for putting me at ease in a situation I was trying not to panic in.

"Ha! You wish!"

"Yes, yes I do." He said looking over his shoulder and doing another all over body scan, only this time not one out of concern.

"Ok, so getting back to the matter at hand, we have to stop Alex, he's planning something insane and he's the last in the bloodline and…"

"Calm yourself Keira girl, I know what he intends but soon he will be far too busy with my own plans."

"And that is?" I asked knowing I would regret it pretty damn quick and I was right.

"Simple…I plan to kill him…which is what I should have done at the auction." He said as if it was the most natural thing in the world and we were discussing the weather.

"Oh yeah, that would have gone down well… 'And can I get a bid on this next lot, going cheap thanks to the recent blood splatter damage'…yeah that would have been peachy." I said making him laugh and it vibrated along the narrow stone tunnel that only barely allowed for Lucius' height.

"You never know, it might have increased the value, as I am sure all who meet him want to see the evidence for themselves of his bloody end."

"Yeah, I sure know how to pick em." I said rolling my eyes when he replied,

"You said it not me, darlin."

"So where are we going?" I asked as we'd travelled far enough to come to a door at the end.

"*You* are getting your sweet ass somewhere safe, whilst I deal with your boyfriend."

"What are you gonna do, break up with him for me?" I said finding the term boyfriend for such a man too disgusting to think about.

"Oh I am going to break something alright." He replied seriously giving me the unwanted visual that Alex had a lot of pain coming his way. I decided it was best not to know too much for what Lucius had planned so I decided silence was the best option as he opened the door.

"After you." He said bowing as he held open the door for me and I couldn't tell if he was just being himself or if it was for my benefit at trying to ease my worried mind. Either way I stepped through the door and climbed the few of steps that led up as if we were coming out of a basement. I gave myself a mental shake for obvious reasons as I still had a few issues with basements.

I then stepped into a room I hadn't seen for a while and one I never really understood but to me it looked like something you would have expected to see in a supernatural museum. Only this museum had been clearly vandalised as there was now glass all over the floor.

"Your handy work?" I asked tiptoeing around the shards.

"Guilty." He said waving his sword at me, one that I knew used to be in the hand of the statue that had now shifted to the side to allow for us to get up to this level.

"Come on trouble, let's get you out of here." He said taking my arm and leading me out of the room when something hugely important smacked me in the face causing me shout out,

"RJ!" And I wrenched my arm free and turned towards the opposite door.

"Keira what are you…!?"

"We have to go back! It's my friend…he has my friend, it's how he got me to open the door in the first place...! Please Lucius…*please*, we have to go back." I felt his arms go around me from behind in order to calm me down.

"Okay pet, calm yourself. Just let me get you to safety and…"

"No! I can't leave her, not again. She's by that big tree." I said interrupting him and when I heard the big sigh from behind me I knew he was reluctantly giving in.

"Alright Keira girl, we'll do it your way, but you are to stay by my side no matter what." I knew by the sound of his tone he meant business and I nodded my understanding as he came round to face me.

"Then let's go. The Crypt is this way."

We made our way to the crypt in silence and I could tell Lucius was thinking this was a bad idea. My only hope was that Alex hadn't made it there before us, which I knew Lucius must have been thinking the same as I was practically running to keep up with his long strides. The sound of my feet echoing in the massive hallway was combined with the sound of the stone gargoyles turning their heads as we went past.

"Nosy bastards." Lucius grumbled after growling at them in warning.

We came to the last door and Lucius pulled me in behind him. Then with one look that told me both to keep quiet and stay close to him, he opened the door. The frigid cold air that hit us made my hairs stand on end and the eeriness to the silent crypt wasn't a comforting one. In fact there was no comfort to be found in this cavernous space, even if there had been a brass band playing some happy Disney tune. The only comfort I found was that I could see RJ's pink hair against the dull pale grey of the ginormous tree at the centre.

"Over there." I whispered from behind him, pointing in her direction and Lucius shot me a look over his shoulder as if to say, 'No shit Sherlock'. He then continued to look all around the room as if listening out for something important and I gathered it was probably for signs of Alex. He must have been satisfied because he nodded for us to move over to where RJ still remained unconscious. As soon as we got closer, I made to go around Lucius, forgetting myself at the sight of my friend when he blocked me with the arm holding the sword.

"What did I say?" Lucius growled scolding me.

"Sorry." I whispered shrugging my shoulders and making him roll his eyes at me. I watched as he placed his sword beside her before picking her up in his arms and to be helpful, I picked up his weapon for him as he clearly had his hands full.

"No! Don't touch…" He started to say but it was too late. I picked up the heavy weight of the weapon and sucked in a sharp startled breath. I closed my eyes and my spine straightened from the shock of what was happening. I was quickly being transported back to a different time, one where the vision was over taking my reality.

It was dark, it was wet, and it was foggy but it certainly wasn't inside the ancient crypt I had been stood in moments ago. I could even smell the damp earth I was now looking down at and I could feel the cold penetrating my thin clothes. I then looked up at the night sky and saw the darker patches of thick cloud where the moon was trying to break through. I felt something dripping down my hand and lifted it to see dark blood running down it in rivulets but yet I felt no pain. What was going on here? And that didn't even look like my hand?

"Caliburnus." I heard myself saying, feeling my lips move yet like my hand, it hadn't been my voice either. No…

It was Lucius'.

I was now Lucius.

This was when the fog started to lift from the ground in a wave towards me. It loomed like a living entity in between my legs and it looked so thick, it was almost as if I could reach out and scoop it up with my hands. But the nearer it got the clearer the sight before me became.

I was stood at the edge of a lake and I lifted my bloody hands in front of me seeing the strong hands of the man I knew. It soon became clear what was happening, and it wasn't a surprise when something started to emerge out of the murky water. I now knew exactly what was happening after I touched that sword as it had formed some kind of physic kinetic link straight into Lucius' memories. And now that very weapon was rising up out of the water, only instead of fingers of stone it was the hand of both the dead and the living, changing in and out between flesh, bone and decay.

The sword gleamed like a beacon just as the moon finally escaped the shadows of the clouds and just as Lucius' bloody hand reached out to grab it, I was suddenly transported back.

"Wh…what was that?" I asked shaking my head trying to regain my senses enough to focus.

"Are you alright?" Lucius asked coming up to me and holding my face in his hands. I frowned down at the tingling in my own hand and then looked up at him to give him my uncertain answer,

"I think so."

"Well that will teach you to touch another man's equipment

without asking." He said on a forced laugh that I could tell was faked to mask his concern.

"Thanks for the tip." I said only now noticing that he had placed RJ back on the ground to come to my aid.

"We need to leave." He said looking up abruptly as if hearing something in the distance.

"Good plan." I said watching as he decided to sling the limp RJ over his shoulder so that he could reach down and this time, grab his own sword. We started walking towards the door when my foot caught on something.

I tripped, falling to the floor and for the second time coming up close and personal with the mosaic tiles that painted the picture of a raging storm beneath me. Lucius had just made it to the door before he turned.

"Keira!" He shouted making my name boom around the space but even hearing it repeated as it echoed off every surface wasn't enough warning before I was grabbed.

"Get her out of here!" I yelled nodding to RJ as I turned in time to see Alex yank my foot with one of the vines that had been lassoed around my ankle. I quickly found myself skidding along the floor as Alex both pulled the vine and ran towards me. I looked back at Lucius and saw him practically throw RJ down and slam the door behind her.

"GET OFF ME!" I screamed up at him as he continued to drag me back and closer to the tree. I looked back to see an enraged Lucius storming our way with nothing but murder in his red eyes. Then I was brutally hauled up by my neck as I reached my destination and was swiftly slammed up against the tree.

"Let her go, Nephilim." Lucius said with deadly calm.

"How about I let her blood go instead?" Alex said holding my neck to the point I could barely breathe, and my fingernails scratched at his hand squeezing my throat. He brought his face closer to mine and sneered saying,

"Let's see how fast you bleed."

I decided to take this opportunity to forget about the breath I needed to survive and used the last of my strength to hurt him. So I lashed out as black spots appeared in front of me and only just managed to press a thumb into his eye until I heard him crying out in pain. I tried not to think of the gross factor and let my adrenaline and need to defend completely take over. Thankfully it was enough for him to let me go but due to the lack of oxygen I didn't make it far. My legs gave out and my blurring vision barely took in the sight of Lucius erupting into his demon side.

"KEIRA!" I knew the moment my name started ringing in my ears that I needed to move but it was too late. I was now being forced backwards and my arm was being held outstretched to the side.

"Too late, Vampire!" Alex said and then all I felt was a pain ripped from my past. Alex had sliced my wrist down to the vein and the searing agony had me screaming till my lungs burned.

"Now let's see if your screams can really wake the dead!" Alex spoke to the room, clearly lost in his madness. Then without another thought I felt him thrust my bloody arm into the vines that surrounded the tree and had encased the colossal trunk within its protective cover.

"NO!" Lucius roared but it was too late. With my arm firmly embedded my life had already started to flow back into the dead tree forcing it to once again take on a new life. It held me locked there just like the door's vines had done, feeding from me like a suckling child in need of nourishment. This was when I noticed that Alex had taken careful steps back to look around the room as if waiting for something. My fogged mind only took in parts of what was happening, and the colour of evergreen was soon blurred tubes in front of me. What were those I wondered as I felt myself being drained of energy.

It was only when the rumbling started that I was able to piece it all together. Feeding the door, a drop of blood was like injecting a small amount of adrenaline into a dead heart and getting enough from one beat to gain access to the Temple. However what Alex had done was to fuel that heart with enough power to pump a constant beat, with my blood acting as the catalyst.

The lush green life travelled along the veins as if chasing the dead away and pretty soon the whole tree was full of life once more, standing tall in all its superb glory. Although we soon found out this wasn't the only dead thing to make its appearance to the land of the living once again.

"Wh…what…haaave…you donnne?" I asked slurring as I was finally released and fell backwards being too weak to stand.

"I invited some friends to the party." He said laughing as the vast space shook like it was some aftershock from seismic waves that kept rolling through the levels of the earth beneath us. I saw the dust and debris raining down from the ceiling and I looked back to the walls when the thundering came from all around us.

I saw Lucius stop and look around the room as if he already knew what was about to happen and only in my wildest of nightmares would I understand. Because this was the point when my life turned into some horrific zombie movie.

I had to squint my eyes to begin with as the first shadows emerged from the crypt's holes but soon it started to look more like a wall of black was closing in on us. Like a swarm of bees all moving around each other, it was hard to pinpoint just one. It didn't make sense until the first line of bodies drew closer and Lucius raised his sword.

"Oh God no! You…you raised dead!" I whispered as I

managed to sit up and cradle my wounded hand to my chest, putting pressure on the bloody slice made there.

"No… *you* raised the dead, dear Catherine."

"Is this best you can do before you die at my hands, Nephilim?!" Lucius shouted, taking a better stance and looking truly magnificent with his flaming phoenix wings stretched out behind him. He looked ready to take on an army and as the first bodies came into detailed focus I sucked in a worried breath, realising how true that statement was.

Lucius was going in to battle and he was doing it alone.

The living dead didn't walk and stumble along like mindless drones as they did in most movies. No, they went at him with purpose as if he held the key to their resurrected survival. It was like a horde of bodies that looked like their dry flesh had been pulled downwards as it hung from the elongated bones like weighty material. Black holes for their eyes, mouth and nose held no features from their past lives and the most distinct body part was the lines of ribs that showed through the sheer stretched skin that looked as thin and as breakable as tissue paper.

"LOOK OUT!" I screamed as the first wave attacked him from behind, but I needn't have feared as Lucius cut them down with one swipe, taking five in one go. I watched in pure amazement as he flung his sword around at such speeds it almost looked like the blades on a propeller going round. He spun, ducked and bent at the waist in a series of movements that was so efficient no one really even got close to him. But the more he cut down the more that steadily replaced them.

I was just watching as he flipped his body around and out to one side arching his weapon downwards which took out another three with one move. Then I was grabbed from behind and with my dry blood still coating the wooden dagger it was held to my throat.

"Time for us to get back to our own private party." Alex said and in his excitement I felt the spray of spit hit my ear and neck.

"Let me go!" I said trying to struggle but giving up quickly when I felt the bite of pain under my neck. I could see Lucius trying to make a path to get to me but each time he tried he was attacked from a different angle. I knew he needed help, just something to give him that small window so he could get to me but more importantly… *to Alex.*

So with this new plan in mind I drew in a deep breath and tried to block out the throbbing pain in my arm. I knew I had but one chance at this and I had to make it count. So I tried to relax and blank my mind in order to draw in some energy. I had no idea how to do this, so I tried the only idea I had and that was to concentrate on not only everything else around me but seeing it all differently. Not looking at what was in front of me as a person or an object but looking at it as an aura. Something that conducted an essence like the supernatural beings did in order to feed. I had to see the world in their eyes and feel out the different energies like Draven had told me about.

It was only then that the world for me changed and for once instead of seeing a place of horror, it became a place of beauty. Colours lit up all around the tree of life and even each of the battling dead became a red glow that filled the room with crimson light. It was almost blinding and if I hadn't had a blade to my neck, I would have shielded my eyes. But in the end this became a means of drawing in this newly discovered energy as a way to protect myself. Like my mind took over and started to absorb the auras around me in long streams of colour now travelling towards me. The sole purpose of this was to make the world less bright but in doing so it made me feel strong…very, very strong.

My body stiffened and I felt the blade start to cut into my skin but instantly, like my arm, it started to heal.

"This can't…you…you can't do this!" Alex said in confusion behind me and just like that night at the ball, my body went stiff as if I was being injected with raw power of the likes I had never known. I felt it seep not only into my veins but also into my very pores as it was absorbed into my skin making me glow.

My mind felt as though it was on a euphoric cloud, floating away to a better place and it was only when I heard the crashing of stone that I looked down. I was shocked to still see my feet on the ground and the thought sobered me enough to look to where the noise had come from. There I found Lucius pulling his body free of the wall he had been thrown into and the sight made me angry.

Actually not just angry but…*furious.*

Very quickly all the energy that had once calmed my body and mind was now only focused on one thing. My fingertips started to tingle which I knew was a sign something was coming. But before I could think too much about it a mighty power shot from my hands and all those thin streams of colour I had drawn into me, blasted forth in a line. It blew me backwards with the force but the damage done in front of me was incredible. It had knocked a wide path in the mass of fighting dead bodies like Moses parting a sea of bone and old flesh.

Lucius saw this and speared the last in his way, leaving his sword embedded in bodies and wasting no time in using the opportunity created for him. He flew over to us, now he no longer had bodies reaching for his wings and within seconds Lucius landed just as Alex was backing up. I fell down on one knee as the energy once consumed was now zapped out of me, leaving me feeling weak. I just had enough in me to raise my head and look up in time to see Lucius grab Alex by the neck, wrench it to the side and plunge his fangs viciously into his flesh.

This was the animalistic side to Lucius I had never seen before and for someone who usually played their cool demeanour like a fine tuned instrument, it was a chilling sight to witness. One so disturbing I wanted to look away but in the end I forced myself to watch. My eyes took in the space around us and at the continued danger that was no doubt headed our way. Thankfully though it seemed they were now weary of me and gave us all a wide birth.

Of course, it's always at the point when you think you have finally won when assumption does a round house kick to your gut, knocking you back on your ass! I knew this when something strange started to happen as Alex stopped struggling and his gurgled sounds of blood rushing up his throat started to turn into a sadistic laugh.

Lucius unlatched his embedded fangs and stumbled backwards.

"Lucius?" I said his name trying to get him to focus on me as it now looked like he was intoxicated. He held his neck with one hand and used the other to feel behind him as if he was about to bump into something.

"Impossible…" Lucius croaked out and I cried out in panic as he fell to one knee. Alex straightened up and wiped his neck like he had nothing but a bug bite that he didn't even need to scratch.

"Is it?" Alex asked cracking his neck to the side and coming over to kick Lucius in the side, knocking him over to his back.

"Stop it!" I shouted but Alex took no notice of me.

"You're… not…Nephilim." Lucius managed to get out as it sounded like now his throat was closing up completely.

"Ah but you just needed to have a taste to finally figure it out, well I am glad you know the truth before you die."

"NO!" I screamed thinking it wasn't possible! Lucius couldn't die, he just couldn't!

"He...he will...kill you!" Lucius said forcing each word through his bloody lips.

"The King can't kill me, just as you couldn't and just as no one can...for I am..." He paused and then turned around to face me showing me the real face of Alex Cain before killing all hope with the truth...

"The Venom of God."

CHAPTER FOURTY-THREE

KEIRA

THE FINAL TRADE

As I woke, I was starting to get used to the feeling of cold hard stone beneath me. But what I wasn't used to was the frozen numb feeling like a dear friend had just died. I didn't want to believe it and my mind was reliving the last ten minutes as if I was stuck in some auditorium in Hell. I would be sat there all alone and screaming at the screen just as I had done in real time at seeing the life leave Lucius' body.

It just wasn't possible. Someone like Alex couldn't kill Lucius, how could he...? He wasn't powerful enough. No! I wouldn't believe it and I just couldn't believe it. No one was strong enough to do that...no one!

"No." These thoughts made me whisper to myself as I felt the tears still following the tracks down into my hairline. I couldn't even care enough that I couldn't move or the fact that I

had fainted after seeing what was the last thing to pass through Lucius' lips before he left this earth.

"My Keira, forgive me."

I had reached out my hand to his and tried to use the last of my strength to crawl to him. I had called out his name over and over. I had screamed it until my lungs crashed but there had been no response. There was no cocky reply. No calm collected sarcasm. There had been nothing but the fight going out of his body and the light fading slowly from his beautiful eyes.

No, my friend had gone.

Lucius was gone.

"Ah awake I see." Alex said at my side from where I knew I was strapped to the altar awaiting whatever ritual the psycho had in store for me. I wanted to tell him to go fuck himself but as he approached the altar, I turned my head from him, not wanting to give him the satisfaction of seeing me crying for my friend. However, this wasn't enough for him and he grabbed my chin painfully and forced my head back round.

"Aww poor little bitch, crying for her bloodsucker."

"Don't touch me!" I snapped ripping my face from his hold no matter the pain it caused me.

"Whoa! Brave now aren't we? Well let's see how brave you get when lover boy turns up and the fun really begins!" He laughed down at my disgusted face before kissing me and then pushing himself backwards before I could bite him.

"I will smile when Draven kills you!" I said with more venom in my voice than I had ever heard before. That was the thing about truly hating someone. The levels you find yourself rising to when someone threatens the ones you love become like an infection you can't rid yourself of. It had been like that for Morgan. Waking each day with this weight bearing down on your soul that he could hurt your family at any time was crushing.

However, the type of murderous hate you feel for someone who has taken someone you loved from this world was like no other. It flooded your veins with the raw need to do harm at unspeakable levels and its bitter twisted obsession for revenge burrowed deep beneath your skin. I think this feeling must have been where the saying 'making your skin crawl' came from as one look at this vile creature and the repulsion I felt made me both shiver and want to throw up!

"Then you will die with tears in your eyes and nothing but pain on your face!" He threatened smirking at the idea causing me to turn my head to save myself the sight.

"I'd prefer to make the lady smile." A new voice boomed powerfully around the Temple.

"Draven!" I shouted looking back and seeing the man I loved come to my rescue. He walked slowly into the centre and naturally commanded the space around him without even trying. I however wasn't surprised to see Alex so lost in his madness that he failed to realise this.

"Draven it's a trap!" I screamed but he just swiped his arm downwards as a way of dismissing the fact and said,

"I know, Love."

"Ah! Finally our guest of honour arrives. So good of you to join us, if you had come any later there might have been parts missing off your little bitch...*I was getting bored.*" Alex said adding this last part leaning forward like it was a secret and Draven's demon snarled at him.

"If I find you have harmed her...!"

"You will what exactly!? Oh, that's right...you actually think you're in charge here don't you?" Alex walked around Draven, although I noticed still keeping his distance. Draven folded his arms looking unimpressed and forbidding in his black clothes that were ready for the fight ahead. Alex opened his arms and then putting his outstretched arms behind him he brought his face forward and said,

"Let's enlighten you should I…? Keira, if you would please *sing for us.*" And then with a click of his fingers the bloody Pentagram around the altar started to burn and sizzle before the flames erupted out like gunpowder had just been ignited. It was in this moment that my nightmare *really* began.

"AHHHHH!" I screamed in agony as my skin soon felt like it was being split apart.

"NO! KEIRA!!!" I heard Draven roaring my name over the sounds of my suffering and in my blurred vision I could just make out him running towards me. But there must have been something that was blocking him as he couldn't make it past the circle of fire.

"I will kill you for this!" Draven said exploding into his other self and it wasn't only his wings that came into play. One long sword grew from his hand until the tip touched the floor. I could feel my back bowing with the strain my body was being put under from each laceration to my flesh. It was as though some invisible entity was stood over me with a knife and just slicing away at me. But wait, that wasn't just it…I was starting to remember…but it couldn't be, could it?

"You die, Nephilim!" Draven promised and I saw him holding out his sword, pointing it at Alex.

"No, I don't think so. You see if you don't do what I want and do it soon then every old injury her body has ever known will come back for a revisit and you know I have heard that she has received quite a few nasty cuts since knowing you…so times a'wasting…oh and look, it's the time she sliced her own wrists, fuck, but that must be hurting her so bad right now." Alex said and the twisted bastard was right, it was hurting me… *bad.*

I didn't know what was worse, when I did it the first time or the duplication of events now, because no matter what people told you, after feeling something once, it still doesn't prepare you for ever feeling it again.

At first it had started as simple grazes and bumps every child gets growing up. But then the accident of when I fell down the stairs and broke two fingers came back with a snap of bone. Even the time that I fell from the tree and winded myself came rushing back to me. I was soon gasping for air and dragging it in panicked painful gulps, along with feeling the spasms in my diaphragm. But now came the worst part as the cutting of every imaginary blade slice into my skin as if I was holding the mirrored glass as I did that fateful day.

"KEIRA!" Draven ran at me again only this time he tried to use his sword against the invisible barrier that kept us apart. However, every time upon impact it just sparked like grinding metal against metal and nothing was achieved other than a wasted effort.

"Stop this! Stop it now!"

"There is but one way and unfortunately for you killing me isn't it, as she will just eventually bleed out, with or without your healing influence." Alex said picking his nails casually with the tip of his wooden blade. I screamed out again as my time with Morgan and Sammael and their treatment of me was starting to lash out at my abused body.

"Then what?! WHAT IS IT YOU NEED ME TO DO!?" Draven's demon thundered out.

"It's simple really. I just need you to take her place and take a little trip for me." Alex said grinning and looking unthreatened by Draven's mounting rage.

"NO! Do…don't do it! Ahhhh!..NO! He…he, wants to Ah… release…*the Titans!*" I managed to push out the words of warning through the bursts of pain my body was going through.

"Keira!" Draven shouted my name and I could just see the distress in his eyes at seeing the hurt reflected back in mine.

"Draven...don't do...this." I muttered knowing like a deep rooted certainty that he was willing to put the whole world at risk just for me. This was confirmed when he whispered back,

"I must." And just as I cried out, he turned back to Alex and snarled,

"Do it!"

"Excellent!" Alex said clapping his hands and kicking away from the pillar he was casually leaning against. He then clicked his fingers once more and I vaguely heard him saying something in another language before finally my exhausted body was given its rest from agony. I slumped back hard onto the stone and looked down to see far too much blood leaving my body. It was flowing like miniature canals through the carved symbols that were all around the altar dripping along the grooves as I lost more of my life too. I actually feared I didn't have much blood left and knew if I didn't start to heal quicker and soon, my body was likely to go into shock.

But I also realised that if Draven and I hadn't made love when we did I would have died long ago. I looked up at the man I loved just as the flames from the Pentagram died down and noticed he was looking back at the exit as if waiting for something.

"Oh I wouldn't worry about them, your family and council will be occupied enough with my dead army." This was when I knew that Draven hadn't come alone but thanks to my blood, they now had a zombie battle to fight. Draven growled at Alex as he walked past him and came to me, no doubt now feeling the weight of worry from all sides.

I felt his hand on my cheek as he pushed the hair from my face.

"It will be alright, my love." He whispered down at me.

"Oh how very touching. Now get your bitch off the altar and lie down!" Alex snapped and Draven with one hand still gently on me, his other hand found Alex's neck and squeezed. I saw first the shock that made Alex's eyes bulge before they started to turn black.

"AHHHH!" I screamed in pain again as I started to feel the growing burn from when Lucius had touched me in my dreams so long ago. I could even feel his fingers imprinted on my flesh and this time I couldn't bear it again.

"Alright, alright, release her!" Draven shouted after letting go of Alex's neck. As soon as my screams turned to whimpers and moans Draven scooped me up and walked me away from both the table of my torture and my torturer. He lay me back down on the marble floor and I looked up at him, pleading with tears in my eyes and a tremble in my voice,

"Don't do this…*please.*"

"Ssshh now, this is the only way." He whispered down to me and I shook my head not trusting myself to speak from fear of sobbing. Draven was just about to bite into his own arm to speed up my healing process when Alex said,

"Huh uh, I don't think so. After all, remembering her dripping in that pretty colour will act as great motivation I think!" He said highly amused. I looked past Draven to then see Alex drawing his own blood with a syringe and I knew this would be my only chance to tell Draven what I knew.

"He wants to use you, Draven. He is going to get you to use his blood to release the Titans, but you can't! You can't do it!" I said whilst Alex was busy gaining the key in his blood to no doubt give to Draven.

"Keira you need to trust in me now…can you do that?" He asked putting his forehead to mine and I couldn't help it this time… I cried for him.

"But Lucius…he…he…Draven, he killed Lucius!" I said trying to catch my breath on a caught sob.

"Lucius is right where the Fates need him to be and you need to also trust in that." The tone of Draven's voice told me all I dreaded to know and confirmed the reason for my broken heart.

Lucius was gone.

I managed to drag myself up against a pillar and was left helpless and healing too slowly to do anything but cruelly watch as Draven took my place. He was stripped to his trousers after he was forced to take back control of his other form. Alex had strapped him down just as I had been, and it was painful to watch as Draven took it without putting up a struggle. He just kept his eyes to mine and gave me the strength I needed to watch this.

"I must say, all that planning and all that waiting really paid off. To think that all it really took was one simple spell, one switch of a cursed, purple jade necklace and bam! It draws in a King even as powerful as you like a dog to a bitch in heat." Alex said walking round Draven and with a long pole in his hand, he started using the burnt blood as a way to draw symbols in the Pentagram.

"You?!" Draven hissed as the realisation hit us both.

"Yes me! Of course after you left your Chosen One for good all I needed was to have a seed planted firmly enough to grow. One that made you believe you needed to be contained and to do that there was no place like Hell's greatest prison." Draven growled and tensed at hearing this but as for me I was frozen in shock. I was trying to process everything that had happened and soon realised the depths Alex had gone to just to make it all possible that Draven could get back into Tartarus. That was why when I took off the necklace Draven had stopped needing to be chained to his prison. The curse had been broken but Draven still had the ticket carved into his flesh.

"So now all that is left is to send you back there with the key that is my blood to free its prisoners." On hearing this from Alex, Draven started to laugh, and I frowned unable to see what he could have found funny in that moment.

"You mean '*prisoner*'." Draven said after the laughing ceased and he turned his deadly purple gaze back to his enemy.

"You don't get to speak about him!" Alex fumed and Draven taunted him further.

"Belphegor sends his regards asshole!" Draven said and Alex lost it. He punched Draven across the face making me cry out. Draven just laughed harder and it was an unnerving sound that echoed around the room.

"That Gorgon Leech's shit for brains doesn't know the first thing about loyalty!"

"Your father was a fool for trusting him, but he was an even greater fool for trying to take what's mine, but I gather that foolhardy stupidity runs in the family." I didn't understand who they were talking about, but I was about to find out.

"We shall see who feels like the fool after you release him, and we finally have the Titans on our side."

"You really think the Titans will follow your rule." Again Draven laughed and shook his head but Alex was the one who looked smug.

"And who do you think my father really worked for and still does, even as he remains buried deep enough in the belly of Mount Tartarus."

"You lie." This time it was Draven who lost his edge of controlling the situation.

"All Cronus has waited for is a key to be passed into Hell. And as my dear mother was mortal with the blood of Kings flowing free in her veins it was left up to my father to create the new King of men. But I still wasn't granted access into the deeper levels of Hell and neither was my father. So that is where *you* came in." Alex said poking his chest at the word 'you' that he spat down at him.

"See originally the plan was to take your bitch here and use her as leverage but then Daddy dearest fucked up using that pathetic mortal and getting himself thrown into the very prison he was trying to gain access to." Draven started struggling when he heard this, and one chain snapped before Alex walked over to me and forced Draven's submission by holding the dagger to my throat.

"Do you want to see more of her blood, is that it?! 'Cause I will gladly oblige." Draven's demon rumbled out a growl before calming enough for Alex to put away the threat.

"That's better. Now, let's get back to it should we? You will take this blood into Tartarus and use it to first free my father, then you will give the rest to him. Only when I see my father back here will I give you back your Electus."

"This won't end well for you. Nephilim." Draven promised as Alex stalked back to him and just as he grabbed the chain and pulled it tight across Draven's bare torso he leant down and said,

"Oh but haven't you heard…the Nephilim was my brother, before I killed him of course!" And then after slipping the vial of blood into Draven's pocket he stepped back and clapped his hands. Draven's body, like mine, was suddenly surrounded by flames, reaching up until I could no longer see him.

"DRAVEN!!!" I screamed but it was pointless because what Alex told me next meant that once again my past was coming back to haunt not only me but Draven as well…

"Oh don't you worry, he'll be back and with him an old friend of yours."

"What are you talking about?!" I snapped having enough of his games.

"My Father is…" I held my breath and waited for the end of all my hope to come crashing against the walls I had guarding my mind. As now I finally realised, they were all pointless in this battle. Because who exactly was the Venom of God and why had the same blood that ran through Alex's veins become poison to Lucius?

The answer was but one name…

"Sammael."

ABOUT THE AUTHOR

Stephanie Hudson has dreamed of being a writer ever since her obsession with reading books at an early age. What first became a quest to overcome the boundaries set against her in the form of dyslexia has turned into a life's dream. She first started writing in the form of poetry and soon found a taste for horror and romance. Afterlife is her first book in the series of twelve, with the story of Keira and Draven becoming ever more complicated in a world that sets them miles apart.

When not writing, Stephanie enjoys spending time with her loving family and friends, chatting for hours with her biggest fan, her sister Cathy who is utterly obsessed with one gorgeous Dominic Draven. And of course, spending as much time with her supportive partner and personal muse, Blake who is there for her no matter what.

Author's words.

My love and devotion is to all my wonderful fans that keep me going into the wee hours of the night but foremost to my wonderful daughter Ava...who yes, is named after a cool, kick-ass, Demonic bird and my sons, Jack, who is a little hero and Baby Halen, who yes, keeps me up at night but it's okay because he is named after a Guitar legend!

Keep updated with all new release news & more on my website
www.afterlifesaga.com
Never miss out, sign up to the
mailing list at the website.

Also, please feel free to join myself and other Dravenites on my
Facebook group
Afterlife Saga Official Fan
Interact with me and other fans. Can't wait to see you there!

facebook.com/AfterlifeSaga

twitter.com/afterlifesaga

instagram.com/theafterlifesaga

ACKNOWLEDGEMENTS

To my Dravenites,

As always you guys are the first I wish to thank and will forever feel blessed for all your amazing support as I continue to take this journey.

This last year has certainly been another emotional rollercoaster for me but as always I feel the support from my fans is a strength I gain like no other. For this I cannot thank you all enough.

I hope you all enjoyed part one of The Pentagram Child as much as I enjoyed writing it. And as always I strive not to let you down.

I would like to offer special thanks to those who not only continued to believe in me but also helped make this book possible.

My sister who we all love for her extraordinary vision and talent in giving Afterlife the front covers they deserve.

To my wonderful Mother who does an amazing job at editing my books and keeps me grounded through hard times. I would be lost without you and love you dearly.

Also a shout out to my Father who adds his own grumpy humour at times when it is most needed (The want to tear your hair out days)

A big shout has to go to all those mentioned in the list below and also every single one of you who find yourselves fans of the Saga. I wish I could name you all but these are just a few to show my love to those who make it their mission to spreading the Afterlife word. Cocktails on me!

ALSO BY STEPHANIE HUDSON

Afterlife Saga

A Brooding King, A Girl running from her past. What happens when the two collide?

Transfusion Saga

What happens when an ordinary human girl comes face to face with the cruel Vampire King who dismissed her seven years ago?

Transfusion - Book 1

Venom of God - Book 2

Blood of Kings - Book 3

Rise of Ashes - Book 4

Map of Sorrows - Book 5

Tree of Souls - Book 6

Kingdoms of Hell – Book 7

Eyes of Crimson - Book 8

Roots of Rage - Book 9

Afterlife Chronicles: (Young Adult Series)

The Glass Dagger – Book 1

The Hells Ring – Book 2

Stephanie Hudson and Blake Hudson

The Devil in Me

OTHER WORKS FROM HUDSON INDIE INK

Paranormal Romance/Urban Fantasy

Sloane Murphy

Xen Randell

C. L. Monaghan

Sci-fi/Fantasy

Brandon Ellis

Devin Hanson

Crime/Action

Blake Hudson

Mike Gomes

Contemporary Romance

Gemma Weir

Elodie Colt

Ann B. Harrison